Other People's Marriages

Also by Shane Watson

The One to Watch

Shane Watson

Other People's Marriages

MACMILLAN

First published 2005 by Macmillan
an imprint of Pan Macmillan Ltd
Pan Macmillan, 20 New Wharf Road, London N1 9RR
Basingstoke and Oxford
Associated companies throughout the world
www.panmacmillan.com

ISBN 0 333 90810 4 (HB)
1 4050 5096 9 (TPB)

3 5 7 9 8 6 4 2

A CIP catalogue record for this book is available from
the British Library.

Typeset by Intype London Ltd
Printed and bound in Great Britain by
Mackays of Chatham plc, Chatham, Kent

for Andy and Ginty

I would like to thank my agents and great friends Sarah, Felicity and Susannah, and my constantly supportive editor Imogen Taylor.

One

If a stranger had stumbled upon the Cunninghams'
eighteenth anniversary party they would probably have
assumed it was a celebration for Valerie Cunningham's
birthday. Archie Cunningham was nowhere to be seen,
and from a cursory glance round the drawing room,
taking in the pale linen furnishings and the clusters of
photographs – formal portraits of the children, and
various posed shots of Valerie from her graduation day
right up to her recent Himalayan trek – you could have
been forgiven for thinking this was the home of an
affluent widow or divorcee. Most likely divorcee, Anna
thought to herself. There was something decisive about
Valerie's deportment, something in the frisky tilt of her
bobbed blonde head that knew no unpleasant surprises,
no unscripted alteration to her plans. Anna watched
her as she stood by the open French windows at the far
end of the drawing room, a vantage point from where
the hostess could survey the party taking shape in the
garden and keep an eye on the front door at the same
time. She was holding herself in that upright, self-
conscious way that a too tight, strapless cocktail dress
will dictate: her shoulders a little too square, her soft
chin raised to counteract the slight welling above the

bodice. Every so often she glanced over to where Anna was sitting and beckoned her to join the throng, mouthing something indecipherable, before breaking off to brush cheeks with yet another guest whom Anna failed to recognize.

On the basis of previous Cunningham parties, Anna calculated that at this point Archie Cunningham would be downstairs in the kitchen easing the corks out of champagne bottles with an expression of intense concentration, despite the fact that an army of waiters had been hired for this purpose. Archie was notoriously party shy, particularly when the parties were organized by his wife. Earlier that evening he had returned upstairs to change his shoes, gone to repark the car and taken a call from his office, all just as the first guests were arriving.

'You see what I have to put up with?' Valerie had asked, motioning for one of the waitresses to answer the door. 'I hope *that's* going in your book, Anna, the way men always sabotage their wives' social plans. Without fail.'

She had bared her teeth for a moment in the hall mirror, smoothing her palms hastily over her wide, tightly packed hips, and twisting to check the effect from either side.

'I mean if Archie had his way, we'd see you and the Dickensons and Tony and Jean once a week for the rest of our lives and that would be that. They just have no idea, do they?'

Anna smiled to herself as she reached across the arm of the sofa and plucked a silver-framed photograph off the polished side table. The black and white image was three, perhaps four years old: a posed group portrait with Valerie seated to the left, and the children, Charlie and Charlotte, arranged in descending order of height, all spruced up, their hair brushed flat and gleaming against their heads. If you looked closely you could just make out, at the far right of the picture, the edge of Archie's trouser leg and the fuzzy white cracks where the photograph had been bent back on itself to fit the frame.

'What have you got there?'

Anna looked up at the sound of Ruth Dickenson's voice and registered a blur of mulberry-coloured print and the smell of musky scent as her friend snatched the frame and dropped onto the sofa beside her.

'Aaaah, look, aren't they adorable?' Ruth rested her head against Anna's shoulder as she held the picture up to the light. 'You wouldn't recognize them now, would you?' She grinned at the photograph, revealing the gap between her front teeth that made her look like a kid in a bubblegum commercial, even though her lips were painted a dark cherry red and her breasts barely contained by an empire-line dress.

Although they were roughly the same age, and although Ruth was married and the mother of a three-year-old child, lately Anna had begun to feel as though she was a different generation from her friend. She had reached the stage when she wanted an ordered, organized life. She planned, as did most of their contemporaries, so that everything ran as smoothly as possible and you knew where you were going from one year to the next. But Ruth's life didn't seem to have changed significantly from the days when they were at college. She still dyed her hair in the sink with an assortment of tints that always came out more or less burgundy. She still ate takeaway kebabs, had her credit cards confiscated and drove a Volkswagen Camper, and she and Dave continued to suffer the kind of Sunday morning hangovers that made getting dressed out of the question. It was a way of life that Anna couldn't begin to explain to Richard, her boyfriend, who was a man who deliberately kept every Friday free for 'them', who, only last Sunday, had installed a low-level wardrobe especially for her shoes. She wouldn't have known where to begin.

Ruth leant across Anna to replace the photograph and then sat back, examining her from under lazy eyelids outlined with slightly too much kohl.

'What are you doing sitting in here all by yourself, anyway?' she asked, prodding Anna playfully in the ribs. 'Observing the rituals of the married classes by any chance? I'll bet you're wondering what it would be like to have eighteen years under your belt, aren't you? Me too.' Ruth rummaged in her bra cup and produced a skinny, bent roll up. 'I mean, that's more than four times as long as Dave and I have been married. Although I don't need to tell you that, of course. You've got it all down in your *notes*.'

She winked at Anna and Anna smiled back affectionately, discreetly checking the place where Ruth's fingers had grazed her pale cashmere top.

'Eighteen years though.' Ruth paused, lighter poised. 'Do you ever wonder, Anna, when you're working on your book, tip-tapping away . . . d'you ever stop and think, "What if?" You know . . . what if things had turned out differently and you'd got hitched, at some point?' The flame danced on top of the lighter and Ruth dipped her head to make contact, inhaling greedily. 'Because, I mean, you're bound to, aren't you? If you spend every day for three years analysing people's marriages. If you're writing a *book* about marriage. You're bound to wonder what it might have been like.'

For a fraction of a second Anna contemplated changing the subject but the slight, curious tilt of Ruth's eyebrow confirmed this was not a realistic option.

'All right. Yes,' Anna said, 'there've been times when I've thought, "Would that have been the answer?" But obviously it wasn't, for me.'

Ruth's chin jutted expectantly.

'Well, I wouldn't be with Richard, would I? You know his views on marriage. Our view.'

'Right.' Ruth blinked. 'Where is he, by the way?'

'Ashtanga. There's some specialist in town.'

They sat in silence for a moment, Ruth grinding the remains of her blue nail varnish against her bottom teeth.

'And the fact is,' Anna continued, 'if I was married, if I had a family, I wouldn't have had the time to write a book like this.' She smoothed out the sleeve of her cashmere top, running her hand down to the wrist and then straightening the hem across the back of her knuckles. 'I mean, of course it's made me think about the issues. That's my job. But not about *me* especially. I'm . . .' she paused, an upturned palm floating in the air searching for the comfortable, at ease with herself aura that this particular speech required. 'I am completely . . . fine.'

Ruth nodded hesitantly. Her face was tensed as if she were preparing for an uncomfortably loud noise. 'So you don't ever think about Danny, then?' she asked.

'Hmm?'

'Danny. Fortune. You don't ever wonder how that might have turned out?'

'Danny?' Anna gave a little astonished laugh. 'Why are you bringing him up?'

'Well. You know.' Ruth shrugged. 'I've thought about it. So you must have. I'm just being nosey,' she added, reaching across to give Anna's knee a reassuring tweak.

It was a perfectly reasonable question, Anna knew. Not only that, but Ruth always told her everything as if it were the most natural process in the world; she'd spent the past three years sharing her innermost thoughts even though there must have been times when she hadn't much felt like it. Anna reached behind her neck and started to gather her hair slowly and methodically over one shoulder.

'I suppose I *have* thought about it,' she said airily, 'but that was another lifetime, wasn't it? It was years ago. I mean, do you spend a lot of time thinking about your boyfriends, before Dave?'

'A bit,' said Ruth. 'Yeah, actually I do.'

'All right, girls?' The sofa trembled behind them and they both looked up to see Dave Dickenson leaning against the back, a brimming glass of margarita lapping at his bottom lip.

'Having a bit of a sesh, are we?'

'Yes, thanks,' said Ruth. 'What do you want?'

'I came to look for you, my Muss,' said Dave, and then, catching his wife's distinctly unimpressed expression, 'Er . . . and our hostess sent me in to flush out the party-phobic husband. Anyone seen him?'

Dave took a slug of margarita and cast his eyes around the room, his thick black eyebrows raised in anticipation.

'Have they decorated in here again? I don't remember that –' he thrust his glass in the direction of a lattice-fronted, silk-lined bookcase '– and where's the telly gone?'

A look of panic crossed Dave's face as he spun around 180 degrees in both directions, scanning the walls and floor frantically.

'There's one in the study,' said Ruth flatly. 'They don't go in for the entertainment-centres-in-every-room-including-the-downstairs-bog policy.'

'Poor Archie,' Dave muttered. 'Eighteen years good behaviour, and the fella can't even watch the snooker in his own living room. Come to think of it, there's not much he could do in here.'

'Dave! Shoosh!' Ruth flapped a warning hand in his direction.

'Sorry, sweetheart. I love Val, you know I do. I just feel sorry for Archie, that's all. We blokes need to stick together, you know, or homo erectus' – Dave waggled his eyebrows – 'will be extinct by the year two thousand and fifty. We men were not made to live in scented cages.'

'No,' said Ruth, 'apparently you were made to live sandwiched between a couple of speakers within arm's length of a fridge.'

'I am perfectly serious, Muss. There was a thing on the telly about it – the feminizing of Western culture and how it's actually having a physical impact on the male *form*.' The eyebrows hopped up and down independently before settling in a quizzical double arch. 'Anna, do you know about this? Because if you don't, I think you should look into it. Seriously. Could be vee-ry significant for your book. This may mean the end of union between the sexes *as we know it*.' Dave craned his neck and lowered his voice to a whisper. 'Smaller willies. It's a fact. Possibly no willies at all eventually, by the time the newspapers are all given over to "Get the Look" and "Heal Yourself with Yoga". Ah . . . now I don't mean anything by that, Anna. I know Richard is . . . I respect . . . yogists. Honestly I do. It's the, you know, bigger picture I'm worried about.'

'Well, look on the bright side. If everyone else's are shrinking . . .' Ruth tried not to smile, she sucked her lips over her teeth but her throaty laugh escaped regardless making her beaded earrings jangle.

'Yeah, very funny.' Dave squinted at his wife affectionately, mouth puckered, dimples dimpling in his trademark blend of wry smile and schoolboy smirk. Anna noticed a green dry-cleaning ticket still safety-pinned to the inside hem of his jacket and the words BOOK MOT scrawled in biro on the back of his hand. 'Anyway, some of us are luckier than others,' Dave continued, 'some of us have wives who are not hell bent on turning us into house pets. And I thank my lucky stars that I married my Muss and not some . . . *woman*.'

Dave drained the margarita, placed the glass on the mantelpiece, dragged his fingers through the front peak of his woolly black hair and then, with a smart clap of his hands, announced that he was off to look for their host.

'By the way, Muss,' he hissed when he reached the

door into the hall, 'you're driving. I think I'm over the limit.' He steadied himself with an elbow on the door frame. 'And girls, keep it clean, will you? I don't want anything ending up in that book that I wouldn't be happy for my mother-in-law to read.' And with that, Dave turned and disappeared down the corridor.

Ruth rolled her eyes and fished in her bra for another roll up.

'How you can get that sloshed in a couple of hours beats me. He never used to . . .' Her eyes met Anna's and she paused for a moment, fingers wedged in her geranium-pink D cup.

'All right, maybe he did. Perhaps the difference is I was always half cut too. But you can't carry on like that for ever, can you?'

'I don't know. Maybe not.' Anna's tone was expressionless, non-judgemental. These days she lapsed into it automatically whenever the talk turned to other people's relationships, whatever the context. She'd been gathering information about her friends' marriages for so long now that there was no distinction in any of their minds between on and off the record; book time and real time.

'Anyway –' Ruth extracted the cigarette and smoothed it out between her fingers '– better not start now. I'm seeing you for our update tomorrow, so you'll get it all then. How's it going by the way? Nearly there?'

'Sort of. Nearly there with you and Dave, and Archie and Valerie, and most of the case studies are coming together. I've just got a few gaps to sort out. The recent second marriage, that couple I thought I had fixed up? They fell through yesterday.'

'Oh?'

'He decided it was going to be too intrusive.'

'Well –' Ruth dusted some stray ash off her knee '– there is a bit of that, isn't there? I mean, you need to be prepared to find out a few home truths in the process.' The ash was all gone but still she carried on, rhythmically brushing. 'I suppose at the start I thought it was going to be more basic, you know: who does the cooking? Who gets to choose the holidays? How often d'you have sex? A, B or C? But then . . . it's like anything, isn't it? The more you delve into something, the more you start questioning what it's all about.' Ruth glanced up from her lap and must have seen the anxiety in Anna's face. 'I'm not saying it's a problem,' she added hastily. 'It's just . . . revealing, that's all. And that was the whole point, wasn't it?'

'But you don't regret it, Ruth, do you?' Anna leant towards her on the sofa. 'I'd feel terrible if you regretted it.'

'Noo, no regrets! I just feel a bit different now, that's all. We're all different. Look how much you've changed!'

Ruth spread both hands in Anna's direction and for a moment both of them contemplated her pristine, mostly cashmere outfit; the dainty silver wristwatch; the French-manicured fingernails; the single diamond on a chain at her throat.

'When you started on the book you were living at ours, remember?' Ruth said, her eyes expanding in mock disbelief. 'No Richard. No money. No job. D'you remember? You had that funny Rod Stewart haircut and that tweed coat.'

They both laughed, Anna quickly lowering her eyes in case Ruth should be encouraged to reminisce any further.

'Still. We're OK, aren't we?' Anna asked.

'Oh yes,' said Ruth. 'You've got a book contract, a gorgeous partner, a fabulous flat . . . not to mention a great new haircut. And I'm married to my best friend. I'd say that's officially OK.'

'Ruth?'

'Hmm?'

'I've always wanted to ask, what's Muss short for exactly?'

Ruth took a drag of her cigarette, one dark eyebrow gliding upwards towards her ruby-tinted fringe.

'It's short for moustache,' she said, when the eyebrow had reached its limit. 'Touching, isn't it? Yeah, well, we can't all have Richards I suppose.'

When Anna and Ruth decided it was time to go in search of Dave and Archie, they found them both downstairs, sitting at the kitchen table, and Tony Alcroft pacing the floor, apparently enlightening his friends as to the lot of the divorced man.

'I mean, you call it a day precisely so you don't have to keep on bending over backwards just to keep them in a half civil mood,' he was saying, 'and then you discover . . . Hi there girls! Come on in and join the party!'

Tony raised an arm over his head and beckoned them enthusiastically before returning to his theme

'And then you discover that marriage was only a bloody dress rehearsal for the serious jumping through hoops that starts the moment you separate. Take tonight –' Tony ran a hand swiftly through his lustrous blond hair, the substantial signet ring on his little finger leaving a slight furrow in its wake. 'My oldest friends' eighteenth wedding anniversary party. I mean, I was only Archie's best man. My night, right?' He paused for effect, one hand resting on his hip. 'And Jean . . . Jean wants to bring Herman.'

'Herve,' Archie said.

'I'm sorry?'

'He's called Herve, apparently.' Archie removed his spectacles and started to polish them briskly on his shirt tail. 'Herve with an H.'

'Okaaay, Herve . . . Since you insist. Anyway, that is the kind of selfishness you come up against all the time. My friends, their anniversary, she wants to bring some . . .'

'Bloke,' interjected Dave, nodding vigorously.

'No, not *bloke*. Hardly. Boy. Some . . . youth. I mean you see to *me* that shows a lack of sensitivity, a basic lack of awareness of other people's feelings, and frankly' – Tony was pointing his finger now, wagging it in Archie's direction – 'that is what makes the difference between thirteen years and eighteen. Am I right? Anna, come on.'

Tony was shimmying across the floor now, tucking his pink shirt firmly into his straining white moleskin trousers as he went. He grabbed Anna by the shoulders and ushered her back towards the Aga, propping her against the rail and then stepping away with a flourish of his hand to indicate that the floor was now hers.

'You tell us, Anna,' Tony said. 'It's all there in your

little notebooks, all those . . . case studies, whatever they're called. You've got the whole thing sorted out – the dos and don'ts, the clinchers and the deal breakers. Everything it takes to make a marriage.'

Tony folded his arms and settled himself solidly against the edge of the kitchen table.

'And I'm betting,' he continued, puffing out his chest, 'that if you look at Archie and Valerie's marriage, or Dave and Ruth's for that matter –' he gave a little courtesy nod in Ruth's direction '– I'll bet you that nothing more complicated than good old-fashioned sensitivity is the secret of their success.'

This sort of proposition was put to Anna with increasing regularity these days, particularly in the kitchen at parties. So she knew from experience that she was not actually expected to give her considered opinion, but rather to reinforce whatever line the questioner was taking. She took a long breath and gave a little leap of her eyebrows, a gesture which she found generally covered it.

'What did I tell you?' crowed Tony, slapping his palms against his thighs. 'What did I tell you?' and he made for the fridge to get another round of beers.

'Sensitivity?' Ruth murmured. 'That's really your final answer?'

Anna shook her head. 'But don't worry,' she said. 'I'm working on it.'

Two

Tony insisted on driving Anna home from the Cunninghams', despite the fact that it took him twenty minutes to remember where he'd parked the Porsche.

'Oh, come on, Anna, can't we be in the book?' he pleaded, when they eventually found the car in the next-door street. 'I don't mean *we*, obviously. I mean me and Jean, separately. I feel a bit left out, to be honest. We are the only two in the gang who aren't part of it, you know?'

'Tony, it's not like that,' Anna said. 'All the contributions are anonymous so no one's identifiable anyway. Besides, you're not married.' Anna fastened her seat belt and double-checked the catch. 'The book is about marriage. You and Jean are divorced.'

She glanced over at Tony who was ducking his head to either side of the steering wheel as if avoiding sniper fire. 'If you remember, that's why you weren't included when everyone else came on board; you were both a bit tied up talking to lawyers.'

'Yeeess, but' – Tony was juggling the steering wheel on his knees now as he reached behind him fumbling for the cigarettes in his blazer pocket – 'when you think about it, Jean and I probably know more about what it takes to keep a marriage going than the rest of them put together. We're the before and after shot; the two halves of the picture. It's all very well looking at the successful marriage, but you don't really know if it is, do you? Today's perfect couple could be tomorrow's car wreck.' Tony propped a cigarette in the corner of his mouth, and reached for the cigarette lighter. 'In fact, I'd go further. I'd say that the everything's cosy and rosy marriages are precisely the ones that are most likely to go belly up in the next couple of years.' He dragged deeply on the cigarette, scrunching up his eyes and adjusting the rear-view mirror.

'Why d'you want to be in it, anyway?' Anna lowered the passenger window an inch or so and leaned towards the gap. 'It's a big commitment, and it's intrusive and disruptive. You should talk to the others. They started out thinking it would be a bit of a laugh and now, three years on, they're sick of the sight of me.' She paused and turned to look at Tony. 'You have to be scrupulously honest you know. You can't get away with fudging it.'

'Naturally, darling!' Tony angled the rear-view mirror towards him and gave his wheat-coloured hair a root-lifting tousle. 'Trust me! I only want to do my bit. And I know how to sell a story. All right, it's *research*.' He licked his finger and started to rub at the base of his right sideburn. 'I appreciate that. But it's still about getting to the meat of it; knowing what your audience is after. This is the story of our lives after all!' Tony lifted both hands off the wheel and thrust them at the windscreen, causing a woman on the zebra crossing ahead of them to stop and peer into the car. 'It's *the* story, isn't it?

Marriage and why the giddy fuck we do it. It's got to be the all-time biggie.'

Tony was an actor, or rather he had been an actor in what his ex-wife Jean had christened the 'Anyone for tennis?' mould. During the late seventies and eighties he had featured, sometimes in major supporting roles, in almost any film you could mention involving Brideshead era Oxbridge days, First World War flying aces or Edwardian country houses, though 'downstairs' was never his thing. These days he got the occasional call up for an Agatha Christie, or a murder series set among the glittering spires – Tony called them 'cameos' – and, in the longer gaps between filming, he gave Jean the benefit of his advice on running her antique business.

'I know what you're thinking,' Tony said, straightening his arms on the steering wheel. 'You're thinking, "If I let Tony on board he'll get carried away and take this in directions I hadn't dreamt of." But I promise I'll behave. Oh, go on, be a sport, Anna. I haven't got much else on at the moment, to be honest.'

Anna raised a hand in surrender. 'All right,' she said. 'I'll have a look and see if I need any more on marital breakdown.'

'Good girl.' He patted her knee. 'You won't regret it, I guarantee. One thing' – Tony shifted his weight in his seat and leant an elbow on the gearbox – 'we mustn't mention the smoking for insurance reasons. And I'm thirty-eight . . . all right, thirty-nine, but absolutely no advance on that. I've got my film work to think of.'

*

Upstairs at their twin sinks the Cunninghams were having their usual party post-mortem; Valerie stripped down to the reinforced all in one that had facilitated the wearing of the strapless dress, and Archie neatly parcelled up in her jade satin dressing gown.

'God, Vicky!' Valerie was saying, rubbing her hands together briskly and then slapping the underside of her chin with the back of her fingers. '*What* does she think she looks like? Poor Jerry. And Deirdre. I mean, really . . . you know, marvellous if you happened to be twenty-five and a size ten, perhaps . . .'

Archie looked blank but nodded all the same.

'Their new house is an *absolute disaster* of course. I knew it would be. They wildly over-budgeted and there isn't enough room for the children, not if they want a live-in nanny, and God knows Deirdre couldn't do without round the clock support.' She stabbed at the bridge of her nose with a ball of cotton wool. 'Who did you talk to, Archie?'

Archie, who was working along his back teeth with an electric toothbrush, took a moment to reply.

'Dave,' he mumbled. The cotton-wool ball froze, mid air. 'And, er, Tony . . .' Archie was watching Valerie closely in the mirror. 'And Anna,' he added, tentatively.

'So. Anyone apart from our oldest friends?' Valerie said, resuming her dabbing. 'Charlie Morehouse, for example? Why do you think I asked him, Archie? Hmm? Do you think it might have had something to do with the fact that he's now on the board of governors at Wellsley? The school where your daughter will most probably be spending her A-level years?'

Shane Watson

Archie jammed the toothbrush back in his mouth and bent over the sink.

'What about Matthew Roberts? Ring any bells? Producer of every British film that anyone has ever heard of? Lives in Thriftville Gardens?'

Archie dabbed his mouth. 'I don't think so,' he said. 'Sorry, darling.'

'Well, it doesn't matter. I told Matthew you're mad about sailing.'

'Sailing?'

'Yes.'

'Why?'

'*Darling* . . . because they have a summer house in Aldeburgh to which they invite the chosen few and their families, and I'm thinking about Lottie. The you-know-whos are learning to sail there.'

Valerie paused to consider her husband. She was several inches taller than him in her crocodile slingbacks and quite a bit broader. In fact, he seemed to be drowning in her dressing gown: the shoulders drooped off him and the satin lapels overlapped at the throat so that his small, smooth, olive-coloured head looked like a delicate wood carving on a presentation cushion. On his feet he was wearing some towelling slippers she'd bought at her health club, which seemed to be an almost perfect fit.

'Who are the you-know-whos?' Archie asked innocently.

'Oh, for God's sake, Archie!'

'I've no idea . . . honestly.'

'Harry and Wills,' hissed Valerie. '*Prince* Harry and *Prince* William. They're down there for the whole of

August and Matthew is entrusted with introducing them to the right sort of people.'

Archie was folding his flannel carefully into quarters. 'Darling, Charlotte is fourteen,' he said quietly, placing the flannel to one side and picking up a tortoiseshell comb.

'Yes,' said Valerie, 'which is why she needs to start moving in the right circles. Archie, please don't look at me like that. If you take the fashionably casual approach to this sort of thing you invariably come unstuck. Look at your sister. Classic product of the "just play it as it comes" generation. Last had a boyfriend five years ago, tried the cottage in the country for a year, now onto the salsa lessons. Officially single and desperate. And all because the poor girl was led to believe that side of things would somehow, magically, take care of itself.'

Archie gave his silky brown short back and sides a last rake with the comb and smiled patiently at his wife in the mirror.

'All right. What about Anna then?' Valerie asked. 'Lovely girl. Pretty. Nice little figure. Everything going for her. But still single.'

'I thought she was living with Richard?' said Archie.

'Pre-cise-ley.' Valerie rested both hands heavily on the sink in front of her, leaning her weight onto her arms as if she were physically exhausted from the sheer effort of opening Archie's eyes to the realities of life. 'Living – with – Richard, as in unmarried. *Committed*' – she swivelled her eyes, to underscore her already unmistakeable contempt for the word – 'to a man who won't stand up in public and declare his feelings for her, and who, furthermore, doesn't believe in having children. I mean, she's no better off than your sister, she just *looks* as if she is. And it's exactly the same problem. Anna thought she had all the time in the world.' Valerie traced an arc through the air with her bare freckled arm, making her cantilevered breasts wobble violently. 'All the time in the world to mess around with this charming boy and that feckless boy, and now, of course, she's no choice but to take whatever's on offer. Even if it's tantamount to a glorified flatmate.'

'Oh, I don't think she would see it like that.' Archie had slipped one foot out of its slipper and was swivelling it from left to right, examining the state of his recently clipped toenails. 'Not everyone is cut out for marriage after all. I can quite see that Anna might feel she's better off focusing on the things she knows make her happy.'

He glanced up at Valerie who had cocked an ear in his direction and was assuming an expression of eager expectancy.

'Really?'

'Yes. After all, there's more than one way to live your life, isn't there? And, let's face it, plenty of lives have been ruined by trying to meet other people's expectations.'

'Is that right, Archie?'

'I think so.' Archie cupped Valerie's elbow and then stepped lightly around her and padded through the bathroom door into their bedroom.

'Well, that's all fine and dandy,' Valerie called after him, 'but if she's so thrilled with her situation, then what's she doing writing a book about marriage? Archie?'

Archie hesitated, one hand poised at the top of the white damask bedspread, and then slowly started to peel it off the bed.

'Why not write a book about "life partners", if that's the perfect solution?' Valerie continued, raising her voice to compensate for any distortion as she slathered her cheeks with night cream. 'It's obvious she's just trying to get it all sorted out in her head. Poor Anna. I mean, it's no coincidence she got a burning urge to write the thing immediately after it ended with . . . whatsisname.'

'Daniel,' said Archie, pulling back the bedcovers. 'Daniel Fortune.'

'Yes, that's it. Well, don't tell me there'd have been any book about the whys and wherefores of marriage if that one had worked out. There wouldn't have been the incentive! Archie? Are you listening to me?'

Valerie stood in the bathroom doorway, her face coated in a light film of grease, the sides of her blonde bob pinned back at the temples with silver hairclips. Archie looked up from his book and smiled.

'Not that it could ever have worked out, mind you,' Valerie said. 'Which is exactly my point. Too much time spent looking in the wrong places. Frankly, I could have told her where she's been going wrong, and saved her all this trouble.'

'Well, you are telling her, my darling, in a manner of speaking. You are giving her the benefit of your experience during the course of your interviews.'

Valerie nodded absent-mindedly. 'I suppose so. Though she always seems to be far more interested in asking meaningless questions about – I don't know – our mutual taste in music, than she is in getting down to the real essentials of what makes a marriage work. I can't help sometimes thinking I'd do a better job of it myself.'

'Daniel was rather dazzling, mind you,' Archie said, fingering the pages of his book. 'Such a romantic figure, with his guitar and all those floppy velvet clothes. Do you remember? And Richard is extremely personable, albeit in a rather different way.' When he looked up Valerie's eyes were closed.

'Honestly, Archie,' she said eventually, reaching over to flick off the bathroom light, 'sometimes I think we're both living on different planets. I really do.'

After listening to Dave wrestle with his seat belt for several minutes Ruth brought the van to a stop a few streets away from the Cunninghams' house, and took charge of the situation.

'You were trying to get it in the wrong slot,' she said.

'No I wasn't,' Dave grunted, still fumbling with the clasp. 'This thing is a bloody crock. We need a new car. We neeed' – he was impersonating someone now, someone smooth – 'perhapsh a Jenshen, and there just happensh to be a faschinating little model in the dealer nexsht to work.' Dave raised one bushy eyebrow and shot his cuffs.

Yes, it was Sean Connery. It was always either Sean Connery or Michael Caine or Russell Crowe in *Gladiator*. Ruth pretended not to have noticed. She checked the mirror and pulled out into the road again.

'We are not getting a Jensen,' Ruth said. 'Where would we get the money for a Jensen?' Out of the corner of her eye she saw the eyebrow slink back into position. 'And don't you dare say, "What's your problem, Ruth Munton?"'

Sometimes her take-off of his Belfast accent was absolutely spot on, and this was one of those occasions. Dave's mouth twitched in appreciation.

'I just think . . .' Ruth hesitated. Here we go, she thought, do try not to be too much of a bitch. It isn't his fault that you've been warming up to this all month, or, more accurately, most of this year. 'I just think . . . we should have moved on from you fantasizing about flash cars, or sneaking off to buy the latest TV, which you know we can't even fit in the sitting room. I mean, it isn't just about getting away with whatever you can, is it?'

Ruth looked in the rear-view mirror and tugged at her fringe. She'd cut it herself in the bathroom the night before and, back at their flat, it had seemed sort of French New Wave: a little bit kooky, a little bit avant-garde. But after an evening looking at Anna's sexy and successful hair, watching her trap the glowing honey front bits between two fingertips and flick them expertly over each shoulder, she felt like one of the Munsters.

'The thing is, Dave,' she said, pushing the mirror away, 'you might mock Archie and Valerie's life. And yes, Val is a bit over the top at times, and she can be a bit tough on him. But, actually, they are just a regular married couple when it comes down to it – making compromises, and negotiating and, you know, having shared . . . plans.'

She'd wanted to say ambitions, but that was definitely a no word. And why had she brought up

Archie and Valerie, the one couple who were the living embodiment of everything they'd promised never to become, and a large part of the reason why they hadn't got married long before they did? This wasn't what she wanted to be saying at all.

'I'm not saying we should *be* like Archie and Valerie,' Ruth added, in the nick of time.

Dave had already swivelled his head in her direction and was giving her the same look he gave her when they were playing backgammon and she was about to screw up: a look somewhere between a second chance and a warning.

'I don't know why I even mentioned them,' she said, picturing the silk-lined bookcase, the kitchen with the hand-made oak table, and the bathroom, with the his 'n' hers basins and the bath raised up on that platform, all carpeted in white.

'Anyway, all I mean is, we should be thinking of the future.'

Oh Christ, *thinking of the future*? This was turning into one of those conversations your brain identified as 'significant' and then – without seeking your permission – started to unload all the relevant clichés it had been storing up for just such an occasion. Like when you were finishing with a boyfriend and, although you thought the circumstances were exceptional, your brain and his brain were busy digging deep into the dusty carpetbag of things you say when you break up: 'It's not you it's me.' 'I love you but I'm not *in* love with you.' 'I just don't think I can give you what you need.'

'Exactly what do you mean?' asked Dave.

Ruth gripped the steering wheel tighter. 'Well, we are

in our late thirties.' She craned her neck to look in the wing mirror, trying to give the impression that her main preoccupation was the progress of the car behind. 'I just think we should . . . I dunno, be behaving differently. That's what life's about, isn't it? Moving on to new stages and taking on new challenges . . . I mean we don't always want to be going to other people's parties and talking about the things that have happened in *their* lives.'

Out of the corner of her eye she could see Dave's fingers drumming on his trouser leg, his lips thrust out determinedly as if he were about to plant a kiss on the windscreen. She knew what he was thinking. He was thinking that she was one tiny step, one breath away from uttering those forbidden words. He was thinking: 'We said we'd get married on the condition that nothing changed, that we didn't become like married people, Mr and Mrs Thank-you-but-no-we've-got-an-early-start-we-are-a-couple-after-all. And now she's about to tell me she thinks we should grow up. Well, can't say I wasn't warned.'

The first time they'd had the marriage conversation Dave had tried to pretend it was to do with his job in drama development for Onyx TV.

'See, take *Friends*, for example,' he said. 'Only worked as long as they were all single. Pregnancies, fine; ex-partners, great; past marriages, no problem. They could all get off with each other as often as they liked. But as soon as marriage entered the equation the series was doomed. That's when the audience stopped believing. It just couldn't have worked.'

'Dave,' Ruth said, stifling a yawn and reaching for another slice of pizza, 'they wouldn't all have been living across the hall from each other any more. That's why it wouldn't have worked.'

Dave gave a dry laugh, as if that was precisely the knee-jerk response he'd been expecting. 'Aaaah, there's more to it than that,' he said knowingly. 'Friends *single* equals sexy, fun, limitless possibilities. Friends *married*, on the other hand, means tensions, domestic drudgery, power politics, kids. Kids are the death of drama, especially young ones. What do you do with them? It's the writer's nightmare.'

'Dave,' Ruth said, 'tell me you're trying to give me a hint about your position on marriage.'

'Yep, that's what I'm doing.' He nodded sheepishly.

'Thank God for that. I thought you might be turning into Mr TV Bore. And Dave,' she leant towards him, and whispered in his ear, 'if I wanted to get married you would be the first to know, but at the moment nothing could be further from my mind.'

And it was the truth. Then it was anyway.

Ruth glanced at Dave again and this time he was watching her through narrowed eyes, feet up on the dashboard, evidently picturing the sequence of incarnations that would inexorably lead to Ruth the twenty-stone wife with the full beard. She knew him well enough to know exactly what he was imagining, down to the last detail. First, there was the humungous weight gain, and simultaneous shift into roomy cotton trousers with elasticated waists. Then there was the short, tidy, librarian's bob, the spreading bikini line and corresponding underwear; the cardigan with tissue-filled pockets, the habit of taking said tissues positioning them over the two index figures and rotating them inside each nostril, in public.

'I'm not suggesting anything radical,' Ruth said and simultaneously saw herself standing in Archie and Valerie's drawing room, cradling a baby in the crook of each arm. Terence, the vicar from their local church, was there, his hands folded up inside his big white sleeves. 'So Ruth, have you decided who is to be the father of these two?' he was saying, smiling beatifically. And, as she hesitated, Jasper, her boss at the agency, stepped forward out of nowhere, oozing hair gel and aftershave. 'Bit of a surprise I'll grant you,' Jasper murmured, giving her one of his winks. 'But one thing you've gotta give me, I do know how to look after the ladies. No woman of mine has ever wanted for life's luxuries, let alone had to drive me home drunk. And you'll need money for those kiddies—'

'Ruth? *Ruth*! We should have turned left at the roundabout!' Dave was slapping the side of her thigh and pointing wildly over his shoulder. 'D'you want me to drive? I can remember exactly where we live, and it's over there . . . behind us.'

'Shut up.' Ruth flicked the indicator and turned sharp left down a side street. 'I wish you *were* driving but, unfortunately, you are completely pissed. Again,' she added, turning her head to look him straight in the eye.

God, was it really four years since they'd lain on the bed in the Henry VIII suite at the Hesmondley Arms, gazing up at the Tudor rose embroidered canopy, listening to rice raining against the mullioned windows?

'Right. Now it's time for our special marriage vows,' Dave had said. 'Repeat after me: I Ruth Hermione sex slave Munton . . .'

'I Ruth Hermione Munton . . .'

'Do solemnly promise that I will never be guilty of the following wifely behaviour: nagging her husband about his drinking, untidiness, childish sense of humour, taste in music-stroke-TV programmes, on the under-standing that I too am mad about booze, a bit of a slut etc., and that is how we intend to stay, for better for worse.'

'Yep, all that. Right, now say, "I Dave Michael Fabulous Shag Dickenson . . .'

'I Dave-the Shag-Dickenson . . .'

'Do solemnly promise that I will never be guilty of the following husbandly behaviour . . .'

'Bring it on!'

'Expecting hot dinners or cooking in general.'

Dave shook his head vigorously.

'Imagining domestic stuff will suddenly become second nature to wife.'

'Never.'

'Suddenly expecting wife to dress and behave in wifely demure fashion.'

'Youhavegottabekidding!'

'Assuming wife will temper party antics, drinking, etc., now that she's a married woman and can be relied on to drive home from parties.'

'Strictly taking turns.'

'Expecting wife to adopt wifely reluctant approach to sex and no longer want it three times a day.'

And that was as far as they'd got.

Dave was leaning forward, trying to look her in the eyes, despite the fact that they were firmly fixed on the road.

'What does *again* mean, exactly?'

'As in, not for the first time.' Ruth sounded a lot more confident and considerably tougher than she actually felt.

'Well, excuuuse me! I didn't realize you were clocking up my units. Since when has it been a crime to have a few drinks at an old mate's party? Anything else you want to have a go about?'

'I am not going to have this conversation when you're drunk.'

'What conversation? I've still got no idea what we're talking about. We were planning for a future without wide-screen TV is about where I'd got to . . .' Dave paused and raised a finger in the air. 'Wait a minute. You've been talking to Valerie, haven't you?'

'No.'

'Yeees you have.' Dave waggled the finger at her. 'All right, Anna, then . . . Aaaah ha! Definitely Anna.' He was smiling his sloping, got-you-now smile. 'It's the book, isn't it? You've been comparing ideal relationship notes and you think yours is a bit rough around the edges, a little bit lacking. That's it, isn't it?'

He loomed towards her suddenly only to be pulled up sharply by the seat belt.

'Ooof! Christ! Look, Roo, you don't want to be with a guy like Richard. I'm telling you.'

'Who said anything about Richard?'

'That's what this is really all about. Come on. Every woman's dream Richard.'

Dave pronounced the name exactly the way Richard did, slowly and deliberately, with the same long blink and meaningful nod. Then he pretended to smooth his hair out of his eyes, in slow motion, with both hands.

'This is *not* about Richard,' Ruth said.

'Bollocks it's not. You've been round there in their white *apartment*, among the original art works –' Dave punctuated the air with snappy quotation marks, another habit of Richard's, '– and Richard has rustled up a little something delicious – obviously no meat products, wheat-free, nat-ur-ally. And after that, he's just had time, before he pops off to Earth, Wind and Fire—'

'Planet Earth,' muttered Ruth.

'Whatever . . . he's just had time to ease out your shoulders a bit. Work on all that tension that your old, carnivorous, alcohol-abusing husband has been cranking up over the weeks and months. And before very long you're thinking –' Dave placed a finger in the natural cleft of his chin and raised his eyes to the roof of the van '– "Hmm. This is what my life should be like. Living in the pages of *Wallpaper* magazine, with a husband who's got a degree in massage."'

'Do you mind?' Ruth said, edging away from Dave as if he were interfering with her ability to drive. 'I find it a bit depressing, I must say, that you have to make this about you and your problem with Richard, instead of about us. I knew I shouldn't have told you about that massage. I should have known you were the only man alive who still thinks massage is a fancy word for fore-play.'

Dave gave a loud snort.

'He's an alternative *therapist*, David. That's what he does. Partly.'

'*Partly*. Look, let's not get too carried away with how multi-faceted Ricky boy is, OK? He owns an organic food shop – two organic food shops – and he's a trained back rubber and yoga instructor. Big fucking deal.'

'Please, can we get off the subject of Richard and back to us?'

'All I know is, that's when it all began. When Anna moved in with Richard and started doing the interviews for the book from their flat, and you got to see him doing his stuff surrounded by all that . . . white leather.'

'That's when what began?'

Dave slumped forward in his seat as if he'd been asked to explain something exceptionally basic for the umpteenth time. Then he bunched his fist in front of his face and glared at it.

'Suddenly it's time for us to move house,' he said, flicking his thumb out to the side. 'Time for me to get a new wardrobe.' Up sprang the forefinger. 'Time we cut down on our drinking.' There was the middle finger. 'And, while we're at it, looked into health-club mem-berships, despite the fact that you have never broken out of a walk since I have known you.' Dave waggled his ring finger, pausing to flick at the skinny wedding band with his thumb. 'And then there's all the newfound enthusiasm for having *dinner parties*, for people we barely know, who have to have champagne when they arrive and a place to put their coats other than the end of Billy's bed.' He lowered the hand and turned to face her. 'Plus, there was that whole cashmere-blanket episode.'

Ruth looked at him as if he were insane. She knew exactly what he was talking about.

'Oh, come on,' he said. 'In the *Psychoanalysts' Book of Symbolic Gestures* I'm quite sure there's a whole chapter on the things: cashmere blankets as purchased by women who, earlier on in the day, didn't have enough money to put petrol in the car but then, all of a sudden, are prepared to fork out the price of a week's holiday in Spain for four feet of mushroom *wool*.' Dave's open palm came crashing down on his thigh with a crack. 'That's a decorative length of wool that can't actually function as a blanket because it would *wear out*.'

Now he was making the same face he made when pretending to be a mad squirrel for Billy's benefit: eyes stretched as wide as they would go, eyebrows straining to reach his hairline.

Ruth turned her head away from him so she was forced to squint sideways at the windscreen. She could see herself standing in the shop, holding the blanket up to her face, trying to remember when she had handled anything so luxurious. When she'd got it home she'd waited for a long time before removing the blanket from its tobacco-coloured tissue paper, and then she hadn't been able to find a suitable place to put it. In the shop it had been folded, lengthways, at the foot of a bed covered with a thick pelt of rabbit fur – one plain note in the midst of an orgy of opulence. But, back in their flat, it seemed ostentatious and dowdy at the same time. She'd tried it spread across the bottom of their Indian cotton bedspread and it lay there, looking up at her accusingly, like a duchess in a cheap motel. She'd tried it folded on the seat of a chair where it looked like nothing at all. By the time Dave got home, the blanket was draped self-consciously over the back of the discounted sky-blue sofabed, the duchess as asked to pose by *OK!* magazine.

'I quite like it,' Dave had said, when she drew his attention to it later on that night. 'Having blankets around the place reminds me of university, when the sofa was the guest bedroom. But it's a bit of a depressing colour, isn't it?'

'What d'you think it means then?' Ruth said, feeling for the gear stick. 'You tell me what the blanket means.'

Dave was silent for a moment, she could feel him weighing up the options: the safe tease versus the riskier observation. 'It means your oldest friend has got a cashmere kind of boyfriend,' he said quietly, 'and you want one too.'

They were outside their flat now. She glanced up at the windows and saw the Lone Ranger and Tonto slowly circling the ceiling of Billy's room, bathed in an eerie blue light. She twisted her head around and, keeping the revs higher than was strictly necessary, reversed the van into a parking space.

When Tony swerved sharply to avoid an imaginary object in the middle of Brompton Road even he had to agree that the best course of action was to drive directly to his mews house, a few minutes away, from where Anna could ring for a taxi.

'But you're coming in for a drink,' he said, yanking the cigarette lighter from its socket and branding the end of another cigarette with such determination that it bent in the middle. 'You haven't seen the house since I've done it up. You're going to *love* it. *Love* it. I love it. It's me, you know? My thing. Not . . . bloody . . . I dunno . . .' The cigarette was tracing small circles in the air now. 'No azaleas! In those painted tin container things. Or dog ornaments. Those bloody sheep with the bushes behind them, trees, whatever they are . . . and those china *whippets*.' Tony fell forward over the steering wheel as if the word itself were the final straw. 'Whippets. God! She had the whole fucking whippet oeuvre.'

Anna looked at her watch. 'I thought you liked whippets,' she said. 'What about Tinks and Hopper?'

Tinks and Hopper were Jean and Tony's dogs. They had gone up the aisle with them, sixteen years before, each dog wearing a giant tulle flower attached to its collar, to match the hand-painted tulle dress that Jean's old friend, Zandra, had made specially for her.

'That is completely different,' said Tony, grinding the cigarette into the ashtray, and jutting his chin at her. 'Besides, Tinks and Hopper are *lurchers*.'

He snapped the ashtray shut and then, without indicating, turned sharp right through an archway into a cobbled mews bristling with tubs of geraniums and cars, most of them zipped up inside branded sleeping bags. Tony's house was down at the bottom on the right, but no sooner were they through the arch than he yanked the steering wheel hard to the left, turned off the engine and killed the lights.

'Duck!' he hissed, skidding down in his seat until his eyes were just level with the dashboard. When Anna failed to respond instantly he reached up a hand and grabbed her arm, forcing her to collapse sideways across the gearbox.

'What are you doing?' she asked crossly.

'Ssssh,' whispered Tony. 'It's Jean and a man.'

'So? Let go, will you? The gear stick's digging into me.'

'Quiet . . . I knew she was seeing someone!'

'Yes, Herve.'

'Not Herve. Someone.'

Anna closed her eyes, 'Tony. It's one o'clock in the morning.'

'Exactly.' Tony was gingerly pushing himself up on his elbows, tilting his head back to get a clearer view of his ex-wife and her companion. 'And who the hell has she been out with until this hour? I knew it. When she didn't kick up a fuss about not being allowed to bring Herve to the party, I knew she had to have something else up her sleeve. Wait . . . there . . . Bugger. He's staying out of the light deliberately.'

'Of course he isn't.'

Anna wriggled back into the passenger seat and slowly straightened up so that she and Tony were level, hunched and staring straight ahead, like astronauts in their re-entry capsule.

'Tony, has it occurred to you that it might not be all that healthy, living in the same street as your ex-wife?'

Anna glanced sideways at Tony who was peering intently into the dark, teeth clenched. 'What are they doing?' she asked.

'I don't know. Looks like he's trying to come in for a nightcap.'

'Well, that is what we were about to do, after all.'

'Yes, but we are *friends*,' hissed Tony. 'That man is not a friend.'

'How do you know?' asked Anna.

'Because, if he were a friend I would know him.'

Anna widened her eyes in amazement.

'Anna, women do not make new male friends in their late forties, everyone knows that. The men aren't interested, for Christ's sake! Oh God, I can't see a bloody thing. What does he look like to you?'

'A black shape, about three inches taller than her.'

'Really?' Tony edged up in his seat. 'Three inches, you reckon?'

'Look, Tony. Don't you think . . . I mean Jean is going to have admirers. Inevitably. He might turn out to be perfectly all right. You never know.'

Tony's head snapped left, his chin was wedged onto his chest giving him the appearance of a man who could move nothing apart from his eyeballs which, as a result, were rather overdeveloped. 'What's she told you?' he said, glaring at her.

'Nuthiiiing.' Anna sighed exaggeratedly.

'Is it anyone I know? Anna . . . ? You don't have to say anything, just blink once for yes. Is it Rollo Haines? I bet it is him. He's been sniffing around since Easter, with his bloody skiing chalet. Has he got a bald patch? Can you see?'

Anna, despite her reservations, obligingly stretched her neck to get a better look and instantly shrank back. 'They're coming this way!' she croaked, gripping the door handle. 'What are we going to do?'

Tony's head sank down in his shirt collar, his eyes flicking from left to right. 'You'll have to say something,' he whispered.

'Me?'

'Pretend you needed to ask her something urgently . . . and I said I'd drop you off.'

'But Tony—'

'Please. *Please*.'

They could hear the scrunch of feet approaching on the cobbles. Tony gave Anna a last pleading grimace, took a deep breath and shot up in his seat, deftly flicking his hair out of his eyes as he made his ascent.

'Hiiiii there, Jean,' he called, lowering the driver's window. 'Anna here wanted a word with you, and then we thought it a pity to interrupt, so . . .' he was gesturing at Anna with his left hand, groping for her arm. Obediently she leant across his lap and smiled up at the couple now standing a few feet away from the car.

'Hi,' Anna said. 'Sorry.'

Tony put an arm around her shoulders and gave them a friendly squeeze designed to convey that she was the kind of woman who needed to be indulged, and he was the kind of guy who couldn't say no. And, from the way the stranger dipped his head and smiled shyly down at his trainers, Anna could tell that Tony had been unable to resist a quick what-can-you-do? roll of the eyes, just to press home the point. The upper part of Jean's face was obscured by shadow, but the slight twitch of her pointy upper lip confirmed she was not so easily taken in.

Tony relaxed his grip on Anna and thrust his hand out of the window in the man's direction. 'I don't believe we've met,' he said, in a voice that could have been heard in the next street. 'I'm Jean's ex-husband. I live just across the mews.' There was a pause and then Anna felt Tony give the stranger his full-strength rich and successful smile. This was the golden smile that had – so the story went – persuaded the head of a leading men's tailoring company to cross the room at a cocktail party, back in 1979, and offer Tony the job of fronting their advertising campaign, right then and there. 'And that was in the days when there was no such thing as "the face of",' Tony would always say at this point in the story. 'I mean there was Daks man, but the models changed with every campaign. There was no precedent for picking an actor, let alone making him responsible for conveying a whole lifestyle . . .'

'It's all very cosy,' Tony was saying, his hand still extended. 'I keep a spare set of keys actually. Makes her feel safer.'

The man was looking sideways at Jean, his hands thrust into his trouser pockets, apparently waiting for some kind of lead.

Jean took a step towards the car and bent down until her narrow oval face was level with her ex-husband's. 'Tony, this is Geoff. Geoff is the Cable and Co. emergency plumber and he's just sorted out a leaking pipe. Geoff, this is my ex-husband Tony Alcroft.'

Geoff took a small hop to the left, raised a palm and croaked, 'All right?'

'Now.' Jean nudged a coil of silver hair off her face and bent towards the car, the better to give Tony the full impact of her fool-detector gaze, 'what's all this about, Anna?'

Anna opened her mouth to answer and found herself gaping stupidly at the windscreen.

'Um . . .' she said.

Tony tightened his grip on her shoulders.

'Never mind.' Jean straightened up, gathering her cashmere wrap briskly around her, making the pom-pom trim dance. 'Anna, darling. I'll pick you up on Saturday morning as planned. And Tony, if I catch you spying on me again there's going to be trouble.'

Jean stepped away from the car, planting her feet at an angle in the way that models used to.

'I'll be off then,' the plumber said hastily, raising an arm in farewell. 'See you, Mr Alcroft. Mrs Alcroft.'

'Thanks, Geoff,' Jean said, 'only please, call me Jean.' She turned her head fractionally in the direction of the Porsche before adding, 'After all, I *am* supposed to be divorced.'

As she swung off down the mews Tony followed her progress intently, his neck craning as she turned the key in the lock of number 25 and stepped through the door with a swivel of her heel. When the door closed behind her, he slumped back in his seat with a barely audible moan.

'So, where are you off to on Saturday?' Tony asked eventually, as if they'd been momentarily interrupted mid-conversation at some social gathering. 'Anywhere nice?'

'A wedding, some young relative of Jean's,' Anna

replied. The whole night had taken such a surreal turn that it felt perfectly normal to carry on talking crouched in the now rather chilly Porsche. 'I'm only going because Jean thought the couple could be my guinea pig newly-weds. And, no, she is not taking anyone.'

'Look,' said Tony, 'I don't want this . . . incident to give you the wrong impression. I have a regular girl-friend, which is more than you-know-who. And what she said, about the spying.' He shook his head sadly. 'I just like to keep an eye on the situation. She wouldn't be the first divorcee to be taken advantage of in this town.'

Tony sat back, tilted the rear-view mirror towards him and pressed the heels of his hands along his temples. 'We should definitely do it,' he said, addressing his reflection. 'Your book, I mean. I'm telling you, you don't appreciate what a bloody complex thing marriage is until the day you get divorced. You really bloody don't.'

Three

When Ruth arrived at the flat for her ten o'clock appointment with Anna, it was Richard who answered the door. He was wearing an aqua-coloured cashmere sweater and truncated cargo pants. His bare feet were tanned and smooth and scrubbed. They looked like the kind of feet that Calvin Klein might put on a billboard in Times Square, intertwined with Kate Moss's, and the words 'Excellence, a New Experience in Extremity Moisturizer'.

'Is something the matter?' Richard asked, glancing between Ruth and his toes. 'You look a bit distracted. Come on in, I've just made some juice.'

Of course he had – a deluxe blend of freshly squeezed organic fruits, high in energy, packed with taste. The only juice they ever had in their house was Tropicana, and that was used as a mixer.

Richard led the way into the flat, gesturing with long, tanned fingers for Ruth to deposit her coat on the white leather sofa. His hips swung loosely as he walked, like a dancer's.

'Babe?' he murmured, tapping lightly on the cherry-wood door of Anna's study. 'Are you ready for your ten o'clock?'

Even though Anna had been living in Richard's flat – or apartment as Richard called it – for over two years now, Ruth still felt like a child on a movie set whenever she came here. In fact, before Anna moved in with Richard, Ruth had assumed that flats like theirs were pretty much all locations for hire, occupied by slick media types in TV dramas but never by real people. She was not the envious type as a rule, but this flat, with its three shades of white colour scheme, floating fireplace and shiny painted wood floor, had triggered feelings that she was not proud of. Even more disturbing, whenever she was in the flat she could feel her confidence ebbing away. On the pavement outside she was the same old Ruth, the Ruth who couldn't resist a floral hair clip or another ethnic cushion. But once inside she was needy Ruth, who felt out of place in her Oxfam leopard-skin coat and unnatural lipstick. If she really had to put her finger on it, Richard's apartment made her feel fat.

'Here we go, Ruth.' Richard handed her a glass of peach-coloured liquid and Ruth took it, uncomfortably aware of the contrast between his Excellence hand and her own, with its wristful of fraying friendship bracelets and chewed, partly painted fingernails. 'Anna won't be a minute, she's on the phone to her editor.' Richard smiled and, not for the first time, Ruth was dazzled by the whiteness and uniformity of his teeth. 'How's it going, by the way?' he said.

'Oh, fine thanks. OK.'

If Ruth felt fat in Richard's apartment she felt fat and naked talking to Richard in Richard's apartment. She always got the sense that he was suppressing the urge to tell her not to touch anything, or longing to drag back her shoulders until she stood up straight. Once, a few nights after a party at Richard's apartment – during which she had upturned a saucer of plum sauce on the white sheepskin rug – Ruth had a dream in which Richard turned up at their flat, wearing protective clothing, and asked her to strip and lie on the bed in order that he could 'clean' her. She hadn't even thought about telling Dave.

'Well, I'd better get going then,' Richard was saying. 'Help yourself to anything you want; there's some yoghurt and berries in the fridge.' He wandered over to the door, plucked a leather bag off a hook on the wall, and gave her a high-five kind of wave.

'Yoghurt and berries,' she could hear Dave muttering. 'Yoghurt and *berries*. And that's a handbag. You can dress it up any way you like, but *that* is a handbag.'

'Bye, Richard,' Ruth said. 'See you,' and as the door closed behind him she heaved a sigh and let go of the stomach muscles she had been sucking in since she arrived.

It was nearly three years since Anna had started going out with Richard. They had all been introduced, Richard to the gang, over dinner in a new restaurant at the end of Richard's road.

'Well, well, well,' Dave said, when Richard rose from the table to greet them, which was Dave's way of saying, don't know how to deal with this one, not at all.

'I was not being unfriendly,' he said later, on the way home in the van. 'I just don't know many men who wear

Thai fishermen's trousers. And don't come the worldly chick with me. I saw your face.'

The truth was, Richard was very different from most men of their acquaintance. Physically, he was in another league: leaner, cleaner, a lot firmer. He had one of those peaky hairstyles that identified him as one of the grooming classes (Tony's hair was full of something, but that was different) and a chunky silver ring on the third finger of his left hand that suggested he was not only right up to date with current trends, but in touch with his feminine side. Open-minded. Also, he was brown all the time, an even depth of brown that Dave hadn't managed to achieve even after a month in South America. It wasn't that Richard was good-looking, exactly, but the effort he put into his appearance made him striking, in the same way as, say, a highly waxed new car. He was a bit younger than the rest of them, of course – thirty-four – but it wasn't that. The point was, Richard appeared to be physically in charge of himself, while Dave and Archie, and even Tony, gave the impression of being at the mercy of the ravages of time, their punishing schedules, and the unpredictable calorie content of food. Richard looked like he was the captain of his own tight ship and fully prepared for all eventualities. Then there was the question of what he did for a living. Besides co-owning a successful organic food shop, Richard was an alternative therapist.

'Really?' Dave said, when Richard volunteered this information, having just asked the waiter if there was any meat product in the risotto. 'Well, well, well.'

'Of course I don't think it's *funny* to be a therapist,'
Dave protested, as they were getting ready for bed later
that night. 'But that was the last straw, wasn't it? Come
ooon. The watchimicalit-designed apartment, the fitness
thing, the vegetarian thing, the "passion" for cooking.
The clasping-hugging thing. I mean' – he picked up the
cushions stacked against the bed head and tossed them
Frisbee style, one by one, into the far corner of the bedroom – 'what is Anna doing with him?'

'Well, that's three answers, for starters,' Ruth told
him. 'Great flat. Great body. Great cook. You'd go for it.'

'Exactly.'

'What d'you mean, "exactly"?'

'I mean he'd make someone a lovely girlfriend.'

The second time they met, Richard had organized
for them all to go and see an avant garde Belgian circus
troupe who were performing in a giant purple tent in
Battersea Park. Even at this stage, the pattern of their
collective relationship was more or less established.
Ruth, Jean and Valerie were impressed and intrigued ('I
can't remember when Archie last took the initiative and
organized an outing,' said Valerie on the phone that
evening. 'Of course, now he's threatening to be delayed
at work.') Whereas the men were sceptical or, in Dave's
case, downright hostile. 'Who does he think he is?' was
Dave's response when Ruth first told him about the invitation. 'We don't need multicultural entertainments. We
have our own things to do on Fridays. It's like being a
student all over again.'

Still, once they were actually seated in the magenta
big top, stars twinkling overhead, even Dave had
started to enjoy himself.

'I think this is rather fun, "a whole new experi-ence",' Tony said, elbowing Dave and pointing to the review quote on a nearby poster, and Dave nodded grudgingly and gave Ruth a small apologetic smile. But that was before it became clear that Cirque Braque was a whole new experience in audience participation.

Dave would later recall his sensation of mounting terror as he glanced up to see two body-painted Cirque Braque performers swooping down from the canopy on elasticated ropes, aiming straight for him. And then the physical lurch as he was hooked under the armpits and sprung out of his seat and up into the dark of the big top, where they proceeded to toss him between them like a banana in a monkey house. All might not have been lost had Dave not looked down during one of his fly pasts, and seen a row of anxious white faces staring up at him and in the midst of them one brown face, smiling and cheering, his hands raised over his head in tremendous applause.

'Hi Ruth.' Anna was padding across the wooden floor carrying a small lacquer tray on which was a white plate, streaked with traces of berry, and a slender vase containing a single lily. She was wearing white jogging pants and a pale cashmere sweater the exact same shade as Richard's.

Ruth had a sudden flashback to her own breakfast that morning. She'd woken up to find Dave rattling around in the bottom of the bedroom cupboard, appar-ently looking for a tie.

'Oh, be a love, and get us some breakfast, Dave,' she'd said.

'Awwww,' he'd groaned, giving her a pained, this-is-all-I-need look. 'What d'you want, then? Quick!'

'Something nice,' she'd replied, blearily. 'Whatever you had.'

Fifteen seconds later she was presented with a bowl of dry cereal containing three bits of dehydrated strawberry, and a spoon.

'If we're out of milk, isn't there a plan B?' she'd asked.

'Nope,' Dave had said, and he'd reached into the bowl, taken a handful of cereal, and popped the nuggets into his mouth, one by one.

'I saw Richard,' Ruth said, stepping to one side so that Anna could put the tray down on the worktop – the spotless, unobstructed zinc worktop. She snatched a glance at Anna's bottom, neat and smooth in the white jogging pants. 'You've got the same sweaters, I see . . . lovely.'

'Yes,' Anna smiled sheepishly, 'his mother bought them for us actually.'

Of all the aspects of Anna's beautiful life with Richard, this was perhaps the most extraordinary. Not only was Richard a study in sympathetic, life-enhancing behaviour, his mother was Martha Stewart, without the ruthless competitive edge. Last Christmas she had given Anna the present of a long weekend at a spa, whereas Ruth's mother-in-law had given her an implement for making carrots into matchsticks and two packets of flesh-coloured tights.

'You and your luxy life.' Ruth sighed. 'God, it hardly

seems possible that you were living in that grotty flat by the Westway with a –' She had been going to say 'with an anti-capitalist musician' but something about the tense downward curve of Anna's mouth made her think again. 'It's funny, isn't it, the way things turn out?' Ruth babbled on, rubbing a finger backwards and forwards along the shiny surface of the counter. 'If you'd asked me, back then, which of our lives would change the most, I'd have picked Val's. I mean, I know it works in its way – her and Archie – but I suppose I'm surprised she hasn't gone on one of her trips and just decided to stay and organize the third world. Whereas Tony and Jean . . . I never imagined they'd split up. And I wouldn't necessarily have pictured you like this.' She hesitated. 'You know? Living the designer dream.'

Ruth glanced up. Anna was rinsing the plate in the sink, her light-brown hair hung down her back in a perfect glossy sweep ending in a line so sharp it might have been measured with a spirit level. Ruth wondered if she was wearing a thong or those knickers like mini shorts that she'd seen in the magazines. Would they be the ones designed by an ex-model, or just the hand-wash-only sort? And what about the bra? It didn't seem to make even the faintest line across her back; or maybe she wasn't wearing one? Could that be all the yoga?

'People do change,' Anna said, wiping her hands and turning round to face Ruth. 'That's sort of the point of the book – looking at how they change and how their relationships adapt over time.'

Ruth nodded. 'You were lucky though, weren't you?' she said. 'That you changed while you were in-between men? Between Danny and Richard, I mean?

You could start all over again, go for something completely different. Because Richard *is* so different, isn't he? To me' – Ruth propped her chin on her fist and gazed dolefully at a list on the refrigerator which began with the words 'Richard to Buy' – 'Richard seems like another species. I mean, when I started seeing Dave, whenever it was—'

'Nineteen eighty-six,' said Anna.

'Right . . . back in the days of disco. Well, there weren't any men like Richard around, were there? Not one. They just didn't come in that description. It was either sexy bastard, or wimpy nice bloke, or your mate you quite fancied. None of this being capable of buying you clothes and being interested in how you felt and knowing all about PMT and loving watching girly crap on the telly. It just wasn't on offer. That's what I mean, you see. You became available just as the first range of "modern men" were coming on the market.'

Anna gave a little shrug and leant back against the sink. 'Maybe,' she said, staring down at her feet. 'It never really felt like that.'

'Oh, come on,' Ruth moaned. 'Humour me. Tell me what it's like to be you, Anna, pleeease. Tell me what it's like to live with a real, reconstructed, twenty-first-century bloke.'

'I don't know,' Anna said. 'I've got used to it, I suppose.' She was smiling but busily twisting her hair over her shoulder, the way she always did when she felt uncomfortable.

'Oh, go on,' Ruth persisted, 'give us some examples . . . anything.'

'Well, OK . . . I don't know. He'll sometimes do

49

things like . . . cook dinner, and maybe set up a table in the bedroom.'

Ruth nodded cautiously.

'Or . . . he takes me away for weekends, mostly to spas. And he likes to go shopping, which I suppose is pretty unusual . . . Oh, and for my last birthday he gave me thirty-eight little presents, one for every year, and hid them all over the flat.' Anna shrugged. 'Is that the sort of thing you meant?'

Ruth was still nodding, but now she had the expression of someone who has just thrown out an old bit of junk, only to see the identical piece on display in an antique shop complete with telephone-number price tag.

'Yep,' Ruth said. 'That's the sort of thing. So . . . what happens about the housework and stuff? You do all that, right? When it comes down to it?'

As she was asking the question Ruth realized that she didn't actually want to know how Anna and Richard's life worked, only how it didn't work, only the parts that bore some passing resemblance to her own experience.

'Er . . .' Anna was gazing at her feet again, the rope of hair in her hand twisted so tight now that it was buckling. 'I suppose . . . well, I suppose Richard takes care of most of it, actually.' She gave a small, nervous laugh. 'Sometimes I do the shopping, but then, if he's going into Planet Earth, it's all there. And he's quite particular about brands and things.' Anna glanced up and Ruth saw she had the same anxious expression she'd had at the Cunninghams', those same, almost pleading, eyes. 'Anyway, that isn't everything, is it?' Anna said.

'Nooo! Of course it isn't,' Ruth agreed, louder than she'd intended.

Suddenly Ruth had a vivid picture of Dave unpacking Tesco carrier bags on the seat of the sofabed, one eye on the TV, as he spread before him a tenth of the requested shopping list, plus one or two surprises. ('A double-headed garlic press! You've got to admit that's worth £4.99. I had no idea they sold all this stuff!') Simultaneously, she saw Dave cooking dinner for them both – utilizing most of the purchases, all the spices in the cupboard, four Pyrex dishes, three frying pans – and she felt a familiar knot tightening in her stomach.

She'd analysed this one before. The knot was partly to do with guilt that she had passed the 'Thai curry? Wow! Great!' phase of their lives and was now firmly at the 'I hope you're going to clear all that up' stage. Partly it was due to straightforward irritation that the palaver Dave made out of cooking their dinner – their far too coconutty, exceedingly creamy dinner that she was usually about as in the mood for as a mud wrestle – had nothing to do with pleasing her, or making her life easier, and everything to do with making him feel like a creative, modern kind of guy. And then, mixed up in there, right in the tight, pinched heart of the knot – which could sometimes take a full night's sleep to ease out – was the knowledge that she was being unreasonable. She was a useless cook; Dave was at least enthusiastic. He left a mess but, to be fair, so did she. Dave had always prided himself on his curries and it was pointless, not to mention mean-spirited, to find fault with him now.

As Ruth contemplated this, the image of Dave,

with his rolled-up sleeves and his bubbling pans, was substituted for a much earlier scene involving a boyfriend she hadn't thought about for years and years. They were standing in a kitchen, inches apart; she was looking at her fingernails.

'Is it something I've done?' he'd said.

'No,' she'd said. 'It's me.'

'God. What sort of person could do this on a guy's birthday?'

'A desperate one,' said Ruth. 'One who doesn't want to be doing this any longer, and can't think of any convincing reason why. All I know, is I don't feel happy any more, and that's all I can tell you.'

'Ruth?' Anna was standing right in front of her, a hand on each of her shoulders. 'Are you all right?' She glanced at her watch. 'We should get on with it really, or it'll be lunchtime.'

'OK,' Ruth said. 'Just tell me one thing first though, Anna. Do you think it's because you were a bit older that you knew Richard was the answer? Do you think you had to go through all the other stuff first before you were ready to give the Richard-type of bloke a chance?'

Anna was gazing past Ruth, somewhere just to the right of her head. She had a strange, grim expression, as if steeling herself before diving into a freezing cold lake.

'No,' she said quietly. 'I think I just had to face the fact that the whole way I approached relationships was wrong, that I didn't have the first idea what I needed. Well, you know that. It was you lot who got a grip of me in the first place, remember?'

*

In fact, the relationship summit around Valerie's kitchen table, six weeks after Anna had broken up with Daniel, hadn't been quite the productive experience Anna had hoped it would be. When she arrived at the Cunninghams' house, Valerie, Ruth and Jean were pacing the kitchen floor and there was an atmosphere that suggested they had already fallen out over where, exactly, Anna was going wrong.

'Valerie's got a flow chart,' Ruth whispered, widening her eyes.

'I have not got a *flow chart*,' snapped Valerie. 'I've just got a few prompt cards. There's no point doing this at all, if we aren't prepared to do it properly. What do you think, Jean?'

'I think it's riveting.' Jean removed the cigarette from between her lips and held it aloft. 'Cards, charts, whatever. I can't wait to hear the tips myself.'

'Good,' said Valerie, glaring at Ruth. 'At least someone else is taking this seriously. Shall I kick off, then?'

The first card was labelled 'Features that Could Be Improved On'. Ruth fluttered her eyelids theatrically as Valerie slid it onto the kitchen table.

'There are those who don't think this sort of thing is important,' Valerie said, methodically lining the edge of the card up with the side of the table, 'but I'm afraid I'm not one of them. No one is saying there's anything wrong with the way Anna looks, but, in my opinion, it's an area where there's room for improvement. Which brings us to the first point on the card: "The importance of the feminine".' Valerie studiously avoided looking over at Ruth, whose hands were cupped round her face, before continuing. 'For example, hair.'

Shane Watson

'What about hair?' snapped Ruth.

'Well, I believe that hair conveys a lot of important messages. Longish, pretty, well-kept hair tells a man that you are on his side. It says that you're both in agreement as to what it means to be a woman. And, at the moment –' Valerie gave a nod in the direction of Anna's heavily layered homage to Rod Stewart circa 1974 '– Anna's hair is just a little bit unisex. And messy. And men are – let me finish, Ruth, thank you. Men are very simple creatures. They don't like challenges. They don't like surprises. Feminine women make them feel more masculine. It's very straightforward.'

'What about a nurse's outfit?' mumbled Ruth. 'They like those. Or a tennis skirt. That could do the trick.'

'Right!' Valerie said. 'Moving on . . .' She presented a new card at arm's length before snapping it down crisply next to its predecessor. 'So, the second point I wanted to address is: "Making Yourself too Available". Now, I don't want to get into . . . sex . . . and when is the right time and all of that. Her voice, normally quite low was rising and getting louder by the second. 'I just think there is something to be learned here, about pacing, and about . . . making men work. Not just offering yourself up as a foregone conclusion.'

'Oh, this is hopeless!' Ruth groaned. 'You'll have her in a wimple next! Besides, we all know it isn't what Anna's *doing* that's the problem, it's the men she's *going for*. Surely, if there's any advice we're equipped to give, it's what she should be looking for in a partner?'

They all, simultaneously, turned to look at Anna, as if to remind themselves what they had to work on. Valerie gave a small grudging nod.

'All right, so let's start with the first priority,' Ruth said. 'He's got to be someone you respect.' Her eyes flickered first to Valerie's face and then to Jean's. 'Jean? Respect has got to be up there, hasn't it?'

'Darling, Tony was playing Max Huthering, the unscrupulous Cornish baron, when we met . . . I can't say *respect* was the first word that sprang to mind.'

'All right. OK. Friendship then. You need to have a really strong friendship.' Ruth scoured their faces for confirmation. 'Well, of course you have to be best friends! Surely?'

'I don't know if that's necessarily quite right,' Valerie said.

'I certainly would never have called Tony my best friend.' Jean wrinkled her nose as if she found the phrase distasteful. 'Friends are generally reliable and considerate. I'd say Tony was more like a child . . . more like a princeling really.'

'Oh, please!' Ruth slumped back in her chair. 'Well, tell us, Jean. What does matter then?'

Jean sighed. 'In my opinion?' She looked around the group as if she wasn't entirely convinced they were ready for the rules according to Jean Alcroft. 'I'd say you want someone who amuses you and who is amused by you. Ideally, someone who never expected to end up with a woman like you, so he's continually amazed by his own cleverness at having brought it about.' Her eyelids descended to the point where she needed to tip back her head in order to see. 'And I think it helps,' she added, 'if you give them the impression that you're not terrifically bothered either way.'

'Dare I say it,' Valerie said, under her breath, 'but someone who can pay the bills is not a bad start.'

'Oh, well, silly me,' Ruth said, 'for imagining marriage might have something to do with compatibility, or even love.'

It was at about that point in the proceedings that Anna had decided to write the book.

'Right, then. Here we go.' Anna edged the tape recorder across the seat of the sofa, a few inches closer to Ruth's knee, and pressed the record button. 'So, Ruth, what shall we start with? Any changes to your circumstances, new developments, that sort of thing?'

Ruth leant back against the beige suede upholstery and gazed up at the mirrored ceiling, wondering, as she always did when she was in Anna's office, how Anna managed to keep the suede from marking and whether or not she and Richard ever had sex in here. 'None,' she said, absent-mindedly. 'Billy's still a typical three-year-old, drawing on the walls, trying to drive me to the brink. We're still living in a two-bedroom flat over a wine merchant, or in heaven as far as my husband is concerned. Oh, and I've been promoted.' She leaned forward and enunciated primly into the microphone like a witness for the Senate House Committee. 'So I now officially have a few of my very own theatrical and film clients. Otherwise, not a dickie bird.'

'Has the job promotion changed anything?' Anna made a note on her pad and looked up at Ruth expectantly. Ruth noticed, for the first time, that the very corners of Anna's eyelids were finely outlined in something pearly and white which must be, she imagined, what beauty writers meant by highlighter. 'Dave all right about the promotion?' prompted Anna.

'Oh, Dave's over the moon. More money for playing. Dave thinks it's the best thing that's happened all year.'

'But you're not so sure?'

Ruth examined her thumbnail.

'We can come back to that. Let's get on with . . . reasons for being married. Any change there – in terms of expectations, or benefits?'

Ruth took a deep breath. 'You could say that,' she said, glancing down at the tape recorder.

'OK.' Anna flipped over the page of her notebook. 'Can you tell me what, specifically?'

'Well . . .' Ruth hesitated. Her eyes shifted upwards to the bookshelves behind Anna's head. 'You know when people say all you want in a partner is a best friend, someone you can go through life with, hand-in-hand, chuckling all the way?'

Anna's eyes drifted up from her notebook, her expression even more than usually neutral.

'That's what I thought I wanted. I thought that's what any sensible woman wanted. And now I don't,' Ruth said. 'That's what's changed.'

'And why would you say that was?'

Ruth wondered, for a moment, if inside Anna was shouting 'Eureka . . . some action at last! Marital discord, here we go!' But then, that wasn't Anna's style. If the truth be known, it was Ruth who was hungry for some drama, not Anna.

'I've got older,' Ruth said bluntly. 'I've got a

three-year-old kid, a full-time job and I'm knackered.'
Her eyes met Anna's and they stared at each other for a
few seconds before Ruth took up the invitation to elaborate. 'There comes a point,' she said, 'when you
couldn't give a toss about being able to tell each other
anything, and knowing everything about each other,
when all you want is someone to take care of you.
Someone who is going to fix the roof so you don't have
to. Someone who's going to forbid you to walk home
late at night, rather than make you toss a coin for who's
going to pick up the takeaway. God . . .' She rolled her
eyes and slumped back against the sofa. 'To think the
equal partnership was the holy grail of relationships for
us. We must have been stark raving mad. Why didn't
someone tell us? I mean they were prepared to bombard
us with all kinds of other useless bloody advice about
what to do with our lives.'

Anna started scribbling 'BURDEN OF EQUALITY' in
small capitals at the top of the page, angling the pad
very slightly so that Ruth was forced to push up on her
fingertips to read it.

'You can say that again.' Ruth sighed, curling her
legs up on the seat next to her and prodding at the fraying wedge soles of her espadrilles. 'How about, "Don't
forget to marry someone with a bit of money and a good
work ethic who thinks you're fabulous and won't let
you lift a finger"? What would have been wrong with
that?' She automatically took the magazine that Anna
was offering her and placed it, as indicated, under her
feet.

'So what do you want now, exactly?' Anna asked.
She had put the notebook aside and was resting one

elbow on the back of the sofa, her fingers pressing lightly against her milky temple.

'Oh, you know, plans. Long-term, rigid, down to the last detail plans. A nice house, with nice things in it. A proper, clean car, not a van full of furniture and old Ribena cartons. I want to have parties, with lots of interesting people and expensive wine and three kinds of glasses. I have turned into *that* woman. I actually do want all the clichés – the kitchen extension, and the bit of decking for eating outside, and a bathroom with his 'n' hers basins and glamorous acquaintances who admire me for having put it all together with such flair.' Ruth's eyes flickered around the office. 'And what I mind is not so much that most of our friends have got all that, but that Dave shows no sign of wanting *any* of it. He thinks all that stuff's for marriage moonies and if you so much as redecorate the bathroom you're one of them, on the road to becoming Mr and Mrs Precious Materialists. He thinks we're above all that. But I want it. Not all of it, just . . . some of it.' Ruth paused. 'And I want more children.'

Anna blinked. 'OK,' she said cautiously.

'Well, not OK. OK, if I was married to a man who was fully mature.'

'But you've already got Billy.'

Ruth rolled her eyes. She fished in her tapestry handbag for a cigarette, found a stray one in the bottom and clamped it between her lips, waving a hand at Anna to indicate it was just a matter of finding a light and she'd be ready to continue. 'The thing is, Dave wanted us to be like a couple of kids who accidentally had a couple of kids,' she mumbled, striking a match and screwing up her eyes. 'Nothing was meant to change. And with Billy it didn't really. But I can't do that any more. Taking your baby everywhere you go, all of you sleeping in the same room on your one week's holiday a year. Somehow that all seemed faintly Bohemian at the time. But now . . .' Ruth eyed the tape recorder and lowered her voice. 'You know, I don't have sexual fantasies any more. I have fantasies about dependable men with fat salaries who take me out to dinner and write out enormous cheques for cleaners and nannies. I was having one about Jasper only yesterday. *Jasper!*' Ruth grimaced. 'Oh God, we can't be this predictable, can we? Anna, tell me I'm not falling into some classic mid-life pattern. I bet you've got a chapter on this, haven't you?'

'Of course not,' Anna said, starting to scribble again. 'Does Dave know how you feel?'

'No,' said Ruth, craning her neck to see what she was writing.

'What would his reaction be, do you think?'

'Huh! I can tell you exactly. He thinks I'm discontented because of this,' Ruth pointed at the notepad, 'because of your book, because it's got me comparing our marriage with other people's. He thinks we should never have moved further into town, because we can't really keep up, and being in the book has just exacerbated the problem.'

Ruth's eyebrows floated upwards as if she were giving this possibility serious consideration for the first time. 'I think I've just got bored of being me,' she said quietly. 'Good old Ruth whose life is a bit of a shambles. Actually, I've had enough of being Daveanruth, the great hairy blob that passes for two adult lives.' Out of the corner of her eye she could see Anna writing 'LOSS OF INDIVIDUALITY' and then, in smaller letters underneath, 'When Being the Couple Becomes all-Consuming'.

'D'you know what it feels like?' Ruth said. 'Like being in one of those pantomime horse suits. Being the back end of a pantomime horse with a front end that's got no sense of direction, and no concern for the fact that you're bent over double, blundering around in the dark, relying on them to stop you from falling into the orchestra pit.'

Anna was scribbling 'CONTROL, LACK OF, see Women's Subconscious Desire to Be Protected and Led. (Note: frequently surfaces in mid-life, when the contrast between the mother's experience and their own becomes more evident.)' She circled the full stop and underlined the word 'mid-life', pulling her shoulders back and straightening her neck as she glanced over what she had written.

'I mean, I know I'm lucky in a way,' Ruth said. 'In lots of ways. My mother, for example, thinks I'm the luckiest woman on God's earth. The fact that Dave cooks and plays with Billy and never orders me around the way my dad used to order her. She'd have a canary if she could hear me now. "You lot don't know how lucky you are," she'd say. "He's spoilt you, that lovely David."' Ruth laughed, but Anna was too absorbed in her note-taking to join in.

'Anna? I was just wondering' – Ruth gestured at the notebook – 'in among all those headings and subheadings – have you got anything on romance? Because, you know, I'm with you about the burden of equality and all that. But sometimes I think, if Dave just came into the kitchen one night and, instead of elbowing me out the way to get at the drawer with the bottle opener, he put his arms around me and said, "I love you, Ruth, and I still think you're the most gorgeous thing I've ever seen" . . .' Ruth smiled sheepishly. 'Well . . . then I wonder if I'd really care about the decking and the twin basins. D'you know what I mean?'

Anna raised a finger to indicate she'd be with her in just a second as she wrote 'ROMANCE as cure. Looking for the SIMPLICITY of earliest relationships. Also seeking INDIVIDUAL ATTENTION – see the female loss of identity after having children.'

'Yeah,' said Ruth softly, 'that's what I thought.'

Four

Valerie was at the wheel of the Toyota Land Cruiser talking into the mic of her tape recorder, a combination which never failed to make her feel powerful (somewhere between one of Tom Cruise's accomplices in *Mission Impossible* and those behind-the-scenes women with the permanent headsets who organize the lives of people like Robbie Williams). The journey over to her mother's house in Maida Vale was the ideal opportunity to catch up on what she called her 'book diary' – an on-going, tape-recorded account of her daily routine, embellished with the occasional observation she thought might prove useful for Anna's book. The fact that Anna had shown no interest in the diary, and had even gone so far as to tell her it was a waste of her time, was not going to deter Valerie one bit. Of all the people involved in this project she was clearly the one who took her responsibilities most seriously, and there was no doubt in her mind that Anna would be grateful for her attention to detail at some point in the future.

'Eleven a.m., Saturday,' Valerie murmured into the mic, in a voice she fancied was not unlike a certain celebrated newsreader's. 'This morning, so far, have chosen the new bedroom carpet, employed a gardener –

every other week, so nothing Archie can complain about
– and fixed up a lunch meeting with Susie Walker to talk
about the Good Life charity sale. Note –' Valerie raised
a finger off the steering wheel '– observation number . . .
oh . . . eighty-something: when a woman's children are
away at school she inevitably wants to find something
to fill her day. So, for example, Susie Walker, whose
husband is senior partner at Cazulets, hosts the Good
Life sales. And I – because Archie is, for the moment, a
junior partner – deal with the organization . . . Errrm,
and now there's just time before lunch to drop round to
mother's and wish her a happy birthday.'

'You said we didn't have to have *lunch*,' said a voice
behind her.

Valerie pressed the stop button on the tape recorder
and glanced sharply in the rear-view mirror. Her
daughter, Charlotte, was slumped on the back seat, the
sleeves of her grey hoodie pulled down over the tips of
her fingers, and the hood itself hauled so far forward
that her face was only visible from the curled top lip
down.

Valerie smiled brightly into the mirror. 'Some of us
will have lunch and others will have what they can . . .
what they want,' she quickly corrected herself, her jaw
tensing as she tried for the life of her to remember the
appropriate response.

That Monday, Valerie had sat through an hour-long
appointment with her daughter's psychiatrist, who was
of the opinion that Charlotte's eating problem wasn't
improving because she still felt she was being controlled.

'If you mean by that, organized. If you mean by that, given a routine and involved in plans, then, yes. I am certainly guilty as charged,' Valerie said, smiling grimly at the psychiatrist. 'Lottie is fourteen years old.'

The psychiatrist was one of those soft-spoken, dumpy women who take twice as long as necessary to say what they mean and make you feel clinically hyper-active by comparison. Valerie could only just resist the temptation to finish the woman's sentences, or lean across the desk and thrust her wristwatch under her nose, jabbing a forefinger at the minute hand. It wasn't that she didn't want to discuss Lottie, she just didn't want to discuss her with someone who had studied painting interpretation for three years and had the remains of a digestive biscuit nestled on the ledge of her bosom.

'Look,' said Valerie. 'Charlotte has got her O levels coming up – or whatever they're called now – and if we don't get on top of this, her boarding school won't have her back. It is crucial they see we have it all under con-trol. Absolutely crucial.'

Valerie paused, waiting for the psychiatrist to take her point and suggest some fast-track solution, some-thing that would tide them over until the school holidays when they could all go away, as a family, and Lottie would have more than enough activities to distract her. Instead, the psychiatrist nodded non-committally, turning over papers on her desk as if they were medieval relics which might, at any moment, turn to dust.

Valerie took a deep breath. 'It would be a disaster if they weren't to take her back,' she continued. 'Look, with respect, I'm not sure that you . . . Marion . . . I'm not sure you can fully appreciate the effort that has gone into getting Lottie to where she is now. We cannot let this get in the way. There's just too much at stake.'

'Mrs Cunningham,' the psychiatrist pronounced every syllable of the name laboriously, 'it is precisely this emphasis on achieving, no matter what, that I believe your daughter is reacting against.' Valerie opened her mouth to speak but the psychiatrist continued. 'There is no snappy solution to this. Charlotte needs time. Not time spent in productive activities, but time to find her own level, her own pace.'

'I'm afraid that isn't good enough,' said Valerie. 'You'll have to give me some kind of game plan. I can't just sit here and wait for her to get better.'

And that was when the psychiatrist had come up, albeit reluctantly, with some rudimentary guidelines: no pressure to eat, no pressure to join in, gentle encouragement to communicate but only on subjects outside 'the judgement zone'.

'Is that all right, my darling?' Valerie peered into the rear-view mirror. Lottie's cheek was resting on the back of her hand. The wrist was a strange purply-red colour, and Valerie could see the bones of the joint jutting up under the skin like a luminous bolt.

'That tape's for Anna's book about marriage, isn't it?' Lottie said. It was more of an accusation than a question, but then all Lottie's utterances these days were so many ways of saying 'I hate you'.

'Yes, darling, it is.' Valerie stretched her neck to see if she could make eye contact with her daughter, her eyes darting from the road to the mirror and back again like an eager quiz contestant waiting for her clue.

'So how come you never say anything about Dad, only what *you've* done, *your* Himalayan thing and *your* bridge and *your* charities, and your . . . everything. It's never about both of you, is it?'

Lottie's jaw was moving as if she were chewing something but the likelihood of that was extremely small. Valerie's eyes stayed glued to the mirror. Let her talk, Marion had said. Don't be tempted to second-guess her questions or cut her off. If she's saying something you don't agree with, hear her out.

'My friends' parents . . .' Lottie hesitated. 'Even some of the ones who are divorced do more stuff together than you and Dad.'

'So, you'd like it if Daddy and I were divorced, would you?'

'I wouldn't *like* anything!' Lottie was running her thumbnail rhythmically up and down the middle of her lower lip. 'I just don't see what the point is! All you do is order him around and all he does is hide in his study and look miserable. I bet he'll run away soon, like Grandpa.'

'Darling, your father's not going anywhere.' Valerie was almost singing now in her effort to appear open and reasonable. 'You know he's devoted to you and Charlie. Aren't you looking forward to seeing Charlie, by the way? He's back from his French exchange today.'

'What if I told you I was a lesbian?' Lottie whined. 'You sooo couldn't handle that.'

'Charlotte,' Valerie said, 'the way you look you'd be lucky if a blue-faced baboon was interested in you.'

Lottie's eyes widened, the thumb dropped from her mouth into her lap.

'I'm sorry, darling,' said Valerie. 'But I can't just sit here and take it. You're going to have to meet me halfway.'

'You don't know how to do halfway.' Lottie was peering at her sideways now, her left eye scrunched up as if she was terrified someone might notice it was a dazzling turquoise blue. 'You can't do anything except *your* way.'

'Well, I'm trying. I'm prepared to give it a go if you will. Ah . . . oh hang on a minute.' Valerie broke off suddenly, lowered the driver's window and leant out into the street. 'Excuse me,' she called, straining to attract the attention of someone on the opposite side of the road. 'Hello! Yes, you. I saw that, and I suggest that you leave a note for the owner of the Citroën because I have made a note of your registration number . . . And the same to you, too,' she added, as she raised the window again. 'Now, where were we, darling?'

There was no sound from Lottie, nor any sign of her in the rear-view mirror, and when Valerie turned to look over her shoulder she discovered her daughter lying flat, face down on the back seat, with her hands covering her ears.

Ever since Tony's divorce, Tony, Dave and Archie had met up most Saturdays for a pint before lunch. It had started out as a way of showing support for Tony, now that he found himself with all this free time at the weekends. Before the divorce, Tony's Saturdays had been spent helping out in Jean's antique shop, and they all knew how much he was going to miss that: demonstrating the music boxes to rapt teenage girls, mischievously holding the dowagers' £50 notes up to the light. But now nearly three years had passed, Tony was well and truly back on his feet, and the weekly trip to the Shuttleworth Arms had evolved into an opportunity for all of them to share their worries and air their grievances. Pretty much anything, with the exception of work, was considered worthy of the group's attention – although they had drawn the line at Dave's problem with piles, and anything to do with Archie's household renovations was off limits, on the basis that they were never-ending.

This particular Saturday, Dave started the ball rolling while they were still settling into their usual booth.

'Ruth has got a thing about that wanker Richard,' he said, slipping an arm out of his parka, his eyes focused firmly on the undisturbed pint of bitter on the table in front of him.

Tony slammed his vodka and tonic down on the table. 'Ruth is having a thing with *Richard*?' he hissed. 'Anna's Richard?'

'Not *having* a thing. Jesus, you're eager! She's got a thing *about* him.'

Tony looked confused, as if this distinction was not one he was familiar with.

'Well, how d'you mean, a *thing*?' he asked, raising his glass to his lips and peering at Dave over the rim.

'I don't know exactly. She fancies him. I don't know if it's more than that.'

Archie cleared his throat and took a slug of his white wine.

'Are you sure?' asked Tony. 'I thought we were all agreed that Richard was an arse, Ruth included?'

'Yeah, but they're like that, women, aren't they?' muttered Dave, reaching for his pint. 'One minute they're banging on about how it's personality that counts and a good sense of humour and the next you're in the park and they're all gawping at the fit blokes with their shirts off. What do I do now though?' He took a deep breath, which seemed to instantly disagree with him, and lowered the pint back onto the table. 'She's always round there, y'know? What if Anna isn't even there and it's just the two of them on their own? Jesus.'

'Now, come on, old chap.' Tony slung an arm around Dave's shoulders, dislodging the pistachio cashmere sweater draped around his neck. 'How long have you been with Ruthie?'

'I dunno. Years.'

'And how often has she been unfaithful during that time?'

'Once . . .' Dave looked up from his pint and shrugged. 'Well, it was more of a snog really, and not since we've been married.'

'Weel then.' Tony squeezed Dave's shoulder. 'What are you worrying about? Ruthie just isn't that kind of girl. God! Anyone can see that, can't they, Archie?'

'Definitely.' Archie nodded eagerly.

'She's been behaving strangely though, honestly. Spending money on weird things . . . candles for the bedroom, aromatherapy oils . . . She hates all that stuff, normally. That's a Richard development. That's all happened since she's been round there doing the book. And she's started wearing these . . . slimy nighties.' Dave dragged both hands down the front of his jumper as if he were trying to wipe them clean of some cloying substance. 'You know, satin with lace down the front, like the kind of thing you wear to the national soap awards? She's never had a *dress* like that before, let alone a nightie.'

'Dave, chum, come on.' Tony removed his arm from around Dave's shoulders and gave him a playful dig in the ribs. 'Women, shopping, fluffing, wasting money on bits and bobs, giving themselves a bit of a you know . . .' Tony tickled the air with his fingers. 'It's all part of the deal. Especially when they get a bit nostalgic.' He took a swig of his drink, folded his arms and ran his tongue across his front teeth. 'You want to know when you need to worry? I'll tell you. When they step up the waxing appointments so they're back to back, regardless of the weather, and mooch around in the bathroom like teenage girls . . . When they suddenly decide that they've been neglecting their girlfriends and need to see much more of them. And when, overnight, they discover some new musical taste and have to listen to the album constantly, and in private.'

Tony widened his eyes and gave a sharp nod in Dave's direction as if this were top-secret information he had divulged against his better judgement.

'*When*,' the eyes were at full stretch now, 'they start to develop an overwhelming interest in some pursuit they've never so much as noticed before.'

'Such as?' Archie asked, rubbing his spectacles with his handkerchief.

'Tennis,' said Tony.

Archie held the spectacles up to the light and then put them back on with his characteristic rabbity twitch of the nose. 'You seem to be a bit of an expert all of a sudden,' he said, blinking at Tony.

'Yeah,' said Dave, 'how come you know so much about it?'

Archie sat up suddenly, pressing his spectacles hard against the bridge of his nose. He peered at Tony and then gave a start. 'No! Not . . . Jeanie?'

This suggestion made Dave laugh out loud and his eyes were still scrunched up with amusement, his head still swaying from side to side, when he glanced up from his glass and saw Archie and Tony staring at each other, without a trace of humour.

The fact was that, without really realizing it, they had come a long way since those first meetings in the Shuttleworth Arms. In the early days, the unspoken policy had been to distract Tony with conversations about anything and everything, bar wives and finances. The fact of the divorce was never openly acknowledged, except for that one time when, out of the blue, Tony asked them back to 14 Eldred Mews, and announced that this was to be the new regime: he and Jean no longer living side by side but on opposite sides of the street. And, for one reason or another, the subject of why, exactly, he and Jean had gone their separate ways had never come up. Theirs had always been a turbulent relationship, everyone knew that: it was no secret that they'd had disagreements about money, and what was referred to as Tony's 'flirting'. So, their friends had just assumed that a combination of Tony's uncontainable charm and Jean's over-tested patience were to blame, and Dave and Archie assumed that Tony would volunteer the details when he was ready. Normally, of course, Valerie and Ruth could have been relied on to fill in the gaps in the story, but it seemed that Jean was no more interested in talking than Tony. On the one occasion when they had tried to pin her down, Jean had apparently flared her nostrils, thrust her hands deeper into the pockets of her coat, and said simply, 'Men are idiots. There's nothing more to say.' And, since it was Jean, that was the end of the matter.

Tony was gazing over in the direction of the bar now, apparently transfixed by the lifeboat collection box.

'The fact is,' he said, closing his eyes for a moment in painful contemplation, 'Jean was unfaithful to me . . . with her tennis coach.'

Dave and Archie stared at him, incredulous.

'I'm afraid so.' Tony gazed mournfully at both of them in turn, giving full exposure to this rare outing of his utterly wronged expression, before lowering his eyes and waiting for the inevitable barrage of sympathy.

Dave and Archie simultaneously shifted their attention to each other, mouths gaping, like two football teammates confronted with a bad offside ruling.

'I don't believe it!' said Dave. 'Surely you were the one with the itchy pants?'

'Exactly,' Archie chipped in. 'Jean was always giving you a second chance, not the other way around.'

Tony gave a loud sniff, the sign that he was drawing on reserves of patience. 'Granted I'd had my . . . indiscretions. One or two meaningless flirtations. But' – he brought an open palm down firmly on the thigh of his pressed Levis – 'that was hardly in the same league. This was Jean. With *another man*.' Tony let the enormity of this sink in, before adding, 'I tell you, I wouldn't wish that feeling on anyone, not even my worst enemy.'

'But, a *tennis* coach.' Dave screwed up his eyes as if he were trying to see through a rain-drenched windscreen. 'Jean loathes any form of exercise! You couldn't get her to lift a ping-pong bat.'

'Which is precisely why I had my suspicions, right from the moment she came home with a Lilywhites carrier bag and three sets of Slazenger balls!' Tony stretched his neck and gazed blankly out over the now crowded pub, perhaps casting back in his mind to that day when Jean had bounced through the door of number 25, in her sparkling new Adidas trainers and white pleated skirt.

'So when did you . . .' Dave's eyes flickered in Archie's direction. 'When exactly did you find out?'

'Oh, by degrees, the way you do. But I suppose the penny really dropped when she came home with a hair-do like Mrs Rochester's and claimed he'd given her a head massage on the sidelines.' Tony gave a derisory snort and drained the last of his vodka.

'Richard gave Ruth a massage,' Dave said quietly. 'He gave her a full, all-over body massage when she was round at their flat. Everything. With her top off.'

Tony stopped jiggling the ice in his glass and they sat there together in silence while Archie give his spectacles another polish.

*

'It's me . . . sorry, darling, running a bit late.' Jean's surprisingly low, unmodulated voice crackled over the entryphone, reminding Anna, as it never failed to, of World Service bulletins and fifties mannequins with silk headscarves and hand-span waists. Anna pressed the communicator button and leant towards the mouthpiece.

'I'll be straight down; anything we need for the journey?'

'Flask of coffee,' Jean replied, drawing on one of her menthol cigarettes.

'Sorry, we don't have coffee. Fennel tea? Peppermint?'

There was silence on the other end of the entry phone and then the sound of Jean slowly, deliberately, exhaling. 'Never mind, darling. Just get your pure self down here. There's a traffic warden hovering and I'm on a double yellow.'

Witnessing Jean behind the wheel provided, Anna had always thought, a vital clue to her personality. You could have known her for years and not discovered half of what you learned from spending a few minutes driving in her company. The actual vehicle she drove – an old Jaguar, with deep-red leather upholstery and walnut features – was revealing in itself. Inside, from the front seats forward, the car was in relatively good condition. The back seat, however, was draped in grey blankets covered in a thick coating of dog hair, and the ceiling and doors had been so badly clawed and chewed by Tinks and Hopper that, in places, you could see the metal framework underneath. No one would ever have associated the elegant, six-foot, pewter-blonde, in her habitual uniform of pristine white shirt and black tailored trousers, with a car like this. And then there was the way she drove, as if she were indulging the whim of some overly fastidious government official; as if she honestly couldn't see the point, but would give it one more set of lights, one more stretch of motorway, before she finally pulled over and said in her delicious head-girl tones: 'As far as I'm concerned this is a complete waste of time.'

Anna looked up from examining the Jaguar and saw that Jean was watching her with a glimmer of amusement, although that was really only a guess. Jean had the sort of frozen, expressionless beauty that was fashionable in fifties fashion plates and seemed to go hand-in-hand with a Valium-like equanimity. Emotion was not something much required of her facial muscles. When she smiled, she smiled as if she'd been told to by an upstart photographer, stiffly and without genuine enthusiasm, but her eyes more than compensated for the glacial composure of her face. She made them up with a slick of black pencil as thick as a mouse's tail, plus several layers of mascara, and underneath all the smoke and grit they were a vivid violet colour, strong and bright as a light source.

Jean gave Anna a slow, mascara-caked wink and opened the driver's door, beckoning for her to get in on the passenger side.

'You don't think it puts men off, do you?' she asked, clasping the rear-view mirror and adjusting the collar of a tweed jacket so narrow in the shoulders it could have been made for a child. 'That would be a pity. Though I like to think a proper sort of man wouldn't blink. In our circle the doggy back seat is proof of one's social credentials, don't you think?'

One of the things Anna most liked about Jean was the way she spoke to her as if they shared the exact same lifestyle, automatically assuming that Anna knew various pillars of London society, was familiar with the smartest restaurants and on nodding terms with all the old-established fashion and interior designers. But what she found particularly flattering was the way Jean would talk, without a moment's hesitation, about the habits and foibles and details that separated people like 'them' from all the rest. Sometimes, when Jean was making some particularly extravagant observation on both their behalfs, Anna would feel a twinge of guilt and reflect on how easy it was to be seduced, not by money or power but simply by the promise of belonging to the right gang. Not long ago, she'd read an article about the snobbery and elitism at a girls' boarding school and had broken out in a sweat wondering if she would have been on the side of the bullied writer or determined to win favour with the smart set, regardless of what cruelties it involved.

'Still,' Jean continued, starting up the Jaguar and gliding out into the traffic, 'I suppose it might scare away the less robust types. Look at Tony, he couldn't wait to get back into his pearlized Porsche with the in-built dustbug. What *were* you doing, by the way, joining him on his stalking mission?'

'I was coming back to ring a cab, and then we spotted you,' Anna said. 'I think Tony mistook your plumber for Rollo Haines.'

'Typical.' Jean snorted like a thoroughbred pony. 'Doesn't stop to think that I can't stand the man. Honestly, why is it that the only thing men really respond to is competition with other men? His greatest fear is that I'm going to hook up with someone terrifically grand or, alternatively, horribly young and virile.' Jean turned to Anna and narrowed her eyes mock-schemingly. 'I'm ashamed to say the whole Herve episode would have been over in a flash if it hadn't been for Tony turning it into another of his mid-life crises.'

'He was gorgeous, though, wasn't he?' Anna reminded her.

'Uhhh.' Jean half closed her eyes and put a slim pale hand to her mouth. 'But *sooo* dull. Excruciating. The man thought Bora Bora was a pop group. I only brought him home to get him to work the video, but then when I saw Tony training his little binoculars on my bedroom window, well, I just had to let him stay. And after that it was too much sport to give up lightly.'

When Anna had first met the Alcrofts, eight years previously, she didn't know quite what to make of them. Tony was so smooth he was almost comical, brushing his lips against the back of her hand, permanently running his fingers through the thick doorstep of his then still naturally blond hair. A cricket sweater was habitually slung about his shoulders, although it transpired that he'd never played the game, and he wore a pair of large-framed sunglasses embedded on top of his head. All in all, Tony was the English-public-school type, as conceived by a mediocre European film director with a passion for the props of upper-class life. He had, for instance, taken up riding, not long before they met, but gave it up as soon as he realized there was nowhere he could be seen in his new jodhpurs and handmade boots, other than in the saddle.

'It was such a shame,' Jean had told Anna in a lowered voice. 'He did look divine, but once he was actually on the horse his backbone just seemed to collapse.' After delivering this information she had blinked once, very slowly – semaphore, as Anna was later to discover, for 'you should have been there'.

And then there was Jean, herself: beautiful, aloof, watching the world through a skein of cigarette smoke from behind the desk of her tiny interior decoration shop. She was just over forty when Anna first laid eyes on her, already glamorously grey and heavy lidded, with hips as narrow as a jockey's and that pale, sun-protected skin that makes even the healthiest tan look vulgar. Right from the start, she struck Anna as a woman who could have had anything she wanted, but who had no great ambitions beyond her bath and gin and tonic that evening. Yet, even so, it seemed surprising that she had ended up with Tony, of all people.

It was only later on that Anna started to understand: Tony and Jean were like a double act with Jean playing the straight man and Tony taking centre stage, fussing and creating and drinking in the attention. There was no platform for Jean's dry wit without Tony's histrionics, and without Jean's elegant example hovering in the background Tony would never have had the confidence to be himself. He was the attention-seeking, charming child that they had never had, and she obviously adored him.

'Ask me what it was like,' Jean was saying.

'What?'

'Herve.'

'Oh. What was it like?'

'Terrible! Like wrestling with an undefrosted turkey. Weights apparently, and plenty of them. He was only twenty-three, you know, less than half Tony's age.' Jean widened her eyes, appalled at her own audacity. 'Still, she can't be much older than that.'

'Who?'

'Who? The TV one.'

'Oh. Belinda.'

'Belinda is it?' Jean raised one elegant mink-coloured eyebrow, so that Anna was in no doubt she regarded this as an intimacy too far. 'I gather he's now referring to her as his *girlfriend*.'

'Mmmm.' Anna stared straight ahead. 'I don't really know. To be honest, he seemed more interested in talking about my book. He thinks you should be in it.'

'Me?'

'You, both of you.'

Jean tipped back her head, righting herself just in time to brake behind an overtaking Volvo. 'Well, fuckitydee,' she murmured, 'that definitely calls for a coffee stop.'

Anna twiddled her watch nervously. 'You know it's getting on for eleven?'

'Perfect, we'll be there early afternoon as planned. Darling, it's only Cornwall, it's not in a different time zone. Now . . . do tell me the plan.'

Valerie's mother had finally finished arranging the flowers that Valerie had brought for her birthday. The

arranging had been undertaken with a kind of grim resignation, as if Valerie had arrived with a bit of broken
furniture and presented it to her mother for mending.
Finding the vase, and then the scissors had been a
Herculean effort; cutting the string and unwrapping the
cellophane had caused her to breathe heavily and cast
her eyes around the room in near desperation. Though
of course there was no question of Valerie being allowed
to help, and her offering to had only exacerbated
the problem. Now Valerie watched as her mother
gathered up the yellow flowers she had systematically
discarded, snapped them in half, one by one, and
deposited them in the kitchen bin.

'It's a pity they don't go in for foliage,' her mother
said, in her thin, dowager's voice.

Valerie flinched. 'I'm sorry, Mummy. I suppose I
thought it was neater without.'

Her mother said nothing. She reached out a hand
mottled with liver spots and centred the vase on the
marble-topped table, then continued slowly and joy-
lessly to adjust the angles of the flowers.

'Well . . .' Valerie closed her eyes for a moment as
she attempted to summon up some topic that might
meet with her mother's approval. 'Charlie's coming
home today from his French exchange. He'll be here for
a few days and then he's off again on his sailing course.
And . . . Archie's just been asked for a day's shooting at
the Ballstocks'. So, that'll be something. Wonderful
house.'

'I know the house.'

Valerie smiled at the acknowledgement. If her
mother could be said to enjoy anything, it was recalling

her days as a young debutante and the glittering house parties and balls to which she had been invited before she'd met Valerie's father.

'He's at work all week,' her mother said, tugging a lily a fraction to the right and then forcing the stalk downwards despite the resistance of its neighbours, 'you would think he might want to spend the weekends with you.'

'Well, it's just the one weekend. And it isn't for a while.' Valerie took a slug of her sherry and looked at her watch. 'The party went well, Mother. I'm sorry you weren't there . . . not that I didn't completely understand about your bridge. But it was quite jolly. We had two hundred in the end, although it's difficult to tell if people use more than one glass . . .'

She took another sip of sherry and glanced over her shoulder into the adjoining room where she could see the television flickering and the point of Lottie's sweatshirt hood just visible above the sofa back.

'Eighteen years of marriage.' Her mother swivelled her hooded eyes to meet Valerie's. 'You think that's a time for self-congratulation, I suppose.' The mottled hand snapped off an arm of peony leaves, taking a new bud with it. 'I can tell you, it's a time for vigilance. Your father took up golf about now, do you remember?' Valerie lowered her eyes to the floor. 'You were fourteen, the same age as Charlotte.'

'Mummy, it's your birthday, we shouldn't be—'

'You must be their conscience and their guard, Valerie. There isn't one of them who would not yield to his base instincts if unchecked. I see it in Archibald as clear as I saw it in your father.'

'Mother—'

'I was naive. You don't have that excuse, I've made sure of that.'

'I know, Mother.'

'I wanted you to know what had been kept from me. The way men are. Deny that, and you risk everything.'

Her mother's top lip quivered as if she had caught the faint aroma of something distasteful. She walked across the floor to her chair by the window overlooking the square, smoothed out the seat of her tweed skirt and sat down slowly, her back turned to the room. It was the signal that she had said her piece and now required to be left alone. Valerie called to Lottie, taking care to keep her voice at a level tolerable to her mother's nerves, and they said their goodbyes from the far side of the Aubusson rug, each raising a hand and flickering their fingers vaguely like people waving off an aeroplane from inside the terminal – hopeful but not expecting to be seen.

'And don't bother to bring flowers again,' Valerie's mother said, still facing the window, 'it's not something you are particularly good at.'

'Have you noticed that Granny only has photos of her?' Lottie said, as they made their way down the stairs of the mansion block. 'Just like the way you only have pictures of you and your . . . triumphs.'

She was looking at Valerie out of the corner of one eye, dragging her sweatshirt sleeves further down over her fingertips. Valerie stepped briskly ahead, grasping the banister with one hand, wobbling slightly on the heels she had worn for Susie Walker's benefit. She flapped her handbag-carrying hand in Lottie's direction to indicate she was not about to dignify this observation with an answer.

'I'm not surprised Grandpa left her,' Lottie continued, undaunted. 'Anyone can see Granny asked for it.' She paused for a second to gauge if her words were having the desired effect, then raised her voice. 'It's obvious she just wanted him around for his money, and to prove she could get married and have children.'

Valerie stopped in her tracks. She looked back up the stairs to where Lottie was propped against the banister, twisted into a sullen tangle. 'You don't know what happened with your grandfather,' Valerie said quietly. 'You don't know what Granny went through.'

'So he went off with someone' – Lottie's jaw swung open – '*big deal.*'

'Charlotte, you have no idea what you're talking about.'

'Yes, I do. It happens all the time. I know loads of girls whose dads have gone off with other women. Loads. And I know why they do it, too. Because their wives are only interested in money and houses and whether their children are at the right parties, and the fathers are so bored of being just, like, bossed around all the time, and then, like, coming home from work and being . . . shouted at and told to make more money and made to go out all the time with people they don't even like just because they're rich or whatever.'

At that moment the doors to the mansion block buzzed open and an old lady thrust a basket on wheels in through the opening. She peered up the stairwell and Valerie smiled down at her.

84

'You don't think it's possible that the men might sometimes be at fault?' Valerie said, lowering her voice and jabbing her head in the direction of the old lady in the hope that Lottie would do likewise.

'Yeees. Obviously. But mostly it's the greedy wives wanting more and more and more . . .' Lottie's eyes flickered contemptuously over Valerie's size sixteen hips in their somewhat tight wool skirt. The old lady with the basket on wheels shuffled forward, her rheumy eyes trying to focus on the source of the voice at the top of the stairs.

'I think it's disgusting,' said Lottie, even more loudly. 'I think it's disgusting that your generation just treat men like they're cheque books.'

The old lady blinked and shifted her focus to Valerie, her expression now enquiring and slightly anxious.

'It's all right,' called Valerie brightly, descending the last few stairs and patting the old woman's shoulder reassuringly as she passed. 'My daughter's just rebelling against the way the world works. It's nothing to worry about.'

'The thing is,' Dave said, 'I'm pretty confident, in that department.'

They were onto their fourth round now, a breach with normal procedure on account of the fact that their Saturday lunch 'quickie' had turned into a crisis meeting.

'We did that national sex quiz thing on the telly the other night.' Dave glanced over at Archie, who was suddenly looking anxious. 'Don't worry, mate . . . you didn't really miss anything. Anyway, we did pretty well. Actually, we got twenty out of a possible twenty-six, which put us in the "recently met and going strong" category. But, you know what? It's nothing to do with that. It's nothing to do with our relationship, full stop. This is all about being a woman now, this feeling of . . .' he screwed up one eye the better to focus on the problem, '*discontent*. They think they're missing out. On everything. They genuinely believe that out there' – he flung an arm in the direction of the fugged-up, dimple-paned pub window – 'are all these women living lives straight out of a tampon ad: satin nighties, log fires, those poncey roll-top baths stuck right in the middle of the room. They honestly think everyone else is getting four hours of sex a night, followed by a long, albeit one-sided, conversation on the subject of . . .'

Dave looked around the table for assistance.

'Er . . . their weight,' said Tony, 'what you thought of the women at the party, what you think of their best friend . . . great isn't she? Though, actually, funnily enough, she is really, really screwed up . . .'

'Recipes,' volunteered Archie. 'That's what I get. Recipes and decorating, but I quite like that in a way. It's amazing what you learn. Did you know those taps with the porcelain bits on them cost £750, minimum, not including installation?'

'We got our whole flat recarpeted for that,' said Dave, dreamily. 'Anyway, my point is that all this stuff is dangerous. It's dangerous because they think that's what their lives *should* be like and men don't fit into that picture. We're just not made that way.'

'Apart from Richard, you mean?' Archie was looking at the bottom of an empty glass again.

'I have to say,' Tony said, 'as someone who has returned to the dating scene after a long break, that women do have rather different requirements now – and I'm afraid Richard may be nature's way of answering them.' He shrugged apologetically. Dave clenched his fists and pressed them against his mouth. 'For example, these days you don't want a woman to think you can't cook,' Tony continued. 'Can't cook equals reactionary misogynist. Likewise, you must be interested in celebrities – ignorance of the big C hierarchy is the pulling equivalent of collecting model trains – ditto fashion designers. Then you've got to be prepared to indulge in the most *minute* analysis of other people's behaviour.' He closed his eyes and inhaled deeply through his nose. 'Everyone, but everyone, deserves a detailed psychological profile, and you'd better be interested in what they've got to say. It's a bit like tarot cards in my day, only even more testing.' Tony paused, his eyes settling on Dave who was now hunched grimly over the table as if deliberating a crucial chess move. 'I'm talking about the *younger* generation, mind you,' he added, ducking his head so that it was level with Dave's. 'Not *Ruth*. Ruth's a good, straightforward girl.'

'So what's Anna doing with Richard, then?' Dave said quietly.

'Weeel.' Tony spread his hands wide. 'Anna was burnt, wasn't she, by that musician fellow? Totally shattered her faith in men, and Richard was her recovery plan. He is to the lost woman what the Arizona clinic is to the cocaine addict. It's written all over him: "Spa

Richard".' Tony gestured as if to an imaginary billboard in mid-air. 'They check in looking for serenity and security, and they never check out.'

Dave nodded, without much conviction, and reached for his companions' empty glasses. He stood up from the table gingerly, as if he was worried his trousers might fall down at any moment, and shambled towards the bar; there was a horizontal dent in the back of his woolly hair where it had been resting against the top of the banquette.

'God, Ruth!' hissed Tony as soon as Dave was out of earshot. He rearranged the sleeves of his sweater across his chest and folded his arms over the top, taking care not to crease the shell-pink, sea-island cotton shirt.

'Well, we don't know . . .' Archie whispered.

'Archie, old boy, much as I love Dave, I think the fact that he's noticed anything at all makes it a virtual certainty.' Tony shook his head with an expression of painful lessons gleaned through personal experience. 'I mean it does happen. As I know only too well. And it's one thing when a man has an affair but it's quite another if a woman takes a lover. Quite another. Men are designed to fool around; they can separate sex' – he placed the edge of his left hand next to his beer mat and rubbed it backwards and forwards as if slicing a cake – 'from the important relationship in their lives. Women can't. It's as simple as that.'

Archie looked mildly intrigued and then, almost wistful. 'Valerie isn't interested,' he said. 'Or, at least, she isn't interested with me. Not much.'

'How much is not much?'

Archie hesitated. 'Well, lately, not at all. She's

always tired. She thinks it's an imposition on top of looking after the children and the charity work and the book contributions. She gets quite angry if I even suggest it.'

'What about after a few drinks? I thought she got quite revved up on a glass or two?'

'Worse if anything. Locks herself in the bathroom with the tape recorder. I mean, I don't mind. I wouldn't mind, rather, if I thought she was happy. But . . .'

'How long has it been then?'

'Oh.' Archie raised his eyes to the ceiling. 'I suppose—'

'Couple of months? Six months . . . come on Arch! If you can't tell me, who can you tell?'

'Two years.'

'*Two years?*'

Archie glanced furtively at the surrounding tables.

'Sorry, old boy, but two *years*.' Tony made a face as if he'd got a whiff of bad milk. 'Why didn't you say something sooner?'

'Well—'

'Good God! No one should be expected to go without for that long, even you, Arch.'

'Go without what?' Dave was hovering next to the table clutching a pint, a vodka and tonic and a glass of wine.

'Sex.' Tony flicked a thumb in Archie's direction.

'Val not up for it?' Dave asked, as if enquiring about her willingness to join their five-a-side-team.

'Well, she . . . No. She was never particularly keen and now . . . now it's sort of tailed off altogether.'

Tony shook his head. 'You just can't tell. Not with

their generation. I always thought Jean could take it or leave it.'

Dave and Archie nodded solemnly, out of solidarity rather than recognition.

'I mean, when Jean and I got together the men did all the work and the girls were sort of laid back and inscrutable. That's just the way it was. One knew they were having a good time, obviously, but they didn't much go in for . . . histrionics. Whereas with the girls now . . . my God, you get a running commentary.' Tony reached for his vodka and tonic and took a long slug. 'Absolutely nothing is left to one's discretion. It's exactly the same in restaurants – you know, nothing can be as it comes. It's all got to be "this on the side" and "that without the sauce".' Tony glanced quickly between the two of them. 'I don't want to moan, of course. There are men who'd give their right arm to be in my position,' he added, looking down at the limb in question and flexing his fingers, confidently.

Tony was acutely conscious of his responsibilities as the trail-blazer of the group, more accurately the only man they knew who was out there on the dating scene, benefiting from the newly generous attitude of women towards sex and commitment. He was something of a hero to his friends – to put it bluntly – and he felt it was inappropriate, on those rare occasions when things weren't going quite as well as they might have, to disappoint them. Tony hadn't been to public school, himself, but had frequently imagined what it would have been like to be captain of cricket, standing on the steps of the pavilion, dressed in his whites, while a lot of lesser boys crowded around him like hungry birds. And this feeling, he reckoned, must come pretty close. The boys looked up to him. Simple as that.

'What would you do if you were me, though?' Dave was still hunkered over his pint glass, hands clasped around its base. 'D'you think I should confront her?'

'Oh no, no.' Tony and Archie shook their heads in unison. 'Never get them in a corner,' said Tony. 'You've got to come around the back, so to speak.'

'What about a few treats?' Archie's smile looked strained as if it was in urgent need of recharging. 'Perhaps something nice for the house, or clothes. Val's always very keen on those.'

'He's right,' said Tony, stretching his arm out along the top of the banquette, surreptitiously checking his watch as he did so. 'There aren't many things that some well spent cash doesn't solve. Why d'you think there are so many bloody kitchen extensions in our lives? No offence, Arch. Yours is one of the very best.'

'I could help if you like,' said Archie. 'We could do a bit of a shop together. I'm rather good with things for the home and all that.'

Tony looked sideways at him. 'You all right, Archie? You seem a bit . . . neurotic.'

Archie didn't reply; his mobile was ringing and from the expression of preparation on his face it was evident the caller was Valerie. He pressed the answer button.

'Darling, hello.' Archie waggled his eyebrows to indicate that for the next minute or two they would have to indulge him as he would be speaking in code. 'Nice visit with Granny? Mmm. Yes. Well, I wasn't going to accept but all right then, if it's so important to y— All right, to me as well. No. Just a couple. Four, and Dave's just got us anoth— Right. All right, my darling, see you in a minute.' The call ended, Archie rested his elbows on the table, put his hands over his mouth and appeared to be suppressing a belch for several seconds before he spoke again.

'She wants me to go shooting at the Ballstocks',' he said, addressing his words to the ceiling. 'I don't shoot. I dislike it and I'm not good at it. But if I don't go I'm a disappointment. Do you ever feel like . . . ?' Archie hesitated, his cheeks flushed dark pink. 'I went to the ballet the other day . . . took Lottie and a couple of her friends. And I sat there in the dark and thought how much I'd have liked to have been a set designer. How much I'd have enjoyed that.' He smiled wistfully. 'Sometimes I think it would have been better to have been born a woman and then one would have had the choice . . . none of this compulsion to prove oneself stronger and more virile than the next person.'

Archie's eyes drifted back to meet theirs: behind his spectacles they looked tired and blurred, limp with midday drinking. 'Lord . . . Valerie was right! Four glasses of wine and I'm making a complete bore of myself.' He stood up suddenly from the table and reached for his coat. 'Better get going then. Same time next week?'

'Week after,' said Tony, 'I've got a little job in the South of France.'

'Right, week after it is then.' Archie pulled on the coat, wriggled his shirt collar and cuffs into place and headed off across the pub.

'What was that all about?' asked Dave, when the doors had swung closed behind him.

'Oh, just Archie feeling the pressure. I'm afraid dear

Val's knocked the stuffing out of him.' Tony tilted an eyebrow in Dave's direction. 'It's always the way, with women. They think they want to be in control and then the more power you give them the more they resent you for it. You've got to let a woman know who's in charge; makes them feel safe.'

Dave snorted dismissively. 'You're joking, aren't you? Try telling that to Ruth. The last thing a woman wants now is to be "taken care of" – no offence, mate, but that attitude went out with the great smell of Brut.'

Tony pouted and rotated the signet ring on his little finger, examining the effect front and back. 'It makes you think though, doesn't it . . . Archie's little outburst? Makes you wonder what, exactly, Anna's got tucked away in those research files of hers. This book could be quite interesting reading after all.'

'Yeah.' Dave sounded dubious.

'Oh, you'll be all right, chum. It's just a hiccup. Take it from an old hand.'

'Maybe. The only thing is . . .' Dave hesitated. 'You and Archie are my best mates. And I'm grateful for all the advice. I am. But it's just that, when it comes to our marriages, I can't help feeling we don't have a lot in common.'

Tony peered at him, his chin tucked into his chest, bottom lip thrust out.

'I mean Roo and I are like best friends,' Dave continued. 'We don't play games. She doesn't bully me like Valerie bullies Archie, or want what Val wants. And your life is just completely different from any of ours these days – I mean you're not even married.'

'You're right.' Tony prodded the base of his glass.

'We probably aren't the best equipped to advise you. On the other hand, it's all the bloody same in the end, David. Young girls, old girls, Valerie, Jean, Ruth – when they're married and they've got a couple of kids . . . one kid, you're back to a level playing field. They all want the same things. They all complain about the same things. They're all hiding stuff in the back of their wardrobes, and fantasizing about houses in the Dordogne, and regretting their loss of independence and the fact that they didn't get out there in their hot pants while they had the chance.' Tony gave a stiff nod and raised his glass to eye level. 'They may start out different, but they all end up in the same place, and you, old cock, are no bloody different from the rest of us. One for the road, then?'

Five

Jean and Anna arrived at the wedding roughly two hours early, as planned, allowing Anna just enough time to interview the bride before the ceremony and giving Jean an opportunity to catch up with her first cousin, the bride's mother.

'So, what sort of questions have you got for Allegra?' Jean asked, as they turned into the gates of a large Georgian house, skirted with marquees glaring white in the afternoon sun.

'Oh, you know.' Anna reached down for her handbag and patted the side pocket, double-checking for the outline of her tape recorder. 'Why now? Is she worried that twenty might be a little young to be settling down? Whose idea was it? That kind of thing.'

Jean brought the Jaguar to a lazy stop in front of the house. Two pasty-faced young men dressed in black trousers and white shirts were manoeuvring an urn of flame-coloured gladioli through the door, white pearls of sweat forming on their foreheads. 'Well, I can answer those for you,' she said, squinting at Anna through the smoke from her cigarette. 'Allegra's pregnant; Mikey is loaded. I think we can safely say it was her idea.'

For a moment Anna thought she was joking, but

then Jean slid her one of her long, heavy-lidded stares. 'Really? So what do the parents think?'

'Darling, they'd have inseminated her themselves if they'd had access to the Montague sperm. It's called making a good match.' Jean's eyes drifted in the direction of the house, lingering critically on the ground-floor windows and the formal arrangements of lilies positioned in each of them. 'You think I'm exaggerating?'

'No . . .' Anna hesitated. 'Well, yes, actually. I can't imagine Allegra and Mikey aren't in love. Why marry these days if you're not in love?'

'Well, there's the small matter of the Montague estate, and the flat in Chelsea, and a rather neat little pied-à-terre right next to the Uffizi. Besides –' Jean raised a hand in acknowledgement to a man in a green overall who was gesturing for her to move the car into a neighbouring field '– what on earth else was Allegra going to do with her life? Really, Anna,' she added, as she started up the engine and the shoulders of the man in the overalls visibly relaxed, 'I don't think I'd realized what a romantic you are.'

'Me?' Anna laughed. 'Don't be silly. I'm nothing of the sort.'

Jean hauled the steering wheel hard to the left, giving the impression that it was terrifically heavy, or that her long, elegant arms were as weak as flower stalks. 'I do hope writing this book isn't going to disillusion you,' she said softly, as if she hadn't heard Anna at all.

'They're all in here!' Bunny Wells gave Anna a bold stage wink as she turned the handle of her daughter's bedroom door. 'Now, don't be too long, will you? Allegra hasn't even had her bath yet.' She let the door fall open and then took a sudden step backwards, fanning her hand wildly in front of her face.

'Eurgh, the *smoke*. 'Legra! Would it kill you girls to open a window for a change?'

'Sorry, Ma,' drawled a bored, surprisingly deep voice.

'It's the dress I'm worried about.' Bunny was bustling across the carpeted floor towards the nearest window, beckoning for Anna to follow. 'We can't have it reeking of Silk Cut in the church. Now –' she threw open the sash window and adjusted the shoulder pads of her silk print dress '– it's time you girls got ready. Allegra has someone to see her.'

Allegra was lying sprawled on a double bed in between two sullen-looking girls wearing tiny logoed T shirts and knickers. The bride-to-be was dressed in a substantial pink bra and matching briefs; she had curlers in her thick, stripey-blonde hair, ropes of cotton wool threaded between her toes and round her substantial neck was clamped a choker that looked like a 2d version of the coronation crown. On the carved gilt bed head behind them was a poster of George Clooney, covered in shocking-pink lip prints, and Anna noticed the paper remnants of tattoo transfers discarded on the linen pillows.

'Come on.' Bunny approached the bed clapping her hands together as if she were shooing puppies. 'Out you all go. We haven't got long, the cars are coming at four thirty.'

The friends smiled sickly smiles at their hostess,

slithered off the bed in silence and padded out of the room without giving Anna a second glance.

Bunny tapped the back of Allegra's bare calf. 'This is the lady who's writing the book, 'Legra.' She gave Anna another reassuring wink.

'Hi,' said Allegra, waggling her splayed fingers and blowing on the freshly painted nails. Her brown eyes flickered over Anna and came to rest on her mother's face with a bold, accusatory stare.

'I'll leave you to it, then,' said Bunny, making briskly for the door. She paused on the threshold for a moment, turned and flapped a freckled hand in her daughter's direction. 'Remember, this could be for a *book*, darling.' She emphasized the word 'book' as if it were one Allegra might not instantly recognize. 'So nothing silly, darling. All right?'

'Good, mind if I . . . ?' Anna placed the tape recorder gingerly on the end of Allegra's bed. 'It just saves me from having to jot down any notes,' she explained, although Allegra was clearly not remotely concerned. She was lying on her front now, propped up on her elbows, idly rubbing a large sapphire engagement ring against the back of her right hand.

'What's this for again?' she asked, without looking up.

'I'm writing a book about marriage,' Anna replied, brightly. 'Why people do it . . . what makes it work . . . that kind of thing. And you and Michael would be my newly-weds. So far, I haven't got a couple who are, literally, just starting out.'

In her mind, Anna was already weighing up whether or not she should cut her losses and invent some excuse to leave, or plough on in the hope that Allegra had a personality change.

'You're Jean's friend, aren't you?' Allegra asked, still admiring her ring. 'Did she tell you I was pregnant?'

'Jean? Um . . .'

'Well, I'm not. I thought I might have been, but Mum said I should tell Mikey that I was anyway. That's what she did, with Dad.'

Allegra dragged her eyes up to meet Anna's, focusing for a moment with undisguised indifference on her cream silk trouser suit and matching sandals. 'You'd better not put that in,' she added, returning to the ring.

Anna nodded, mesmerized. For several long seconds she was at a loss for something to say. 'Weren't you . . .' Anna leant slightly forward on the dressing-table stool. 'Aren't you worried that he might think you tricked him?'

Allegra's top lip curled. 'Nooo,' she said, the cocked lip substituting for the words, 'you are so sad'. 'Mikey wanted to get married. All my friends do. He didn't care. He was just glad to have a reason.'

Anna felt a sudden rush of adrenalin. She could see the triangular diagram that was to be the centrepiece of her introduction, with the words Trust, Equality, Communication floating over each of the three points.

Allegra was watching her with an expression of mild curiosity. 'Are you married?' she asked, in a tone that suggested she already knew the answer. 'No,' Anna said, 'but I'm—'

'Living with someone, right?' Allegra's gaze was challenging. 'Why not get married? I mean if you're already living together?'

'Well,' Anna cleared her throat, 'let's get back to you, Allegra . . . why would you rather get married than live with Mikey?'

'Cos everyone knows that people who live together are keeping their options open. Or they've, like, done it once and they don't want to risk all the hassle again.'

'That's rather simplistic, don't you think?'

'Maybe, but it's true.' Allegra rolled over onto her side and propped her chin in the palm of her hand. 'Didn't you ever want to have children,' she asked, 'when you were younger?'

Anna laughed, though the noise that came out sounded more like a bark. She shook her head and smiled patiently intending to convey that nothing was quite as black and white as it might appear to poor, unworldly Allegra in her ivory tower; that her question was naive and inappropriate and, frankly, embarrassing. But Allegra was oblivious to such subtleties. She looked at Anna much the same way she might have looked at someone who didn't ride, or lived in a house with a street number, and waited for her answer.

'I . . .' Anna began, folding her hands on her knee. 'This really isn't about me, Allegra. But, since you ask, marriage and children are just one of the options open to women.'

Allegra sucked on her top lip, her neck thrust forward between her shoulders.

'And there are plenty of us who feel perfectly fulfilled as we are. As a matter of fact –' Anna's eyes wandered out of reach of Allegra's blank stare '– those sort of decisions have a great deal to do with social convention. Often people who want . . . all of that, are actually seeking to conform as much as anything.'

Allegra's eyebrows lifted a fraction. 'Whatever,' she said. 'Is there anything else? I really should start scrubbing up or Mum's gonna have a fit.'

The reception – Allegra's father announced, from his position on a raised dais at one end of the marquee – would consist of dinner followed by dancing to an Irish band.

'The seating plan is just there, if any of you failed to spot it,' he bellowed, using the table on which the cake was displayed for leverage, and pointing with a purple hand in the direction of an easel. 'Anyone who's lorst, have a word with the wife and she'll sort you out. Right. Tuck in everybody!'

Jean took one last, lingering drag of her cigarette and let it fall on the grass at the entrance to the marquee, where Anna finished it off with the sole of her sandal.

'I must say,' said Jean, 'I think Bunny could have been a bit more imaginative. She's put me on a table entirely made up of widowers and divorcees. I feel as though I should be wearing a tabard with the date of my decree nisi on the front and my alimony terms on the back. Who have you got?'

Anna scrunched up her eyes, trying to visualize the seating plan. 'Er, someone called Gerard something, a couple called Shawcroft, and one called Tantyl . . . Tintyl . . . one of those Cornish-sounding names.'

'Tyntallin?' Jean cast her eyes around, suddenly intrigued. 'That will be interesting.'

Anna attempted to look enthusiastic, apparently unsuccessfully.

'Tyn-tal-in.' Jean enunciated each syllable. 'Anna, you must have heard of the house? You know it, of course you do. It's the one with the lake and those twin islands. They're always filming something there.' She cupped both hands and held them out level in front of her, as if they might spark a memory of the geography of the park. 'Anyway, his wife Henrietta was an old school friend of mine. She died, unfortunately, and he's just married again – American apparently.' Jean lowered her voice and dipped her mouth towards Anna's ear. 'She's some kind of psychic . . . they say she puts him in touch with Henrietta.'

'Oh, stop it.' Anna slapped Jean's hand lightly.

'I'm only repeating what I've heard. Well, time to bite the bullet, I suppose. Don't forget, I want every detail.' Jean squeezed Anna's arm and glided off into the warm candlelit glow of the marquee.

The Tyntallin couple were seated on the opposite side of the table to Anna, separated from each other by an anxious-looking mousy woman, and an empty chair. Anna didn't need to see their place names to confirm their identity; the American stood out from the other women in the marquee like a glass of fresh lime in a smoke-filled pub.

'Mr Jock Beech-Ham,' she said, leaning across to read the card above the empty place with the asset-maximizing instinct of a model – pressing her shoulders back and her chest forward and lifting her white-blonde, roller-curled hair daintily off her collarbone. She looked up flirtatiously and fixed her eyes on Anna's neighbour, a florid-looking man with a stomach that was keeping him at arm's length from the table. 'Well then, now who knows where the naudy Mr Beech-Ham might be?'

Anna's portly neighbour adjusted his napkin. 'No idea,' he said flatly, addressing his lap, 'could be the one with the kidney stone.'

The American shifted her gaze to Anna. 'Well, lucky us,' she said, her voice full of amusement. 'Hi, my name is Lily Tyntallin, and this' – she gestured with a hand limp under the burden of its double diamond rings – 'is my husband, Tarka Tyntallin.'

Anna murmured her name in reply and paused, waiting for some acknowledgement of the introduction, but Tarka Tyntallin remained swivelled round in his chair with his back to the table, his weather-beaten fingers tapping impatiently on the white cloth.

'My husband is a little exercised,' Lily explained from behind her hand. 'A lot of the staff working tonight are employed on his estate, and he feels awfully responsible.' She smiled at Anna, narrowing her pale blue eyes, bestowing the gift of her confidence directly into her lap. 'You're from London, I can tell,' she said, pressing her glossy shoulders in Anna's direction. She was wearing a strapless yellow silk dress, and whether it was the dress, or the manicured fingernails that plucked modestly at the bodice, or the shiny hair, curling upwards at the ends in a jaunty flourish, she reminded Anna of a bright fifties debutante – prim and adventurous, naive and sophisticated all at once. 'Oh, don't get me wrong, I adore it down here. Everyone adores it down here.' Lily flashed a smile, her eyes flickering around the table. 'But you can just spot that urban . . . fizz.'

The mousy woman blinked at her uncomprehendingly.

Lily winked at Anna and took a sip of her mineral water. 'What do you do, Anna?' Her delicate, ring-laden hand reached out across the table. 'Something wildly glamorous, I'll bet? Let me guess . . .'

'I'm researching a book about modern marriage,' Anna said and, to her surprise, felt her face growing hot. 'I'm just in the finishing stages,' she added, 'only a few months to go before it's all done.'

'Modern English marriages,' whispered Lily, making each word sound charmed and exotic. 'Oh my, is that a book I wanna read! Tarka gave me a map of the area, so I could get to know my new home, but forget maps. This book is what I need, right? The mysteries of the English relationship laid bare.' She brought her palms together in front of her pale, glossy lips and looked suddenly serious. 'You don't have a chapter specifically on the psyche of the upper-class English male, by any chance?'

'My wife loves to play the ingénue.' Tyntallin's voice was so low it startled Anna. He was looking down at his plate now, his face obscured by a shock of hair the exact colour and texture of steel wire. 'That's what she would have us believe, whereas she is, in fact, something of an expert on men, English and otherwise.'

Lily's hand retreated into her lap, her smile stretched tighter across her face. 'Oh, Tynt, all I meant is that your world is somewhat . . . just a bit different from what I'm used to. Well, inevitably. I mean, I'm a New Yorker.' She cast her eyes around the table, looking, with increasing disillusionment, for a sign of sympathy or recognition.

'How long have you been married?' Anna asked quickly.

'Oh!' Lily beamed with gratitude. 'Well, almost a year, incredibly.' She shook her head prettily as if ridding her hair of blossom fall. 'And what a year! Good grief. Such a lot to . . .' she glanced in the direction of Tyntallin who was turning his fork over and over in his hand, his eyes boring into the tablecloth. 'Well, "to get used to" makes it sound like it hasn't been terrific. Which is nodadall the case. But the fact is, last spring I was renting a little studio apartment in New York City with this one little window box.' She placed her hands a few inches apart on the table to indicate just how little it had been. 'I'd never even visited this country. Barely even been outside the States. And now I'm a wife and a stepmother with a stately home to run and a garden that's the size of Central Park.' Lily raised her hands in a gesture of wonder. The mousy woman gazed at her expectantly, poised for the crucial piece of information that would make sense of what she had just heard.

Lily looked suddenly weary. 'I am absolutely the luckiest person in Great Britain, I know that,' she said softly. 'But, you know, it's kind of a steep learning curve. Do you deal with that at all in your book, Anna? Second marriages. Second wives . . . settling in?'

The whole table seemed to swivel their heads in unison to look at Anna; she had the strong sensation that somehow a lot was resting on her answer.

'Of course,' she said. 'I have a whole section on second marriages.'

Lily gave a little start at this news and Tyntallin lifted his head slowly. 'Actually, you might find it helpful,'

Anna added, taking care to avoid Tyntallin's gaze. 'It's very common, it seems, to feel overwhelmed, particularly where there are children involved.'

'Three!' Lily put a hand to her throat. 'Three, the youngest only just out of diapers . . . and seven staff. That's not counting the grounds . . . people . . . whatever.' She snatched another furtive glance at her husband. 'Oh, I'd be fascinated to see what your studies have to say. Just fascinated. Because, I figure there's a whole . . . process that you have to go through, whatever your circumstances. And I think if a person just knew, at the outset, what it involved. You know. If someone just told you what you could expect, and how long . . .' She hesitated. Out of the corner of her eye, Anna saw Tyntallin raise his chin and suck in a long, steadying breath.

'Tell us, if you would,' he said, 'what exactly qualifies you to write this, er . . . definitive study of marriage? Are you married?' And then, before she could answer, he added, 'Obviously not.'

Anna felt the colour rising to her cheeks. 'Excuse me?'

'No *ring*.' Tyntallin gestured to her left hand, pressed flat against the tablecloth. 'You still go in for those in London, I suppose?'

Anna dragged the hand into her lap, gripping the fingers between her knees. 'My marital status is of no relevance, whatsoever. I'm a writer and researcher. What qualifies me is my experience . . . as a journalist.'

'Ah.' Tyntallin's mouth twitched. 'Yes, of course. Specializing in . . . ?'

Anna hesitated. 'Social observation,' she said, more loudly than she had intended.

Tyntallin bowed his head in acknowledgement. 'Really. Well. So you'll have us summed up in a nutshell by now. You've already discovered all the important facts about my wife, after all: her beauty, her nationality, her fondness for the sophisticated things in life, her healthy scepticism about the countryside.' He lit a cigarette, grimacing as he inhaled. 'And you already know who I am: a farmer and landowner, therefore a reactionary relic with no understanding of the modern world, least of all women. So, there we have it: the beauty and the boor. The flower of New World optimism gasping for air in the stultifying twilight of the feudal system.'

'Oh now, Tarka!' Lily laughed nervously and reached for her husband's arm across the table. 'Just because Anna is from London and used to be a journalist . . .' She leant towards Anna, her eyes willing her new friend to let the moment pass. 'You'll forgive Tarka I know,' she murmured. 'It's just he . . . we, feel like we're under siege sometimes. Like everyone's against us. And then it all gets mixed up.'

'I,' said Tynatallin, 'am perfectly clear who the enemy is. Excuse me.' And with that he stood up, gave a small awkward bow and stalked off between the tables.

When the Irish Band could be heard in full cry in the next-door tent, Anna excused herself from the table and headed for the relative calm of the house. Here and there people were propped up against fireplaces, or loitering in packs, queuing for the lavatories. Two girls compared tears in the hems of their dresses with the incurious expressions of those who are not required to worry about such trifles, and boys who looked too young to be shaving lit each other's cigars with furrowed brows. Anna raised a hand in greeting to Mikey, the groom, who was leaning against the back of a sofa, his arm flung around the best man's shoulders, and then, side-stepping a tray of coffee, found herself in the doorway of a small study.

The room was empty, with a fire in the grate and two armchairs placed, invitingly, on either side of the fireplace. Anna crossed the carpeted floor, lowered herself into one of the chairs, stretched out her legs and contemplated what to do next. She considered looking for Jean but then the possibility of bumping into Bunny, and being herded back into the tent for a dance with her neighbour at dinner, put an end to that idea. She thought of ringing someone – maybe her parents, to double confirm that Jean would be dropping her off there the following morning – but there was no real reason to. It would have been nice to talk to Ruth and elicit some sympathy for the way she'd been treated by that Tyntallin man. (Wouldn't Ruth go mad on her behalf? Wouldn't she have hated him too?) On the other hand, she didn't want to risk waking up Billy. The safest bet, of course, was Richard, only she already knew what he would have to say: 'Babe, why are you letting it get to you? Those people are unevolved. I'm disappointed that you are still seeking that kind of approval' – or something along those lines anyway. And then it occurred to Anna that she was alone at a wedding, and she hadn't been alone at a wedding for as long as she could remember. Over the years she had probably been to hundreds of the things, but almost always accompanied by whoever her boyfriend was at the time. And now that she thought about it, every one of them had felt subtly different as a result.

In the same way that it was agonizing watching sex on screen in the company of a man with whom you could be having sex in the near future, attending a wedding with a man who you might end up spending your life with was a strange, and often awkward experience. If you were at the start of the relationship it was just plain exciting: an excuse to play at being a couple; an opportunity to show off the way you complemented each other and bask in all the talk of 'for ever and ever' without actually being associated with it. Those were the aphrodisiac weddings.

Once you'd been going out for a year or so, the thrill factor had pretty much worn off and weddings had become a time for sober reflection. Now you weren't flirting and knitting fingers during the vows, you were listening hard, comparing yourself to the couple standing at the altar, each of you wondering what the other was thinking. Another couple of years down the line and the duration of the ceremony was spent conducting an inventory of your relationship, flicking through those mental snapshots: him at Christmas lunch with your family; the time he didn't want to get wet bringing in that boat on holiday; the moment when you stopped to look at flats in an estate agent's window and saw, reflected in the glass, the way he was looking at you, almost as if he suspected you of some betrayal. And then you'd glance up at your boyfriend, and you'd see from his expression that he was bored, disengaged, all the mild curiosity that had been there on previous occasions replaced by a kind of aggressive detachment.

Later on still, there were those weddings when the events of the day appeared to have been orchestrated expressly to illuminate the chasms in your relationship. You were late, fractious, there was nowhere left for you both to sit. And when you were forced to cram together on the end of a pew he was restless, adjusting his tie, straining to have less contact with you, when once he would have been grinning and nuzzling, grateful for the opportunity to get this close. Those were the weddings when you looked around the congregation at the married couples, the men smiling indulgently at their wives in their bobbing hats, the wives briskly brushing dandruff off their husband's collars, rooting happily in their pockets for handkerchiefs and collection change – those were the times when you had to admit you were not one of them.

'Hi. Am I interrupting?' It was Lily. She was standing shyly in the doorway holding her handbag in front of her knees, a pale-lemon cardigan draped around her bare shoulders. 'I've been looking all over for you, Anna. I wanted to apologize.' She walked over to the fireplace and propped her bag on the mantlepiece, unclipped it and reached in for a packet of cigarettes. 'I didn't mean to involve you in . . . Well, hey. I guess I hardly need to tell someone who's writing a book about marriage how things can get a little—' Lily broke off to light her cigarette and then waved it dismissively in the air.

'Of course,' said Anna. 'I understand.'

'Tynt doesn't like me to smoke.' Lily gave a little giggle and tweaked the cardigan tighter around her shoulders. 'It's one of my secret pleasures. One of a growing catalogue, actually.' She turned her head and saw that Anna was watching her, waiting for her to elaborate. 'Oh . . . just, there's a coupla things that drive him crazy, like my shopping, for instance, and my sports car. Boy, does he hate that sports car. Apparently it gives out totally the wrong message. Rule number one of living on an English country estate . . . never be seen to be spending money on anything besides the roof.' Lily cocked her head on one side and eyed Anna mischievously. 'Forgive me for latching on to you like this. But, you know, females under the age of fifty are rarer than nail bars around here. Everyone is awfully kind, of course, but there's no one for miles who I can actually talk to.' Lily rolled back her head and closed her eyes. 'And I'm an American, for heaven's sakes! A twenty-eight-year-old, California-raised, red-blooded American woman! I love to talk. That is like my number one reason for existing.'

'Can't you talk to . . .' Anna hesitated, unsure how to refer to Tyntallin.

'My husband? Oh sure. But not about how truly, totally terrifying it is to be the wife of a perfectionist in a country that rates Americans somewhere just above pond life.'

Lily seemed to drift off for a moment, momentarily mesmerized by the smoke floating upwards from her cigarette. 'I mean it's hard for him too, y'know?' she said quietly. 'Not only has he lost a wife but he's been landed with someone who thinks it's her constitutional right to get it all out on the table. Where I come from that's just a basic given. Where Tynt comes from, it's sort of contemptible.'

Lily turned away for a moment to reach for an ashtray and when she turned back again she was smiling brightly. 'I did get him to talk though,' she said triumphantly. 'When we first met that's all we did. But that was different, of course. We weren't *married* then.'

'I hear you're a psychic,' said Anna. 'I hear that's how you met.'

'A what?' Lily stared at her blankly and then put a hand over her mouth and started to giggle. 'Oh my God,' she squealed. 'The American witch, right? That woman who seduced the poor, vulnerable lord? Well, I guess it's all the same thing around here, but actually I'm a counsellor. I *was* a counsellor, I should say. And, yeah, Tynt came to me for bereavement counselling, while he was taking time out in New York. Oh wow –' she gave a little knowing chuckle '– lucky I didn't meet him before Henrietta died, or they'd have pinned that one on me, for sure.'

'I'm sorry,' said Anna, embarrassed to have been implicated in such ignorant gossip.

Lily scrutinized her for a moment, her head listing to one side as if she were assessing Anna's trustworthiness, computing what little information she had at her disposal. 'I really have to go,' she said suddenly, reaching for her handbag. 'But we should definitely keep in touch. Could we do that?' She reached into the bag and took out an address book, opening it at a clean page. 'Would you write down your details for me? Then perhaps you'd come and visit us? Tyntallin really is beautiful, especially now, in summer. And you never know, you might get some good material out of it. Second wife and a foreigner too – there's gotta be something in that, right?'

Lily was trying her best to sound light-hearted, but Anna saw how her mouth dragged at the corners.

'I'd like that,' she said, quickly. 'By the way, you've got me down under F. It's E. E for Emery.'

Lily nodded. 'I know. I forgot, so I just figured I'd put you under F for friend. Pretty dumb, huh? See what country life does to you?' Without meeting Anna's eyes she took the address book, turned and clipped across the study and out of the door, the skirt of her yellow dress swinging jauntily as if she hadn't a care in the world.

Six

'Who knows what he was thinking?' Jean said. 'A man in his position has all kinds of motives for marrying.' They were driving along the motorway the morning after the wedding. It was overcast and drizzling and Jean was steering with her fingertips as was her habit when she was concentrating on something of genuine interest. 'Maybe he thought she had some money to shore up Tyntallin for another generation? Maybe he felt he needed a mother for those children, and that it would help if she was young. I was surprised, though, I must say.' Jean slid the car into fourth gear and left her pale fingers draped over the gear stick, like a handkerchief. 'Tarka never struck me as the type who would go for a pretty little thing. His first wife, Henrietta, was a farmer's daughter – not what you'd call high maintenance.'

'And who said Lily is "high maintenance"?' Anna said.

Jean turned to look at her. 'You're worried about the American, aren't you? I shouldn't, darling. The fragile-looking ones are invariably the toughest.'

Anna nodded, but still she couldn't help remembering how Lily had looked as she was driven off after the reception – pinched and owl-eyed, staring out into the darkness, while Tyntallin towered over the wheel, glowering to left and right as if challenging anyone to question his right of way.

'I never got a good look at her,' Jean continued. 'But he's as dashing as ever. He's still got those very intense grey eyes that look as if it physically hurts him to focus on you. Did you notice? And that wonderful croaky voice. I had rather a thing for him, as a matter of fact, years and years ago. He was so much more manly, even though he was younger, than the boys we were used to going around with.'

Anna sighed heavily and turned her head to look out of the window. She was not in the mood for indulging Jean's world view. After a night spent in the company of Tyntallin and his peer group, it suddenly didn't seem so harmless after all.

'I must say I thought he'd worn well,' Jean continued, 'compared with the lot on the gay divorcees table. It's the *way* men go bald, isn't it? It's not the actual hair loss, it's those sad little outcrops they will insist on leaving, like high-tide markers, as if knowing where it used to grow makes it any better. And then, of course, the ones who live in the country have that *skin*.' Jean paused for a reaction, but Anna kept on staring determinedly out of the passenger window. 'Every one of them looks like they've been rubbed between two bits of sandpaper. Take Reggie Porter. He used to be dazzling before he moved down here –' Jean made a sweeping gesture with her left arm, causing the car to glide gently towards the slow lane '– now he's got everything but the limp and the wall eye. Mind you, when I had a crush on Tarka, I was rather enthusiastic about the whole country experience.'

'Oh, Jean, what *are* you talking about?' Anna twisted round in the passenger seat and glared at her friend. 'The man is a reactionary, arrogant, bully. He's a pig to his wife, obviously. He was appallingly rude to me. He actually accused me of being unfit to do my job because I wasn't married! And he insinuated that I had an agenda. That my work was just a way of . . . confirming my own prejudices. Because I live in London! Because I used to be a journalist!'

Jean sighed and lifted a hand off the wheel in a gesture of resignation.

'Well, I'm sorry,' Anna snapped. 'But it's people like you who romanticize people like him, that encourage people like her to believe that they are somehow . . . extraordinary. When, in fact, what they are is unspeakable.'

Out of the corner of her eye, Jean saw Anna shift her position so that her back was turned squarely towards the driver's seat. It seemed to her that Anna was rather over-reacting, but then clearly the entire wedding had been something of a disaster as far as she was concerned. Allegra had, apparently, been 'confrontational'; Mikey was monosyllabic and then drunk; and Tarka had, evidently, ruined her entire dinner. Then, this morning at breakfast, after a night spent under the Wells's roof, Anna had been forced (her words) to listen to her hosts singing Tarka's praises at the same time as criticizing the shortcomings of 'the American'.

'You notice the worst they could find to say about her was that she hadn't turned up to some country landowners' fundraiser,' Anna had scoffed, as they loaded their overnight cases into the boot of the Jaguar. 'Oh, and the fact that she "might" be vegetarian.'

Jean sneaked another look at Anna, rigid and aggrieved in the passenger seat, still wearing the silk trouser suit she'd worn for the wedding, her other outfit having proved too lightweight for the sudden change in the weather. Poor Anna. She did so mind about women being treated justly, especially by the men they were involved with. Sometimes Jean wondered if there wasn't more to it than professional concern. For all that she had this very house-trained boyfriend and a successful writing career it seemed that Anna was not, when it came down to it, terribly happy with her lot. Nor was she quite the same Anna that Jean used to know. That Anna was softer and more relaxed; she laughed a lot and drank too much and always laddered her stockings within minutes of putting them on. And the funny thing was, considering the work she now did, that Anna had been a rather better listener.

'You are watching for the turn-off to your parents', aren't you, darling?' Jean said, gently reaching over and giving Anna a conciliatory pat on the knee. 'Of course, you're absolutely right about Tyntallin, but you're an idealist, you see. You get to my stage of life and everything becomes a lot simpler. Frankly, he could be sleeping with the butler for all I cared, so long as I had the run of that fabulous house.'

Jean breathed in deeply, drawing her shoulders up to her ears as she pictured the library with its peach silk wallpaper, the two fireplaces, each mantlepiece bristling with Meissen figurines, the Sargeant portraits lining the length of the room, most of them ten feet tall in their giant gilt frames.

'Really, I think I could put up with anything,' she said dreamily, glancing over at Anna, sizing up the risk before adding, 'and I'm sure little Miss Lily thought much the same.'

'She met him in New York, as it happens. And she'd never set foot in this country, so the idea that she was after the heirlooms doesn't wash.'

'Really?' Jean's eyebrow twitched. 'Maybe she got a tip-off from the other side.'

'She's a *counsellor*, not a clairvoyant. She gave him bereavement counselling, in New York. And she's twenty-eight, not nineteen.'

There was silence in the car for a moment. Anna sat stiffly, tugging her folded arms tight under her ribcage. And then Jean asked, 'Is Tarka an earl? I've completely forgotten. Oh, how maddening. I know, why don't I ring Tony on the mobile and ask him? That'll really get him going.'

As the Jaguar pulled up outside the Old School House, Anna could see her parents rallying themselves in the kitchen. Her mother was hastily untying her apron, shooing her father towards the front door with little jerks of her newly set grey bob, and from the slightly fretful expression on Minty's face, and the way she kept glancing between the door and the oven, Anna could tell that there was a crisis about the lunch. But then it was a very long time since things had run smoothly in that kitchen. Her parents were in their mid-seventies, sprightly and enthusiastic, but utterly closed to the introduction of new technology, including a replacement for their ancient and unpredictable cooker. Their attitude was that they had worked long and hard getting to know the appliance's idiosyncrasies and, having got this far, they weren't about to give up on it now. It was quite a good example, Anna often thought, of the difference between their generation's attitude and that of their children's; and it didn't just apply to the material things of life.

As Anna stepped out of the car and made her way around to the boot of the Jaguar, she saw that Minty had moved through to the sitting room and was now busy tidying the place on the sofa where her father had been sitting moments before. Her lips tut-tutted and her head wagged as she smoothed the cover, retrieving bits and pieces from down the sides of the cushions, and placing them on the occasional table, among the sea of ornaments. Next door, in the kitchen, Anna watched her father fill his wine glass from a bottle next to the sink, his bottom lip clamped tightly over the top one, spectacles glinting in the light. Then he looked up suddenly and gave her a hearty wave, blissfully unaware that he had sloshed the first few inches of his drink onto the floor at his feet.

Jean blew a kiss to her parents, waved one last time, and Anna stood back and watched as she reversed down the few yards of drive and out onto the street. As the Jaguar slipped away, with a last forlorn toot of the horn, she could feel the proof of her adult life vanishing with it, and the clock turning back and back to the time when it was just her, Freddie and Minty. She often wondered if this was a feeling common to people who didn't have their own children, or if it was just to do with the fact that she wasn't married and therefore, in her parents' eyes, permanently stuck in the limbo between adulthood and still seeking a direction in life.

'Darling!' Her parents were both at the front door now, both hovering on the threshold, arms outstretched. 'Come on in, darling,' they chorused, each kissing Anna on opposite cheeks as she squeezed through the narrow space between them, dragging her suitcase behind her.

'So, how was the wedding?' Minty addressed the question to Anna's legs and then, looking up at her hesitantly, eyes tensed, asked, 'Did you wear trousers?'

Anna had anticipated this particular line of enquiry; it was a reasonable question from someone who would have expected a visit from the vicar if she had turned up to church without a hat, and Anna was old enough, and comfortable enough with herself, to indulge it.

'Oh, for God's sake,' she wailed, dropping her suitcase on the floor and flailing her hands in exasperation. 'Yes, I wore this trouser *suit* to the wedding.'

Her mother nodded, still peering at her with those pale sensitive eyes, making Anna feel simultaneously like a spoilt adolescent and the kind of brittle, harsh career woman who strikes fear into the hearts of children and old ladies.

'I wore trousers, all right?' she repeated, because the whole women-who-wear-trousers-and-work-and-have-opinions-are-a-threat-to-civilized-society attitude was, after all, what she had been battling all weekend.

'They're very nice,' said her mother, bravely, forcing herself not to look at the trousers. 'I just thought you might have worn your lovely dress with the . . .' she made a frilly gesture at her elbow to indicate the one she was referring to, 'since Richard wasn't going to be there.'

Ah, of course. This was what it was all about. Quite early on in her relationship with Richard, Anna had made the error of mentioning, in passing, that Richard preferred her in trousers, which was then instantly added to the list of Things They Didn't Like About Richard. Also on the list was the fact that Richard was a practising Buddhist ('Is he doing it to be fashionable?' Minty had asked); that he had talked during an episode of *Morse*, when it was clear that Freddie was having trouble grasping the plot as it was; and that he had never heard of Rommel's Desert Rats (both Minty and Freddie felt cheated at not having served in the war and could spot a potential conscientious objector at a hundred yards). Then there was Richard's knowledge of yoga, which Minty and Freddie persisted in associating with acrobatic, and quite possibly gender non-specific, sex. (They had never actually said as much, but Anna knew this from the way her father tucked his hands under his armpits and hummed whenever Richard was in the room.) And, of course, Richard's refusal to eat meat, even when it had been purchased at some cost, and prepared in a labour intensive way, for Freddie's birthday.

But the main reason why her parents always referred to the man she lived with in that special tone – with that palpable degree of effort – was because Richard had made it a point of principle to inform them of his views on marriage and children. The each to his own speech had not had quite the effect Richard had come to expect from his audience. Less than a minute into the main philosophical position and Freddie was chortling nervously, pointing his finger randomly at various objects around the sitting room, and not long afterwards Minty had got up from her chair, without a word, and retreated to the kitchen.

'And how does he think he'd be here, living the high life, if no one had bothered to bring him into the world?' she had muttered when Anna tried to drag her back. 'Who does he think he is, wanting to live with you, without even having the decency to buy you a ring?'

It was quite straightforward: Anna had been to a wedding, on her own, and her parents had been silently hoping, possibly quite noisily praying, that during this window of opportunity their daughter might have caught the eye of someone, anyone, so long as it wasn't Richard.

'Look,' said Anna, 'I know this is all about Richard. And I don't want to go there, all right?'

'Go where, darling?' asked Freddie.

'So, did you meet anyone nice at the wedding?' Minty was peering through the glass of the oven door, one hand shielding her brow like an Indian tracker.

'Er, nooo.' Anna was uncomfortably aware that her hands were resting on her hips and her head slung defiantly out to one side; all that was missing was the regulation grey pleated skirt and striped tie. 'If you really want to know, I was on a table with a lot of crusty old squires and their wives and the only person I had anything at all in common with was an American counsellor.'

'Oh? Very nice. And what was he doing there?'

'She, actually.' Anna rolled her eyes in disbelief. Freddie was now tugging at the handle of the oven door while Minty swatted at him with the oven glove. 'Not yet,' she hissed. 'You'll let out all the heat. Ssshh . . . I can't hear what it's doing.'

Anna's eyes travelled upwards to the shelf above the cooker where she could clearly see an oven timer and a meat thermometer, both of which she had given her mother, caked in a layer of dust.

'I don't suppose you're interested now,' she said, her foot jigging impatiently, 'now that the counsellor's not a *man*.'

'Oh no, darling, of course we're interested in your party,' mumbled Minty. 'It's just that we're coming to a rather crucial moment with the joint.' She straightened up and patted her damp pink face with the oven glove. 'I do hope you weren't this cross for the party, Anna darling. It was a wedding after all.'

That evening, once the news was over, Freddie switched the TV off and he and Minty sat side by side on the sofa preparing to be interviewed by their daughter for the last time. At this point Anna was always struck by two contradictory emotions. On the one hand she was over-whelmed by how much of a unit her parents were: you looked at them and saw not two individuals but a couple; two people who seemed as inevitably linked as Siamese twins. The other feeling was a mixture of frus-tration and irritation. Both Minty and Freddie were as cooperative as she could reasonably have hoped, but their actual interest in her book was non-existent and, if anything, they were slightly embarrassed by it. It wasn't the personal nature of the questions that made them feel awkward, but simply the fact that their daughter could take relationships so seriously; that she was bothering to ask the questions in the first place. Sitting here in front of them, with her tape recorder at the ready, Anna found it almost impossible to suppress the image of herself in front of a cardboard greengrocer's, forcing her parents to buy pretend packets of sweets, hour after hour.

'Right, where d'you want to begin?' Anna said. 'With the update questions, or the "when you met" stuff?' Generally she found it was better to take quite a snappy, businesslike tone with them, or they tended to drift off.

'Well, erm.' Minty lifted her bi-focals to her face and peered at the sheet of typed paper in her hand. 'Your father and I weren't quite sure what you meant by "an anecdote that demonstrates . . . when you were first aware of your mutual commitment".' Minty turned to Freddie as if to give him one last chance to come up with the correct interpretation, then looked back at Anna and shrugged.

'It just means, when you knew that you were ready to commit to each other, for life,' Anna said patiently. 'When you knew you wanted to get married.'

Minty nodded and returned to the piece of paper, running her finger tentatively under the relevant words.

'Everyone has that moment, don't they?' Anna coaxed. 'When they realize that this is the one, and they don't need to look any further?'

Freddie was looking up at the ceiling and tapping his

whisky tumbler against the table as if trying to communicate with someone on the floor above.

'Well, I don't know,' said Minty. 'Do you mean when your father proposed? Because that isn't much of a story. I was sitting at a table with Julia Onslow and Mike Leighton, who were courting, and when Julia went off to get a drink Mike turned to me and said, "Do you want to get married?" Then your father popped up from somewhere and said, "She's marrying me, chum, so push off." And that was that.'

Freddie nodded. 'After that Mike asked Julia and she said yes . . . so everyone was happy.'

'That was their fiftieth anniversary we went to last month,' Minty added, to prove the point. She peered at the paper on her lap again and shook her head. 'I don't know if we were quite so interested in commitment and all of that, we just sort of got on with it in those days.'

Anna flicked the top of her pen irritably and tried again. 'How about, what made you think you were right for each other? The thing that separated Dad from . . . Mike, say?'

'Oh, well.' Minty gave her a look as if to say that should have been perfectly obvious. 'Your father and I were a very good fit on the dance floor. I often think your generation would have been a lot better off if you'd learned to dance like we did. You can tell an awful lot about a man from the way he waltzes.'

Freddie looked at her as if he couldn't quite remember having ever waltzed, let alone with her.

'I don't suppose you've ever danced cheek to cheek with Richard?' asked Minty, warming to her theme.

'No, Mother, but I sleep with Richard, so I think we've probably got beyond that stage.'

Freddie sucked his lips over his teeth and adjusted his spectacles.

'That's as maybe,' Minty said, peering at Anna as if she suspected she might be sickening for something, 'but I'm not so sure.'

'Right,' said Anna. 'I'm not going to get distracted, thank you. Now, have either of you, since we last spoke, noticed a new dimension to the relationship?'

Anna's bedroom at her parents' house was a slit of a room furnished with a narrow single bed, a chest of drawers, and a wall of shelves stacked with old books, magazines and photograph albums. She had gone upstairs early intending to read, despite the noise of the television blaring in the sitting room below, but every time she got to the top of a page her eye caught sight of the photograph album spines on the shelf, each carefully labelled with a date and sometimes a subject: 'India 1986; Cornwall 1987'. All her recent albums were in London, of course. These were the ones with the peel-back pages and the marbleized vinyl covers that Richard had suggested were better left here for the time being. The photographs they contained were a different species from the ones recording her life with Richard. Those were glossy and painstakingly choreographed, each a miniature work of art: there was a whole black and white series of her walking in a wheat field, for example, and you couldn't see her face in any of them. But these old albums were crammed full of faces: laughing,

bleached-out faces with eyes half shut, and bodies blur-
ring as they jostled in front of the lens. In one or two
there was an attempt to include a landmark, but the
people were always there in the foreground. You never
really had a picture without a face in those days.

Anna turned on her side so that the albums were
behind her, out of view, and tried to concentrate on the
book. But even though her eyes travelled obediently
along the lines her mind was juggling snapshots,
dangling them just out of focus so she couldn't quite
make them out. In the end, there was nothing for it but
to place the bookmark between the pages, sit up against
the rocking, pine headboard, and reach up for the album
marked 1997–2000.

The pages of these albums were never quite how
you remembered them: everything was less vivid and
smaller and the captions were sloppily written in
different strength biros by a hand that seemed only
vaguely familiar. Then there were all the people you'd
forgotten about, the places you couldn't quite identify,
the clothes you never remembered owning. But the
biggest surprise were those pictures that had been
elected to your personal Hall of Stars: the ones you had
mentally airbrushed and digitally altered, so that when
you came across the real thing they never quite lived
up to expectation. Anna was always prepared for disappointment. She turned the pages of the album, occasionally pausing to squint at a caption, but keeping
moving, aiming to get somewhere. And then suddenly
there it was, long before she expected it, right in the
middle of the page where Danny had glued it five years
before.

It was a colour photograph of the two of them, standing in a half embrace, clutching a dark red blanket around their shoulders. A sliver of Danny's bare, brown chest showed through the gap where the edges of the blanket didn't quite meet; and below the rug his calves and feet were bare alongside the flares of her jeans. He was looking at the camera, grinning, and she was looking up at him, smiling, and there was something about the shape of them together – the bendable, relaxed way they fitted together, and the outline of his arm around her shoulders, pulling her closer towards him – that never failed to bring it all back. She stared at his green eyes, the little beard that he'd grown for the summer, the thick black curls mingling with her own ropy, salt-tangled hair. She tried to remember what they'd been saying in those seconds before the shutter clicked; what it felt like to get into their sleeping bag that night, clutching toes, knitting fingers, wriggling closer and closer.

Anna turned over the page, and then another, until she found the picture of him leaning into his guitar, fingers arched on the frets, eyes closed. The caption read 'Portobello concert for flood victims: Danny raises the roof'. It had been his thirty-fourth birthday and afterwards they'd gone back to Tony and Jean's. She turned the page again, and there they all were, propping up the walls of their tiny mews kitchen: Jean casting her trademark forbidding glance at the camera; Tony striking a muscle-man pose in front of the fridge; Ruth pointing at Dave's protruding stomach, while Dave clinked beer bottles with Danny. 'You're really happy, aren't you?' Ruth had said that night. 'I've never seen you this happy. You're not going to let him get away, are you?'

'Darling?' There was a fluttering of fingers on paint-work and Minty opened the bedroom door an inch. 'Are you all right in there?'

For a second Anna had the urge to stuff the album down the side of the mattress but Minty was already hovering beside the bed, glancing from Anna to the photographs and back again.

'Oh, you're looking at your albums!' Minty bent and extended a papery hand to guide the page into her line of vision. 'Goodness, didn't Ruth look better then, without the fringe? There's David. Dear David.' Minty paused to rally the enthusiasm in her voice. 'And Daniel!' she gasped, pushing it too far, 'now he was a good-looking boy, wasn't he? Whatever became of him, Anna?' She scrunched up her nose in concentration so that her top lip was pulled clear of her gums and she appeared to be snarling at the picture. 'You'd have thought you'd have heard something,' Minty added.

'Well, I haven't.' Anna tried to pull the album out of her mother's reach, which she took as an invitation to settle herself on the edge of the bed.

'Your father thinks he must have been a bit unhinged,' murmured Minty, 'to have gone off like that. And then not even a letter. Fancy asking someone to marry you and then not even a phone call? He must have had some sort of nervous breakdown, Ginny said.' At the mention of their neighbour Anna let out a low moan. 'Well, she does know a bit about that sort of thing. Their son, Derek, was in and out of those places. He's never been quite right since those malaria pills.' Minty looked up from the photograph and peered at Anna. 'Do you still worry about it, darling?'

'Nooo!' Anna flicked over the page and proceeded to scour the prints with the aid of a finger.

'He probably just realized he wasn't up to it. And better to have found out before it was too late. I had a girlfriend who was left at the altar. Terrible. Her hair turned white, poor thing.'

'I know. You've told me several times, Mother. Why are we talking about this now?'

'Because of the photograph.' Minty shifted on the bed. 'And because, I wouldn't like to think that you were still . . . carrying a torch for Daniel.'

'Carrying a torch! Mother, I live with Richard. We are a *couple*. If you don't mind, I was just looking at some *photographs*.'

Her mother smoothed her hand lightly over the duvet cover, glancing up cautiously, as if expecting it to be slapped at any moment.

'And,' Anna added, as an afterthought, 'if you remember, I was supporting Danny all the time we were living together. He was a penniless musician, with no prospects – to quote you – and you thought he was an anarchist. That time the queen got shot at you rang me up and asked if it was him! So please, do not pretend you had your hopes set on Danny.'

'I'm not saying we did.' Minty was gazing at her hand now, as if it were a sick puppy she didn't expect to last the night. 'Your father and I were very worried, as a matter of fact, about how the two of you would manage, if you did . . . but we just thought . . .' She looked up at Anna, her eyelids fluttering. 'We just thought that when you were with him you always seemed so happy.'

Anna opened her mouth to speak and instead felt it sliding away, and hot, fat tears flooding her eyes.

'Oh, darling,' Minty crooned, hooking an arm around her daughter's shoulders.

'I'm not crying because of that,' sobbed Anna.

'What, darling?'

'The happiness thing. I am happy. I'm just happy in a different way. And I wasn't centred then. I wasn't in control of my life. That's the whole point.'

Her mother looked at her nervously, as if she were about to say something inappropriate in front of a room full of elderly relatives.

'It might have seemed wonderful, but . . .' Anna caught her breath, twisting the duvet cover in her hands, 'it wasn't healthy for me. That's what you and Dad don't understand.'

Tears were sluicing down her face now. It was as if she'd accidentally tripped a wire and unleashed three years' worth, rather than the everyday frustration quota that was currently required.

Her mother gave her shoulder a squeeze. 'We just want you to be happy, your father and I,' she said, 'that's all.'

They sat in silence for a moment, Minty absent-mindedly stroking the back of Anna's hair, Anna dabbing her nose with a tissue while she groped for the convincing clincher.

'The reason I'm crying,' she said, eventually, 'is because I shouldn't have let myself become so dependent. No one should have so much invested in one other person.'

'But, darling, you thought you were going to marry

him,' Minty said, gazing at her with puzzled watery eyes. 'Isn't that what marriage is all about? Trusting someone with your future?'

'Yes if it's you and Dad.' Anna sniffed, scrabbling under the pillow for another tissue. 'But not these days. No one wants to feel that kind of responsibility. You could scare a man away if you let him think he was responsible for your happiness. You've got to take charge of your own life.'

Minty was nodding and humming very softly. 'Might it help,' she asked, her arm tensing slightly around Anna's shoulders, 'if you told me what really happened?'

What really happened? What had actually happened was that Danny had walked out of her life, for ever, the morning after the night they got engaged. What her therapist said had happened – or implied anyway – was that Anna had been so carried away with the idea of getting married that she hadn't been listening to Danny. And the reason she wanted to get married so much, was because she had failed to take full responsibility for her own life.

What her friends said had happened varied. Ruth was of the opinion that, forced to choose between his life and the real adult world, Danny had bottled out and taken the easy option. Valerie said – though not right away, obviously – that Anna had made it far too easy for him, and that if you provided for a man he was bound to end up resenting you. Jean didn't have a particular view, but she did volunteer that she'd always thought Danny was 'pretty shifty'. 'And men with guitars, darling,' she'd said, intending to leave it at that if Anna hadn't begged for clarification. 'It's the international symbol of self love. Everyone knows that. Not if you're Willie Nelson, obviously. But if you're a nice middle-class London boy . . .'

What had happened according to Danny's keyboard player, Mike, was that Danny probably felt 'sort of hemmed in', and as a result had 'split'. Not that she and Danny weren't great together – and everyone appreciated that she'd done a lot to straighten him out – but with Danny the music was always going to come first, and he really needed the space for it to come together. 'The pram in the hallway,' Anna had murmured, staring out of the window of their flat, the telephone barely in contact with her ear. Mike hesitated on the end of the line. 'Yeah, I don't mean like actual space for equipment. More like space for his head, y'know . . . room to breathe. Tell you what, if he gets in touch I'll ask him to give you a call.'

What Anna thought had happened changed quite a bit between the time she realized Danny had really gone, and six months later, when she finally accepted he wasn't coming back.

She'd woken early, on that Saturday morning, and Danny's side of the bed was empty. In retrospect that waking instant gave her a desperate, sinking feeling but, at the time, she was merely puzzled for a split second and then filled with joy as she remembered the events of the night before. She lifted her left hand from under the bedclothes and examined the green felt-pen diamond cluster drawn on the third finger, smiled to herself as she pictured Danny buying breakfast in the shop on the corner, maybe picking up some flowers from the stall down the street. Then she'd slipped out of bed, pulled on her dressing gown, and started to tidy up the empty bottles and remains of last night's dinner. Anna remembered glancing in the shard of mirror propped against the wall, pulling the cord of the dressing gown tight and yanking open the collar, determinedly moulding the lumpy towelling this way and that, imagining it was creamy duchess satin – maybe with a seed-pearl border.

At some point Ruth had called, and they'd made a plan for them all to come round that night, to celebrate.

'But I won't ring the others just yet,' Anna told Ruth, 'because Danny should be here too. He wouldn't want to miss that.'

Then she'd tidied up some more, moving on to her clothes, finding she was suddenly inspired to throw out anything tired and black and washed out, and it wasn't until Archie and Valerie rang at midday that she realized Danny still hadn't returned.

'Oh, he'll be looking for the ring, poor boy.' Archie chuckled. 'Valerie sent me straight out the morning after I proposed and told me not to come back until I had something that she couldn't fit under a glove. Either that or he's sneaked off to write you a love song.'

It was at that point she'd noticed Danny's guitar was missing and decided to phone Mike, the keyboard player, who confirmed that none of the band had seen him since Wednesday. By three o'clock Anna was in tears, at four she rang Ruth, and after that it was all a bit of a blur.

Anna wasn't sure when, exactly, everyone turned up

at the flat. She remembered Archie, sitting quietly in the corner ringing round all the hospitals; Tony leaning forward in his seat, murmuring questions she couldn't answer. Where were Danny's family? Did he have any other friends, besides the band? Had he said anything out of the ordinary?

'Yes, actually,' Ruth said, scooping a protective arm around her friend's shoulders. 'He asked her to marry him.'

Anna had lifted her face from the clod of tissues for a moment. 'No, he didn't,' she whispered. 'I asked him.'

'It doesn't matter who asked who,' Ruth said gently, lifting a lock of Anna's hair out of reach of the soggy tissues. 'The point is, the last time you saw him you were planning on spending the rest of your lives together.'

Anna had nodded, but she knew then that she had driven Danny away. She knew by the way Tony was sucking in his lips and Valerie's eyes were flicking round the group, and she thought back to the night before and how Danny had stood at the window looking out into the darkened street.

'What are you thinking?' she'd asked.

He hadn't answered her at first. Then he'd turned to look at her, smiling. 'I'm thinking about tomorrow,' he'd said, 'and all the days after that.'

'You're not pregnant, are you?' Dave asked, and then froze. 'What? Well, that could put the frighteners on a bloke, I just thought it was worth . . .'

'No, I'm not,' Anna answered. 'But he wouldn't have minded anyway. We wanted to start soon, we'd talked about it.'

The night before they'd even discussed their children's names. She'd made suggestions while he'd scrawled them on the top of his music sheets – Ivy and Clodagh and Sam. 'I'd like to write a song for Ivy,' he'd said and smiled as he formed the letters, dreaming, she'd thought, about their little girl Ivy with the long black curls and the pony print wallpapered bedroom and the kitten that had to sleep next to her bed.

Two weeks after Danny left, Anna had got a post-card in the mail. It said: 'I'm so sorry. I love you, but I can't do this. I wish I could. You will always be in my heart. Danny.'

'Arsehole,' pronounced Ruth when they came round to view the evidence for themselves. 'Look at the way he's signed his name! He thinks one day this is going to be sold in an auction of Danny Fortune memorabilia. Look at the tail on that Y. Give me a break.'

'He says he loves me,' Anna said, in the cracked wispy voice people get when their lives have collapsed around them. 'Maybe he just needs some time?' She remembered how she'd searched their faces for corrob-oration, gazing up at them hopefully from her nest in the corner of the sofa.

'Sweetheart, we don't even know where he is,' Jean said gently. 'I don't think he's planning on keeping in touch.'

'Well, it's from somewhere in Ireland.' Valerie held the postmark up to the light. 'Anna, I've been meaning to ask you . . .' She closed her eyes, the signal that what she was about to say might cause discomfort. 'Have you checked that nothing valuable is missing?'

Ruth groaned.

'Well, someone had to say it. What about all that money he owes her? There's no mention of that in the postcard.'

'That was a loan. He didn't *take* it,' Anna protested.

'Well, it's a permanent loan now.' Valerie clucked. 'As if you had that sort of money to lend in any case. I didn't like it at the time. He never told you what it was for and then he was in such a rush to get his hands on it—'

'I think there's more to the postcard,' Anna interrupted, hugging her cardigan tighter around her shoulders. 'He didn't need to say he loved me if he was trying to say goodbye. He could have just said, "Sorry, but . . . I think it's for the best", or something.'

'Or how about this,' said Ruth, folding her arms. 'How about, "Sorry I lived with you for three years, led everyone to believe that I was a permanent part of your life, said I wanted to marry you and have your children, and then walked out of the door one day and never came back. Sorry about that."'

'Do you think there's someone else?' whispered Anna.

'No,' they all chorused. And she felt better than she had done in days.

Over the following weeks Anna was offered lots of alternative explanations for Danny's behaviour, but the one that made the most sense, the one that kept repeating in her head, was that her own unwomanly behaviour was to blame.

'Unwomanly?' said Ruth. 'How d'you work that out?'

'I just shouldn't have been so available.'

'Is this Valerie, and the thing about the money?'

'No. It's about what men really want. You can't be unreservedly, helplessly in love. They need you to be one step away from completely attainable. I knew that. I overwhelmed him. I pushed him. *You* told me to,' she added accusingly, looking up at Ruth. 'You said I couldn't let him go, so I pushed him.'

'By asking him to marry you?'

'Yes, mainly.'

'Anna,' Ruth was wearing her I'll-say-this-only-once expression. 'Don't be an arse. If he took fright at that, what was he going to be like when you were actually married? How was he going to cope when the twins had whooping cough, you had post-natal depression and your parents were living in the spare room?'

Anna frowned.

'That's different,' she said.

By around week five, Anna had developed her unwomanly theory and arrived at a list of six core reasons why Danny had left her. One, she had invested too much of her happiness in him, and was not sufficiently independent. Two, she was not self-contained or serene and therefore lacked the necessary mystique to keep men interested. Three, she smoked too much. Four, she didn't make enough noise in bed. Five, she was too bourgeois in her outlook and preoccupied with public gestures – i.e. marriage – when really there was no earthly reason why they couldn't have carried on just as they were. Six, she only shaved her legs in summer, had never had a manicure and had never owned any nice underwear, alluring nighties or similar.

'I think you're approaching this the wrong way

round,' said Archie, when she gave them her list over dinner at the Cunninghams'. 'Shouldn't you be reminding yourself of all the qualities Danny was lacking in?'

'Absolutely,' agreed Ruth.

'Mind you, noise is important,' said Dave. 'I mean, isn't it?'

That was the dinner that had sparked the idea of the relationship summit, though it was decided, straight off, that no men were allowed, on the grounds that they would only confuse the issue.

Minty's lips quivered as she stifled a yawn.

'And that's more or less it,' said Anna. 'Then I met Richard, and he helped me realize what I really need from a relationship.'

She had relayed the whole saga – minus most of the detail and all of the references to financial loans and sex – while still huddled in her mother's embrace, and now, as she shifted in the bed, Minty's arm fell limp behind her.

'Ooof. It's gone to sleep.' Minty groaned as she levered herself up against the headboard.

'Well, you said you wanted to know what happened,' Anna said huffily.

'Oh, darling, I did! And I'm so relieved it's all behind you.' Minty cleared her throat. 'You don't think – now you're on an even keel again – you don't think it might be good for you to get back in the swing of it?'

'What do you mean, "get back in the swing of it"?' Anna instantly thought of the party that Richard had just refused on both their behalfs in favour of an Ashtanga and meditation weekend in Wales.

'I just mean it was very nice of Richard to see you through a difficult patch, but now you might want to let yourself . . . relax a little bit. You were always a great one for the up-all-night riot.'

'Rave.'

'Rave. And now you barely drink, let alone . . . all of that.'

'Mother! You should be pleased that I look after myself. I had very high acidity levels. My liver was stressed. Besides, I'm older now.'

'I know you are, darling. But what if after all this effort to live this very . . . healthy life, you get run over by a bus outside your front door?' Minty looked suddenly guilty as if she'd been surprised reading some unsuitable literature. 'At least if your father or I go tomorrow we'll know we've had a lot of fun,' she added, blinking nervously.

Anna stared at her mother. She was picturing Richard arranging the taupe cashmere cushions against their leather bed head, plucking one from the back, spinning it on its side and positioning it, just so, in the centre of the arrangement. And then, disconcertingly, Richard was leaning across her in bed, reaching for the ylang ylang oil which he had taken to incorporating into their sex life, along with a painstaking eight-point massage, working inwards towards the perineum.

'Darling?' Minty was peering at her. 'You look as if you're in pain. Are you all right?'

'I'm fine,' said Anna. 'I just wish you wouldn't assume you know what I want. I'm different now.

Everything's different. And you and Dad are just going to have to get used to it.'

The following morning Anna was in her parents' kitchen when she received a call on her mobile.

'Hi there,' said a clear American voice Anna instantly recognized as Lily Tyntallin's, 'isn't it a beautiful day! Oh, forgive me, is this a good time?' She sounded fresh and energetic and slightly breathless, as if she'd just come in from a game of tennis on the lawn. Anna could picture her in her neat, white mini-dress, her hair pulled back in a stretch navy hair band, the racket dangling from her diamond ringed hand.

'Of course,' said Anna. 'I was just about to make some lunch.'

'Gosh! I'm still in bed.' Lily giggled. 'Well, not actually in bed, but sort of loafing.'

Anna's mental picture scrambled and then settled on a wide, four-poster bed draped in damask. Lily was propped up against the pillows wearing a dressing gown, a pearl-grey satin dressing gown with the initials LT embroidered on the pocket, and next to her on the bed was one of those old-fashioned cane breakfast trays, laid with a linen cloth and bone china.

'Listen, I know we only just met,' Lily was saying, 'and I know in Britain you have to have been introduced like a minimum of ten times before you can even pick up the phone – but I just had this great idea. How are you fixed for the weekend?'

'Well . . .' Anna started to reply but Lily could not contain her excitement.

'We're giving a dinner party!' she squeaked. 'Well, I am, anyhow. I'm asking all the people that I wanna see, otherwise it'll be the Shawcrosses and the Loseley Wellards', as Lily enunciated the names her voice dragged, like a record winding down, 'and the point of this party is to have some fun. Oh, say you'll come, Anna. Tynt's in London on Thursday, you could drive down with him. Make it a long, long weekend.'

'No . . . I mean,' Anna winced, 'thank you, that would be lovely. But I couldn't come until Friday, at the earliest.'

'OK. Great! Not too late though. The dinner's Saturday, but I'll need *lots* of time to show you around.' Lily caught her breath and Anna could see her spinning around the bedroom, trailing her fingers along the hand-painted wallpaper, tracing the arcs of humming birds and pink orchids and pale-green bamboo. 'Y'know, Anna, I just can't wait to have someone to show this place off to, someone who isn't thinking "What *has* she done to the flower arrangements? Who does she think she is wearing *white pants* in the English countryside?" Someone sympathetic! Oh. Hold on a moment, Anna.' There was a muffled sound as Lily adjusted the receiver against her ear. 'Mrs Gordon? Mrs Gordon? Hi. Could you please tell cook I'd like a caesar salad, dressing on the side, and I'll have it in here, there's no need to set up the dining room. Sorry, Anna. I'm downstairs now,' Lily lowered her voice to a whisper, 'and by the looks of it this lot have never seen a lady in a velour pant suit.' She giggled. 'So. D'you need train times?'

'No, I'll be fine,' Anna mumbled, readjusting her picture of Lily in her surroundings, adding a ponytail, a visor, French windows open onto rolling lawns, a chef with a tall white hat and checked trousers.

'Super. Just let me know when you're arriving and I'll pick you up. We'll have so much fun, Anna! And it'll be so good for Tynt. Just the two of us tucked up here is enough to drive any man crazy.'

'So the children are away then?' Anna asked.

'Hmm? Oh no. The kids are here. All right then. Until the weekend. Can't wait for you to see my perfect life.'

Seven

'Charles?' Archie was standing at the bottom of the kitchen stairs, one hand on the banister, the other cupped around his mouth. 'Charlotte? . . . You two, supper's almost ready. Come and get it!'

He turned his head to smile over his shoulder at Valerie. This was one of those moments when it all made sense; when they were here at home, as a family, just enjoying being together. But for some reason Valerie was untying her apron with the swift precision that indicated her patience had finally snapped.

'What did I tell you?' she hissed, flapping the apron towards the ceiling. 'Don't draw attention to it.'

Archie hesitated. His instinct was to say nothing at all, but Valerie was waiting for a response, chin jutting, lips tensed. 'It, my love?'

'*Food*.' Valerie slung her apron over the Aga rail and gave it a sharp yank. 'How many times do I have to repeat myself? We're not supposed to make a *thing* of it in front of Lottie. What are you looking for, Archie?'

'The carving knife.'

'If you think you're carving, you've got another think coming. Get the plates out of the oven if you want to do something useful. Charlieee!'

Valerie opened her arms wide and Archie turned to see their son loping down the kitchen stairs, skinny arms folded across layers of T-shirts, the waistband of his jeans clinging precariously to his groin.

'Charlie, come and sit down. Archie? Offer your son a drink.'

Archie saw his wife roll her eyes at Charles in mock exasperation, and Charles respond with a flicker of a smile and a backwards step. 'Right! What about a beer then?' Archie said. 'I've got some of those little French bottles—'

'Oh, give us all a glass of wine for heaven's sake!' Valerie jabbed the carving fork into the chicken and waved the knife in the direction of the wine rack. 'Or maybe Charlie would like something stronger? Have whatever you like, Charlie. Go on!'

'That's OK.' Charles was looking at his feet. 'I'm fine.'

Valerie stared at her son for a moment, her mouth fixed in an expectant smile. He shifted his weight but kept his head bowed and his eyes fixed on the ground, the only means he knew of avoiding taking sides. Archie felt an overwhelming urge to cross the room and take the boy in his arms, nuzzle the funny, gelled hair that looked like wind-whipped corn, but Valerie had forbidden any such spontaneous displays of affection. 'Don't you realize how much you are embarrassing him?' she had announced, after some recent school event. 'The boy is sixteen years old. He doesn't want you fawning all over him as if he were a child.'

Archie remembered her choice of words because it had struck him how peculiar it was that growing up is associated with removing yourself physically from the people closest to you. No more sitting on knees, no more running for comfort into the arms of the ones you love. He tried to picture the last time he had held, really held, another human being. And then he remembered last Friday afternoon in Mark McLintock's office standing chest to chest with his old friend, gripping him across the back, appalled to learn that Mark was among the casualties of the cutbacks, yet, at the same time, strangely happy to be experiencing this rare moment of intimacy with someone he had known for over ten years.

'Dad? Mum needs the plates.' Charlotte was standing beside him at the Aga. Her hands were stuffed up inside her jumper, pushing the wool away from her body with stiff pointed fingers. He noticed there were shadows like slivers of bat's wings under her eyes and her lips were a muddy violet colour; it was far too hot in the kitchen but Charlotte looked half frozen, the colour of a corpse.

'Well, my pretty thing, she shall have them,' Archie said, snapping open the oven door, and when he looked up again she was actually smiling, not in a way that showed her teeth, of course, not looking him in the eye, or even in the face, but smiling nonetheless.

'Sweetheart?' Archie clasped her skinny wrist through the oven glove. 'Are we terrible parents? Are we? Do we make your life insufferable?' Charlotte shook her head, retreating from him. 'We just want you to be happy, my angel,' he whispered. 'I wish we could all just be happy.'

'Archie.' Valerie's tone was upbeat, with base notes

of pure threat. 'Lottie, why don't you help yourself?' She jerked her head to indicate that Archie should step away from his daughter, immediately. 'Leave her alone,' she mouthed. 'Just sit down and talk to Charlie.'

When was it, Archie wondered, that women had decided husbands were just another aspect of their lives that had been sent to try their patience? Or had it always been the case? He remembered his own mother treating his father with a certain deference and care at all times, but had she done so simply out of a sense of social propriety? Maybe the only difference between marriage then and now was that women no longer bothered to disguise who was calling the shots? Maybe they'd always thought their menfolk were useless fools but, back then, had simply found it more expedient to work around them, rather than advertising their perpetual frustration and displeasure? As it was, things had shifted to the point where Archie was beginning to suspect there was a sort of kudos in having a husband who you had relieved of all responsibilities, bar bringing home a salary. He wouldn't have been at all surprised if Valerie and her friends sat around their kitchen tables, comparing what their menfolk were not allowed to do, and congratulating each other on having narrowed down their sphere of influence to pouring drinks and putting out the rubbish.

Archie sat down at the table, opposite his son. 'Lovely to have you back, Charles darling.'

'Charlie,' Valerie corrected him. 'Everyone calls him Charlie, don't they, Charlie?'

'Whatever,' said Charles. 'I don't mind.'

'If that's what all your friends call you . . .' Valerie

twisted round to face the table as she carved. 'How are your friends, Charlie? How's Rob?' She widened her eyes at Archie as if to say, '*That* is how to talk to your son.'

'He's OK.' Charles was looking mournfully down at his plate. Archie watched as he slowly picked up his cutlery and started to investigate its contents as if they might be booby-trapped. Next to him, Charlotte sat slumped like a penitent in front of a much smaller plate, evenly distributed with a layer of peas and what could only be described as a morsel of chicken. She appeared to be attempting to pick up one of the peas without revealing the tips of her fingers.

'How was France, Charlie?' Valerie wriggled into her place at the end of the table, mouth open in anticipation. 'I was there exactly this time last year, you know.'

'Did Dad go?' asked Charlotte, accusingly.

'Oh, you know Daddy. He had to work. Besides, he doesn't understand the French.'

'I love the French, sweetheart! It's where we spent our honeymoon, after all. I have extremely happy memories of that hotel in Paris and our little bedroom, tucked away in the eaves.'

Charles and Charlotte both looked up from their plates, suddenly intrigued.

'Well, Charlie wasn't in Paris,' Valerie said, 'and we want to hear about Charlie's trip. Lottie will want to know all the details for when she goes next year.'

'I'm not going.'

'Of course you are. It's very important to be fluent in French. But we won't worry about that now.'

'Actually, Mum,' said Charles, 'it wasn't that good.'

Valerie either elected not to hear this, or genuinely missed what her son had said because the telephone had started to ring. 'I'll get that,' she trilled, darting up from the table. 'Hello? Oh, Louise!'

'Oh God,' moaned Charlotte.

'Yeees. We'd love to! How adorable. A swimming pool? Oh, they'll be thrilled . . .' Valerie had hooked the receiver against her shoulder and was rubbing her hands slowly up and down her stomach. Something about the tautness of her smile told Archie that by the time they retired to bed she would be in a fever of discontent with her lot. He predicted, as he watched his wife pressing her hands to her hips, that there would be another diet resolution, probably a declaration about needing more challenges in her life, and, almost certainly, a debate as to why it was that everyone else they knew could afford a second house in the country. 'Lovely! See you then,' Valerie said.

'It's the new woman next door,' Lottie muttered. 'Mum's found another "friend" to compete with.'

'As a matter of fact,' said Valerie, resuming her place at the table, 'she's asked us to stay at their house in Suffolk, and there are going to be lots and lots of young people your age.'

'Marvellous,' said Archie.

'Oh, not you, Archie. It's mothers and children only. She says if you want to give Jimmy a ring . . .'

'Jimmy?'

'Jimmy, her husband. Our neighbour. If you want to give him a ring, he'll probably be at a loose end too. Well, it is the *summer*, Archie. You can't expect us to stay cooped up here in London all the time.'

'I'm not going,' said Charlotte.

'You won't have to swim if you don't want . . .' Valerie hesitated.

'I'm not going. I want to stay here with Dad.' Charlotte fixed Archie with a look that somehow managed to exclude everyone else at the table. 'Dad, why don't you just have an affair, like anyone else would?' she said. 'With someone who even notices you're alive?'

'Shut up, Lottie.' Charlie glared at his sister.

'Well, someone's got to say something. It's so sick.'

'What's sick, my angel?' Archie reached out to her across the table and suddenly, without warning, his daughter's eyes were drowning in tears.

'This *family*.'

'Why don't you just eat, instead of blaming Mum and Dad?' growled Charlie.

'Why don't you hang out with people who are maybe, occasionally, *girls*?'

'Oh, now,' Archie said. 'Whatever either of you do is fine with us, just so long as you're not harming your health.'

'Charlie? You like girls. You've got lots of lovely girlfriends.' Valerie tilted her head appealing to her son for confirmation.

'It's OK, Mum. Don't worry about it.'

'No one's worrying! No one's worried about a thing. I'm certainly not.'

'Right,' Charlotte said. 'Everything is just *perfect*.'

'Now, now, that's enough, all of you.' Archie wasn't sure, as he started to speak, what was the best way to conclude this happily. Valerie was watching him, her fingers white around the bowl of her wine glass; Charles and Charlotte were busy examining the edges of their place mats.

'The thing about marriage,' Archie said, 'is that it isn't at all like it is in the films. Sometimes it's hard work, and occasionally it's really rather hellish, and you wonder what on earth the point is. But what matters, you see, is that you care enough about each other to make it all worthwhile. What matters is that you both know – despite all the little disagreements and irritations – that you are with the one person who understands you and accepts you for what you are.' Archie smiled broadly at this point, to demonstrate that, under these circumstances, he was well and truly capable of over-looking a mere lack of appreciation. 'So, you mustn't worry about your mother and me. Whatever you may think, we have an understanding—'

'Archie, for heaven's sake.' Valerie raked her hair nervously. 'Do you really think Charlie wants to hear all this? Honestly. I wouldn't be surprised if he turned round and went straight back to France again.'

'That's OK,' said Charles.

'Well, it isn't OK with me – we should be having fun! Tell us about all the *petites filles* in wherever it was, Charlie . . .' Valerie shivered as if she were caught in a draught and raised her wine glass for her son to refill.

'Just give up, Dad,' Charlotte whispered. 'She doesn't even get it.'

When Ruth got home that same evening, Dave was sprawled on the sitting-room floor reading *Hello!* with MTV flickering in the background, while Billy stacked bricks around his father's bare feet. The flat was heated to a sub-tropical temperature and Dave was wearing his Hawaiian shirt to make the most of it, and swigging beer out of a frosted glass.

'I'm back,' she said, in a tone chosen to convey that she was also tired, a little low, and generally 'not in the mood'. She thought it said, quite clearly, 'I need a bath, I need you to deal with Billy, and look at the state of this place.' And, if Dave had been listening very closely, he might have heard, like a signature refrain whispered in the background, 'When are you going to grow up, Dave? Look at you. Look at us.'

'Heeey! Heeere's Mummy. We've got a surprise for yooo.' Dave rubbed his hands gleefully, leapt to his feet and started delving around behind the sofa. As he bent over, the tail of his shirt drifted away from his jeans revealing a belt of pale skin scored with the imprint of the carpet, and Ruth felt an unexpected wave of mild revulsion.

'There!' He was upright again holding aloft an exceptionally large carrier bag. 'Come and get it, Mrs Dickenson.' Dave pronounced the name Duckernson. It was his name, and that was the way he had always said it, but right now Ruth wished he didn't.

'What is it?' she asked, glancing at her watch.

'*It* is a present,' said Dave, attempting to lift the bag above his head like a prize cup.

'It's a peasant,' repeated Billy, nodding his head wildly, 'from ve shops.'

'I'll give you a clue,' Dave said. 'It's not dirty under-wear, but it is per-rity stee-mee. And Billy chose it. Well, he chose the colour. And obviously he paid for it, out of his little set-aside education fund that Granny gave him.'

Dave was grinning. The present, balanced on his shoulder waggled precariously. For a fleeting second Ruth was reminded of the time he had come home from the market with a cardboard box full of oranges and tequila propped on his head.

'Let's make a baby,' he'd said, 'right now. I have the ingredients for the conception cocktail and we have the technology.'

'We hope,' she'd said.

'I love you, Ruth,' he'd said. 'We are going to have beautiful, wonderful babies.'

'You've never even had a hamster,' she'd said. 'What if we're no good at it? What if it changes everything?'

'Why should it?' he'd said. 'Getting married didn't change us. There is a risk involved though. What if . . .' and his eyebrows had danced like puppet caterpillars, 'what if the wee man's too good-looking? I mean really *offensively* good-looking. That could happen.'

She'd looked at him then with his Airedale hair, and his triangle of dimples, and his kind, crinkly eyes and she'd hoped their son would be exactly like him, in every way.

'Roo?' Dave's smile had shifted down a gear. 'Are you ready for your present or what?'

She flicked her head impatiently in Billy's direction. 'Have you given him his bath?' she said. 'And don't call me Roo,' she wanted to add, 'call me Ruth. It's a woman's name. Roo is the name of an Australian life-guard.'

'Er, nooo, I haven't actually.' Dave swivelled his eyes

hard to the right and then to the left. 'We've been waiting to give you a per-res-ent, you see. From the shop.
We're dressed up for the occasion.' He pointed to his
hibiscus-print shirt and to the package on his shoulder
and then, when she still refused to meet his eyes,
lowered the bag very slowly onto the sofa seat. Billy
looked from the bag to his father and back; he had the
tense expression of someone trying to catch a noise
barely audible to the human ear.

Dave bent over and ruffled his hair. 'Looks like
Mummy wants to wait for her surprise, Billy. Off you go
now and get your jim-jams on, we'll give her the present
later.' Billy hesitated, his suspicions aroused by the note
of false enthusiasm in his father's voice. 'You know, the
longer we wait,' whispered Dave, 'the more excited
she'll be.' This seemed to do the trick. After a moment's
consideration Billy patted the present, as if rewarding a
dog for good behaviour, and then shot off in the direction of his bedroom.

Ruth forced a little indulgent smile to show that
there were no hard feelings. 'One of those days, I'm
afraid,' she said, depositing her handbag on the hall
table and shrugging off her jacket. 'I just need . . . a bit
of space.'

Out of the corner of her eye she saw Dave do a
double take. 'A bit of space' was up there – along with
'spiritual person' and 'issues' and 'personal growth' and,
of course, 'no thank you, we've got an early start' – at
the top of the list of phrases that defined people who
were the antithesis of *them*. The old Dave and Ruth
had no concept of 'a bit of space'. When they'd chosen
their double bed they'd gone for the smaller, almost

queen-sized model, because the one that gave you room to spread out, with a clear runway of empty mattress in between, made them both feel lonely just looking at it.

'I think I'll have a bath,' she said, smoothing down the skirt of her dress, trying to find a reason not to have to look in his direction.

The truth was Ruth disliked this person who demanded time to herself, who looked irritably at her watch and refused to play along, even for the sake of her little boy. She felt as though she should be wearing a belted mac and high-heeled boots, like Meryl Streep in *Kramer vs Kramer*. She felt like the enemy, bringing her selfish ideas, her personal separate hopes and worries, into this home that once had no personal, separate anything. And she was conscious that had she been watching this scene unfold a few years ago, she'd have given herself nil points for her performance.

'What is her problem?' she'd have said. 'So she knows it's a cappuccino machine, because he tried to persuade her she wanted one for Christmas. So she's given up coffee, and there's no room for it in the kitchen, and they certainly can't afford it. So, what? Why be such a bitch about it?'

But that was the way it happened, wasn't it? You spent the early part of your relationship priding yourself on being easy-going and undemanding – the kind of woman who made your partner's male friends green with envy – and the rest of it trying to claw back all those precious concessions so carelessly relinquished.

Does everyone arrive at that day, Ruth wondered, when they look at the gap between their husband's shirt and trousers and feel the faintest flicker of contempt? Is it just a matter of time, a determinate number of years and months, until you regret never having any privacy in the bathroom; until you start to fantasize about having the bed to yourself, once in a while, and begin to get irritated by the way he always rubs his thighs just before he tells a joke? If you made a list of the things that most attracted you to him in the beginning, was it always those, in order of preference, that began to grate on your nerves first?

'I love the way he's so laid back,' she heard herself saying to Anna, a few months after she'd met Dave. 'I love the way he's got nothing to prove. He doesn't play all these macho games. And I love his Belfast accent "Dayvut Duckenson". Isn't it so sexy? It makes me go weak at the knees.'

'I won't be long,' Ruth called, as she climbed the few steps up to the bathroom and shunted the door open with her shoulder, a necessary manoeuvre ever since the fraying carpet had formed a barrier across the threshold.

Ruth was conscious that what really summed up the difference between her life and that of the Annas of this world, was bath time. For women like Anna, the bathroom was a sanctuary, furnished with favourite objects, paintings and proper armchairs. Whereas the Dickensons' bathroom was a battle zone, always wet and strewn with debris, toys and soggy, no longer legible sections of newspapers. Recently, Ruth had been making an attempt to turn this situation around and bring out the temple in their bathroom. She'd cleared a space next to the taps and arranged bottles of scented oil in clusters, like a prisoner cultivating a window box,

chipping away a corner of hope in a hostile environ-
ment. Just two of the bottles now remained intact,
propped on their sides, wedged between the hippo with
the rubber ring and the frogman with the sunglasses.
The embroidered muslin curtain hadn't fared much
better; a couple of weeks back Dave had managed to rip
it in half when changing a light bulb. That left the bamboo ladder, propped up in the corner, and a small sheepskin rug that had started to smell like Camembert.

'I told you,' Dave had said. 'I told you that thing
wasn't going to dry. They're not designed for men's
bathrooms. Men have body hair, they drip. You've got
to have under-floor heating and the follicle count of a
Japanese schoolgirl if you want to go lining the place
with sheepskin. And tell me' – he'd placed an arm
around her shoulders, at this point – 'what exactly *is* the
ladder for? Hmm? Not towels, that's for sure. You can't
fit them on the little rungs, can you? What you can do,
though, and I've tested this, is fit precisely one pair of
Billy's pants on each.' And with that Dave had started
honking like a seal.

Ruth turned on the taps and reached across for the
bottle of lavender oil, unscrewed the lid and watched as
the droplets melted on the surface of the water. The
question was, did she really want a nice bathroom, or
did she just want Dave to acknowledge that, after all
this time, she deserved at least that? Ruth unzipped her
dress and let it fall to the floor, examining herself fleet-
ingly in the mirror over the sink before scooping the
dress up and placing it on the cork-topped stool. Of
course the other possibility – one she had only allowed
herself to think about in the last few days – was that this

oasis she dreamt of was just a symptom of a wider desire to escape, completely, from everything.

Dave had a theory that one of the reasons the divorce rate was so high was because of the number of women who succumbed to their ideal home fantasies. His line was that when couples embarked on their life together, they were usually young and grateful to have a futon and a toaster. But then, as they got older and more affluent, the women realized they'd never had a chance to sew their decorating oats, and were stuck, for good, with the practical, family-friendly compromise. This had always been the case, of course, but the difference was that now there was a burgeoning singles culture out there to remind them continually of what they were missing.

'When our parents were in their thirties there were no single people,' Dave would say. 'Let alone ones who were spending all their income on leather floor tiles and white sofas. The worst it ever got was the neighbours having a better car or a bigger telly. Now, on the other hand, we have a situation where there's Us – the struggling marrieds – Them – the affluent marrieds – and then, on top of that, there are these niggling little envy stokers, the Loaded Young Singles.'

Ruth sat on the edge of the bath, rolled off her tights and knickers and swung her legs over the side. At about this point in the 'Single Envy' speech, providing they were in their flat, Dave would wander over to the window and indicate the house on the opposite side of the street, which you happened to be able to see straight into, and which happened to be occupied by an unmarried, thirty-something, professional-looking female.

'Exhibit A,' Dave would say, inviting the listener to take in their neighbour's gallery-like living space, the cow-skin rug, the turquoise teardrop-shaped velvet sofa and the flickering gas log fire. 'Hitherto the mildly discontented young wife would look at her life and think, "Oh well, could be worse. Could be on my own in a bedsit with a gas ring and a mangle for company." But what does she think now? Now she thinks, "On the other hand, I could have light-coloured velvet upholstery, and a lav seat that's permanently glued to the porcelain, and a fridge full of make-up and Badoit." I'm telling you, if you said to most of them, "Right, then. You can leave him, but only on condition that you stay here and make do with the Draylon – no lifestyle makeover for you, my dear," I guarantee the divorce rate would drop overnight.' Of course, Dave's theory got aired a lot more often these days.

Ruth slipped down into the water and lay back, nudging the toys out of the way with a practised wriggle of her head and fishing, with her big toe, for the flannel draped over the taps. The thing was, once you let yourself think about all this stuff, your mind started scurrying off into corners, digging around for all those old grievances and suppressed dreams. And after that it was only a matter of time before other people could smell it on you. The girls in the office had started asking her if she wanted to come for a drink after work. Yesterday, a shop assistant had assumed she was looking for something for a special date. And then there was Tim.

Tim Brady was the dynamic new talent (so Jasper informed them) who was going to take PJK forward into the twenty-first century. He'd spent two years working for their sister agency in New York – the one with the real stars on its books – and was now being parachuted in (Jasper's term again) to give the London office an injection of whip-cracking, New York-style deal-making. They'd actually been given a talk specifically about Tim and Tim's particular assets and experience, on the Friday before he started. Some of the girls had stayed late afterwards, to tidy their desks, and every one of them had turned up the following Monday wearing their day-into-evening best. Not that Ruth had. She'd just worn her red dress with the gathered sleeves.

'Roo?' Dave nudged open the bathroom door and stood in the doorway, hands jammed in the pockets of his jeans. 'Got everything you need?'

'Yeah,' she said, fumbling for the flannel. 'I'm fine. You OK?'

He nodded. He was looking at her new lavender silk bra draped over the edge of the stool. 'Listen . . . why don't we go out tomorrow night? Get a babysitter.'

'Tomorrow? I don't know . . . might be a bit late.' Ruth peered up at him, willing him to refuse to take no for answer, but at the same time telling herself that if he didn't, then it wouldn't be her fault if she ended up going for a drink after work with Tim and the others.

'OK,' Dave said. 'Maybe I'll meet up with the boys then.'

'OK,' she said.

'I could pick you up afterwards.'

'No, don't worry,' she said. 'I'll probably get a lift.'

Dave never offered to pick her up. She should have shown surprise, if not gratitude. She could have at least smiled. But that was how it went: you wanted someone to change and by the time you knew it for sure, they couldn't make up the ground fast enough. Ruth reached for the soap by the taps, dipping her head low so that her hair flopped forward, shielding her face like blinkers.

Not so long ago, Ruth would have told Dave all about Tim. She'd have come home on the Monday Tim started, and mentioned that the bloke from the American office had finally arrived, and that, despite all the 'golden boy' talk, he was actually OK. She might have added that Tim had immediately decorated the walls of his office with arty-looking black and white photographs, and that in the corner, where Jasper had kept his trouser press, Tim had a stack of boxes containing brand new chalk-blue shirts. But she probably wouldn't have described the way the new recruit smelt of lemon zest, or the fact that he had that American millionaire's hair – thick and springy and prematurely grey – and the kind of tan you only get from sunlight reflected off snow or water. She wouldn't have commented on his confident telephone manner, the bold, deal-maker laugh, or the way he rolled his silver pen between his fingers when the conversation turned to difficult matters. All of this and more would have gone unmentioned because, not so long ago, Ruth wouldn't have noticed it. This time last year Tim would have been just another new face at the office; marginally more interesting than most, but, essentially, part of the furniture.

Now he was an altogether different prospect. Now Tim was someone who reminded you what life could be like if you came into work fresh from a power shower and a just-squeezed orange juice, hungry for what the day had to offer. He was a walking advertisement for his lifestyle: groomed, energetic and confident, and worldly, of course. (Tim spoke Spanish and Japanese and thought nothing of going abroad for the weekend, at a day's notice.) Just being in his company, just dropping a file off in his office, made you feel part of something powerful. As Jasper had said, Tim asked for 20 per cent more. What he hadn't mentioned was that Tim also inspired you to book a hair appointment to have your bottle colour covered up, and to invest in new under-wear, and nibble on raw vegetables during your lunch hour. And, of course, Tim was the reason behind the escalated level of female staff interaction in the ladies'.

Just before lunch was the peak time for exchanging gossip over the washbasins and, since Tim's arrival, Denise, his secretary, had become the unofficial chair of these sessions. It was Denise who decided what was and wasn't a plausible contribution to the agenda, and, nat-urally enough, it was Denise who provided most of the information. So far they knew the basics – where Tim lived (off Ladbroke Grove), how old he was (thirty-seven), his salary (more than Jasper's), his intention to rent on the coast where he could keep a boat (what sort of boat Denise was unsure) – but they were still groping in the dark for solid facts concerning Tim's sex life. He definitely wasn't married, but the question was, did he have a permanent girlfriend, or a series of girlfriends? Last Friday they'd had a few leads.

'That Tania called twice this morning,' Denise informed them, dipping her chin as she sized herself up in the mirror. 'I think she wants to move in. I think she's got a kid as well.'

'Howdyouknow?' a few of the girls had enquired, huddling closer.

Denise shrugged. 'He was askin' about parks in the area. Could be she's got a dog though. D'you think this top is too tight on the arms?'

'Noooo,' they all chorused, running their eyes over her as a formality. 'So, is he going to let her, then?'

'Nah. He's not really interested,' Denise said confidently. 'Not his type. If you want my opinion, I think he quite fancies Ruth.'

Ruth, who had been applying more kohl to her eyes, slipped and smeared a black line all the way out to her temple. 'Don't be daft!' she said, as six pairs of eyes swung around to settle on her and commenced scanning-in her new profile: Ruth the potential enemy, Ruth the mole in their midst, Ruth who wasn't quite as ambivalent as she pretended to be. 'Why would he be interested in *me*?' she protested. 'I'm married! I can't even put on eye make-up! Give the guy some credit.'

Some of the eyes swivelled back in Denise's direction and waited, unblinking, for her professional verdict.

'He makes little comments to you,' Denise said, looming towards her reflection in the mirror, widening her eyes and opening her mouth. 'I see him looking over at you, and then he'll nip across and make some . . . comment.'

'Yes,' said Ruth. 'Like, "Where are the Imogen Drake publicity shots?" Honestly, Denise. Of course he doesn't *fancy* me. Men like that . . . well they don't need to look at anything above thirty, do they?'

She was back on course, the folded arms were loosening up. Some of the girls were even smiling affectionately, grateful for the reality check, happy to be single and twenty-something and still in the sexual running.

'Yeah, well.' Denise tugged her skirt down over her bottom. 'What about by the lifts, last night? He wasn't talking about publicity shots then, was he? You were blushing.'

'Oh, that. I was humming something,' Ruth said, 'and then he asked me if I was a singer. I suppose I was flattered.' Strange as it sounded, it was the truth. And when Ruth had hesitated, Tim had looked her straight in the eyes, smiled and said, 'I thought so. I could tell.'

'Whatever,' said Denise. 'Have it your own way,' and the meeting was officially adjourned.

The funny thing was that, up until that moment by the lifts, Ruth was simply enjoying being someone other than Good Old Ruth. Tim Brady was her motivator – the equivalent of one of those parties you have to go into training for, on account of the guest list being made up of above averagely good-looking people with above average standards of maintenance. Ruth was perfectly well aware that the approach of her fortieth birthday, the introspection encouraged by Anna's book research, and casting Tim in the role of 'man to impress' were not unrelated. You didn't need a degree in psychology to work out that she had been craving some excitement and so she'd set about manufacturing it, in a safe, containable sort of a way. She'd wanted an excuse to make some changes and Tim was that excuse.

But by the lifts, somewhere between his question and that look, everything had been bathed in a kind of dewy clarity. One minute she was standing next to a work colleague she'd elected to slightly fancy; the next she was engaged in a no-contact erotic communication that left her breathless. It was as if some code word had accessed her nerve centre, and all of a sudden she was acutely conscious of his lean fingers reaching out to press the call button, the slow considered way he swivelled his wrist to look at his watch, the outline of his shoulder muscles under his shirt. Then he looked at her again, a long, straight look full of questions, his eyes narrowing for a moment before, with her permission, he let them travel lightly down her body. In those few seconds Ruth had opened herself to him and he had seen who she was, and what she had the potential to be: the woman, the singer, the actress, the free spirit, the Ruth that everyone else had chosen to ignore.

'See you,' he'd said as he stepped into the lift, and she had smiled to herself, luxuriating in his wit and wisdom, and in the pleasure of being so well understood.

'There's a new bloke at work,' Ruth said, sliding down in the bath water. 'He's just arrived from the States. Bit of a slave driver, of course. You know how they are.'

Dave gave her a stiff smile. 'It was a cappuccino machine, by the way. The present. You probably guessed.' He looked down at his shoes, glancing up for just long enough to catch her smiling back, had she been.

Now was the moment she should have said

something, her chance to tell him what was wrong. What could she say though? 'Dave, I need you to look at me differently. I need you to treat me differently. And I know there are people who can see more in me. Men who think of me as someone special and beautiful.' How could she say that? How could you ask your best friend to look at you the way Tim had looked at her? How could you expect your husband to see you as intriguing, unexplored, a golden prize to be won? And even if he could, would she honestly be able to look back at him without thinking, in some tiny corner of her mind, 'I wonder if he ever paid the gas bill?'

Ruth heard the click of the bathroom door, lay back in the bath and closed her eyes.

Eight

Anna stepped off the train onto the platform of Tyntallin station. She released the handle of her suitcase on wheels, hauled the strap of her laptop bag further up her shoulder and made for the exit at a snappy pace, intended to disguise her mounting nerves.

The truth was she was excited to be here, flattered to have been asked, even hopeful that the weekend might provide some useful material for her book. On the other hand, she wasn't at all sure what to expect. In her suitcase she had packed everything from jeans to her best cocktail dress, four kinds of footwear, plus Wellington boots, and a tennis racket. She had also, at Jean's suggestion, brought a small crib book on eighteenth-century antique furniture and a torch. But, as she passed through the swing doors of the station and raised her hand to shield her eyes from the early afternoon sun, Anna knew at once that she'd miscalculated on all fronts.

Perched on the boot of a gleaming red sports car – a denim miniskirt pulled taut across her slim brown thighs, snakeskin sandals waggling on the shiny chrome bumper – was her hostess, Lily Tyntallin.

'Hey!' Lily called, pushing her sunglasses up onto the crown of her head and flashing a smile that seemed too bright for these soft-tinted surroundings. Anna was suddenly aware that they were being watched from all sides – in rear-view mirrors, under cover of the raised boot of a hatchback. She allowed herself to be clasped tightly around the shoulders before stowing her suitcase and taking her place in the passenger seat, smoothing the skirt of her trench coat carefully underneath her.

'Journey all right?' Lily asked, flipping her sunglasses into position and throwing her bare arm over the back of Anna's seat as she put the car into reverse. 'You seem a little tense, Anna. Is everything OK?'

'Yes, thanks.' Anna stole a glance at her hostess's mocha-coloured thighs. The hand that was lightly guiding the steering wheel had pale manicured nails, each one a perfect creamy oval.

'Like the nails?' Lily retrieved her arm from the seat back and flicked her blonde hair out of her eyes. 'I found a woman in the village. Ohmigod, the relief! And so cheap! I have to say I'm almost converted.'

'I hope I've got the right clothes with me,' murmured Anna, gripping her laptop on her knee. 'I didn't really know what to bring.'

'Oh, sure you have! It's very relaxed. Listen, I never have the right thing. Tynt says I look like I live in Miami Beach. I think it's because I wear sandals. No one in Britain wears sandals, did you ever notice that?' Lily switched her head from left to right as they approached a T-junction and then, tucking in her chin, made the turn at high speed.

'You think this is going to be an ordeal,' she shouted above the noise of the engine, 'because the English so get off on making this sort of thing an ordeal, right? But, I say, what is the point of having a beautiful house where people are afraid to come visit, because they don't know if they have the right "kit"?' Lily wrinkled her nose in distaste and shrugged her bare shoulders. 'I want to fling open the doors and let in some light. I want to fill the house with artists and poets and writers – people like you! And you're gonna help me. Hey, look.' Lily stretched out an arm and pointed to a stand of oak trees flashing by on their left-hand side. 'See it? Through the trees? There. That's the house. That's Tyntallin.'

It was some time before they turned off the road, through a set of high, newly painted iron gates, and then several more minutes until the house came fully into view on the far side of an oval lake. It was vast to Anna's eyes: a long, tall, pale-grey building clad up to the top of the second-floor windows – she counted nine of them in all – in some sort of creeper. Above the line of creeper was another row of smaller, square windows and above those a shallow slate roof. There were wide steps leading up to a central front door, covered by a pillared porch, and in front of the house, between the broad sweep of gravel and the lake, endless green lawns interrupted here and there by big, fluffy trees.

'Like it? Pretty big, huh?' Lily let the car idle for a moment, watching her friend with amused curiosity. 'First time I saw it, I couldn't speak either. People always say "Wasn't that the most magical moment of your life? Coming over the brow of the hill and seeing this place and knowing it was going to be your very own home?"' Lily's lips twitched. 'But you know what I thought? Really? I thought, how the heck can I compete with *that*? You know, the first time I saw it was the evening of our wedding?' Lily glanced nervously at Anna, as if she suspected this fact was open to misinterpretation. 'My husband wanted it to be a surprise, of course,' she added, quickly. 'We didn't plan a honeymoon, because the children had been disrupted enough. So we married in London, and came right back here that afternoon, me still in my little oyster satin number.' Her hand floated to her chest, absent-mindedly tracing the neckline of the dress. 'I remember the way he looked when we got to this spot in the road, that mixture of pride and affection and peace. I tell you, I felt almost jealous.' Lily slid down in her seat and relaxed her head against the head-rest. 'Actually, completely, totally jealous. And scared. I felt like a kid. A kid a long way from home.'

Anna hesitated. 'Didn't you tell him how you felt?'

Lily turned to look at her; there was something strange in her expression, something guilty, as if she felt disloyal talking about her husband behind his back. 'I couldn't do that,' she said. 'If you've lived this way, all of your life, you can't understand someone else's anxiety, or how they could ever have a problem with it.' She gave a little frown. 'But you know what? I called my mom that night, and I was like, "Mom, I didn't know I was going to be the second Princess Diana! You don't know what I've taken on here. You would not believe this place." And she was really calm, my mom, she said, "Lily, it's only a house. He is still the man you met and fell in love with."' Lily enunciated the words like a mantra, nodding to herself.

'And is he?' Anna asked the question she knew Lily was asking herself.

'Oh, well, sure!' Lily laughed lightly, slipping the car into gear and moving off down the drive. 'I just don't get to see him so much, that's all. He's really, really busy and I'm not number-one priority any more.' Lily rolled her eyes self-mockingly. 'It's real life kicking in, you know?' She stretched a hand out to touch Anna's knee as if it was she who needed the reassurance. 'Listen, I know you and Tynt didn't exactly hit it off at the wedding, but he's really such a gentleman, Anna. Such a good man. His staff are devoted to him. Everyone's devoted to him. And he's really very open-minded.'

Anna braced herself, smiling and raising her eyebrows in an attempt to look persuadable.

'Honestly. He has all these wonderful plans. He's into organic! And he's looking at . . .' Lily whirled a hand in the air.

'Wind energy,' Anna volunteered, suddenly feeling guilty, knowing that this litany of Tyntallin's good deeds was all for her benefit.

'Yes! Windmills. I mean people are very resistant to that kind of stuff around here. Plus he has rare breeds . . . sort of small little cows and . . . he does an awful lot with the country landowners' organization . . .' Lily's voice faded along with her confidence in her subject.

'Well,' said Anna, 'that does sound . . . something.'

'I know.' Lily's eyes were shining, grateful. 'He's a bit of a local hero actually. There's a lot of disappointed women around here, that's for sure. And let me tell you, they have *all* been around for tea. Oh yeah. And they never touch a drop, or say a single word to me, they're so busy craning their necks to see what changes have been made to the jewel of the county.' She giggled. 'Sometimes I feel almost guilty. I see them looking at me and thinking, "Why her? What does she have to offer?" Boy, if they knew the half of it. I wanna say, "Ladies, help yourselves. Take it all, just leave me the man."'

They were drawing close to Tyntallin now. Gravel crunched under the wheels of the sports car and Anna had the strange feeling that they were shrinking as they swept up to the front of the house and parked in the shadow of the entrance porch.

Inside the house, Anna's first impression was of a mossy coolness, stone floors, high ceilings and the smell of silver polish.

'Don't ask me,' Lily said seeing Anna gazing up at a full-length portrait hanging on the staircase. 'I so should know, I've been told a million times. The clock on the wall, I'm pretty sure is Louis Quinze.' She said Quinze like cans, cocking an eyebrow as if it didn't sound quite right, even to her own ears. 'That sword over the fireplace belonged to one of Tynt's relatives who was big in, like, the Crimean War, I think. And those terrible things –' she pointed to a pair of ebony statues flanking an open double doorway on the opposite side of the hall '– they belonged to Queen Victoria. That's his excuse, anyway.'

Lily shrugged, and gestured for Anna to follow her through the doors into a long, narrow room that seemed to extend along the whole west side of the house.

'The library,' she whispered over her shoulder. 'Isn't it wild?'

The room was wallpapered in peach-coloured silk, with tall windows that opened onto a terrace, and a series of islands of furniture arranged along its length like individual stage sets. Seated right at the far end, a newspaper draped across his knee and a cigarette smouldering in the cleft of his fingers, was the unmistakeable figure of Tarka Tyntallin. He rose slowly at the sound of their approach, discarding the newspaper and taking one last, hard drag of his cigarette.

'Did we keep you?' Lily called, her voice shattering the soft peach gloom like the cry of a tropical bird.

'I asked cook to feed the children,' he said, by way of an answer. 'I didn't think they should be made to wait any longer.'

'Oh . . .' Lily hesitated. 'I'm sorry. Well . . . Tynt, you remember Anna? She's our guest of honour for dinner tomorrow.'

Tyntallin dipped his head in acknowledgement and abruptly extended a stiff arm towards the adjoining room. 'I trust you had a good journey,' he said, not bothering to look in her direction. 'I'd offer you a drink but I'm afraid Mrs Gordon might blow a gasket.'

Lily described the room they were to lunch in as the Garden Room.

'The dining room's already been laid for dinner tomorrow,' she explained, ushering Anna towards a round table next to some French windows overlooking row upon row of rose beds. 'Not that it's going to be grand, adall,' she whispered, gesturing for Anna to take a seat next to Tyntallin. 'I keep saying that, don't I? But it's true. It's going to be chic but relaxed, just like a New York party.'

Anna nodded, with as much enthusiasm as she could muster, her eyes shifting from Lily to Tyntallin who had assumed his usual defensive position, hunched over his plate, an unlit cigarette dangling between his fingers.

'We're having butternut squash risotto to start,' Lily continued, realigning her cutlery with the flat of her palms. 'And then a fabulous fish dish with, like, pak choi and snow peas. My husband usually deals with the menus, so this is sort of an experiment,' she confided, lowering her voice. 'Well, my husband and Mrs Gordon.'

Lily gestured to the various dishes that were being planted smartly on the table in front of them by a small, grey-haired woman wearing a light-blue overall.

'Trouble is,' she said, 'he's so darned good at it all. He had to be, of course, he had no choice. But I'm learning!' She smiled over at Tyntallin. 'And then I've got plans for parts of the garden, haven't I? And the cottages . . . They're a little drab. Is that fair, Tynt? Just a tad on the dingy side. I wanna have a go at freshening them up, give them more of a Shaker sort of feel.'

Lily cleared her throat and started to fuss with her cutlery again. Anna looked at Tyntallin, expecting him to make some comment, to offer his wife some small encouragement. But he said nothing.

'Anyway,' Lily's eyelids fluttered, 'there is stuff that I can do, here and there.'

'Of course there is,' said Anna. 'There must be so much.'

'Oh, but you can't just rush in. I realize that, of course. It's sort of . . . you know, for so many reasons.'

Anna nodded, but she was watching Tyntallin. He

had nudged his empty plate to one side and was staring at his unlit cigarette as if he couldn't quite remember what it was designed for.

'Mrs Gordon will need some help in the kitchen tomorrow night,' he said suddenly. 'And what are you planning to do with the children?'

'Well.' Lily's hand clutched at her glass. 'I rather thought Jenny might be avail—'

'Have you asked her?'

Lily opened her mouth to speak and then gave a little shake of her head.

'Then, I suggest you do. On Saturdays she usually goes to see her mother. My wife would like to do more, you see,' Tyntallin said, lifting his eyes to meet Anna's, 'so long as it involves socializing, or shopping, or embellishing her appearance. She's not so keen on the more mundane aspects of domestic life.'

'What did I tell you?' Lily giggled, as if this were one of their favourite marital routines. 'I've got to get into those quilted waistcoats and galoshes before he'll be satisfied. And ditch the beautician, of course. Though I am bringing employment to the village, honey, you have to admit.'

Lily's voice had a wheedling tone. Anna noticed her shift her weight onto one hip as she stretched out a leg, trying, without success, to make contact with her husband under the table.

'No one could fault your dedication when it comes to keeping the village occupied,' Tyntallin said drily.

'Well, that's because I love it.' Lily beamed. 'As a matter of fact, I thought I might take Anna in after lunch, and leave the guided tour of the house to you, my love.'

'No, that's OK,' said Anna, quickly. 'I don't need a tour. I'll be fine, really.'

'Oh, but there's so much to know, and I haven't a clue. Everything sort of falls into place when you see the work that goes into maintaining a house like this. The passion. It makes you realize just how dedicated you have to be to live this life.' Lily blinked at Tyntallin, still hopeful of some sign of approval.

'Maybe later then,' Anna murmured, focusing on the plate of Irish stew that had been set in front of her. 'Actually, I'm not sure I can manage all this. Salad would be plenty.'

'Mrs Gordon,' bellowed Tyntallin.

'Sir?'

'Another plate, please,' Tyntallin flicked open his napkin, not bothering to disguise his irritation. 'I'm afraid our guest has Lady Tyntallin's horror of food. She will be having salad only.'

With a nod, Mrs Gordon promptly removed the stew to the sideboard and returned with a clean plate, taking care to place it with the crest at precisely twelve o'clock.

'I didn't mean to . . .' Anna started to apologize, but at that moment all eyes turned in the direction of a hollering sound coming from the library, and a second later a tall, red-faced woman was standing, legs astride, in the doorway.

'There you are!' she cried, raising her hands to reveal circles of sweat under the arms of her short-sleeved dress. 'What a time to be having lunch!'

She thundered across the oak floor towards Tyntallin, the soles of her trainers flashing with each step, and then stopped suddenly in the middle of the room.

'Is that going spare?' she asked, indicating the stew steaming on the sideboard. 'Oh very well then. Mrs Gordon, would you be so kind as to lay another place next to my darling brother?'

Anna, transfixed up until this point, glanced at Tyntallin who was pouring himself a glass of wine apparently oblivious to the interruption. Only when his sister leant over the back of his chair and gave him a hearty kiss on the cheek, enveloping him momentarily in a thick curtain of wiry brown hair, did he mumble something in greeting.

'I'm Margot,' she said, extending a hand to Anna. 'You must be a friend of Lily's. And you, Lily dear, are looking as blooming as ever. Still on the no carbs, I see!'

Margot took her place at the table, scrutinizing her sister-in-law with small brown eyes. 'Now, Tarka, you know why I'm here.'

Tyntallin continued chewing on a mouthful of stew, betraying no sign of either knowing or caring.

'My dear, you've been avoiding me. And very naughty it is of you. We simply must talk about the hunt ball and how on earth we're going to manage it.' Margot took a mouthful herself, shaking her head as she dealt with it. 'This year it was to be mine and Henrietta's turn to do the organizing,' she continued, in a muddier tone. 'So, I'm going to need some support from you, and Lily of course.'

'A hunting ball?' asked Lily

'That's it.' Margot fished along the edge of her gum

with a sturdy little finger. 'Is something the matter, my dear?'

'A ball to raise money for hunting foxes?'

'Yes, dear. It's a frightful bore, in a way, but all in a good cause.'

'Oh, I couldn't.' Lily clutched her napkin in her lap. 'I can't have anything to do with that. I'm sorry.' Margot froze in mid chew. 'I'd like to help with something else though. Maybe something to do with conservation? I did a lot of charity fundraisers at one time.'

Margot stared at Lily across the table. For what felt like a minute no one spoke or raised a fork to their mouths. 'Good heavens,' Margot said, eventually. 'I must say, I wasn't bargaining for that. That does rather . . .' she slid an anxious look in Tyntallin's direction.

He did not look up from his plate, but Anna saw how his jaw clenched as he chewed and the knuckles of the fist resting to the left of his plate were suddenly bone white.

'I know what you're thinking,' Lily said. They were walking after lunch in the gardens below the terrace. Here, the lawns were patterned with newly mown stripes and there were crescent-shaped rose beds, bordered with box hedges, and a fountain struggling to maintain a steady spray in the light wind. Lily's arm was hooked through Anna's, and she was smiling up at her, oblivious to the faint knot between her brows.

'You're thinking, "What is she doing?" You're thinking that I had a life of my own – a great life – and now I've given it all up, for the sake of a man who doesn't seem to appreciate me.' Lily gave Anna's arm a little squeeze. 'I'd think the same in your position. But you have to understand what Tynt has been through. He's not angry with me. He's angry with Henrietta for leaving him with three kids, and with himself for falling in love when he wasn't expecting to. And you know, even though I had no idea about the scale of this –' she swept her arm from right to left, taking in the rose beds and the lake and an island with a Palladian temple at its centre '– I still knew that marrying Tynt was not going to be easy.'

Anna peered at her. 'How did you know?'

'Because I've seen it often enough in my work – the anger, the grief and the guilt that goes with these situations. It's typical for "the outsider"' – Lily pointed a finger to her chest – 'to be used as a punch bag. I mean in counselling terms, Tynt is what we call "pre-stable", which is like unstable, only without the stigma.' She winked at Anna. 'Hey, I'm the counsellor, remember? I can handle it. Besides, he's sooo cute.'

Anna stared straight ahead.

'Oh, come on,' Lily said teasingly. 'Don't tell me you haven't noticed. I saw you casting an approving eye over him at the wedding . . . right before you fell out.'

'I noticed how he treated you, that's all I noticed.' Out of the corner of her eye Anna could see that Lily was watching her intently. Wouldn't she know, with all her experience, couldn't she see that she was deluding herself; that what might have started out reasonably happily was now painful to watch. Humiliating?

'Hey . . .' Lily yanked playfully on Anna's arm. 'So,

now that we've established I am *not* the victim in this, can we talk? Because it's so insane sometimes, the whole business, and I'm really hoping you can shed some light on it.'

They'd come to a stop by a bench next to the fountain. Lily sat down, swinging her legs up beside her on the seat. 'You know what it is?' she said, caressing a snakeskin heel. 'It's like I've trapped him against his will. I mean obviously that's what everyone round here thinks, but he thinks it too, in a way. If you're going to be married and you're someone like Tynt – and this is the part I'm only just beginning to understand – it has got to be a selfless choice. If it looks like too much fun, then everyone feels bad. It's almost like I remind him of some weakness in himself, something he should have resisted.' She reached an arm up in the air and stretched, her hand clutching at the warm, rose-scented air. 'I think that's why he doesn't like me to dress up now. When we were in New York I'd wear such fun stuff and he loved it . . . do my hair up with streamers.' Lily paused for a moment, gazing up at the sky. 'I guess he was just him then . . . not the master of all this.'

'And he never told you who he was? He never warned you?'

'Oh, he said he had a house in the country, and a farm, so I'm picturing a little patch of grass and a barn, like something out of *Babe*. Now I know that's British code for, like, "a major place" I'd be more alert.' Lily let her head drop back against the bench. 'I wanted to ask you, Anna. Do you think it would be different if I wasn't an American? I mean do you think an English person would just sort of get this, automatically?'

'No,' said Anna, 'I don't.'

'Really? I wonder. Cos no one . . . they all seem to sort of resent me for not knowing the part. It's like, if you don't know the rules, don't ask to be in the game.'

'What does he say?'

'Well, to begin with, he just said, "Be yourself."' Lily tugged the heels of her sandals tighter in to her body. 'But what he meant was, "Be yourself, and know how to deal with the servants, how to run a fifteen-bedroom house, what, exactly, to do with my kids . . ."'

She glanced up at Anna, anxiety dragging at the corners of her eyes.

'And these kids are unhappy kids, you know? They've been through a lot. But getting them to, maybe, see someone? That's not even up for discussion. I guess that's what I mean about me being an American and sort of coming from another place. Because there's just some stuff, some attitudes, that I'm not at all used to.'

Lily uncurled her legs and let them drop to the ground, her head drooping forward so that Anna could no longer see her face.

'Like what?' Anna asked gently.

'Oh, just English stuff, I guess. Nothing really . . . just, you know, habits and things. I really don't wanna—' Lily dug her heels into the grass and rocked her feet backwards and forwards. 'You're not gonna put this in the book, right?'

'Of course not.'

'Not that there's anything so secret. It's more . . . how he wants me to be, now that we're here. He doesn't like for me to wear lip gloss any more, or smoke. He totally hates the idea of hair dyeing.' Lily pulled at a strand of bone-white blonde hair. 'Like only Tynt wouldn't know this is bleached to hell. And he doesn't like underwear that isn't fifties high-school-plain and he insists on me having these nightgowns—' Lily stopped suddenly. Her eyes flitted in Anna's direction. 'But it's the rules that really drive you crazy: the knives that go with the cheese but never with the fruit; the correct shirt for lunch but not for dinner or for church; the right flowers to have in your borders though never on the table.' Lily looked up at the sky and swivelled her neck from side to side, rolling her shoulders up and back. 'At lunch, I said I was working on the garden. What actually happened was I told them, where I come from, chrysanthemums are not the most elegant, and would they please plant something else for this summer.' Lily gestured with a nod of her head to the border running along the base of the terrace, a brilliant blaze of orange chrysanthemums and red-hot pokers. 'That's so what you have to get your head around. The gardener likes chrysanths, I'm just the American who has to be humoured. You know, I read that exact same thing happened to Princess Diana . . . at Highgrove.' Lily's eyes bulged. 'I'm not kidding! Only it was with the kitchen part. Can you believe that?'

'You shouldn't put up with it, Lily,' Anna said. 'You don't have to put up with it.'

'Oh, but I'm as determined as a dog with a bone. I wanna succeed at this, Anna. I wanna make my husband happy. And if it means putting up with a little bit of this and that – well then, so be it. Excuse me.'

Lily broke off to retrieve a mobile phone from the pocket of her skirt, mumbled a few affirmatives, and flipped the mouthpiece shut, grinning at Anna triumphantly.

'That was the florist, my table arrangements are ready. Well,' she jumped up from the bench, thrusting out her chest and raising her chin high like a cheerleader, 'if Mr Greystone won't grow me my lilies then I'll just have to get them elsewhere. Come on, Anna, let me show you the dinkiest little village in the whole of England.'

'Oh, Lady Tyntallin. We were just about to ring you,' said the woman in the florist. 'We thought you'd want the arrangements delivered, as usual.'

'No, no.' Lily cut her short, snapping her credit card down on the counter, 'we were coming in anyway. Tell you what,' she spun around and addressed Anna over the raised collar of her rabbit fur jacket, 'I'll be a minute or two here. Why don't you get going and I'll catch you up. Head down towards the bakers . . . that's where it all happens.'

Anna did as she was told, pausing outside on the pavement to let a pair of women pass with their entourage of whippets. It was, indeed, a pretty little village. Directly ahead of her was a small green, with a squat stone memorial at its centre, and beyond that a row of pastel-painted timbered shop fronts with mullioned windows. Far down on the right-hand side of the street, she identified the baker's by the silhouette of a wheat sheaf suspended over the doorway, and next to it, the sign of a bookshop – a golden lion with a stack of volumes under his paw. Anna crossed the road, slightly self-conscious in her neat trench coat and pale suede boots, and made her way diagonally across the green in the direction of the bookshop.

'Can I help you?' asked the woman behind the desk when the jangling of the bell over the door had subsided. She had a kindly, scrunched-up face and the expression of someone who wanted very much to be of use, so Anna found herself swallowing the reflex refusal, and asking to be recommended a novel.

'Something new?' asked the woman, her mouth open in anticipation. She had come out from behind the desk and was making her way towards the shop's central display table. Something about her rolling gait, the brightness of her small brown eyes and the care with which she reached out and straightened the sign on the table that read 'Some of our Favourites' made Anna feel suddenly, inexplicably sad.

'These are a few we particularly like,' said the woman, gently patting a shiny-covered hardback. 'Did you have an author in mind?'

'Not really,' said Anna.

The woman nodded sympathetically. 'Well, would you be in the mood for something romantic? Because . . .' she felt her way across the books and plucked a fat paperback from the middle of the table, 'this one is rather special. It's a modern love story, with a slight magical—'

'Oh.' Anna smiled hard at the woman. 'I'm not sure. Maybe something a bit less . . .'

'I know.' The woman put the book smartly back, as

if she had not approved of its selection in the first place, and clasped her chin as she surveyed the alternatives. Anna could see that she had dented the woman's confidence, broken the bond that had temporarily existed between them. 'Something less romantic,' she repeated, ignoring the bell as the shop door opened behind them. 'Something perhaps . . . what about this one? It's a thriller, set in Prague. Very clever, apparently.' She handed Anna the book. 'I'll be with you in a moment, sir,' she said, looking past her.

'This looks perfect.' Anna smiled, glancing over the reviews highlighted on the back cover: gripping, gritty, a dark tale with a chilling twist.

'Lovely,' said the woman. 'Will that be it then?'

'I think so,' said Anna. 'Thank you for your help.'

'Not at all.' She carried the book back behind the desk and rifled in a drawer for a bag to put it in. 'My husband died six months ago, so it's a great treat for me to help out in the shop. Gives me something to do, you know. I do love books, but it's the company I enjoy really.' She licked her thumb and after several attempts found the opening in the bag.

'I'm sorry,' said Anna.

The woman looked up, her expression at first grateful and then puzzled. 'May I help you, sir?' she asked.

Anna turned to see who she was addressing and found the stranger was standing so close she could smell the leather of his coat.

'May I help you?' asked the woman again, this time with a hint of anxiety in her voice.

Anna lifted her eyes from the man's chest.

'It's all right, we know each other,' he said.

'Oh, right.' The woman sounded relieved. 'Well then, that'll be 10.99, please. And I'll just pop in one of our bookmarks.'

'That's grand,' he said, answering for Anna, his green eyes creasing at the corners.

He was browner, thinner, and his hair was less wilful, but still long enough to droop in his eyes. She scanned his face feverishly like a sculptor reunited with their life's work. In a matter of seconds the world had telescoped so that all she was aware of was his eyes, his lips, the bashful smile that was now creeping across his face.

'We've got a leaflet with details of book signings,' the shop assistant said cheerily, unaware of her intrusion. 'I'll just put one of those in too.'

He nodded, acknowledging the gesture, his eyes never moving from Anna's.

'Shall we sit, Anna?' he asked, and the sound of his voice saying her name hit her in the back of the knees and low down in her stomach. She let him guide her gently by the elbow to a sofa in the corner of the shop and lowered herself onto the seat, pressing herself against the arm for support. He sat down beside her cautiously, leaning forward on his elbows, forcing his thumbs together as if trying to test their breaking point. There was just a few feet between them. She could have reached out a hand and touched the back of his head, leant her cheek against the leather stretched tight across his shoulder blades. Then he shifted on the seat, turning his head towards her, and they looked at each other.

How many times had she imagined this moment?

How many times had she gone over what she would say, what he would say, how it would end? Never, in all the hundreds, the thousands of times she had played this scene in her head, had they sat in silence, gazing at each other like drunks on a park bench.

To begin with, the Moment They Met Again had always taken place in the flat they once shared. The doorbell would ring, unexpectedly, but she would be looking fresh and glowing, and she would open the door, laughing – mid phone call perhaps – and there he would be, wearing the clothes he'd left in. Sometimes she'd say something dry and cool like: 'Well, you took your time,' or 'So, what can I do for you?' But the satisfaction of feigning indifference was short-lived, and mostly she would open the door and snarl, 'How dare you show your face here! Do you have any idea what you did to me?'

Then on it would move from there, incorporating some of Ruth's best lines ('A postcard to end a relationship, I'd have expected more from a schoolboy') and a variation on Valerie's theory about making his life too easy ('You like to think of yourself as this sensitive musician. But you know what you are, Daniel? You're a user'). Even some of Dave's observations had found a place in her daily confrontations with Daniel. And for a while, for quite a while, she'd found it comforting to run the various reproaches over and over in her head when she was cooking, or cleaning, or waiting for the bus, or lying in bed awake at night; tightening up a phrase here, eliminating a put down there, honing and shaping the ultimate Who Do You Think You Are Screwing With My Life? speech.

Notably, Daniel never had much to contribute on these occasions. He was chastised, of course. He would say, 'I've missed you, baby' and 'I don't want to lose you' and 'There's never been anyone else', but the actual excuses were hazy and few. What could he say that would sound acceptable to her? What did she want him to say that would restore her trust? For a month or so she dallied with the idea of him having had a complete, but not too distressing, breakdown. She'd invented a broken background for him, a form of post-traumatic-stress syndrome that was triggered in times of extreme emotion. Then, when that palled, she imagined him red-eyed and unshaven in a Dublin bedsit, composing music through the night; frightening, wailing songs with choruses about the killing of the heart and her name whispered to his fingers on the fret board.

The later versions of the Moment They Met Again were slightly different. Anna was less angry and more hungry for answers. ('Did you love me?' 'Was it all in my head?' 'Was I too needy, was that it?') And Daniel had more lines, mostly admissions of his weaknesses, faint flaws he had been working on that he was determined to change, because his life was nothing without her.

'I had a speech prepared,' Anna said, hugging the arm of the sofa. 'I can't remember any of it now.'

'Me too,' Danny said.

'So, this is where you came, then?' As if she really cared.

'No. I went to Ireland. I've not been here long.' He knitted his hands in front of his chin. She glanced at his ring finger; it was bare.

'And you?' he said.

'Still in London. I'm visiting a friend.'

He glanced at her sharply, looking to see if her expression matched the non-committal tone, and then lowered his eyes to the floor. He seemed relieved.

'It must be more than three years,' she said, knowing exactly how long it was. 'Are you still a musician?' She said it to hurt him, to show that she knew he was the kind of man who might appear to have a consuming passion, only to walk away from it one day, without looking back. He gave a flick of his head, the muscle in his jaw signalling a direct hit. She wanted to reach out then and stroke his hair. Her legs begged to drift across the few feet of striped loose cover that separated them.

'You're here for a while?' he asked. He was watching her eyes.

'Just the weekend.'

'Could we meet? We can't talk here. Could we meet later, or tomorrow?' There was a seriousness about him she didn't remember, an intensity.

'All right,' she said.

He put his hand in his pocket and pulled out a biro. They looked at each other; neither had a piece of paper, neither wanted to involve the woman at the desk and jeopardize this fragile state of intimacy. He leant across, gently picked up her hand and turned it over exposing the inside of her wrist, and she watched as he wrote his number in the loping, careful way she would have recognized anywhere. Then he gave her back her hand and they both stood up from the sofa, slowly, consciously avoiding brushing against each other.

'You ring me then,' he said. And before she had time to say she would he was out of the door and in the street, tugging his leather coat around him.

'Funnily enough,' the voice of the woman behind the desk jolted Anna back to reality, 'we get a lot of people bumping into each other unexpectedly. You wouldn't think it, but this is quite a little meeting spot.'

She held out the paper bag containing the book Anna had chosen, her eyes following Danny as he made his way across the green.

'That one's never been in here before, mind you. Though I've seen him about the village, of course. He's the sort you notice, isn't he?'

Anna paid for the book, as quickly as she could, thanked the woman and left the shop, pausing deliberately on the pavement before she let her eyes drift in the direction Danny had taken. The street was empty except for a man in a white apron adjusting a blackboard sign in front of a shop and two adolescent girls, arms locked, springing down the pavement as if it were a trampoline. Anna felt a stab of anxiety and was just about to examine her wrist, to check the phone number was still in place, when a tug on her sleeve made her jump.

'And who was that?' Lily, eyes as wide as saucers, jabbed at her with the arm of her sunglasses. 'I leave you alone for five minutes and you've already met some hip young guy . . . in Tyntallin. In the bookshop of all places!' Lily paused and stepped back on one heel, examining Anna critically out of the corner of her eye. 'Well, who is he? Ohcomeon now. You're not going to go all secretive on me, are you? That's not part of the deal adall.'

Anna could feel herself blushing. 'He's just someone I used to know.'

'Uh huh?' Lily was smiling mischievously, twirling the sunglasses in her hand.

'Someone I used to go out with . . .'

Lily gave a nod and tilted her head, poised for more information.

'It ended pretty suddenly.' Anna glanced down the street. 'I didn't expect to see him again actually.'

'Eeeew. Sort of unresolved?' Lily frowned. 'Oh, I hate that. That's the worst.'

'Well, no. It was such a long time ago. I'm with someone else now.'

'You are? How come I didn't know that?' Lily looked bemused for a moment. 'Well, anyway, what a coincidence meeting him out of the blue like that. Must be fate.'

Anna was now scouring the street, unable to pretend she was just taking in the view.

'Hey. Maybe you should take advantage of it?' murmured Lily, following her eyeline. 'I mean, you don't just meet a guy you have unfinished business with and then leave it at that. If you were in the city you'd go have a coffee, right? Did you get his number?'

Anna pulled at the wrist of her coat, and nodded.

'Well, there you go . . .' Lily paused. 'Wait a minute, exactly what kind of a guy is this? I mean, what's his thing?'

'He's a musician,' said Anna. 'He's in a band. Or he was.'

'Uh!' Lily raised both hands in the air triumphantly. 'That settles it. You have to ask him to dinner. I desperately need him for the mix. Oh, don't look so alarmed, it's just perfect! You get to resolve . . . whatever it was. And I get an addition to my alternative, artistic circle.' Lily spun around clutching her rabbit-fur jacket to her throat with one hand and shielding her eyes with the other. 'Can you still see him?'

'No,' said Anna.

'No?'

'I mean no. I don't think I can ask him.'

'Why ever not?' Lily turned her head to look at Anna; she was smiling but there was something flat and tight in her eyes – the stirrings of impatience.

'It's all too sudden,' said Anna. 'I don't even know if I want to see him again, let alone . . . sit down to dinner with him.'

'Oh, you!' Lily took a few steps and grasped her friend's arm. 'Don't you wanna know how he turned out? Whether he's over it? If he's got someone else? You could take a walk in the garden.' She was looking up at Anna through soft brown eyelashes, her voice was soothing, persuasive. 'You absolutely have to meet again now. You can't just pretend it didn't happen. Anyway, if you hate each other we'll just send him straight home to the pub.'

Suddenly Anna felt foolish and unsophisticated. 'Maybe you're right,' she said.

'You bet I am.' Lily slipped the sunglasses onto the crown of her head and pointed a finger at Anna. 'Give him a call. I'll pick up the bread and then we're done.' She sashayed off down the street, pausing when she reached the green to call over her shoulder. 'I've said eight thirty to everyone else so you should ask him early evening. Trust me. This was meant to happen.'

Nine

At six the following evening Anna was standing in front of her wardrobe, gazing at the various outfits she had brought, and chewing hard on her thumbnail. Now she was here, the black trouser suit seemed far too severe: in it she would look as out of place as a laptop in a fairy tale. The cocktail dress had looked like the most promising option but, on second thoughts, it was just too dressy and self-conscious. And the top she might have worn with the suit trousers – a silvery sequined number designed to look like an heirloom – suddenly seemed cheap and over-bright.

It was partly the surroundings that were to blame: her bedroom at Tyntallin was huge and high-ceilinged, with faded toile de Jouy curtains, a sofa upholstered in threadbare rose silk and a carpet that was still, in tucked-away corners, the colour of strawberries and cream. In this room her clothes felt out of kilter, like those English summer clothes you pack for holidays which, as soon as you open the suitcase, look as drab and heavy as a nun's habit. But it was mainly Danny who was responsible for this crisis. Now, on top of finding something appropriate, something that didn't jar with the house, and fitted the Bohemian mood of the

occasion, she had to think about the effect she wanted
to have on him. Anna needed to look relaxed, as if she'd
barely given her outfit a thought, and at the same time
make him notice her new, size smaller figure. She needed
something soft and sensual, to cancel out his first
impression of her in that business-like trench coat, and
something glamorous that would let him know she was
no longer the fashion-shy tomboy. She wanted something . . . 'Oh God,' Anna said out loud, 'this is hopeless. I need help.'

The telephone beside the bed had a list of extension
numbers pasted to the dial and Anna tapped out the
number for Lily's room. Lily answered at once.

'Trouble choosing what to wear?' she said, before
Anna had a chance to speak. 'Well, whatever you need,
I've got it. Hold on there, and I'll come and get you.'

Minutes later Anna was being ushered into Lily's
bedroom, which was nothing at all like the room she
had imagined for her. The scale was much the same –
there was a four-poster bed and a fireplace – but instead
of pale silk, the bed was draped in black damask, and in
place of the blossom-covered wallpaper the walls were
painted a rich Chinese red and hung with abstract paintings. At the end of the bed, where Anna had imagined a
chaise longue, was a black lacquer chest and on top of
that a selection of exquisite white orchids, each in a separate celadon vase.

'How's your room?' asked Lily. 'Falling apart, right?
This was the same, but I persuaded Tynt I had to have a
change. There was actually, like, a commode in here.'
She pulled a face. 'Why would anyone want that dirty
old junk in their *bed*room? All these pictures, and most

195

of the furniture, are from my apartment in New York.' She glanced around her, smiling. 'It's where I feel . . . you know.'

'Wouldn't you like to have some of these things in the main part of the house?' asked Anna.

'Oh, I guess it's simpler this way.' Lily shrugged. 'I can just come up here when I'm feeling homesick and I've got everything all in one place.' She scrunched up her nose, attempting to make this seem like a cosy arrangement. 'This was Henrietta's room too. So it's not like it was any different for her, not really. You see, he doesn't like to wake me, when he comes in late, and it was the same with her. Also, it's typical of the British upper classes to keep separate bedrooms – I looked it up in a book. The only reason you wouldn't is if you fell on hard times and didn't have the space. It's pretty standard, actually.' Lily gripped her upper arms and gave a little shiver. 'Anyway, down to business. We need to find you the Result Dress.'

Anna opened her mouth to protest but Lily was already flinging open the doors of a built-in wardrobe and dragging clothes off the hangers, giving a running commentary as she went.

'I have this, which is divine. Would you wear red? Or, how about this? But you need a good bra to carry it off.' She twisted around and eyed Anna's chest. 'It is a little low, but it's fabulous on. How are you with cleavage?'

'What are you wearing?' asked Anna. She felt sixteen years old.

'Black sequin pants. They've been approved by Tynt, whereas all of these . . . Uh uh, way too fancy for the part.' Lily held the red dress up against Anna and regarded her at arm's length.

'I don't want anything too . . . you know,' Anna said.

Lily's eyes widened in disbelief. 'He's your ex-boyfriend, isn't he? You want him to curse the day he let you get away. You wanna drive him craaaazy.'

'No. Really, I don't,' Anna said, bending down to rescue something trimmed in ostrich that had slipped from Lily's grasp, 'because I'm very happy as I—'

'Oh forget that!' Lily was yanking more clothes off the rail. 'All this stuff is just going to waste here. Come on! What's the harm?' She thrust an armful of chiffon in Anna's direction. 'You don't always wanna live your life by the book, Anna. Have a bit of fun,' Lily said, hustling her out of the room. 'Go with the flow. Please, for my sake.'

Lily was smaller and slighter in build than Anna but there was one dress – pale turquoise chiffon with bell sleeves and a low boat neck – that fitted her well and made her feel light on her feet and carefree. Lily pronounced it perfect as they waited downstairs in the library for Danny to appear and seven o'clock, the appointed time, came and went. At seven thirty, Lily warned Anna that relentless plucking at the sleeves was liable to cause fraying; and at eight, she offered her something stronger than the champagne they were already drinking.

'So he's a little late?' Lily said, reaching for a cigarette from the silver box on the mantelpiece. 'Don't worry about it, you've got all night.'

But as the evening drew on, and the guests began to

arrive, Anna felt increasingly sick. It was as much as she could do to smile politely at each new arrival when her mind was standing sentry outside on the front steps. For a while she took refuge in handing around a plate of canapés, keeping her eyes on the library doors while she shuffled from group to group, pretending to be distracted by her responsibilities, fending off attempts at conversation with an ambiguous tip of her head in the direction of the kitchen. And then, at last, when the room was resonating with the sound of raised voices, suddenly he was there in the doorway, hands thrust in the pockets of his needlecord jacket, nodding his head in casual greeting as if everyone had been assembled expressly for his pleasure.

Anna hastily deposited the canapés on a side table and made her way briskly across the floor, excusing herself under her breath as she pushed past the chattering bodies and manoeuvred around the jutting elbows. But, as she drew closer, she saw that Danny had been absorbed by a group standing near the door and was already engrossed in conversation. She watched him – smiling and relaxed, unaware of her proximity – and waited, assuming he would raise his eyes to look for her at any moment. But Danny didn't look for her. And when Lily approached the group, a moment later, with a glass of champagne held aloft, Danny accepted it without so much as bothering to meet his hostess's eyes.

Anna felt suddenly hot and faint. She retreated a few steps and leant back against the cool of one of the marble mantlepieces, ignoring the inclusive smiles of two women standing nearby. The past few hours had stripped away any illusion that this was to be a harmless meeting – a chance to flirt and show off her newfound serenity and independence. All Anna had been able to think of was seeing Danny again, and in her excitement she had imagined him arriving in a frenzy of anticipation like her own, thrusting through the crowd, straining for a glimpse of her. The idea that he could be here, and not seize the first opportunity to find her, seemed harder to bear than if he had never shown up at all. Anna tipped forward on the balls of her feet and craned her neck to try and catch a glimpse of him, and found herself looking into Lily's round blue eyes

'Well, he finally showed!' Lily said. 'And he seems to be fitting in pretty well.'

'I should introduce you,' said Anna, trying not to sound hurt.

'Oh, I'll manage. Is something the matter, Anna? You look kind of pale.'

'No, nothing. I think I need some air. I won't be a minute.'

Anna pushed herself away from the mantlepiece and made her way swiftly across the room towards the windows which, tonight, were open onto the terrace. It was cool outside, too cool for most tastes. A lone couple were leaning against the balustrade, looking out over the floodlit garden like passengers at the rail of a ship, their hair lifting softly in the breeze. Anna hurried past them along the length of the terrace, until she was beyond the light of the library windows and protected by the shadow of the house. When she glanced to her left the couple had gone, driven back into the house by the icy-fingered wind that was plastering her dress against her legs and making her grip the tops of her arms. But she welcomed it. The shock was holding back her tears, holding back her thoughts.

'I'm sorry I was late.'

His voice, behind her, made her start. She didn't move. She felt the weight of his jacket covering her shoulders and the touch of his hands shifting it gently into place.

'I've made you angry,' he said.

'Not at all.' She stared straight ahead of her. She didn't want to turn around. Her voice had sounded sharp, cracked, and she was afraid her face would betray her further.

He stepped forward and leant against the balustrade, his back to the stone.

'I think I have,' he said, tilting his head on one side, watching her steadily. 'I should have come to find you sooner. But I didn't expect you to be out here.'

'I like it out here,' she said. 'It clears my head.'

'And has it helped?' he said.

Anna closed her eyes. Her legs were vibrating under the chiffon dress, and she had to clamp her teeth tight shut to stop the shaking spreading throughout her body.

'Why did you leave me, Danny?'

She heard him suck in his breath and shift his weight against the stone. 'I don't know,' he said, his voice barely louder than a whisper. 'I know some of the reasons, but none of them explain . . .' He made the funny clicking noise in his throat he used to make when he disapproved of something. 'I was scared. I was angry, with myself. I was worried I'd turn into my father. I was afraid I'd let you down.' Danny paused. 'I could say I'm sorry, but that doesn't seem to be a big enough word.'

'You should have tried to explain,' Anna said. 'You owed me that at least.'

'I know that.' His head drooped forward, he kicked out a foot sending a loose stone rattling across the terrace. 'But I couldn't bear to see you. Just because I left didn't mean my feelings for you disappeared. I've never stopped thinking about you, Anna, wondering what you were doing. It may be wrong of me to say it, but I never stopped thinking of you as my girl. And then, yesterday, in the bookshop . . .'

The wind whipped against Anna's face making cold tears snake out of the corners of her eyes. She felt numb. She tried to clench her hands into fists but the fingers only flickered in response.

'I don't blame you for trying to bury it,' Danny said. 'I don't blame you for wanting it to go away. You've moved on.'

'Yes I have. I'm with someone. I'm happy. You can't just walk back into my life after all this time and expect those feelings to be . . .'

Frantically Anna fumbled for the button in her head labelled 'In the event of experiencing this intensity of feeling, press here for a reminder of the consequences'. 'Remember how you were then and how you are now,' shrieked the recorded message. 'Remember the pain you went through. Remember how calm your life is versus this cocktail of emotions, this teetering on the brink of madness.'

'You have no idea how much you hurt me,' Anna said. 'I don't ever want to fee—' But his mouth was on her mouth, he was dragging her against him, pulling her up under her arms like a lifesaver rescuing a sodden body from a cold green pond and her frozen hands were searching blindly for his face.

It was the longest dinner Anna could remember. They were at opposite ends of the table from each other, Danny at Lily's end, she near Tyntallin's. Every time she looked up his eyes would be on her face, serious, deliberating. There was a new purpose about him, a determination she hadn't seen before, and yet Danny was still the free spirit, the unconventional, charming boy she had fallen in love with. From the way their host had shunted his shoulders impatiently when they were introduced, Anna was in no doubt that Tyntallin disapproved of Danny's earring, his tangled curls and his relaxed manner, and she felt something like pride that she had been the one responsible for bringing him into this house. Later on, she noticed Tyntallin watching Danny over the rim of his wine glass and knew he was envying his guest's easy affability, questioning how it was that this nobody had managed to make a friend of both his neighbours in the space of an hour, while Tyntallin was still struggling with the pleasantries. 'Look,' Anna had wanted to tell him, 'Danny is what modern men are like: sensitive, warm and easy with women. And he's mine. He's all mine.'

When the time came for coffee to be served in the library, Danny and Anna found each other over by one of the fireplaces, and huddled together, their backs turned to the room so as to discourage interruption. Touching fingertips, they exchanged information rapidly and without ceremony, spilling facts without any need for explanation or elaboration. Danny had formed a new band and they were recording an album in a nearby studio. He shared a room with the drummer, above the pub in the village, an arrangement which worked only because they were in the studio every hour of the day. There hadn't been anyone serious in his life since Anna, and he hadn't wanted there to be. He was broke, but the album was going to change that; it was a serious venture for a major label and everyone antici-pated great things. Anna told him about the book and how it had brought her here, to Tyntallin. She told him how she had thrown herself into her work, after he left, and how she, too, felt she'd found her direction. And she mentioned Richard, but in a way she knew suggested he was already almost forgotten. Danny looked sideways at her, scanning her face for some sign of conflict and, finding none, he smiled and squeezed her hand.

In less than half an hour they had covered every aspect of their lives since they'd been apart that mat-tered, and there was nothing left that either of them needed to know.

'I want to start again,' Danny whispered, leaning his head towards hers. 'I want to do everything right this time, take it slowly.' He frowned suddenly. 'I'll need to find somewhere else to live, somewhere I'd be happy for you to come.'

She laughed, as if it mattered where they were, but he looked at her sharply.

'I need to win you again, Anna. It's important. It's important to me,' he added, softening, reaching out a finger and touching the edge of her chiffon sleeve.

'All right,' she said.

Behind them the room was thinning out and beyond

the library doors they could hear the laughter of departing guests echoing in the hall. Danny looked hard at her, as if he were holding her hand in his and making a vow.

'It's time I was going,' he said. 'But I'll ring you tomorrow, and the day after that. We'll find a way.' And he kissed her slowly on the cheek, tucking her hair behind her ear as he stepped back, just the way he used to.

'Well, that was rather a success, though I say it myself.' Lily flopped down onto the sofa by the fireplace nearest the door and stretched her arms above her head with a jangling of bangles.

There were just the three of them, alone again, among the debris of sticky glasses and discarded mint wrappers. Tyntallin stood in front of the fire, tapping his cigarette ash into the dying embers, and Anna sat on the opposite sofa, conscious that he had been watching her for a while, taking in her dress, her fidgeting hands, the way she had strained to hear Danny's parting words, and Lily's jaunty goodbye: 'You're very welcome, Daniel. I hope you'll visit us again soon.'

'Didn't you think it went with a swing?' Lily clasped her hands behind her neck and sighed luxuriously. 'Isn't it great when people just hit it off?'

Tyntallin dragged hard on his cigarette, his eyes still fixed on Anna's face.

'Anna met an old friend she hasn't seen in years,' Lily continued, evidently used to these one-sided conversations, 'Daniel, the musician.'

'What a coincidence,' said Tyntallin

'I'm hoping it'll mean we'll see more of her.' Lily

winked at Anna. 'It is the summer after all. You don't have to go back tomorrow, Anna, you could stay on. Why not? Spend a little time getting to know your friend again.'

'It's not that simple,' Anna said, more abruptly than she had intended. She shifted her position on the sofa so that she was turned away from Tyntallin's gaze.

'Why ever not?' asked Lily. She seemed excited, euphoric after the success of the party. 'You two were getting on so well, I thought.'

'Well, there's my life in London, for a start. I have a partner.'

Tyntallin exhaled slowly, apparently savouring her discomfort.

'But Danny's the One, right?' Lily was leaning forward in her seat, her bangle-covered wrists clamped between the knees of her sequined trousers. 'He's the love of your life, the one you wanted to marry.'

Anna felt herself recoil, she opened her mouth to speak but Lily was batting a jangling wrist at her.

'Oh, you can't hide stuff like that, Anna! Not from a woman. I knew the moment I saw the two of you together.' She smiled conspiratorially. 'It's none of my busi-ness, but I'd say you'll be coming down here a lot from now on. And I think it's too thrilling, don't you, Tynt?'

Lily looked up at her husband expectantly, but when he turned his eyes on her all the light went out of her face as surely as if he had slapped her. 'Of course, I feel sorry for the guy in London,' she added quietly. 'But I guess I'm selfish enough not to care so much, if I can have my friend nearby.'

'Daniel doesn't have anywhere to live,' Anna said quickly, 'so I think we're jumping the gun a bit.'

Lily gave a little gasp. 'Honey? Aren't we looking for a tenant for Gardener's Cottage?' Her eyes were round and amazed as if something wonderful was manifesting itself in front of them. 'Well, wouldn't this be the perfect solution?'

'Would it? We don't know anything about him, do we?'

'Maybe not who his people are, and all of that. But I thought he seemed charming. And if it would help Anna out . . .'

'Help Anna out?' repeated Tyntallin.

'Please, let's forget about me.' Anna tried to catch Lily's eye but her friend appeared to be oblivious to the menace in his voice.

'Oh, don't worry, Anna. Tynt knows I'd like to have every one of my girlfriends right at the end of the drive! He's getting used to it.'

Lily laughed too loudly and shook out her hair, a tic Anna had noticed surfaced whenever her husband was threatening to turn the mood sour, like the flourish of a picador distracting an angry bull. And then, suddenly, Tyntallin lurched across the floor to where his wife was stretched out on the sofa. Anna saw Lily's hand reach out and automatically grip the arm, bracing herself.

'Why don't you leave her out of it?' he growled as he loomed over her, fists clenched at his sides. Lily opened her mouth. Her fingers clutched a handful of seat cover as she shrank back against the sofa. And then, just as suddenly, he pulled himself up, took a step back and strode past her and out of the room. The whole episode was over in a matter of seconds.

Lily's eyes closed. Slowly the hand relaxed and she curled her legs up under her, carefully smoothing down the sequins on her trousers. She sat there like that for a moment before meeting Anna's eyes.

'Look,' she said softly. 'Ignore him, please. It's just that he hates the thought of people knowing our private business. The cottage is there, empty. It'd be a treat for me to have you guys around.'

Anna stared at her, astonished. 'I couldn't possibly. I can't accept anything from him.' She hesitated. Lily's face was white as a sheet. 'Lily, I saw him just now. If I hadn't been here . . .'

'Oh no.' Lily shook her head distractedly. 'It isn't what you think. It was just bad timing, what with the party and everything. He hates to be social. He hates to be cornered. And we've all had too much to drink. Please . . .' Lily held up a hand to prevent Anna interrupting, her eyelids were fluttering, translucent lilac. 'Look. You found Danny again because of me, so do this one thing for me, will you? Let him take the cottage. Just, please, stay close. That's all I'm asking. That's all I need.' And with that, Lily turned her head and rose from the sofa, waving her fingers behind her back so Anna wouldn't see the tears she'd heard gathering in her voice.

When the phone rang in the Dickenson household at around half-past midnight Ruth and Dave were both wide awake. Ruth was reading her book, *The Phalocine*

Principle, and Dave was fighting the irritation that this was causing him, his cheek pressed hard into the pillow, eyes screwed tight shut. *The Phalocine Principle* was subtitled *Rebooting your Life* and, as Dave was pointing out to Ruth, albeit silently, behind his flickering eyelids, 'You might as well come to bed with *Eligible Alaskan Farmers Illustrated*. I mean, how am I supposed to feel watching you pore over a book on how to *start up* again. That's like me going round to Mum's, putting my feet up by the gas fire, and getting stuck into *Undertaker's Monthly*. "Options for the Close Relative's Big Day".'

The telephone was on Ruth's side of the bed and had one of those rings that sounds like a heavy vehicle's reverse warning.

'Who is that?' muttered Dave, yanking the duvet and rolling over to face her. 'It must be nearly one a.m.'

'Hello?' Ruth pressed the receiver to her ear and Dave watched her face for clues. 'No, no, we were just reading,' she said, nodding at him and mouthing, 'It's Anna.'

'Anna!' Dave hissed, causing his wife to flap her free hand wildly in his direction. 'You're not serious! It's way past their bedtime, surely?'

But Ruth's furrowed brow and fixed, staring eyes suggested she was completely serious, and that whatever Anna was saying on the end of the line more than justified the lateness of the hour. Dave shuffled up in the bed as unobtrusively as he could manage and very slowly leant towards the receiver.

'No! *No!* Where? . . .' Ruth gave Dave a cautionary look and edged away from him across the bed. 'A bookshop? God!' She gave a little gasp, and then another one. 'What were you wearing?'

So far it seemed to Dave that Anna had been involved in some kind of embarrassing accident – something humiliating but not life threatening. Ruth was transfixed. Once or twice she blinked, deliberately, as if trying to improve her focus. Several times she opened her mouth to speak and then was hit by some new piece of information that made her eyes widen and her question obsolete.

'So you still felt . . . ?' Yes, she did. Ruth was nodding now. 'Well, you were in shock . . . I know, I know.'

Dave recognized Ruth's expression from somewhere: that particular mixture of intense concentration and excitement. It was shopping, he thought. She'd definitely had it when they'd looked around that flat they'd made an offer on last year, the one the French couple had beaten them to. Ruth had cried when the estate agent broke the news, which was a bit of a surprise, but obviously it was frustration more than anything. They weren't in any hurry. Ruth loved their place.

'God, you must have been desperate by then!' Ruth was saying. 'All that time . . .' She was clutching her stomach now, and wincing. It must be diarrhoea. Anna had gone to stay somewhere in the country, and they'd fed her something ropey and she'd got an attack of the runs. Poor Anna. Dave leant forward in the bed so he could catch Ruth's eye and contribute a sympathetic grimace to the conversation. She looked straight over him.

'So what did he say?' Ruth was focused now, nodding rhythmically, the phone-a-friend on whom everything depended. And then there it was, the fractional forward-sliding of the lower jaw. Whatever 'he' had said to Anna, Ruth wasn't impressed.

'So that's it, is it?' The jaw locked, maybe quarter of a centimetre in front of its usual position. 'Couldn't he have said he was sorry, at least? At some point between then and now?'

During the course of the answer to this question Ruth closed her eyes and leant back against the bedhead without relaxing a muscle. After an entire minute – Dave was timing it on the bedside clock – she opened her eyes, stared straight ahead at her reflection in the mirror on the door of their wardrobe and said, quite loudly, 'But I thought you didn't believe in fate?' After that there was another long pause and then, equally loudly, Ruth said, 'I thought you didn't believe in chemistry?'

Right. So, there was something else going on here. A man, as in a love interest, was undoubtedly involved. Besides the references to fate and chemistry, Ruth's tone of voice had suddenly acquired that slightly impatient edge that Dave associated with any conversation involving her girlfriends' unexpected good fortune. Not that Roo was mean-spirited. It was more, he thought, that sometimes she felt out of the loop. She got the voice, for example, when Anna and Jean came round after their single girls' expedition to Vietnam. She got the voice when Valerie let slip that they were spending £10,000 on re-landscaping their garden. Come to think of it, she really got the voice when Anna announced she was moving in with bloody Richard.

'What is going *on*?' Dave mouthed, but Ruth cupped a hand to her brow, removing him from her eye line.

'I know,' she murmured, curling her shoulder around so that her back was turned to Dave. 'Of course I understand that . . . Of course I do. He was your grand passion. There's nothing like it.'

Dave's head, which had been lolling in Ruth's direction, snapped upright. He eyed his wife surreptitiously. There was something in her tone that he didn't like, something exclusive, something private. It was by no means certain that Ruth's grand passion, the one she had experienced in order to be able to empathize with her friend so unconditionally, was himself. He couldn't help thinking that it would have been appropriate, under the circumstances, for her to throw him a misty, grateful look. Ideally, she should have put her hand over the mouthpiece and whispered, 'You're my grand passion, Dave. I won't be a minute, my darling.'

'What is going *on*,' Dave hissed, hurling himself down on the pillow and thrashing around as if he were being forcibly restrained. 'It's one o'clock in the morning. Can't this wait?' Ruth cupped the blinkering hand tighter around her temple.

'All I'm saying, Anna, is be careful. Don't rush into anything.' There was a pause. 'Really? Well, if you think . . . No. You're probably being very sensible. You need to get to know each other again . . .' Ruth glanced across at Dave meeting his eyes for a fraction of a second. 'No, I had thought about him, of course . . . Oh, it's their phone? Right. OK . . . Well, try us again when you can. Bye.'

Ruth replaced the receiver, folded her arms and stared at Dave.

'What's the matter with you?' she said.

'What's the matter with *me*?' Dave's eyes darted around the room.

'That was Anna, saying she'd seen Danny.'

'Danny?'

'She's in a bit of a state, as you can imagine.'

'Why didn't you let me listen in? I could have helped!'

'How could you have helped?'

'I don't know. Tips. It's always useful to have a man's point of view. So . . .' Dave swung his hands behind his head. 'Danny's back.' A slow smile crept across his face as he considered the implications of this new development. 'Which means Richard is getting the old heave ho. So we can all go out for curries again, and go on bad-taste holidays, and have nasty drunken parties, with Malibu and hula hoops and . . .'

'Don't you think you should be thinking about what's best for Anna, not what suits your social life?'

'I *am* thinking about Anna,' Dave said, still smiling up at the ceiling. 'She was happy, wasn't she, when she was with Danny?'

Ruth sighed and pulled the duvet cover up under her armpits. 'Yes. But where's he been for the last three years? At least Richard's . . .' Dave turned his head expectantly in her direction. 'At least he's been there for her.'

'Oh, puurlease.'

'At least they've made a life together.'

'They've made an interior scheme together, that's what they've made. They've made a window display.'

'But, Danny . . .' Ruth hesitated. 'I mean it's only an accident that they bumped into each other. It's not as if he'd decided to come looking for her.'

'So?' Dave was picturing the holidays in Ireland, the Guinness tours culminating in the all-night lock-in at the Bridey Hotel. He was imagining Richard strapped backwards onto the saddle of a donkey, being led down cobbled streets through crowds of hostile, rosy-cheeked yokels, including Sir John Mills.

'I'm just not convinced,' Ruth said, 'that if your feelings were that strong you could stay away for all that time and then find them reignited, Bam! In a bookshop.' She turned on her side to face him, doubling the pillow under her head. 'I mean, how could she ever trust him again? Don't you remember when he disappeared, you said you'd always had your doubts about him?'

'Well, he never bought a round, did he?' Dave eased out his neck as he tried to bury the reservations he'd harboured for a while before Danny left; the last thing he wanted was to spoil his enjoyment of this moment. 'But that was then. The guy was young.'

'Thirty-four,' said Ruth, in her try-harder voice.

'Yeah, well, immature then. He'll have grown up. Look, he's not going to get involved with Anna again unless he knows he's changed. What did he say anyway?'

'He said their hearts had recognized each other. He said, "You're still my best girl."'

Dave glanced at Ruth to check if this information had been relayed with at least a trace of irony, but her expression was soggy with sentimentality. He was pretty sure he'd heard those same lines in the Leonardo di Caprio film on TV last night, and was about to tell Ruth as much when she smiled blearily at him, like a child who'd been at the chocolate liqueurs.

'It is really romantic though, isn't it?' she said. 'Apparently Anna couldn't really speak when they met, but she just felt this . . .'

'Electricity,' said Dave.

'Exactly. And after that she couldn't remember any of the bad stuff, all the things she'd been waiting to say to him all this time. She just wanted to hold him; just to lie up against him and feel him breathing. She says it's made her reconsider everything.'

'Has he still got the band?' Dave paused, Ruth was glaring at him. 'What's wrong now?'

'I don't know if he's still got the band,' she said. 'Were you listening to what I was saying?'

'So,' Dave said, 'let me get this straight. You're not sure if Anna should trust Danny, but you're not really interested in finding out about the new Danny, because Anna wants to listen to him breathing, and nothing else matters. Meanwhile, Anna, who has devoted three years to writing a book about the fact that all successful relationships are based on solid, pragmatic foundations – factors like security and trust and a sense of responsibility for one another . . .' Dave paused until Ruth was forced to lower her eyes in defeat. 'That same Anna is AWOL in the country, experiencing the electricity factor, with the bloke who dumped her at the altar.'

Ruth sighed and buried her arm deeper under the folded pillow. 'Chemistry, passion, romance – the three ingredients we're taught to associate with love,' she recited, as if from an autocue. 'Yet research consistently shows, none of them makes it into the top-ten ingredients of an enduring match.'

'Excuse me?' Dave flattened his elbow against the pillow and peered at his wife.

'It's from the book. That's Anna's big line. "CPR provides the spark but not the life support' . . . something like that.' Ruth shrugged. 'She shows me stuff sometimes.'

'Jesus,' said Dave. 'What a load of bollocks. How much are they paying her again?'

'They're not sleeping together.'

'Sorry?'

'Anna and Danny. They've decided not to have sex for a while, until they're sure.'

Dave shook his head briskly as if trying to rid his ears of water. 'They've WHAT?'

'It was his idea. He says he wants to win her back first. He thinks it's important that they should build up trust in each other. Don't look at me like that!'

'Well, give me a break! Danny Fortune said that?' Dave levered himself up on the pillow. 'Danny Fortune said they should lay off sex so that he can win her back? How unlikely is that?'

'I think it shows he's thinking about Anna.' Ruth hesitated. 'She didn't sound all that happy about it though.'

'Well, she'll be gagging for it, won't she? She's had three years of spooky Buddhist hands-free sex. Oh, come off it, Roo, you can't actually feel *sorry* for Dickless. He's so busy thinking about himself, he's so into his own thaaaaang.'

Ruth stared at him and in that moment Dave knew that he had missed something very important in all of this. 'If Richard is going to be miserable and on his own,' Ruth said, 'then I, for one, am going to let him know we're still his friends.'

Jesus! Why hadn't he thought of that? This was not good at all. Dickless had become wronged and lonely and . . . available. 'Fine!' Dave said. 'Oh, and by the way, your mum rang, and I said it was OK if she came to stay.'

It wasn't much of a counter strategy but it was an excellent way of getting his own back. Ruth and her mother did not, for the most part, see eye to eye, but Ruth's mother happened to adore Dave. She quite literally thought he had saved Ruth's life and wasn't shy of saying so, in front of whoever was prepared to listen. 'Ruth never had much luck with men before David,' she would say. 'She always had these ideas about who she was, and what she was going to be. It was such a relief when David came along, so down-to-earth, and such a lovely father. And a gourmet cook, too! She doesn't know how lucky she is.'

'You sod,' said Ruth, reaching for the bedside light. 'That's all I need.'

'Oh, come on!' Dave wailed. 'I was just trying to show a bit of family spirit. And I was thinking about Billy, as it happens. He hardly ever gets to see his grandparents.' He rolled over onto his side and shrugged the pillow under his shoulder.

'Woa,' he thought as he closed his eyes, 'that was pretty convincing.'

Ten

Valerie heard the news from Jean the following morning while at the wheel of the Toyota Land Cruiser.

'I don't believe it,' she gasped, tucking in the earpiece of her mobile. 'After all this time! So what did he have to say for himself? . . . And? Jean, hold on. We simply can't do this over the phone. Come over for coffee. I'll be back in twenty minutes. OK, bye.'

'*We*'ll be back,' said Lottie. 'I do exist, you know.'

'Oh, darling, don't be silly, it's just a figure of speech.' Valerie reached for the tape recorder on the dashboard. 'That was Jean on the phone. You remember Daniel? Anna's boyfriend who disappeared into thin air? Well . . . would you believe he's turned up!' Valerie tapped the steering wheel triumphantly.

'Why am I supposed to be interested in that?' Lottie shuffled down in the passenger seat, pressing her folded arms tight against her hips.

'Well . . .' Valerie paused, wondering as she often did in these exchanges what was the right answer, given their circumstances. 'Because, I suppose, it's rather unexpected. Those sort of things don't happen every day. And because it presents Anna with a dilemma. Now she'll have to choose between Richard and Daniel . . . assuming she has a choice.'

'You make it sound like shopping.'

'There's no need to be quite so po-faced, Charlotte, Anna isn't married after all. Besides, I thought you liked Daniel. You remember Daniel. You thought he was cool.'

'I did *not* think he was cool.' Lottie made a face that might have been appropriate had a severed head been dumped in her lap. 'Why d'you even *say* that? Because he had a guitar? Because he had long hair?' The disgusted expression levelled out into a sneer and, not for the first time, the thought crossed Valerie's mind that Lottie might benefit from an upper-lip wax. Truthfully, the only thing preventing her from making the appointment was the prospect of having to deal with Marion should it come up during their sessions.

'Oh, never mind,' sighed Valerie. 'Let's not argue about it, please.'

They drove along in silence for a moment, Valerie's eyes flicking between the tape recorder in her lap and the passenger seat. Then swiftly, guiltily, she pressed the record button and held the microphone to her lips.

'Sunday, 12 o'clock-ish, in the Land Cruiser. Lots going on, as usual. Just popped into Top Shop to try and find Charlotte something for her party.' In the passenger seat Lottie flinched. 'Some very nice things but nothing she felt was really her. Um. So, really just wanted to make the point that today is one of those days when you can see what I've been calling the "Balance" working at its very best. Archie's playing golf this morning; we're out doing our things; the whole family is meeting up for lunch, and then Archie and I will have some quiet time together this evening.'

Lottie made a retching noise and yanked the neck of her jumper up around her ears.

'And Archie and I have just talked on the phone about a rather nice property that's come on the market down on the Suffolk coast. And that, to me, is a very important part of marriage.'

'What, buying houses?' Lottie glared at her mother over the top of her polo neck.

'Planning,' said Valerie, keeping her voice steady and silky smooth. 'Making plans, together. Having projects to look forward to, whether it's a house, or a holiday, or a party, or whatever . . .' She flicked off the record button and then flicked it straight back on as another thought occurred to her. 'And clearly defined roles, of course. Marriage, like any team, works best when everyone knows exactly what their responsibilities are.'

Valerie injected an added huskiness into this signing off which always made her feel like a reporter in the field. (This is Valerie Cunningham, out and about in London, researching the way marriage works in the noughties.) She checked her hair quickly in the rear-view mirror before glancing across at her daughter, taking in the knobbly ridge of her spine, the violet-hued nails scraping up and down the outside seam of her jeans.

'Really, Lottie. I don't know why you're so scathing about all this. You should be proud that your parents' marriage is going to feature in a book. Who knows? We might be an inspiration to others, in some small way.'

Lottie leant her head against the glass of the passenger window and traced a finger in the condensation.

'Charlotte? You remember what Marion said? She said the car was a very good place to talk. Darling?'

'Obviously she didn't know you're always talking to your tape recorder.'

'Well . . . think of it as my work. Lots of your friends' mothers work. Janey's mother works, doesn't she? Steph's mother practically lives at the office. Lucky for you I'm just contributing to a book and not some ego-crazed banker. Come on . . .' Valerie ducked her chin and gripped the steering wheel. 'I want you to tell me how you'd like your father and I to be. Would you like us to be more like Ruth and Dave?'

As she said this Valerie felt a twinge of disloyalty. It wasn't quite right to use one's best friends as an example but, off the top of her head, she couldn't think of a better way of illustrating the lack of structure and goals her daughter was supposed to crave.

Lottie turned her head very slowly and deliberately in Valerie's direction, the polo neck still pulled up to the bridge of her nose. Her blue eyes settled on Valerie's, unblinking.

'It isn't a competition, Mum,' she said coldly, and turned to look out of the window again, leaving Valerie feeling strangely disconcerted.

'Yes it is!' Valerie wanted to shout. '*Life* is a competition, and who you marry is crucial to deciding where you come in it! Don't you ever forget that!' But of course she couldn't. Lottie wouldn't understand. Marion would have an absolute fit.

Instead Valerie said, 'I'm just trying to find out what you'd like us to do differently. There's nothing wrong with that, is there?'

God, if only she knew, Valerie thought. If only she knew that without constant pushing and nagging on Valerie's part, and considerable behind-the-scenes work on the partners at Cazulets, her father would probably be sitting in the garden at that very moment, painting some useless watercolour.

'Not us,' said Lottie. 'You.'

'All right. Me.'

Valerie was feeling magnanimous, cheerful. She wasn't certain what was responsible for her mood but it probably had something to do with that adorable house coming on the market and, possibly, the news that Richard and Anna's relationship was coming unstuck. She wasn't one to gloat, obviously, but she had always said it was a relationship without solid grounding, like a tent with no pegs. As she had this thought Valerie automatically reached for the tape recorder and depressed the record button.

'Note,' she murmured, letting her thumb linger on the pause button for a moment. 'It's becoming an increasingly old-fashioned position, but I firmly believe that one of the reasons Archie and I are still together, is because we made a commitment in church in front of our friends and families. I don't think it makes it any easier, but, at the same time, it's about more than two people buying a flat together and investing in a few pots and pans. No offence, Anna.' Valerie replaced the tape recorder by the gear stick and met Lottie's scathing look with a generous smile.

'At least Anna's trying,' Lottie said.

'Trying, darling?'

'At least she's doing things that make her happy, not

so she's exactly like everyone else. You'd rather Anna was married and miserable, just so long as she was the same as you . . . so you could compare who was doing best.'

'Charlotte, that is not true. I want Anna to be happy, and the point is Anna hasn't really been happy. Daddy and I, our lives may look very boring to you, but the fact is we are a lot happier than someone like Anna. Though of course now, who knows, if she settles down—'

'When does Dad get to say his bit for the book?' Lottie interrupted.

'Once every six months, the same as me.'

'And has he told Anna yet?'

'Told her what?'

'That you don't do sex?'

Valerie stiffened in the driving seat.

'You don't have to pretend. I've heard you and Granny talking. It's obvious, anyway.'

'Charlotte, I don't know what you—' Valerie stopped. Lottie was gazing at her, a penetrating, unforgiving gaze that, at the same time, contained a flicker of something Valerie hadn't seen for months. Hope. Valerie took a deep breath. 'Charlotte, even if what you said were true, it would not mean that your father and I didn't love each other. Your father and I have a very loving relationship.'

'Well, Marion wants to see you.' Lottie was deathly pale now.

'What do you mean?'

'She thinks it's why I'm ill.'

'You told Marion?' Valerie felt suddenly sick.

'You've been discussing our private life with . . . Marion.'

'Mum! You're putting your private life in a book! Anyway, you're the one who made me go and see her in the first place. You're the one who said we had to talk about everything. You just said that!'

Charlotte's eyes welled with tears. She was plucking at her lower lip, pinching it between her finger and thumb as if she were trying to form a spout. Valerie stared at her. She wanted to explain that there was no comparison between telling your own version of events to a trusted friend, strictly for research purposes, and discussing your sex life with a woman who could have no concept whatsoever of how your life worked. She wanted to say the latter was beneath her dignity, beyond even thinking about; that this whole ghastly eating issue had gone on for far longer than she had been led to expect; and that the idea that she and Archie were now going to be involved in this sort of way, in the most personal and intrusive way, was quite intolerable. She longed to slam on the brakes and scream 'How dare you do this to us. How dare you make our lives into this cheap spectacle.' But the tears were coursing down Charlotte's cheeks and against all her instincts Valerie heard herself saying, 'When does she want to see me?'

'Not *you*,' Lottie wailed. 'Both of you. You and Dad.'

'That's what I meant,' said Valerie, and Lottie let her grip her hand for a whole five seconds.

*

223

When Anna got back from the country, two days later than planned, she found her office answer machine clogged with messages. The first two were from Valerie: the initial one an excitable request for information, and the second an invitation to dinner the following night. ('I've assembled the gang so you don't have to go over it all more than once,' Valerie explained breathlessly. 'We are desperate, Anna. Ruth hasn't got any sort of memory for details, as you know.') After those were a couple of messages from her editor, one from Bunny Wells, and the usual update from both her parents (they each liked to get on a separate extension) informing her that their neighbour had gone into hospital for an operation on his knee and never come out. 'He was eaten by one of those bugs,' her mother announced shrilly, while Freddie incanted the details of the case in the background, signing off with an uplifting, 'Hope you're well!' Finally, last in the queue, was a message from Lily. 'Hi,' she said, her voice soft and almost shy. 'It's about three o'clock, I guess, on Tuesday. Just wanted to say missing you already. I know you've got a life in London . . . I know you've got a book to deliver. But, please, do think about coming back soon. We have an office here waiting for you,' she lowered her voice to a whisper, 'and someone who is crazy about you.'

Anna lunged for the stop button. She knew Richard was away at a seminar on organics, but she felt suddenly ashamed and, for the first time in years, slightly out of control. On the one hand, she was sure what she wanted, but at the same time, leaving Richard for Daniel contradicted everything she had learned over the past three years. She was almost scared to go back to her laptop and continue working on the book for fear that it would all start unravelling before her eyes.

A long time ago, someone had recommended talking to herself when her thoughts became confused while writing – asking herself questions out loud and answering them spontaneously – and on the few occasions she'd given it a go, it had seemed to help. Anna sat down on the sofa in the office, her hands clasped on her knees, and focused hard on her situation.

'What do you *think* is the right thing to do?' she said out loud. Silence. Anna cleared her throat and tried again. 'You've worked hard to find this stability; are you prepared to risk all that?' Nothing. Just tense shallow breathing. She grabbed her handbag, reached inside for her mobile phone, and dialled Ruth's number.

'Roo?' she said, when Ruth answered. 'I really need someone to talk to. I need someone to ask me the questions that I can't ask myself any more. Can you do that?'

'I'll be there in ten minutes,' Ruth said.

They met in the coffee shop at the end of Anna's road. Anna ordered a mint tea and a mineral water; Ruth ordered a double cappuccino and a brownie.

'Bit of a role reversal this, isn't it?' Ruth said, spooning milk froth into her mouth like ice cream and eyeing her friend with curiosity. The woman sitting opposite her looked like Anna, but she was behaving like someone who had just given up smoking, having had a fifty-a-day habit.

'I've tried talking myself through it,' Anna said,

shaking her head in disbelief. 'I just can't do it somehow.'

'That's because you know too much.' Ruth waggled
the teaspoon at her and then dipped it in her mouth
again. 'What you need is a bit of the amateur approach.
I assume the question is, should you stay or should you
go?'

Anna nodded.

'You know you want Danny, but you also want the
security and the lovely white flat, and you need to know
which is ultimately going to make you happiest.'

'I'm confused,' Anna said, still nodding. 'I know
what I feel, but then I should be applying all the lessons
I've learned researching the book.'

'Right. Well, put all the book stuff out of your mind.
Now, just answer me truthfully and quickly, if possible.'
Ruth levelled the teaspoon at Anna. 'If you were stuck
in a car on the M25 for fifteen hours, just the two of you
and a pocket Ribena, who would you rather be with?
Richard or Danny?'

'Well, Richard would be very . . .' Anna's eyes flickered. 'Danny.'

'OK. Something happens in your life, something
good or something bad. You get a book deal. Your dog
dies. You win the lottery. Who do you want to speak to
first?'

Anna sucked in her breath and lowered her eyes. 'I
suppose, Danny.'

'Right. You are standing naked in a room, which
one of them is making you feel most like J. Lo?'

Anna frowned. 'Richard's always very . . . supportive,' she said quietly.

'Not the question, unfortunately.'

'All right.' Anna shrugged helplessly. 'Danny, then.'

'Sex,' said Ruth firmly. 'Who gets the most points out of ten?'

'Well, that depends . . .' Anna spread her hands on the table in front of her and concentrated hard on keeping them symmetrical. 'Richard's sort of a specialist.'

'Yes?'

'But it was always fun with Danny.'

'Not fun with Richard?'

Anna shook her head. 'Not really. We used to have to . . . time it. Anyway. What's next?'

Ruth took a sip of her coffee and watched Anna over the chunky lip of the cup. 'Well, I could carry on, but that's what you'd call a landslide.' She grinned. 'Cheer up, Anna. Richard will get over it.'

'I know he will. I think he might actually be relieved. But, even if this is what I want, Ruth . . . is it the right thing?' Anna gripped the metal handle of her tea-glass holder and stared out across the cafe.

'I don't know. But you tried the right thing and it wasn't quite right.' Ruth hesitated. 'You know, you never seemed . . . you haven't seemed that jolly. Not for a while.'

Anna shook her head, still gazing blankly past Ruth's shoulder. 'I was so sure. I had my whole life worked out. I honestly thought I'd gone beyond all that, not just Danny, but all those crazy feelings.'

'You're never too grown-up for "all that",' Ruth said.

'I feel I've failed.'

'It's not failing if you can't stop loving someone.'

227

'I don't just mean Richard. I mean the book.'

'Oh. That.' Ruth signalled to the waiter for another cappuccino.

'Me and Richard . . .' Anna leant across the table and lowered her voice, 'we're the twenty-first century model relationship. It's *us*, in the book. And not only that . . . this . . . what's happened to me . . . contradicts my whole thesis about relationships and what makes them last.'

'Hmm.' Ruth pursed her lips. 'I had sort of noticed that.'

'But I think I can get round it, don't you?' Anna was reaching across the table now, using Ruth's spoon to emphasize her point. 'Because there are all the other examples that bear it out . . . There's Val and Archie, and you and Dave—'

'Anna, I . . .'

Anna looked up from the table expectantly.

'Oh . . . nothing, really. I was just going to say, we're at that confusing stage of life, aren't we? There was bound to be some sort of hiccup.'

Anna's eyes glistened. 'I've let you down, haven't I?' she said. 'I was supposed to have all the answers and now . . . I'm just a bit all over the place.'

'Actually,' said Ruth, 'I find it strangely reassuring.'

Minty and Freddie were due for tea at Anna's flat, later that afternoon. These days they liked to come for tea, rather than supper, because Freddie couldn't see to drive after dark and Minty was no longer allowed behind the wheel of the automatic since she had accidentally slammed it into reverse, annihilating Freddie's golf clubs. They were coming for tea on this particular day, midweek, because they had gathered that Richard would be away, although they were pretending it was because they had to be up in town for some unspecified sale. So far they had rung twice to confirm details: once to ask if they should bring some biscuits and milk (the answer was no, as usual), and once to check where they should park. 'Just outside,' Anna had told them, ignoring the sceptical silence. 'Have a look when you get here . . . there's always plenty of spaces.'

'We had to park a few streets away, Anna,' her mother mumbled accusingly into the entry phone. 'There is nowhere to park.'

From where Anna was standing she could see a space large enough to accommodate the Dickensons' VW van. 'OK,' she said. 'Never mind. Come on up then.'

'We've brought a cake,' announced her mother.

'Great. D'you want to come up?'

'Your father isn't very happy about where we've left the car.' Minty lowered her voice to a whisper. 'It's outside that taxi place. There seem to be a lot of . . . people.'

'All right. Well, come up, and we'll worry about that in a minute.'

Anna pressed the entry button and kept leaning on it, ignoring the pleas for more information, until she heard the clunk of the front door closing. Then she opened the door to the flat and stood in the entrance waiting for her parents to round the bend in the stairs. Minty was first, carrying what could only be described as a hamper and breathing heavily. Freddie brought up the rear dragging what looked like a blanket.

'I thought you might need milk,' Minty puffed. 'Your father won't drink the no-fat sort.' Anna took the hamper from her mother, which weighed roughly as much as a case of wine, and staggered ahead of them into the flat. Behind her Minty and Freddie had already started to adopt the body language of tourists in a stately home.

'Well, here we are . . .' said Minty, her eyes wandering restlessly around the room, grasping for something she might compliment. 'Isn't Richard clever?' she said, finally, starting to unload the hamper.

Inevitably they had brought everything you could possibly require for tea, all of it loaded with e numbers, colouring and saturated fats. The hamper also contained tins of soup, sweet corn, olives and tuna fish. Why, Anna was not sure, but this was the ritual. She suspected there was a pasta dish you could make using all the ingredients, and it was Minty's hope that one day Anna would grow out of her organic phase and return to eating this sort of decent and reliable food. As for the blanket, that turned out to be a rug which her parents no longer had any use for and thought might do for 'somewhere' in the flat (they meant the bedroom but could not refer to it directly as that constituted an admission that she slept with Richard). The rug was a variation on a tartan, with quite a bit of yellow in it.

'How is Richard?' Freddie asked, eyeing a framed black and white photograph of a bent elbow. 'Still . . . busy?'

'Actually,' said Anna, stacking the last of the Viennese Whirls on a white platter, 'Richard and I are splitting up.'

Minty froze in the middle of unwrapping the teabags.

'Splitting up,' Freddie repeated flatly, unable to gauge his wife's reaction from where he was standing.

'Yes,' Anna said. 'I'm back with Danny. We bumped into each other and . . . well. We're back together. I thought you'd be pleased,' she added, glaring at her mother.

'Just give us a moment, darling,' said Minty.

'Danny the musician?' her father asked, keeping his eyes firmly on Minty.

'Yes. The musician.' Anna paused to give them both a chance to digest this information. 'He's doing very well. He's making an album.'

The word album appeared to jolt Minty to her senses. 'So he's still a musician.'

'Yes, he's *still* a musician,' Anna snapped, her anxiety about Danny still being a musician, and the commitment involved in being a musician, and what that might mean for their future, surging up like a big red bubble and exploding inside her cheeks. 'Just say you're pleased,' she said. 'I know you never liked Richard.'

Freddie gave a goofy shrug. Minty looked around the room as if checking that Richard was definitely not there before speaking her mind. 'Does that mean you'll have to move out of here, then?' she asked, her eyes flicking randomly from one luxurious article to the next.

'Obviously.'

'Oh.' Minty paused. 'So, where will you go?'

'Who knows?' Anna grinned and spread her arms wide, almost convincing herself that she was the kind of girl who really couldn't care less about a small detail like the whereabouts of her future home. 'For heaven's sake, is that all you can think about?' she said, not daring to meet her mother's eye. 'Where are you going to live? What's he going to do? Can't you think of anything else to say, like . . .' Anna hesitated, trying to think of the sort of thing she would like them to say.

'Has he told you he loves you?' Minty asked.

'Ohforgodssake!' Anna felt the red bubble burst again, this time in her throat. He had said everything but! They were agreed . . . they had an unspoken agreement that because of their history, words like love were, for the time being, a little too loaded to handle. Anna closed her eyes. Should he have said he loved her? She'd wanted to say she loved him.

'Never mind,' said Minty. 'Let's get on with the tea, I think your father could do with a cup.'

'We are in love,' said Anna defiantly. 'And it's a miracle that we met the way we did.'

Minty considered her red-faced daughter. 'Yes, darling, I know.' She reached across to shift the Jaffa Cakes out of Freddie's reach and then braced herself against the table, eyes blinking. 'I was thinking . . . Perhaps Richard would let you stay here, for a while. Just until you know what you're doing.'

'Why not?' Freddie agreed, as if his wife had suggested a rubber of bridge.

'I give in.' Anna groaned. 'I thought you'd both be over the moon.'

'Of course we are.' Minty extended a hand towards

her daughter. 'We just have to look on the practical side as well. We are your parents. We want to be sure that you're looked after, that's all.'

'Please, Mother. I am an adult, I can look after myself.'

Minty looked genuinely surprised that her daughter could entertain such a naive belief. She gave Anna the same look she used to give her when she threatened to run away as a child: the you-and-I-know-better-than-that-now-don't-we? look.

'All right,' Minty said. 'So where's the teapot?'

Eleven

Dinner at the Cunninghams' was a more or less monthly ritual for the friends. Valerie would ring, a week or two in advance, and make a terrific song and dance about finding a date that suited them all, even though Valerie and Archie were the only ones who had what could be described as a 'social life'. The evening always started with drinks, upstairs in the drawing room, and dinner itself was generally one of Valerie's legendary stews, or sometimes a joint of beef, followed by cheese and fruit if anyone had room. But, tonight, as Valerie informed the first arrivals, the formula was going to be slightly different.

'We're having pumpkin risotto,' Valerie said, her tone at once alerting them to the hidden significance of this change in menu.

'Richard's not coming, is he?' asked Dave, looking furtively around. 'I thought that was on the back-burner?'

'No, Richard isn't coming,' said Valerie, staring straight at Jean. 'Anna's coming on her own. Someone else is bringing, someone.'

Dave rapidly scanned his hostess for clues, zooming in on her black crêpe dress, bending over to check her choice of shoes.

'Val, can I pop Billy in the spare room?' Ruth hoisted Billy further up on her shoulder, tugged down the back of his pyjama top and, without waiting for an answer, started up the cream-carpeted stairs.

'Oh my God.' Dave switched his attention from Valerie to Jean. 'It's Thumbelina, isn't it? From *House Proud*?'

'Belinda,' said Valerie with a reverential nod, as if referring to someone recently deceased.

'Right . . .' Dave rubbed his hands together and then, catching Jean's eye, crammed them in his pockets.

'Please,' said Jean, fishing in her bag for a cigarette. 'I can cope.' She placed the cigarette between her lips and then paused, meeting the two pairs of anxious eyes trained on her face. 'Tony and I *are* divorced, you know. We are free to see other people.'

'The thing is,' murmured Valerie, cupping Jean's elbow. 'When Tony rang and asked if he could bring her, I just felt I couldn't say no.' She was looking at Jean the way mothers in cars watch their travel-sickness-prone children, with that subtle mixture of empathy and forbidding. 'Would you rather I'd rung and warned you, Jeannie? I thought on balance, better not.' Valerie shot Dave a look.

'No point!' said Dave, on cue. 'She's only a minor TV presenter anyway.' Jean blinked at him. 'Not even really a presenter. More of a gofer. I don't even watch it. Who does?'

'Exactly,' said Valerie. 'And you always look so immaculate, Jean, I didn't think there was any point worrying you. I have had *everything* out of my wardrobe, mind you. What d'you think?'

Valerie spread her arms wide inviting Jean and Dave to admire the dress which had, in fact, been purchased that morning, specifically for the occasion.

'Very suitable,' Jean said, aiming a thin stream of cigarette smoke at her hostess's cleavage.

Valerie sighed contentedly and gestured for them to go through to the drawing room. 'Oh, and by the way, apparently Belinda doesn't like to talk shop,' she confided as she led the way. 'I wonder, though, d'you think she'd mind having a very quick look at the spare room? I'm just not sure about me and Chinese yellow.'

When Anna arrived, a few minutes later, Dave made a beeline for her, ushering her swiftly over to the drawing room window seat.

'I just wanted to say, good for you,' he murmured, wrapping an arm around Anna's shoulders and giving her an affectionate squeeze. 'It is all very exciting, I can see that.' Dave hesitated, biting his lips together and furrowing his brow. 'But have you really, really thought about this, Anna? I mean . . .' the clacking of Ruth's mules descending the stairs prompted Dave to lower his voice and shift position, so that his back was turned to the doorway. 'I mean – *Richard*. A lot of women would be pretty happy with a man like that. A lot of women.'

'I didn't think you liked him,' Anna said. 'In fact, I think I've got that on tape.'

Dave grimaced, raising his hand in acknowledgement of this possible error of judgement.

'Maybe. Maybe. But we're all capable of misreading

people. And the fact is, Anna, a reliable partner is a rare thing and Richard *is* that thing.' Dave tightened his grip on her shoulders. 'That guy has been there for you, Anna. Can you honestly say that Danny will be your rock? Can you honestly say you know him any more?'

'All right everyone!' Valerie stood in the doorway of the drawing room, palms pressed together in front of her chest. 'Slight change of plan, Tony is turning up with Belinda from *House Proud*.' She angled the praying hands in Jean's direction. 'So we have to get all the latest from Anna, right away, before they arrive.'

Valerie glanced swiftly at her watch and then pulled a chair over to the window, beckoning the others to gather round.

'Val! Honestly.' Anna smiled shyly as she glanced around the group. Jean was decoratively draped in the white armchair, Archie and Ruth were perched on the edge of the ottoman; all eyes were trained on her.

'Well, I think you all know already, but I suppose the news is . . .' she paused, pressing a hand to her mouth as she felt her lower lip start to vibrate, 'Danny's back.'

A cheer went up, albeit low key, and mostly male. Dave leant towards Anna, arms folded.

'I wouldn't commit yourself,' he murmured out of the side of his mouth. 'You don't want to narrow your options at this stage.'

'And nothing's changed,' Anna continued, beaming delightedly at her friends. 'Absolutely nothing. We want to be together. We knew instantly. It was . . . it felt like coming home.'

'That's wonderful, darling,' murmured Jean, reaching out an arm in a crisp white shirt sleeve.

'Wonderful,' echoed Archie. 'It's terrifically romantic, isn't it? All these years and your eyes meet across a crowded bookshop and you just knew, it's like . . .'

Valerie's head swivelled in her husband's direction, severing the thought mid-flow. 'Let Anna give us the details please, Archie. Did he say why, Anna?'

'Why what?'

'Why he disappeared in the first place?'

'Oh. Not really. I think he lost his nerve, mainly.'

Valerie's head retreated an inch or two, sufficient to register her reservations. 'And it was just a coincidence, was it,' she continued, 'your bumping into each other?'

'Or fate,' said Anna, smiling bashfully. 'He'd never been in that shop before; I'd never been to that village. The people I was staying with just happen to have this vacant cottage, which he's moving into this weekend . . .' She shook her head in disbelief at her own extraordinary good fortune. 'It's like a dream. I really think somebody must want us to be together.'

'Not Richard, obviously,' mumbled Dave.

'How marvellous,' Archie said. 'What a place to spend the summer. Can you finish the book there, d'you think?'

'Maybe. I'd like to try. And of course, I won't have a base here any more.' Anna glanced at Dave. 'Not once I've told Richard, which I will do as soon as he gets back.'

'The car's Richard's too, isn't it?' Dave said. He gritted his teeth and clamped his hands under his armpits as if contemplating all the long, grim, carless journeys that lay ahead of her.

'So . . . you're giving it another go!' Valerie nodded to herself, her eyes bulging the way they did when she was trying to distract attention from a less than convincing smile.

'It's a chemical thing,' said Ruth dreamily. 'She doesn't have much choice in the matter, does she?' And then, just as Dave was starting once again to make the case for proceeding with caution, the doorbell rang.

'Right,' said Valerie, gesticulating for them all to stand up and prepare for the VIP's entrance. 'We'll have to put this on hold for a while. Anna, fix the cushions on the window seat, would you? That's it. On second thoughts, let's take her straight down to the kitchen, I think that might be more her sort of thing.'

By the end of the first course (another alteration to the usual plan) the Cunninghams' kitchen table was divided down the middle, literally. At one end Jean, Archie and Anna were stoically conducting a conversation among themselves while, at the other end – beyond the barricade formed by Dave and Tony, craning forward on their elbows – Belinda was demonstrating the miracle of 'tit tape'.

'This always happens.' Belinda giggled. 'Honestly, wherever I go all anyone wants to know is "How d'you keep them from falling out when you're on the telly?"'

Dave nodded enthusiastically and propped his chin on his knuckles.

'But it's really, really simple. You just put it here –' Belinda peeled back the edge of her plunge-front jersey top, exposing one half of a perfectly spherical breast

'– and then . . . zip, zip. And Bob's your uncle.' She snapped her fingers delightedly, making her chestnut ponytail bounce.

'It is quite something.' Tony chuckled. 'Everywhere we go there are people hassling Belinda for information. Should I use eggshell or . . . the other one? Can I risk sea grass in the bathroom? What about tongue and groove and dry rot? It's madness!' He flapped his hands beside his ears like a vaudeville performer. 'She's actually been mobbed in Marks & Spencer's food department.'

Tony glanced over his shoulder to see how this information had been received at the far end of the table. Jean waved her cigarette at him.

'It's true,' said Belinda, who had one of those elusive, England-is-my-second-language accents, even though, so far this evening, she had already managed to mispronounce Rioja and broderie anglaise. 'I find it quite amazing, actually, that all these women are asking *me* for advice.'

'Me too,' said Ruth.

'It's not quite the same, but the kind of attention Belinda is getting . . .' Tony drew back his elbows and puffed out his chest, 'it reminds me of when I was starting out and we were filming *The Four Hotspurs*. Of course, there wasn't anything like the same cult of celebrity in those days—'

'And all the fans were under twelve,' said Jean. 'But apart from that . . .'

'Well, isn't this nice? Here's to the cook!' Archie, now slightly pink in the face, raised his glass in the air, while Valerie rolled her eyes in mock horror and made shooing gestures with her hand.

'Ahhhh,' Belinda said. 'You're all so nice. I was a bit worried, before I met you. Tony said none of you were particularly interested in interiors.'

Jean, who had been tapping her cigarette packet idly against the edge of the table, froze and swung her head very slowly in Tony's direction.

'I meant modern decoration,' said Tony hastily.

'Oh, yes, of course.' Belinda clamped a hand to her throat, putting the tit tape through its paces. 'I know you've got that lovely shop, Jean. I didn't mean . . .' She widened her brown eyes at Tony who was now scrutinizing a wine label intently. 'Anyway, I think it's lovely when a man has such a close group of friends. I think it really says a lot.'

Belinda leant across the table towards Ruth who was pressing her forefingers against her sinuses and making low snorting noises.

'I'll bet you're the strong one in the group,' Belinda said, scrunching up her nose. 'And Anna –' she swivelled to face the other end of the table, forcing Dave to shunt back in his chair '– you're the lynchpin, of course. The one everyone trusts with all their secrets.' Belinda's gaze flickered for an instant to the seat next to Anna's, where Jean was blowing smoke rings the size of lassos, before slinking back to settle on Valerie's expectant face. 'And Valerie, I can see you provide all the warmth and nurturing. Are you a Virgo by any chance?' Valerie wasn't, but that didn't appear to remotely detract from her enjoyment of the moment.

'Well then,' Valerie said, her voice now positively oozing warmth and nurturing, 'everyone for risotto?'

'I'm feeling a bit sick, actually,' said Ruth. 'Is everyone else feeling all right, or is it just me? Jean?'

When the moment arrived for coffee, Tony led a breakaway group consisting of all the men and Belinda, to watch the football highlights in the study. It turned out that Belinda was a passionate Arsenal fan.

'And, don't tell me,' Jean said, the minute they were out of earshot, 'she simply has to have sex twice a day or she goes stark raving mad.'

'Was it awful?' asked Valerie anxiously. 'I have to confess I thought she was rather interesting . . . about the pale with pale rule, and the thing about lining up the carpet underlay.'

'Oh, Val!' Ruth sank her head in her hands. 'It wasn't her so much – she's just a detail in Tony's ongoing mid-life crisis – it was the principle of it. Why should we have to tolerate some tit-taped, half-wit at this stage of our lives? I mean, we've done our time, thanks. We've gone out with the idiots, hung out with the losers, edited it down to the people we really care about – and all for this to happen. Did you see Dave's face?' Ruth lifted her eyes to meet theirs. 'He was glowing. He had exactly the same expression he had when he won the bowling championships.'

'Well, it was never going to be easy, was it?' Valerie said, rhythmically scraping crumbs off the table onto a side plate. 'Calvados, Jean? Another coffee maybe?'

Jean shook her head, tipped back her chin and exhaled another chain of perfect smoke rings.

'It's just depressing,' muttered Ruth, tugging at her

fringe. 'I mean, to have actual confirmation that men genuinely can't tell the difference between a Belinda and a Jean – that's what I can't take. You know, you think, "Oh, well, they might not show that they appreciate us, but of course they do really. They know they'd rather be married to women like us, and not those girls with fake tits and a size-six figure, because they're not snotty twelve-year-old boys." You picture them, don't you, sitting on the tube on the way to work, drifting off for a moment, remembering all the little things you've done that week, without prompting or complaint, to make their lives that bit easier? All the things about your character that make you special? And you imagine them thinking, "How lucky I am to have that wonderful, unique woman for a wife."' Ruth reached across the table for the wine. 'But that's not how it works, is it?'

'Well, it could have been worse,' murmured Jean. 'We could have liked her, and that would have been really awkward.'

'I think you're very cool,' said Ruth. 'I'm proud of you.'

'Oh, darling, I'm far from cool.' Jean raised one of her thin, effortful smiles. 'I've told Tony that if she so much as touches the dogs he will have my lawyers to deal with. Anyway,' she swivelled her legs in Anna's direction, flicking some spilt ash off the thigh of her leather trousers, 'how was the romantic weekend? What a setting for it. You must have been in heaven.'

'Yes, it was lovely,' Anna said hesitantly.

'Oh?' Jean let the cigarette rest against her cheekbone. 'You mean Daniel wasn't quite as wonderful as you'd remembered?'

'No, Danny was lovely. I just wish—' Anna started rubbing at the rim of her glass. 'It's not very happy, the situation down there, and I'm afraid that rather colours everything else.'

Jean cocked an eyebrow in Ruth and Valerie's direction. 'So what's the problem, darling? You've unearthed some skeleton in the Tyntallin closet?'

'You remember when I started on the book, and I was looking for the unreconstructed husband who demanded to be obeyed in all things, even if it meant bludgeoning his wife into submission?' Anna's jaw hardened. 'Well, I've found him.'

'Tynt?' said Jean.

'The one with the fabulous house?' Valerie reached for her spectacles on the dresser.

'I knew it the second I laid eyes on him. He's the original die-hard misogynist; the kind you could only find being nurtured . . . celebrated even, in the depths of the English countryside.'

'Really?' Jean made a pained face but let her eyes stray briefly in Valerie's direction. 'So what ghastly crimes are we talking about?'

'He's arrogant beyond belief, dictatorial and selfish. He's made his wife give up her work. He expects her to cope with all these staff and his children and the running of the house as if it were second nature. And he isn't there himself, half the time.'

'Sounds like business as usual,' murmured Jean.

'And he hits her.' Anna's eyes darted round the table, defying each of them in turn to question this statement. 'He's a bully,' she added, more hesitantly. 'You've no idea what she has to put up with.'

'My goodness.' Valerie put a hand to her throat. 'Anna, should you be getting involved in something like that? Jean? Ruth? Should she be there at all if there are those sorts of problems?'

'I would walk away,' said Anna, 'but I'm Lily Tyntallin's only link with the outside world. And I think I can help just by being there – by letting him know there's someone who's got his number, and reminding her that she's got a choice. I feel as though I've been chosen, somehow.'

'And now there's Danny to keep you there,' said Jean, narrowing her eyes against her cigarette smoke.

'Exactly. It's where I want to be now, for better or worse.'

When the football highlights were over, Tony wandered back downstairs to persuade the kitchen party to join them in the drawing room.

'Archie's opened some stickies,' he said, rubbing his hands together. 'We were wondering if we could tempt you.'

Ruth yawned and pushed back her chair. 'That's our cue to leave, I'm afraid. Anna? Would you give me a hand getting Billy in the car?'

As the two of them headed upstairs, Tony put a hand on Jean's arm and drew her to one side.

'D'you want a lift, Jean?'

Jean swept her hair out of her eyes and fixed him with the look she'd been trying to give him throughout dinner. 'Me in the back and you and your girlfriend in the front? I think I might pass on that, thanks, Tony.'

She sidestepped him and crossed the floor to the Aga, swivelled round and leant back against the metal rail. 'You know it's your turn for the dogs this weekend?'

'Aaaah.' Tony winced. 'Is it really?'

'Yup. And I'm away.'

'Ah. Right. Jean, uh. I've got a bit of a problem. The thing is, I've made a prior arrangement, a foreign arrangement. One involving aeroplane tickets and hire cars and hotel bookings.' Tony's head bobbed from side to side like a metronome as he itemized the obstacles to cancellation. 'Unfortunately it just can't be got out of.'

Jean crossed her arms. 'You booked a holiday?' she said, incredulous. 'Why?'

'I had no choice,' moaned Tony. 'It's Belinda's birthday on Friday, which wouldn't have been quite such an issue if I hadn't screwed up on Valentine's Day. But . . . well, you know what it's like these days.' He looked pleadingly at his ex-wife. 'Birthdays, anniversaries, they're all so terribly important now. They actually expect you to take the day off, and if it happens to coincide with a weekend then that's a guaranteed trip abroad with all the trimmings.'

'Really,' said Jean.

'Tell you what.' Tony took a deep breath. 'You can have the dogs for the whole of Christmas if you take them this weekend. Christmas Eve until the day after Boxing Day – how's that?'

'Done,' Jean said.

'Right.' Tony tweaked the collar of his shirt back into its slightly raised position and thrust his hands into the pockets of his starched Levis. 'Look, Jean, while we're at it, I've been meaning to ask you a favour.' He hesitated. 'It's about Mummy.'

Jean's face softened. Tony's mother, Elsie, was eighty-one and still lived, despite her son's protestations and offers of service flats in Knightsbridge, around the corner from the house in Acton where Tony was brought up. She was five foot four, wore her snow-white hair in coiled rings kept in place with kirby grips, and had such pronounced bow legs, and the rolling gait to go with them, that she was known to all who loved her as Chimpy. Apart from Tony, that is. Ever since drama school, he had referred to her as Mummy, an affectation that never ceased to delight her. And, though he wasn't as eager as he might have been to ask her to functions and introduce her to his glamorous friends, Elsie was the person Tony most adored in the world.

Even so, it had taken him three months to mention Elsie's existence to Jean, and it wasn't until he had proposed, and Jean had accepted, that Tony finally agreed to take her home to meet his mother. It was a winter afternoon, Jean remembered. They arrived at the house and rang the doorbell, Tony made the necessary introductions and then announced he would wait outside in the street, his excuse being that it was a risk to leave his car unattended.

'Poor Tony,' Elsie said, tweaking the net curtain to one side and peering out at her son, grinding his heel into yet another cigarette butt, 'he thinks I might put you off.' She let the curtain fall back into place and fixed Jean with her beady brown eyes. 'But I can see he's no need to worry on that score. He's got something a bit special in you, hasn't he?'

Jean was not put off. She stayed late into the afternoon, perched on a chair by the gas fire, balancing a cup of tea on her knee and a gold embossed photograph album dedicated to Tony.

'Oh, he was always fancy,' Elsie said, identifying the pictures upside down from her seat on the opposite side of the fire. 'He just wanted better for himself really, I saw that.' She gestured with a custard cream in the direction of a picture of Tony, aged about fifteen, wearing a burgundy silk cravat and a Panama. 'Course, it drove his poor father demented, God rest his soul. A man doesn't like his son to have airs in that way, makes him feel nervous.' Elsie crammed the last quarter of biscuit into her mouth and sat for a moment dabbing at the crumbs on her lower lip. 'If I'm honest,' she said eventually, 'I miss seeing him that bit more, but, then again, I know that's the penalty of success. I say to Alice, my sister, "We get to watch him on the TV and he always phones on birthdays, and that's more than a lot of mothers can say." You don't mind, do you, in the end, so long as they're happy?' Elsie had blinked and smiled fondly at the upside-down album.

Tony stood in front of the Aga, arms folded, gazing down at his shoes.

'They've found a, er . . .' he waved his hand in the vague direction of his navel, 'blockage . . . of some sort. They want to go in and have a look. Probably isn't anything to worry about. And she's very chipper about the whole thing, but I . . . I'm not at my best around hospitals, as you know.'

'Of course I'll be there,' Jean said.

Tony looked up and smiled with relief. 'Terrific. It's all set for Monday week. I'll pick you up.'

'Anything I should know in the meantime?' Jean asked, gripping her hair at the base of her neck, revealing the smooth sculptural shape of her head and the way the cheekbones formed a swollen ridge, like the lip of a jug. 'Apart from the fact that we're still happily married?'

'Not really. I might have given her the impression I was up for young Jolian in *The Forsyte Saga*, but there's no reason why that should come up. Thanks, anyway, Jean. You're . . .' Tony paused.

'A brick?' Jean volunteered.

'Yes.' Tony nodded slowly as if weighing up the merits of this description. 'Anyway, Belinda's got one of those early morning calls, so we'd better be off. You're sure you don't want a lift?'

'Quite sure.'

'Right. Good.' Tony started body searching himself for the car keys. 'You think it went all right then?'

'You're asking me?'

'Yes. She went down well, don't you think? Valerie seemed to get on with her like a house on fire. And Ruth, actually.'

'I'm sure you're right,' said Jean.

'She's got four A levels, you know. I only mention it because most people assume she has no qualifications.' Tony lowered his voice. 'Earns a fortune. Absolute *fortune*. They all do. Anyway. Better dash.' He bounced the car keys in his palm. 'Hope we can all do it again soon.'

*

After Tony had left, Jean went upstairs in search of Anna and Ruth and found them both on the spare-room bed – Billy lying spreadeagled between them, pink and sticky-haired in his Thomas the Tank Engine pyjamas.

'I think there's room for a chapter on divorcee etiquette in your book,' Jean said, flopping against the door frame, a whisky glass hugged to her shoulder. 'Only one's ex-husband has the potential to make you feel like an old maid. Am I interrupting? You both have that look.'

'You're not interrupting,' Ruth said, examining her nails. 'I was just asking Anna's advice.'

Jean's gaze drifted in Anna's direction and Anna stared back, eyes widened in warning. 'I think I might be about to have an affair,' Ruth said, still focusing on her nails, so that she didn't see Jean glance across to the sleeping bundle on the bed, or the tight V of anxiety embedded at the bridge of Anna's nose. 'Nothing's actually happened,' she continued, her voice flat and lifeless, like the voice of someone who desperately needed to sleep. 'It's weird, because I don't really want it to. And yet, I like the thought of having the possibility . . . there in the background. It makes me feel alive.'

Ruth lifted her eyes to meet Jean's. She looked sheepish and confused but at the same time something else. Defiant was too strong a word for it. Decided, maybe. It was only now Jean noticed that Ruth's hair, which had been some unnatural shade of purplish-brown for as long as she had known her, was an even tone of silky brunette. The usual cat's cradle of jewellery had been edited down to a single silver pendant, and in place of the ubiquitous lace-trimmed, on-view vest, was a good two inches of well-supported plump cleavage.

'Who is he?' asked Jean

'Someone at work.' Ruth shrugged. 'I know, I know. It's not me at all. But I feel as though I don't want to be me, just for a bit. I need to get away from being the mother, the wife, the reliable friend, the good daughter. Don't you ever feel that? Like you've signed it all away, for the sake of being this person you don't even know?' Ruth sat up suddenly and put her head in her hands, pressing the heels of her palms into her eye sockets. 'Oh God. This is middle age, isn't it? This is the reason for mother's little helpers, and nips of sherry behind the curtains.'

Jean and Anna exchanged rapid glances. Jean mouthed the words, 'Your call,' and Anna shook her head. 'You,' she mouthed back, 'you know.'

'What do you want us to do, Ruth?' Anna asked.

Ruth flopped back on the bed and gazed up at the ceiling. 'Tell me I can get away with it, just this once, and it might even do me good. Tell me it's normal to love your husband and want something more as well.' Her eyes slithered sideways and settled on Jean, still standing in the doorway. 'Tell me not to do it because it'll ruin my marriage.'

'Don't do it, it'll ruin your marriage,' Jean said. 'Men can't cope with infidelity as a rule. That's a woman's game.'

They both turned to look at her as alert as cats in a fish shop. This conversation had been three years coming and Ruth's predicament could wait a little longer.

'My situation was very different, of course,' Jean

said, hastily. 'You couldn't compare it, really. Apart from the fact that I was unhappy.'

Jean took a deep breath and crossed over to the window where she stood, her back turned to the bed, gripping her glass to her chest. She'd never really spoken about what happened. She'd never seen any reason to. But now, because they thought she was the expert, the only one among them with the relevant experience to draw on, it seemed she had no choice.

'Tony had had a couple of affairs, as you know,' Jean said quietly, gazing out onto the empty street. 'I knew they didn't mean anything, I suppose. But knowing something and feeling it are two very different things. My confidence was destroyed. I didn't even realize to what extent. All I knew was there came a point when I couldn't remember how I liked my coffee. I wasn't sure, any more, who I was meant to be.'

Whenever Jean thought back to those last days of her marriage she remembered not the scenes, or the long, wakeful nights; not the girl who came to the mews and hammered on the door demanding to see Tony; nor the pills she had become accustomed to taking before going anywhere in public. What she remembered was sitting alone on that coral-coloured sofa, watching the television and registering nothing. Sitting there, not having the energy to draw the curtains or turn on the lamps, helpless to alter her fate.

'I felt I had to do something,' Jean said. 'I had to prove that I could.'

'With the tennis instructor?' Ruth asked

'Yes. With the tennis instructor.'

'And if Tony hadn't found out? Would it have been worth it?'

'Oh, I wanted Tony to find out.' Jean swivelled round to face them. 'I wanted him to feel mad with jealousy. I imagined how he'd refuse to let me out of his sight, cancel all his plans, take me away and woo me all over again. I pictured the presents in velvet boxes, the two of us curled up in the shop with the dogs and a bottle of champagne, planning our love-saturated future. But that wasn't how it happened.' She smoothed her hair carefully off her face, her eyes focused on something very far away. 'You see, to him what he'd done was just harmless, meaningless, fun, whereas what I'd done was the ultimate betrayal.'

Tony was sitting in the dark, slightly the worse for drink, when she'd got back that evening. He flicked on a lamp and sneered with disbelief at the sight of her in her white pleated skirt and brand-new tennis shoes.

'What exactly are you playing at?' he said.

'Nothing,' she replied. 'I've been having a tennis lesson.'

Jean remembered his incredulous expression, how he had cocked an ear in her direction, like some ancient professor stretched to the limit of his tolerance. 'Do you think I'm a complete, idiot?' he asked, rising from his chair. 'For one thing, it's dark. For another, I saw you and your so called tennis coach *snuggled up* on the bench in the square, as I'm sure did most of our neighbours. God save us, Jean. Some hairy Antipodean teenager. Have you no dignity?'

'How can you say that to me?' she said. 'After every-thing I've had to put up with.'

'Everything you've had to put up with?' Tony repeated. 'Ah. Now we're getting to the truth. Now I see what this is all about.'

'What do you mean?'

'I knew it was only a matter of time. I knew, even if you said it didn't make any difference, you could never settle for less than perfect. Why should the golden girl have to make do?' Tony's voice was a whining imitation of a petulant rich girl's. He was standing in front of her, thrusting his face towards hers.

'Is that what you really think?' she said.

'You're my wife! And you're making a bloody fool of me in front of everyone.'

'Tony, you know this has nothing to do wi—'

'I want to give you a bloody baby!' Tony wailed. His mouth buckled, his hands rubbed up and down the thighs of his trousers as he sucked back the tears. 'Jesus Christ, Jean. Jesus Christ. How do you think that makes me feel, knowing he could give you that? Knowing that two-bit tennis bum could give you the one thing I should be able to give you . . . the only thing I ever . . . Jesus Christ, Jean, you might as well have taken a knife and stabbed me in the heart.'

'He'd made up his mind,' said Jean, downing the last of the whisky in her glass. 'It was as simple as that. There was no reasoning with him.'

'Couldn't you have explained you were just trying to get his attention?' Ruth asked.

'He was so convinced, I just didn't have the strength. I didn't even bother to tell him that we never got further than a fumble in the pavilion.'

'Nothing happened?' Anna gasped. 'Nothing happened and you never told him? But that's terrible!'

'He wouldn't have believed me, so what was the point?' Jean adjusted the collar of her white shirt, scooping her hand up under her chin as if arranging tissue paper around the neck of a bottle. 'The funny thing is, the tennis instructor teaches at our local school now, and do you know what they call him?'

Ruth and Anna shook their heads in unison like rapt children at a magic show.

'Gay Graham. He lives with his boyfriend in Maida Vale.' Jean hesitated. 'I would have told you all this before, but there just didn't seem much point. Whatever way you look at it we made a mess of our marriage; who did what, exactly, didn't seem to matter very much.'

Ruth was examining her nails again, applying the lessons of this story to her own situation, though Jean could see from the set of her jaw that her mind was already made up. They were having this conversation, as one always had these conversations, when it was already too late for it to affect the outcome. Ruth had asked for their advice, but what she was really asking for was their forgiveness.

'I don't want to sleep with Tim,' Ruth said, quietly. 'I just want to be taken out to dinner and kissed and adored and sent passionate text messages and watched across a room. I want to have someone to dress up for and to think about . . . who I know is thinking about me.' She shook her head. 'Sorry,' she said, 'I realize I sound like a stupid adolescent.'

'Well,' said Jean, drily, 'pity Gay Graham's off the scene. Sounds like he might have been just the ticket.'

Archie placed his bookmark between the pages of his thriller and glanced at the clock on the bedside table. Valerie had been in the bathroom for almost twenty minutes, where he imagined, judging from the low murmurs escaping under the door, she was talking into that Dictaphone of hers. He smoothed out the turned-down sheet, removed his spectacles and cleared his throat.

'Val darling?' Archie waited and then raised his voice slightly. 'Lovely party, sweetheart. I thought Belinda took a real shine to you.'

Beyond the bathroom door there was the sound of banging cabinet doors, the chink of glass on tile, and then Valerie emerged, tightening the belt of her dressing gown, one hand hovering over a rectangular bulge in the left pocket.

'Everything all right?' asked Archie, focusing deliberately on his wife's face as she crossed the floor towards the bed. Valerie had taken to wearing a hair band at night and a thing like a gum shield which was supposed to lift the colour of her teeth from a regular white to the fluorescent, Britney Spears kind.

'You're not taking on too much, are you, my love?' Archie asked, as she walked round to her side of the bed, unwrapped the dressing gown and draped it over a chair. 'D'you know,' Archie folded his arms and squinted up at the ceiling, as if a thought had just occurred to him, 'the other day, when I had my session with Anna, we were talking about how busy our lives seem to have become, and I couldn't honestly remember the last time we—'

'We what?' Valerie snapped

'Well, had dinner together, or just sat down and talked. Anna always asks those questions, doesn't she? And sometimes it makes you think.'

'Oh, Archie.' Valerie yanked back the bedclothes and glared at him across the snowy expanse of sheet. 'I've got a hundred and one things going on in my life, the last thing I need is you nagging me for more attention. Anyway –' she sat down on the edge of the bed, swinging her legs up slowly so as not to disturb the line of her linen nightgown '– as it happens we are going to be required to do quite a bit of talking in the very near future. You're going to need to take some time off work.'

'Really? I thought Anna preferred us on our own at this stage?' Archie folded his hands in preparation for his wife's explanation of this new development. He was surprised, because generally there was nothing that gave her more pleasure than their involvement in Anna's book, but there was a severity about her mouth that suggested she was far from happy.

'Not for *Anna*.' Valerie sucked in a long, deep breath. 'Charlotte's psychiatrist, Marion. She wants to see us both, together. Apparently –' Valerie reached for a tube of hand cream on the bedside table '– apparently, Lottie's problem may have something to do with . . . sexual anxiety. Our fourteen-year-old daughter is, according to the professionals, "deeply distrustful of sexual relationships". Those were the exact words.'

Valerie was kneading her hands together now, working the cream into the knuckles, knitting her fingers and sliding the greased palms from side to side. 'I mean, of all the possible problems, they would have to come up with something like that, wouldn't they? It couldn't be the fact that she's too bright for her years, or shyer than a lot of the girls, or frightened of the responsibilities of growing up, in general. It had to be something . . .' Valerie drew her lips tight against her teeth and gave a little shiver of contempt.

Archie watched his wife for a moment, waiting for the beating of his heart to subside a little. 'Well,' he said, 'I imagine they have their reasons.'

Valerie swivelled her head sharply in his direction. 'Is that all you can say? Don't you realize what this will involve? You and I discussing . . . being cross-examined about the most intimate details of our lives by some . . . I can't think of anything more grotesque. It's horrible.'

Archie nodded and waited. His expression was resigned, sympathetic, but inside him a voice was singing, Thank you, God. 'We'll just have to put a brave face on it, my darling,' he said, after a suitable interval. 'If there's a possibility, however remote, that it could make a difference to Charlotte's recovery, we have to show willing.'

'I know that. I know that.' Valerie's voice was cracked. 'I want to do whatever we can. But why should this, of all things, be anyone else's business?'

Archie reached out to his wife and, to his surprise, she let him rest a hand on her forearm. 'Well, it wouldn't be their business, if it weren't for Lottie's situation. And it is voluntary after all. No one's making us.'

Valerie forced a nod. Her eyes were tense with concentration and she seemed not to notice when Archie
moved his hand down her arm, took her fingers in his
and squeezed them tightly.

'What will they expect from us?' she whispered.
'What will they want?'

'Val . . . whatever we can manage, my darling. It
isn't a test.'

Her eyes flickered and Archie saw them drift and
come to rest on the photograph frame on his dressing
table. The picture in the frame was eighteen years old. It
was of the two of them on their honeymoon, leaning up
against a cannon somewhere in France. He had his arm
tight around her waist and she was laughing, her hand
cupping his, her head tilted sideways so that he could
nestle his chin easily against her shoulder.

'I'm not sure that I can do it,' Valerie said. 'I can't
just change because some . . . social worker tells me to.'

'I know, darling. You can only give it a try, for
Charlotte's sake. It doesn't matter to me. I love you just
the way you are.'

Not so long ago, Archie thought, that would have
been more or less true. But gradually, since he'd been
sharing the details of their lives with Anna, the lack of
physical contact had started to seem more significant.
And now he found it was the pretence that everything
was normal that he minded more than anything. Valerie
shifted in the bed, sliding her hand from under his on
the pretext of adjusting her pillow. The embroidered
border around the neck of her nightdress reminded him
of a scarf she'd worn on their honeymoon, tied as a
bandeau top. She would stand by the mirror in the room

of their hotel, trying it this way and that, letting it fall to her hips, exposing her bare breasts. Lately, it seemed to Archie that he might never see his wife's naked body again.

'Why do you think a woman stops wanting to have sex?' he'd asked Anna at their last session, and she had looked momentarily surprised before politely suggesting that he should address that question to his wife. 'I have tried,' he'd explained. 'All she'll say is "The shutters come down, I can't help it." But that doesn't really answer the question, does it?' Anna had then tried to reassure him that most couples experienced these lulls, and afterwards they had stared at each other in silence, both of them conscious that Archie was not the sort of man to complain about a lull, or even a relatively long drought. 'I could recommend someone,' Anna said, eventually. 'If that's what you think you need. But then, Archie, how would you ever get Valerie to go?'

Archie leant across the bed and gently kissed the top of his wife's arm, prompting her to brush the spot with her hand, as if swatting away an insect.

'I'm ready whenever you are, my love,' he said, placing his spectacles and his book on the bedside table and sliding down between the sheets. 'We'll get through this, however hard it is for both of us.'

But after Valerie had turned out the bedside light, he lay there on his back in the dark, grinning up at the ceiling.

As soon as Ruth pulled the VW up outside Anna's flat, Dave leapt out and insisted on escorting Anna to her front door, even though it was a matter of a few yards and every other time they'd given Anna a lift home he'd settled for a wave through the window. Ruth leant across the bench seat and watched the two of them, standing at the bottom of the steps to Anna's building: Dave, palms raised to the night sky; Anna, still and upright as a mannequin. She gave them a minute, then pressed the horn, sat back and waited.

'Oi!' Dave flung open the door of the van and jumped up into the passenger seat. 'What's up with you?'

'I thought Anna needed rescuing. The campaign for reinstating Richard is getting a bit out of hand.'

'Ah . . . Good. Something new for you to be really angry with me about. I wonder if this one will supplant the "rage at Dave's inability to telepathically pick up on my desire to go to the Cuban jazz concert"?' Dave lingered on the words Cuban and jazz with an air of intrigue, as if he'd never had reason to use them before. 'Or maybe it's good enough to overtake, "rage at Dave's decision to decorate the bathroom".'

Dave thrust his head forward as if trying to catch something she might have said. Ruth tried to ignore him.

'The bathroom one is my particular favourite, of course,' he continued, settling back against the seat as Ruth swung the van out into the road. 'What with you having been complaining about the condition of the bathroom since a few months into our marriage. So, naturally, it makes perfect sense that when I decide to do something about the bathroom, you go ballistic.'

'It's just typical, that's all,' Ruth said, regretting the words as soon as they left her mouth, amazed that she was allowing herself to be drawn into another alcohol-lubricated, early morning argument that had nothing to do with what was really on their minds.

Dave, however, was as eager as a dog presented with a stick. He cocked his head, glancing in vain around the van for some witness to this reason-defying moment.

'Typical? And how exactly do you work that one out?'

Ruth looked at him, hesitating just long enough for them both to register the small step into the danger zone.

'Because it's taken you years,' she said, 'and then you get some dodgy Australians to do the work, because you're too tight to do it properly. Because you're going to make a bloody horrible mess, and it'll be this great lark which will take weeks and weeks—'

'It's going to be *great*! What is wrong with you? It's going to be a nautical-themed bathroom like you've always wanted. Tongue and grooooove.'

'I want *more*.'

There was silence in the place where he should have said, 'More of what? More, how do you mean more?' They stared at each other.

'I was in the butcher's today,' Ruth said. 'And there was a woman in there with two little girls, in one of those double prams. And she had this lovely suede handbag and this great, glossy haircut and she was brown and just . . . she wasn't smart or anything but she looked good. And she was ordering this big pie to be delivered for some dinner she was having. And then her mobile rang and she was laughing and whispering into it, and the man on the other end wanted to come and pick her up, so she didn't have to walk home, but she said she didn't mind because it was such a beautiful day and . . .' Ruth stopped. She swallowed. 'She was about my age, and it felt like watching another species.'

'She was *rich*,' Dave said, eyes casting about in disbelief. 'What man picks his wife up from the butcher's in the middle of a weekday apart from someone who is *loaded*?'

'Maybe she was, but it wasn't that. It was the way she was still *her*, with this bag that hadn't been chosen just for its durability and how much baby equipment it could take, and the way she felt about herself . . . She was still a woman, first, despite the two little girls and the chores, and the man who wanted to pick her up knew that. He valued her for that.'

'And I don't value you? Is that what you're saying?'

'I know you do, in a way. But we don't have that . . . you don't think of me like that.'

Dave snorted and swivelled round so he was facing straight ahead, arms folded across his chest.

'You're going to have to be more specific, Ruth,' he said. 'Because I'm getting to the point where all this is starting to sound like bullshit. I'm not interested in some woman in the butcher's, I want to know what's going on with *you*.' Ruth could feel his eyes scanning her profile, alert for any flicker of anxiety or guilt. He waited, the folded arms rising and falling on his chest. 'Actually, I was asking Anna about you back there,' he said. 'I told her you wouldn't talk to me any more. I wanted to know if she had any idea what was going on. She said I should ask you, of course.'

Ruth turned to look at him. His eyes were drooping at the corners, there was a tiny piece of twig embedded in his hair that must have fallen from the trees outside Anna's house. She felt a sudden urge to stroke his woolly head and tell him it would be all right, but at the same time she knew it was too late for that.

'Remember the lists?' Ruth asked. 'At the beginning, when Anna asked us both to put down the reasons why we'd wanted to get married?' Dave nodded. 'Well, a couple of weeks ago I did another one' – their eyes met – 'of the things that have changed, for me since then.'

'She asked you to do that?'

'I told her I wasn't . . .' Ruth fished for a word, any word other than happy. 'I thought it might help to . . . clarify what I'm feeling.' Dave shook his head slowly. 'It isn't what you think,' Ruth said. 'I'm not carried away because of the book. It's very common at our stage, to have these . . . thoughts. To have different needs.'

'Yeah, if you're encouraged to analyse every shagging aspect of your life, every nuance of your relationship, day after day for three solid years. You never even used to think about your *needs*, Ruth. It was us and Billy. Us. And Billy. That's all you wanted before that sodding book.'

'You can't blame Anna,' she said. 'It's not as though it's so unusual for people who have been married for a while to feel . . .' she gripped the steering wheel.

'In a rut?' Dave said. 'Limited, trapped, incarcerated?'

'Shall I tell you what was on the list?' she asked.

'Why not? Go on, make my day.'

'It's all small stuff.'

'Is it really?'

'Dave—'

'No, no. Go ahead. I'm all ears. We used to be able

to talk, but if reciting lists you compiled for Anna is all that's on offer, that'll have to do.'

'All right.' Ruth hesitated. 'Well. I'd like you to show me more respect, notice the things I like, and the things I'm good at. I'd like you to show some interest in my singing instead of making a joke of it.' She took a deep breath. Out of the corner of her eye she saw Dave's cheeks hollowing as he sucked his lips into a figure of eight. 'I need you to listen to me, not assume that you know what I want, and what I think, just because you have done in the past. I want you to show me care and consideration, not think of me like some old pal who's no different from you. You know when you always say, "Don't worry about Roo?" Well, now I want you to worry. Or, at least . . . to treat me like a woman.' She waited.

'That's the lot?' asked Dave.

'More or less.'

They were turning into their street and, for once, there was a space right outside their flat. Normally this would have been a cause for celebration – Dave would have drummed his fingers on the dashboard and adapt-ed some football chant to the occasion – but this time he wasn't watching the road.

'Don't look at me as if I've disappointed you, Dave, I never promised you I wouldn't grow up,' Ruth said.

'Oh! So this is growing up?'

'What was I wearing last night, Dave?'

'I refuse to answer that question.'

'Or the night before. Or at the Cunninghams' party? When did we last have a dance?'

'I'm not doing this.' Dave folded his arms tighter.

'This is undignified. This is bollocks. This is Anna book crap.'

'You don't know, Dave, that's my point, you don't notice that part of me. You've forgotten it and I've forgotten it and I miss it.' Ruth lined up the van in front of the space and twisted around, preparing to reverse.

'Right,' Dave said. 'So if I start respecting your singing and noticing your underwear, you won't bother having the affair. Is that it? Only there's not much point in me turning into Richard if you can have the real thing.'

'It isn't Richard,' Ruth said, and held her breath. There were so many ways she might have confirmed his fears, she would never have imagined three careless words could have managed it so conclusively. There was absolute stillness in the van as she turned the wheel, straining to see behind her, going through the motions automatically, in spite of the voices crowding her head: the things she should say, the things she mustn't say.

'It's no one,' Ruth said, whole seconds too late.

Dave was watching her, not searching for clues any more; adjusting.

She tried again. 'Nothing's going on,' but what was meant to sound dismissive came out as a self-pitying whine.

Dave flinched, his head retreating a fraction as if he'd just been hit in the face by a sulphurous smell. 'Don't, Ruth,' he said and yanked on the handle of the door and stepped down into the street.

Twelve

When Anna arrived at Tyntallin station on the Thursday there was no sign of Lily's red sports car, only a man in an anorak who announced he was from the local cab company and had been booked to meet her train.

'Down for the weekend?' he asked, peering into the rear-view mirror as he drove.

'Maybe longer,' Anna replied, smiling back at him. 'We'll have to see.'

'Ah, well. Weather forecast's good, they say.' The driver paused while he negotiated a junction, feeding the steering wheel through his hands laboriously, twisting his head to left and right and back before he executed the turn. 'I should think that'd be a lovely place when the sun's out.'

Anna nodded in acknowledgement, before turning her head to look out of the window at the passing hedgerows and the fields starting to blur in the milky evening light. She thought of Danny in the studio nearby, hunched over his guitar, earphones slung around his neck, chin easing forward as he stretched out a chord. The band were in the middle of recording now, working through the night more often than not, so when she'd spoken to him on the phone, the evening before, and heard his voice husky and dragging with exhaustion, she had offered to postpone her visit.

'It doesn't sound like you're getting back to the cottage much anyway,' she'd said, trying to sound relaxed, easy going. 'It's probably better if we leave it for a bit.' Anna smiled now as she remembered the black, deep silence on the end of the line and then the sudden change in atmosphere, the catch in his voice as he came up with the idea of her inviting herself to Tyntallin.

'That way you'd be looked after, I wouldn't have to worry about leaving you on your own,' he'd said, all the tiredness gone from his voice. 'And then, when I get the breaks . . . if I get the breaks . . . I'll know you're there, waiting for me.'

'I'm not sure,' Anna had said. 'We'll hardly see each other, and I'll be stuck with that pig of a man.'

'Come on, babe,' he'd murmured, persuasive as ever. 'It's better than nothing, isn't it? And it's only going to be like this for another few weeks, then we can be at the cottage all the time if you like.'

It was the first time Danny had mentioned the possibility of something permanent; the first time he'd acknowledged a future beyond the making of the album. Anna drew her linen coat tighter around her, imagining the little thatched cottage on the edge of the grounds. Their new home. Their very own home.

'What's the cottage like?' she'd asked him.

'Small. Old. It's kind of missing the feminine touch.' In the background she could hear him shifting things around, the click of a boiled kettle, the clunk of a teaspoon against the side of a china mug. 'I miss you,

Anna,' he'd said. 'Just having you nearby would make . . . Maybe it's too much to ask, when I can't promise I'll be able to get away—'

'No, no.' She'd stopped him. 'You're right, it's better than nothing. Of course it is. I'll try and get hold of Lily tonight.' She'd wanted to ask if they could spend just one night alone, whatever happened; she wanted to say, 'I don't care about taking it slowly. I don't care if we have to stay on the floor of the studio. We've found each other again and I don't want to waste any more time.' But the tiredness had crept back into his voice and she knew that, for the sake of his work, for both their sakes, she had to be patient and unselfish. They had time after all.

'Just promise you'll come and get me whenever you can,' she'd said.

The cab had reached that turn in the road where Lily had stopped the sports car on Anna's first visit to Tyntallin. And now the driver slowed almost to a standstill, beckoning with a mottled hand for her to appreciate the pink-streaked sky and a group of roe deer gazing in their direction with a mixture of curiosity and disdain.

'Been 'ere before, 'ave you?' he asked over his shoulder.

'Just once.'

'From America, isn't she?'

'Yes.'

He nodded. 'I 'eard she's made changes.' The driver craned his neck to check her response in the rear-view mirror. 'Spent a lot of money, I 'eard. Put in a meditation room. All sorts of fancy stuff.' The neck stretched another centimetre, revealing a strip of pale skin normally hidden under the rough wool collar and blue knitted tie.

'I'm sure those are just rumours,' Anna said, meeting the driver's eyes just long enough for him to register her disapproval. 'Lady Tyntallin works very hard to fit in and do the right thing.'

The driver made a noise like a tyre deflating. 'I dunno about that,' he said, yanking off the handbrake and moving the car on down the drive. 'She's not one bit like Lady Henrietta, that's for sure. Never comes to church. Never out with the hunt. When the earl's giving one of 'is talks, you'll not see 'er there. Not a chance.' As he spoke he glanced every now and then in the mirror, willing Anna to contribute something to this picture of a spoilt, feckless chatelaine with no sense of loyalty to her husband or home. Anna felt her cheeks flush. She thought of Lily with her wardrobe of unworn dresses, standing at the window of her bedroom watching Tyntallin's Land Rover disappear down the drive.

'Perhaps she isn't made to feel welcome,' Anna said, pointedly. 'I'm sure she would be there, if she felt she was wanted.'

The driver shrugged. 'Praps,' he mumbled. 'Or praps she's got other things to keep 'er occupied. It's a shame though, isnit?' He blinked enquiringly in the mirror, blissfully unaware that his audience had no sympathy for his views or interest in his opinions. 'Lord T wanted a wife to take care of those kiddies, didn't 'e, not to gad about and suit 'erself?'

Anna shifted out of the driver's eye line and turned

her face to the window. They were approaching the house now and she could make out the figure of a man standing at the top of the steps leading to the front door.

'They say 'e was swept away,' the driver continued, nodding his head in the direction of the house. ''E was that desperate to find them a mother and that churned up about Lady Henrietta, 'e just lost 'is 'ead. Didn't even sign a prenap—'

'Prenup,' Anna snapped.

'Thassit.' The driver grinned at her in the mirror. Then the smile fell away and he shook his head resignedly. 'Six weeks 'e knew 'er, before 'e proposed. You're not in your right mind, are you, so soon after something like that? Did you know 'er, Lady Henrietta?'

Anna shook her head, half willing him to stop and at the same time curious to know more about the one part of the story that Lily could not tell her.

'Aah well. She was ill for two years, thereabouts, poor soul. Bedridden for the last six months or more. And 'e wouldn't let them keep 'er at the 'ospital. 'Ad everything she needed brought to the 'ouse.' The driver paused. 'That's a lot for any man to cope with. And then 'e goes an' rushes into this . . . with a young girl.'

'She's twenty-eight,' said Anna.

'That's right.' The driver blinked at her in the mirror. 'Just seems to me 'es not been thinking straight, what with one thing an' another.'

They were drawing up to the front of the house now. Tyntallin was still standing at the top of the steps, one hand thrust in the pocket of his tweed coat, the other fidgeting with the ever-present cigarette. He didn't move to acknowledge their arrival, just raised the cigarette to his lips and continued to gaze out over the park, his eyes narrowed against the setting sun.

'Well, you got Lord T come out to meet you, must be a special guest,' said the driver good naturedly.

'I don't think so,' Anna said, hastily handing over the fare and scrabbling for the door handle. But by the time she had stepped out onto the gravel Tyntallin was already bent over the open boot. He extracted her case in one deft movement, and, with a smart tap on the wing of the cab, sent the driver on his way. Anna stood awkwardly, watching the car as it drove on past the house and then branched off under an avenue of beeches that marked the beginning of the back drive. She knew the cottage lay somewhere at the end of that drive, its mossy walls and thatched roof blending into the surrounding woods. A trail of smoke rising above the trees in the distance made her wonder if Danny had somehow managed to make it back to their sanctuary, and was waiting there now, stoking a fire to get rid of the damp. Could that be possible? She put a hand in her coat pocket and pulled out her mobile, checking the screen for missed calls, even though she already knew there was no signal here.

'Do you have to be somewhere?' Tyntallin asked. 'Or shall we go inside?'

Anna slid the mobile back into her pocket and turned to face him. Tyntallin was staring at her, his expression a mixture of surprise and curiosity, as if he had been expecting an altogether different Anna Emery.

'Unfortunately my wife has not yet returned from her appointments,' he said. 'So I'm afraid you'll have to make do with my company, for the time being.'

Anna tugged her bag flat against her stomach, rapidly calculating whether she could plead a headache and retire to her room, or perhaps pretend that she was expected at the cottage for supper.

'I'm afraid there's no way out,' Tyntallin added, extending an arm towards the front door. 'We dine at eight thirty, perhaps you remember? In the meantime, let me show you to your room.'

'What about the children?' she said, hastily.

'The children?'

'Yes. I've never met them.' Anna hauled nervously on the strap of her bag. 'I'd very much like to. Perhaps they . . .'

'Perhaps they'd like to join us for dinner?' Tyntallin volunteered, an arrow-shaped crease developing at the corner of his mouth. 'And save you the prospect of spending an evening alone in my company? Quick thinking, indeed. Unfortunately, the eldest is eight and the youngest four, and, being a rather old-fashioned household, we tend to have them in bed well before we eat.' The arrow head sharpened to a tight point. 'Nevertheless, you should meet them without delay. So, first stop the nursery, then.'

'I didn't mean . . .' Anna hesitated.

Tyntallin's grey eyes narrowed in on hers, skewering her with a look that made her flush from her cheeks to the roots of her hair, and suddenly Anna was determined to show this man that she was not afraid of him, and certainly not of his children.

'All right,' Anna said. 'If now is a good time, I'd be delighted.'

*

The nursery was at the top of the house, a long, low-ceilinged room with peeling floral wallpaper and a strong smell of plasticine and firewood. When Tyntallin pushed open the door the first thing Anna saw was a giant television screen, lit up and blaring, and, directly in front of it, a small, badly erected tent. Tyntallin crossed the floor, lowered the volume on the television and announced their arrival to the occupants of the tent who emerged, one by one, through the front flap.

First out was a skinny, long-legged girl with lemon-blonde hair that hung down her bare brown back to the top of her pyjama bottoms. This, Tyntallin identified as his eldest daughter, Emily. After Emily came Oscar who looked puzzled at the sound of his own name and adjusted his spectacles on his ginger-freckled nose before volunteering that he was the 'Second oldest. And I've got my own bedroom.' Last to emerge was Maisie, who peered at Anna from under her glossy brown fringe as if she had already severely disappointed her, and then, distracted by something her brother was doing, broke into a smile that engulfed the lower part of her face like the slam of a white clapperboard.

'This is our guest, Anna,' said Tyntallin, watching Anna as he spoke. 'She's been to stay once before, but I daresay you were all locked up in the kennels.' Maisie giggled.

'Is she a teacher?' asked Oscar.

Anna felt the colour rising to her cheeks, she loosened the grip on her bag and tried to relax her face.

'No,' Tyntallin replied. 'She's a spy. Not the sort you have in *Tin Tin*, more like the ones who come to the farm to root around the pig pens.'

Three pairs of eyes swivelled to take in the spy.

'I'm actually a writer,' said Anna, forcing a smile. 'I write books.'

Oscar and Emily looked to their father for confirmation, but he simply continued to watch Anna's still reddening face.

'What happens in your book?' Oscar asked.

Tyntallin tipped his head back and folded his arms in anticipation.

Anna hesitated. 'Well, it isn't really a story, you see.' Oscar stared at her, his expression registering both hope and preparation for disappointment. 'It's more like a book of facts, about people,' she continued, smiling harder and widening her eyes to suggest untold complexities she wasn't able to explain at this precise moment.

'What people?' Oscar demanded, oblivious to her discomfort.

A telephone was ringing in the background. Anna paused, relieved, assuming this would be the natural cue for her and Tyntallin to head back downstairs, leaving the children to play. But Tyntallin was already halfway out of the room, mumbling his apologies.

'You carry on,' he called over his shoulder. 'I'll see you for drinks in the library at eight.'

'What people?' repeated Oscar, his gaze unwavering.

'Married people,' Anna said brightly. Behind Oscar she saw that Emily was studying her over a bare brown shoulder. Oscar absorbed this information, stood his ground for the three or four seconds that courtesy dictated, and then spun around and dived back through the flap of the tent.

'Well,' said Anna, 'this is a lovely nursery, isn't it?'

Maisie lifted her eyes from her Barbie suitcase for a moment and then resumed the tricky task of folding Barbie into the small space that was left alongside the miniature cereal boxes, pausing every now and then to pat down her towelling dressing gown, the sleeves of which were folded up into chunky doughnuts over each wrist. Anna pictured Lily hunkered down on the nursery floor, helping Maisie choose Barbie's outfits like an older sister; someone young and fun to lighten up the children's regimented lives. She took another step into the room and slipped her shoulder bag onto an armchair, her eyes scanning the walls for something they might all talk about.

'Ooh,' she said pointing to the television screen. 'I used to love this cartoon.'

This time Maisie didn't bother to look up; she silently upended the Barbie case and, sweeping her pudgy splayed palms across her forehead, surveyed the contents with a deep frown.

When did it happen, Anna wondered, this fear of being left alone with children? She'd started to notice it a year or so ago, around the time of her thirty-seventh birthday. Quite suddenly she'd become convinced that she was being watched, whenever she was in the company of children; that people she knew, and even people she didn't know, were judging her responses. Old ladies would seem to smile, pityingly, at her self-consciousness. Young mothers would eye her surreptitiously, wondering if she could cope with a child's request for its food to be chopped up, or its coat to be put on. Children she plucked from a tumble, who then automatically reached for their mother's arms, would be hastily apologized for, thereby confirming her as a person who did not have the knack required. And there were the times when she'd be playing with a toddler and look up to catch a friend's half-sad, half-curious expression, as they struggled to comprehend how it would feel to know you were never going to have a child of your own. These days, she thought the children sensed that she was different, too.

'Are you our stepmother's friend?' Anna looked up to see that Emily had retreated to the window seat where she was crouched, watching Anna over the top of her knees.

Anna nodded and lowered herself into the armchair.

'You can get married twice,' Maisie informed them.

'She knows that,' Emily said, keeping her eyes on Anna. 'Did you know our stepmother in America?'

'No, I didn't,' Anna said. And then, because she felt she needed to declare herself, 'I wish I had known her for longer.'

'Have you been in her room?' Emily asked, digging her chin between her knees and flicking Maisie a cautionary look.

'We're not allowed,' said Maisie. 'Not even Daddy is,' she added, pursing her lips in defiance of her sister's hissed threats.

'Shut up! Daddy doesn't even want to go in there!' Emily shouted, kicking out a leg in Maisie's direction and then letting it dangle, the heel tapping rhythmically against the window seat. 'Anyway, we could,' she added. 'It's our house, not hers.'

Anna toyed with the idea of defending the principle of bedroom privacy, but Emily's tapping foot persuaded her otherwise. She smiled brightly and scoured the room again for something to change the subject. 'I bet Lily takes you out for lovely rides,' she said, her eyes lighting on a poster of a grey pony. 'I know she's very fond of horses.'

The girls exchanged looks. 'She's never even taken us for a walk,' said Emily. 'She's always got too high heels on to do anything, and too much make-up, and she's always just lit a cigarette or just made a drink. "Caynt you see I've just poured mahself a lurvely cacktail."'

Emily's imitation of an American accent wasn't much like Lily's, but the droopy hand holding the imaginary cigarette was uncannily similar. Maisie giggled.

'You don't have to stick up for her, by the way,' added Emily, observing Anna's discomfort. 'It's only what we expected. It was Daddy who didn't realize. He's never read any Charlotte Middleton books.' Emily peered at Anna. 'Don't you know about Charlotte Middleton either?'

Without waiting for an answer she bounded across the floor towards the bookshelves and reached up with one hand, gripping the top of her pyjama bottoms with the other.

'There,' she cried, racing back towards the chair and plopping a paperback in Anna's lap. Maisie, meanwhile, had hauled herself up onto the seat and stood on Anna's other side, rocking unsteadily in her sheepskin slippers.

'These are all the ones she's ever done,' explained Emily, running her finger down the previous titles list. *Jill's Miserable Year*, that's the best one about stepmothers, but it's not like us because Jill's parents are divorced. And that one's really good. In that one the father dies because he's an al-co-holic.' Maisie grinned at her sister's daring and eyed Anna nervously. 'But *Sarah's Test* is the actual one that I think could definitely happen. That's when the girlfriend of Sarah's father bewitches him, and he has to do anything she says, including sending Sarah off to this hideous boarding school with damp beds and cruel teachers, and rats.'

Maisie's eyes sought Anna's, her bottom lip wobbled.

'Oh now, that sort of thing doesn't happen in real life,' Anna said. 'And besides, people like your stepmother don't believe in sending children off to boarding school. Americans don't do that sort of thing.'

Emily closed the book and swept her mermaid-blonde hair off her shoulders. 'They do if you remind them of the wife before,' she said. 'Or if they want to have your father all to themselves, so they can start again and pretend you never even happened.'

'What never happened?' bellowed Oscar from inside the tent.

'That's what Mrs Gordon says.' Emily glanced sideways at Anna as if she weren't altogether sure of her information, or how it would be received. 'She said: "She's only interested in one thing and it's not those children." I heard her.'

'Well.' Anna paused. 'You know Mrs Gordon probably just misses your mother . . .'

Emily's face suddenly contorted, as if she'd tasted something exceptionally bitter; her eyes slid in the direction of her little sister who had started tugging at the corner of the book and humming softly to herself. 'You can't say about her in front of Maisie,' she reprimanded

Anna, in the bored tone of a teacher who has given a lesson once too often. 'She'll have dreams now. Anyway, you'd better not talk to us any more if you've got to get ready for dinner. Daddy goes mad if you're late for dinner.'

Dinner was at 8.30 prompt and served in the dining room where the dinner party had taken place, nearly two weeks before. Though the evening was warm, the windows were closed tight shut behind floor-skimming velvet curtains, and there was a small fire flickering in the grate beyond Tyntallin's chair. Anna was half expecting them to be seated one at either end of the table, making an already awkward situation even more uncomfortable. But her place was laid directly to the right of his and, as Mrs Gordon bustled around by the sideboard, eyeing Anna with suspicion, she found herself wishing that they had been separated by eighteen feet of polished mahogany.

'So,' Tyntallin said, watching her over the brim of his wine glass, 'how is the book progressing?'

'Fine, thank you,' she answered, conscious that her tone was clipped to the point of rudeness.

'Cracked the formula, have you, for the successful . . . *relationship*?'

'Not exactly, it's more an exploration of the options,' she said, clamping her hands in her lap and staring at the wall ahead of her. Out of the side of her eye she could see that crease developing again at the corner of Tyntallin's mouth. 'If you don't mind,' she added. 'I'd rather talk about something else.'

'Oh? What a pity.' Tyntallin sat back in his chair, elbows resting on the polished arms, wine glass in hand. 'I was rather hoping you might enlighten me, give me the benefit of your professional insights.'

Anna hesitated, conscious of that lurching in her stomach that she knew so well from the minutes before giving a reading, or a talk to publicize one of her books. 'I don't believe you're genuinely interested,' she heard herself say. 'And even if you were, our ideas of what a relationship involves are so different there wouldn't be any point.'

Tyntallin clasped his glass by the stem and rolled it between his fingers. A bead of red wine hovered on the base threatening to drop at any moment onto the lapel of his cream dinner jacket. 'Is that so?' he said, 'and what would those differences be?'

'I think you know what I mean.'

'I'm afraid I don't. Please . . .' he gestured with a hand the colour of treacle for her to continue. 'Surely you wouldn't shirk the opportunity to educate an emotional pygmy such as myself?'

'All right,' Anna said. 'If you insist. As far as I'm concerned, there has to be respect and equality in any partnership – one person cannot control another person's life.' She eyed him pointedly, before continuing. 'There needs to be kindness, and consideration, and trust. Without those, a relationship becomes a prison.'

Tyntallin raised an eyebrow and leant forward in his chair, a finger pressed to his lips. 'Forgive me,' he said, feigning a puzzled look. 'I understood that the purpose of your visit here was to wait, quietly and obediently, for a man who has already proved himself to be completely untrustworthy and unkind? Or have I misread the situation?'

'You don't know anything about us,' Anna protested, though, to her horror, her voice had shrunk to something small and cracked.

'I know what my wife tells me . . . which is precisely as much as you know about me.'

'I don't have to rely on Lily's information.' Anna glared at him. 'I have seen enough for myself. And I see someone who is cruel and blinkered—' She broke off as she noticed Tyntallin had grown very still and pale, his face tensed as if the light from the candelabra was hurting his eyes. Anna was suddenly conscious of being alone in the house with him, with no car, and no neighbours to run to. 'It isn't for me to judge,' she said quietly, and no sooner had she spoken than Tyntallin's hand came crashing down on the table, making the silver jangle and the candle flames flicker.

'Not judge! Dear God. Isn't that what you do wherever you go? Isn't that why you're here? Because you took a liking to my wife and decided that she needed rescuing? Because you think you have all the answers?' His eyes lifted from his hand and locked onto hers before she had a chance to avoid them. He leant across the table towards her, close enough that she could smell the cigarette smoke on his breath.

'I understand her situation, that's all,' Anna said, reaching for her glass, praying he wouldn't notice how the surface of the wine quivered as she brought it to her lips.

'Ah, of course.' He sat back suddenly in his chair. 'You are very certain of your ground, if I may say so.

Very brave in your defence of someone who you met, oh . . . all of a few weeks ago. Have you ever thought to ask yourself why that might be?'

'Sometimes you feel you can make a difference,' Anna said, hiding behind the wine glass, pressing herself harder into the back of the Chippendale chair.

'Oh, you've made a difference all right,' he said.

They sat in silence as Mrs Gordon appeared to clear away the first course – untouched by either of them – and they were still silent when she returned carrying plates heaped with lamb, the cue for Tyntallin to light another cigarette. He had smoked it halfway down and drunk another full glass of wine before Anna plucked up the courage to speak again.

'I wondered . . .' she hesitated. 'I wondered if that smoke I saw earlier could be coming from Gardener's Cottage?' He gazed at her, unblinking. 'Because, if Daniel was there, for some reason – my boyfriend – then I'd like to go and see him. Only I know there isn't a phone there, and you can't get mobile reception here.'

Tyntallin said nothing for a moment, then he snatched up his knife and fork and started hacking at the food on his plate. 'Tell me,' he demanded, 'why would you have him back?'

She watched him skewer a piece of meat, bite it off the end of the fork and take a slug of red wine, swilling it around in his mouth as he chewed. 'Because love means very different things to you and me,' she said, her cheeks suddenly stinging hot. 'Because love is not about someone conforming to your expectations, and if you really love someone you're not counting the wrongs and rights, you only want them to be happy . . .'

Anna paused. He was watching her again in that strange, half-quizzical way, as if he had mistaken her for someone else, but could not quite place who it was. The look was unsettling: it was as if he knew something about her that she didn't know herself. 'I don't expect you to understand,' she added, lowering her eyes, suddenly conscious of how angry she had become. She heard him lay his knife and fork down and reach for his glass.

'To answer your question,' Tyntallin said, 'the smoke you saw was from one of Mr Greystone's bonfires. I'm sorry to disappoint you. There is no one waiting for you at the cottage. And now, if you'll excuse me, I have matters to attend to.' And with that Tyntallin rose from the table, leaving Anna to the silent reproaches of Mrs Gordon.

That night Anna slept fitfully, dreaming of a cottage with a smoking chimney buried deep in a forest of tangled creepers, and woke damp with sweat, conscious that some sudden noise had roused her. She lay still in the pitch dark of her room, straining her eyes and ears, her body already prepared to confront imminent danger. And then there it was: a series of dull thuds followed by the sound of voices rising in sharp, angry bursts. Anna held her breath. In the corridor outside her room a light flashed on, and a few seconds later she heard the tread of light feet, bare feet, running quickly and softly past her bedroom door, followed by the sound of a door slamming and a key turning in the lock. The footsteps could only have been Lily's, and the door, because of the lock, had to be the bathroom at the end of the corridor. Anna lay there, the sheet clutched under her chin, the sweat now cold on her skin, waiting for she knew not what. And then, after several minutes had passed, she heard the floorboards groan again as Lily crept back along the corridor, this time painfully cautiously, a slow step at a time. She stumbled once, as she passed Anna's door, righting herself with a nudge of a hand or an elbow, and Anna sat up in bed, tempted to go to her and ask if there was anything she could do. But that would have been mortifying for Lily, to know that after all her efforts she had been discovered, fleeing from her bed in the middle of the night.

Long after the light in the corridor had been switched off, Anna lay there in the dark, a dull, sick feeling trickling through her veins as she imagined her friend curled up on her four-poster bed, swollen-eyed and shaking, the lacquer chest she used to keep her old belongings pushed up against the bedroom door.

Thirteen

The following morning Anna was on her way down-stairs to breakfast when she saw that the door to Lily's room was ajar. She called out and Lily answered that she wouldn't be long, but in a faint, uncertain voice that instantly brought back the image of her the night before, cowering in her bed. Instinctively, Anna took her hand off the banister and slowly crossed the landing, suddenly afraid of what she might find behind the bedroom door. She knocked lightly, giving Lily time to pull her dressing gown closed over her bruised collar bone, to roll down the cuffs over her purple knuckles and turn away to shield her puffy eyes. But when she pushed the door open it was the state of the room that caused Anna to gasp.

Lily was standing in the middle of the floor – bare-foot in jeans and vest, her hair pulled back off her scrubbed face – surrounded on all sides by strewn clothes and upended furniture. A vase lay smashed in the fireplace, the broken flowers mingling with loose beads and splayed-open books. The drawers of her cup-boards yawned empty, their contents spewed in clumps over the floor. Even the curtains at the window, great heavy drapes that could have withstood the weight of a small child, hung loose on one side, ripped from their pole.

'Quite a mess, huh?' Lily forced a laugh. 'Not something you really want your guests to see, anyway.'

'What happened?' Anna whispered.

Lily raised her palms to the ceiling, a tight smile stretched across her face. 'Just one of those nights, I guess. You tell me.' She gave a shrug of her bare shoulders, pushed a stray hair out of her eyes and then suddenly the tense composure of her features blurred as if she were being rattled in a drum. Her mouth opened wide, her head listed helplessly to the side, and she started to sob, raw dry sobs that seemed to physically hurt, forcing her lips off her gums and her eyes into tight, black knots.

Anna reached her in a few short steps and gently eased her friend's shaking form on to the end of the bed.

'Oh, God help me,' Lily sobbed. 'God help me.'

'It's OK,' Anna said, although she knew it wasn't.

They sat like that for a while, side by side, Lily leaning into Anna's shoulder, Anna murmuring vague words of comfort and then, bit by bit, Lily told her what had happened.

Tyntallin had been drunk when she got back to the house, late the previous night; drunk and angry. At first she'd tried to defend herself, tried to explain how she'd been driving back from her painting class when she suddenly felt overcome with tiredness, and the next thing she knew she was parked on a verge, looking up at the stars, and it was past midnight. But her excuse only seemed to anger him more. He'd jeered at her, accused her of treating him like a fool, of humiliating him and

plotting against him. 'How have I done that?' she'd
pleaded. 'Please, tell me what you think I've done?' But
he was too angry for explanations. Too angry for anything but name calling. He told her that everyone had
warned him she was a gold digger and that he'd been a
fool not to have seen it himself. He called her a witch,
and an American cow and a liar. He said that he was
going to find out what she was spending his money on,
even if he had to beat it out of her. Then he'd grabbed
her by the arm and dragged her up the stairs and into
her bedroom. Somehow he found her handbag and
tipped out the contents, scrabbling through them, looking for what she didn't know. Then he started ripping
clothes off hangars, dragging things out of drawers,
hurling her precious possessions into the four corners of
the room. 'Look at this place,' he'd shouted at her. 'You
call yourself the Lady of Tyntallin. You're just some
New York upstart who managed to turn my head when
my guard was down. I despise you.'

Lily's eyes flitted anxiously around her as if looking
for some new clue to her husband's behaviour. 'Maybe
the classes were too much,' she croaked. 'I thought one
evening a week would be OK. But it's not what he's used
to. He feels terribly threatened. And then he drinks. And
he's not good with drink when he's stressed. That's when
he starts to get angry with himself, you see . . .'

'Lily,' Anna gripped her friend's hands, forcing her
to look her in the face, 'can't you hear yourself making
excuses for him, even now? For God's sake, can't you
see what's happening here? Listen to me. Did he hurt
you?'

Lily stared at the wall, her face was expressionless.

'He didn't hit me. He—' she lowered her eyes. 'That's how it usually happens. Mostly he isn't interested. Then there's a fight, he gets crazy . . . I used to think it was a guilt thing. A way of getting over the feeling of betraying Henrietta.' She frowned and rubbed at the knee of her jeans, her lip was trembling. 'I'm so sorry to have got you into this, Anna. I'll make it up to you. How can I make it up to you?'

Anna felt Lily's slim cold fingers pressing hard against hers and suddenly she knew what she had to do. 'You know what would help is if you talked to me on tape?' she said. 'Tell me all of it from start to finish.'

'Oh, I couldn't!' Lily snatched her hand away. 'What if Tynt found out? He'd kill . . .'

They both looked at each other. 'It's not going to come to that,' Anna said quietly. 'Nothing will happen because no one else will know. I wouldn't use any of it for the book, it would just be there as a record. Like a diary.'

It would be evidence, Anna was thinking. It would be a detailed account of everything you've suffered, and I would be a witness to it. To all of it.

'I would like to,' Lily said hesitantly. 'I would like to just sort of . . . get it all out.'

Anna nodded. Just do it, please, she thought. Perhaps in the future they could use the tape to force Tyntallin to seek some kind of help. But for now all that mattered was that Anna had some proof of what was happening here, in this house, where there was no one but her to see.

'Maybe it could even help?' Lily's blue eyes searched Anna's face, craving reassurance. 'If you knew all the facts, then you might be able to tell me how to get things back on track. I'm just a little out of my depth here. That's all.'

'That's right,' said Anna, 'it'll make things clearer. I'll go and get the tape recorder now.' As she stood up to go Lily grabbed her arm and smiled up at her bravely. She looked like a child – a tired, trusting, hopeful child. 'I haven't given up, you know,' she said. 'I'm still Lady Tyntallin. I'm still here.'

Later on that afternoon Anna was crossing the front hall, wondering if she might take a walk down the drive in the direction of Gardener's Cottage, when Mrs Gordon appeared in the doorway of the dining room, hands clasped tightly at the waist of her checked blue overall.

'Would you know if Lady Tyntallin is on her way down?' she asked, her voice precise and clear with the hint of a west coast Scottish accent. 'Only Lord Tyntallin was expecting her to pick up the children from school in half an hour.'

Anna hesitated. She had left Lily upstairs sleeping, drained from the night before and from the strain of talking through the events of the past year. 'Lady Tyntallin's resting,' she said decisively, noting the impatient tilt of Mrs Gordon's chin. 'Perhaps someone else could go, just this once. I'd be happy to, if you like. Lady Tyntallin mentioned that I'm insured for the Land Rover.'

Although a solution had been found to the problem Mrs Gordon was evidently dissatisfied with the outcome. She had a pinched, restless look about her as if Anna had somehow wilfully misinterpreted her meaning. 'As you wish,' Mrs Gordon said. 'I was going to suggest a picnic supper by the lake. But if Lady Tyntallin is indisposed . . .' She shot a meaningful glance at Anna, bobbed her head and disappeared back into the dining room.

They had passed the school on the way from the station so Anna knew she would have no trouble finding it. Even so, she was ten minutes late by the time she drew level with the playing fields and, as Anna slowed to turn into the gates, she saw that Emily and Oscar were waiting outside them, squatting on their crayon-coloured rucksacks, scratching with twigs at the gravel under their feet.

'Sorry I'm late,' she called cheerily through the window, and then froze. Oscar had raised his freckled face and was gazing soggy-eyed towards the Land Rover, one small, grubby hand pressing a pair of crushed spectacles to the muddy lapel of his blazer. Heart beating, Anna swung the vehicle across the road, slammed on the handbrake and leapt out, forcing herself to walk rather than run as she approached the huddled pair.

'Oscar? What happened?' she asked gently, crouching down and smoothing out the peaks of his pale red hair.

'He got pushed over,' Emily replied. 'Nobody saw though,' she added, as if this were an unexpected bonus.

Oscar watched his sister spellbound from under

heavy lids, as if only she had the power to interpret what had happened. He took a short juddering breath which made his shoulders shiver inside the too large blazer, and solemnly surveyed the broken spectacles in his hand.

'Who pushed you over?' Anna dabbed ineffectually at the mud on his lapel. 'Didn't anyone do anything?'

Emily shook her head. 'It only happened just now. It was boys in the top form, same as before. First they say, "Your stepmother's a tart", and then when you won't fight they push you.' She looked hard at Oscar, causing a sharp crease to form between her blonde, perfectly arched eyebrows.

'Well, we'll have to tell your father about this,' Anna said and then, noticing that Emily was squinting at her strangely, 'What is it? Is there something else?'

'That's what our mother used to say,' Emily said. 'He knows anyway,' she added, resuming her gravel poking. 'Last time he told us we had to just ignore it. He said, "Some people like to give other people labels and you just have to get used to that." Can we go home now, please?'

At the mention of 'home' Oscar stood up and automatically placed his hand in Anna's, while Emily grabbed both their rucksacks and made for the Land Rover.

Anna watched as they both scrambled into their usual positions on the back seat, slithering under their seat belts and arranging their rucksacks between them like midget paratroopers preparing for a drop. All of a sudden she was conscious of a sharp pressure in her chest and the sight of Oscar, feeling blindly for a pocket on the rucksack to stow his broken spectacles, made her reach across and plant a slow kiss on his forehead. When she closed the door on them, a moment later, Emily was studying her again, from that same sideways angle.

'I'm sorry Lily wasn't here to pick you up,' Anna said, hauling herself up into the driving seat and putting the Land Rover in reverse. 'She's having a rest, but she'll probably be up by the time we get home.'

There was silence in the car, the subdued, tense sound of children waiting for normality to resume.

'You know, perhaps you should talk to Lily, if ever something's worrying you . . . ?'

In the rear-view mirror Anna could see Oscar staring at Emily expectantly while Emily rested her head against the window, her eyes flickering strangely as they half focused on the fields sliding past.

'She'd love to help,' Anna continued, craning her neck to try and catch Emily's eye. 'That's what she's there for. I think she'd be very good at sorting out problems, don't you?'

'You don't know our stepmother very well, do you?' Emily said suddenly, causing Oscar to swivel his head sharply in the direction of the driving seat. 'She actually never comes to pick us up unless she's absolutely forced to by Mrs Gordon, when Mrs Gordon is particularly cross. We never even see her, including at weekends. Not even Daddy does. He says she's got her own gender.'

Emily's eyes widened in anticipation of the reaction to this untested adult word. When none was forthcoming she sat bolt upright, flushed and breathless with her own audacity.

'And she's trouble, because men like Daddy are sitting ducks—'

'Says Mrs Gordon,' interrupted Anna.

'How did you know?' Emily glared accusingly at Oscar who simply dodged the look and pressed himself further back against the seat.

'Because,' Anna said, 'it just sounds like the sort of thing Mrs Gordon might have said.'

Emily looked puzzled and gave Oscar another sharp look, just in case. 'Anyway . . . what Daddy was meant to do was marry one of his and Mummy's friends. One of the ones who's divorced or their husband has died. There's loads of them and they all wanted to.' Emily raised her hands like paws in front of her chin. 'Yooo are sooo fuuunnny, Tynnie daahling. You are sooo clever, Tarka sweeetie.' She grimaced at Oscar and he giggled wildly, delighted to be included in this unparalleled assault of cheekiness.

'Well. Now your father's married to Lily, and I think you should give her a proper chance. It's only fair.' In the mirror Anna could see Emily contemplating this suggestion with one scrunched-up eye.

'Have you ever been to the country before?' Emily said suddenly.

'Why do you ask that?'

'Because you've got funny clothes' – Anna glanced down at her linen coat and pale pink linen trousers – 'and you always want to talk about funny stuff.'

'Do I? What would your mother have talked about, then?' asked Anna, smiling brightly in the rear-view mirror.

Emily opened her mouth wide, thought for a

moment and then, in a sing-song voice, began to list the possible options. 'The ducks having babies, the men coming to do the scum on the lake, how we have to tidy up our rooms before supper, whose turn it is to feed the ponies –' Emily tipped backwards and forwards rhythmically as she announced each new topic '– what's for homework, not getting in Mr Greystone's way, not getting in Mrs Gordon's way, what we can dress up as, why I have to have my hair cut . . .' Emily's voice tailed off. 'Lots of stuff,' she added quietly, pressing her cheek to the window.

'Well, I'm sorry,' Anna said, 'but I'm afraid I don't know about all those things.' And she wasn't sure if it was the note of umbrage in her own voice, or the cool lack of interest in Emily's expression, but something made her face burn and her foot press down harder on the accelerator.

As they approached the house Oscar scrambled round in his seat to point out the gleaming rear wheel of a motorbike, protruding from the bushes at the edge of the driveway.

'Loook!' he shouted ecstatically. 'Motobike! Motobike!'

'That's his,' said Emily, matter-of-factly.

'Whose?' asked Anna.

'The man in the cottage.'

Anna's eyes leapt to the rear-view mirror. 'Daniel? How do you know?'

Emily shrugged and eyed her brother whose euphoria had evaporated instantaneously. The hands that gripped the Land Rover's window frame slid away, and his head flopped lethargically against the seat back.

'Well, the man in the cottage is my friend,' said Anna, scouring the driveway up ahead. 'That means he must have come to see me. Isn't that exciting? He's in a band,' she added, ducking her head to peer through the trees. She was gabbling, she knew, and driving faster than she should have been. 'Can anyone see him? Emily? First one to see him.'

But it was Anna who spotted Danny first, standing in the shadow of a tree to the right of the house, gazing up at the first-floor windows.

'Oh, look,' she cried, 'he's trying to work out which one is my room! He's not even close, bless him. Oh, I do hope he hasn't been waiting long.'

Anna laughed – the too loud laugh of relief and excitement and pride and nerves, all mixed up – and leant on the horn and waved. Daniel hadn't noticed them before but now he turned sharply towards the sound, a hand shielding his eyes against the sun, and slowly, cautiously, raised his arm in salute.

'Poor thing,' Anna murmured, 'he doesn't dare just drive up to the front door and ask to see me.'

She brought the Land Rover to a stop, yanked the rear-view mirror towards her, and peered hard at herself, smoothing her hair flat, reminding herself to be bright and up, not to think about how long it had been, or how long they might have, or when they could meet again. He's here now, she told herself, testing her smile in the mirror, that's all that matters. That's all you need to think about.

'Well, here we are,' she said, turning to look over her

shoulder. 'Would you both like to meet my friend?' But the children were already scrambling out of the Land Rover, tugging their rucksacks behind them, and when Emily was forced to double back for a dropped pencil case she refused to meet Anna's eyes.

'Will you be all right?' Anna stepped out onto the gravel and called after them. 'Emily, will you find Mrs Gordon and ask her to look after Oscar?'

'I want Daddy,' shouted Oscar, his eyes locked onto his sister's.

'So do I,' yelled Emily and the two of them raced, backpacks flapping, across the gravel and up the stone steps without a backward glance.

Anna stood watching them as they disappeared into the mossy gloom of the house, and then she felt the warm pressure of Daniel's body against her back, his taut arms encircling her waist.

'Hey, it's my girl,' he whispered, his lips brushing her ear. 'I've been looking for you.'

She twisted around in his arms and rested her cheek against his white shirt. Her eyes were closed. 'I could have missed you,' she whispered, afraid for a moment that she was going to cry.

'I'd have waited.' He smiled down at her. 'Who wouldn't wait for you? Not that he didn't try to warn me off.' Danny jerked his head in the direction of the house. 'He told me you wouldn't be back. Told me I was wasting my time. He's getting worse, isn't he? I could feel it.'

Anna nodded, but she didn't want to talk about that now. Not now that she had Danny all to herself. 'Let's get away from here,' she said, staring up into his smiling face. 'Can we go to the cottage? Danny? We could go now. Please . . .' She felt like a child begging for a treat. Even more so when he took both her hands in his and gently shook his head.

'I've just come from there, babe. There's been some kind of leak – water and crap everywhere. I'm sorry. The plumber says it could take a while to sort out. Now, come on. Don't give up on me.' He cupped her chin in his hand, but she wouldn't meet his eyes.

'I never see you, Danny,' she said. 'We hardly ever talk. I don't know what I'm doing spending all this time in this house when I never even see you.'

'Hey. Why d'you think I'm here? Why d'you think I've taken time out when the rest of the band are locked in the mixing suite and after my guts?' Danny took a deep breath and leant forward so that his lips were resting lightly against her brow. 'Listen. I know this hasn't worked out the way we'd hoped. I know it's been hard. But we're nearly there now. We're so nearly there.'

Anna shook her head. She was still thinking of their dream cottage, the low-beamed ceiling, swollen and dripping, the legs of the bed standing in a foot of dirty water. She wanted to tell him that it felt like he didn't need her the same way she needed him; that she'd thought she understood about his having to work every minute of the day, but now she wasn't sure.

'It's just that I miss you,' she said.

'And don't you think I miss you?' Danny grasped her hands and pressed them to his chest. His eyes flickered up to the windows of the house, as he searched for the right words to comfort her. 'You know, when we've got the house and the kids and the ducks, we'll probably look back on these few weeks as the most romantic thing that ever happened to us.' He edged his feet either side of hers and pulled her closer. 'You've no idea how much I've thought about you; the plans I've made for us.' She stared up at him and her face must have registered the shaky hope she felt because he gripped her even tighter. 'God, Anna. Don't you know that this is all for you? To prove to you that I'm worth it?'

She smiled. Just being this close to him wiped away all her anxieties like some miracle-action painkiller. 'How long have you got?' she asked, drawing back so that she could look him straight in the eyes. 'Long enough to walk down to the lake?'

'You bet,' he said.

It was after six when they strolled back towards the house, swaying idly arm in arm, the sun low in the sky behind them turning the windows a blazing gold. Anna carried her shoes and scarf in her free hand and nuzzled Danny's shoulder, murmuring random thoughts that came into her head, most of them prefaced with the words 'Do you remember?' She felt mildly drunk, and profoundly womanly – as if her body contained the power to enchant and heal and change the course of lives.

'Come inside for a bit,' she said. 'It doesn't matter about him. It would cheer Lily up to see you.'

Danny shook his head. 'No thanks. I don't need that.'

'Why do you care?' She giggled, pulling him closer.

'I want him to see that he's failed. Let him see two people in love! Let everyone see.'

'I have to get back to the guys before they send out a search party.' Danny stroked the line of her jaw contemplatively as if trying to memorize its contour. 'You're my best girl, you know that? You're the reason for everything.' He held her face in his hands as he kissed her and then, before she had time to plead with him further, turned and started striding out across the lawn, towards the place where the motorbike was parked.

'And you don't have to hide next time,' she called after him. 'Drive up to the house. Park it right in front!'

Danny raised two thumbs in the air but didn't turn around or break his stride, and Anna felt her cocky young lover's smile grow suddenly heavy as he ducked into the shrubs and was gone. The truth was she had wanted to show him off to Lily, to Tyntallin, to the children, even to Mrs Gordon. Anna didn't quite know how the scene might have unfolded, but she had sometimes lain in bed picturing Danny at lunch in the dining room, captivating the children with his stories, making Lily laugh and Margot blush, while Tyntallin looked on with increasing discomfort. And over at the side table, Mrs Gordon would lift her head, watching with disapproval at first, then gradually softening until she stood there enchanted, oblivious to the sound of the bell ringing in the kitchen.

Anna was still imagining the Daniel effect on the household as she climbed the steps of the house and turned the handle of the front door. Once inside, she paused. There was music coming from the library – raucous, thumping, seventies-sounding music, with football-chant vocals and whining electric guitars – and at a volume that the master of the house would never have tolerated. Curious, Anna crossed the hall to investigate, expecting to find a cleaner with a radio, or possibly a workman shoring up the damp corners of the ceiling. But what she saw when she walked through the double doors stopped her dead in her tracks.

Halfway down the library Maisie and Emily were dancing – Maisie jumping and stamping, Emily adopting extravagant poses – while their aunt Margot wove in and out between them, flapping her hands on either side of her head. Beyond them an ottoman had been pulled into the middle of the room to form a stage, and on it stood Oscar, wearing a top hat, and Tyntallin, his face half obscured by a long, fringed lilac wig. Both of them were labouring over the imaginary chords of a plastic sword and a brass fire iron, respectively, although Oscar seemed more preoccupied with trying to copy his father's wide-legged, hips-forward stance. As Anna watched, the two would-be rockers leaned towards each other, mouths stretched wide and, over the background roar of Slade, shouted 'Maa mama weee're all crazeee now!' At the end of the line, Tyntallin shook his head with such ferocity that his wig slipped down over his eyes which, in turn, caused the girls to squeal hysterically.

'Oh, enough!' Margot appealed, pressing a hand to her chest and limping over towards the record player. 'Could we have a little intermission, please?'

The music silenced, dancers and players both slumped to the floor, feigning collapse, and Anna took this as the appropriate moment to announce herself.

'Oh my dear!' bellowed Margot. 'You just missed us cutting a rug to Oscar's favourite song.'

'And DADDY's,' chorused Oscar and Maisie indignantly.

'No, I saw you,' Anna said. 'It looked like fun.' Her eyes slid in the direction of Tyntallin, who was busy rescuing strands of lilac nylon from the waistband of his trousers. He lifted his shirt-tail and brushed idly at his stomach, chuckling to himself.

'You seem surprised,' said Margot. 'Oh, we love our bops. Though I never know whose benefit they're really for, the children's or Tarka's.' She struggled over towards Anna, one hand propped in the small of her back and in a lowered voice added, 'Anyway, it's certainly taken Oscar's mind off things, which was the desired intention.'

They both turned to look at Oscar who had clambered onto his prone father and was now sprawled like a bear on a rock, his hot pink cheek pressed against Tyntallin's plastic silver waistcoat.

'My brother's had a lot of practice getting them to forget their worries,' Margot murmured. 'A lot of practice. And my goodness, he never fails them.'

'Daddy?' Oscar raised his head from his father's chest. 'If Anna is here, should we do Abba now?' He seemed to consider this a basic courtesy, as if Anna might feel left out otherwise. Tyntallin turned his head to look at her; there was glitter applied in gloopy patches to his cheekbones and clinging to the ends of the wig hanging in his eyes. 'Well?' his expression seemed to be saying. 'Are you brave enough to dance with me? Will you risk it this once, for his sake?'

'Maybe another time,' Tyntallin answered for her, still holding her gaze.

'Good heavens, I should think so! That's quite enough for one evening.' Margot's hand cupping Anna's elbow made it clear that she had other plans for the new arrival. 'Now, Anna dear, the reason I dropped by was to have a word with Lily about the flowers for the church. Do you know where she's got to by any chance?' As she talked, Margot steered Anna back across the library and out into the hall. 'Mrs Gordon claims not to have seen her all day,' she continued, when they were safely out of hearing range, 'and Tarka doesn't seem to know any more than Mrs Gordon. It's all very strange.'

'I think she may be upstairs,' Anna said.

'Upstairs?'

'Yes. She's been having a difficult time. I think she wanted to be alone.'

Margot's face paled. So definite and capable a second previously she seemed suddenly quite lost. 'Oh dear,' she said, thrusting out her chin and staring at the flagstone floor. 'I did wonder.'

Over Margot's shoulder Anna could see Tyntallin attempting to stand from a squat position with all three children balanced on his shoulders.

'Perhaps I should stay for supper?' Margot said tentatively. 'See if I can't get her interested in some of the local goings on?'

Anna considered pointing out that Lily's problem was not going to be solved by a few distractions, but seeing Margot's tight, anxious expression she couldn't quite bring herself to.

'That's exactly what I'll do,' Margot said, gathering

confidence. 'I'll stay to dinner and we'll draw up a plan of action. When in the country one has to get involved or one does find oneself at a loose end, that's very well known. Don't you worry about a thing.' She gripped Anna's arm tighter. 'I've got it all under control.'

'But doesn't that make her an enabler or something?' said Valerie, who had been immersing herself in therapy books ever since Marion had referred her and Archie to the Relate counsellor. She shifted the cordless phone so that it was no longer jarring against her pearl earring and, with her free hand, adjusted the arrangement of magazines on the newly upholstered stool.

'I mean, the fact that she's there in the house with them, watching it all go on. Even if she is getting the American to talk, it doesn't sound very healthy, does it?'

'Who knows?' drawled Jean on the end of the line. 'If you ask me she's more interested in nailing Tyntallin than anything else at this stage. Anyway, she's staying down for the rest of the week and after that she's got to come back and sort out the flat. Richard wants to put it on the market.'

'How did he take it in the end?'

'Pretty much as you'd expect. He expressed a lot of anxiety about Anna's emotional health, naturally, and then he announced that he was starting up a healing centre for couples in Ibiza, and had been planning it for months. Offered her an exclusive preview, in return for a chapter in the book.'

'Gosh. No attempt to dissuade her then?'

'Not as such. Anyway, I think she's just relieved he's found a new project.'

'And how's it all going with Daniel?'

'Oh. Fine, she says.'

'But . . . ?'

'Well, she's barely seen him by the sounds of it. Every once in a while he turns up at the house, unannounced, which of course means she's tied to the place and never goes anywhere.' Jean dragged hard on her cigarette and then shielded the mouthpiece as she delivered one of her lung-rattling coughs. 'It all sounds most unsatisfactory if you ask me. I've had Minty on the phone too wanting to know what we all think.'

'Did you tell her . . . ?'

'No, of course not. I said they both seemed happy . . . I didn't admit that none of us have seen Danny since the night of the Portobello concert. Anyway, never mind that. How are you, Val darling? How's the whole . . . thingumy going?'

'Hmm? Oh, absolutely fine.'

Valerie knew that her feigned nonchalance wouldn't fool Jean, but she also knew that Jean would be sympathetic which was why, out of all their friends, she had chosen to tell her, and her alone, about the Relate sessions. Not that the others wouldn't have been supportive. But telling Anna would have meant admitting that she hadn't been entirely truthful about the circumstances of her sex life. And while talking to Ruth might have been a relief in many ways – she was so matter of fact about that sort of thing, she'd probably have managed to persuade Valerie that it was no different from a course of driving instruction – there was always the risk of Ruth telling Dave.

Thinking about it now, Valerie could picture those devilish dimples twitching, the thick black eyebrows arched in anticipation of all the opportunities for merciless teasing.

'So, let me get this straight,' Dave would say. 'Val and Archie are going to a *sex* therapist? As in the three stages of touching exercises, followed by petting with lights off, introducing the lights after week three, and then graduating to full bodily contact with pants on . . . how FAN-TASTIC!'

'Actually, it's perfectly fine,' Valerie said, adjusting her hair in the mirror over the mantlepiece. 'I mean it's ghastly for Archie, obviously, but on the whole . . .' she paused, suddenly mesmerized by the elastic motion of her wide, red mouth. 'At least I've got the measure of the woman we have to deal with, which is the main thing. So long as you give them something to keep them happy, you know?'

This was not strictly true, any of it. The counselling was not fine, at all, even though they were still at the preliminary stage and there had been no mention of 'exercises to practise at home'. It was not ghastly for Archie, who had, on the contrary, approached their sessions with the enthusiasm of a child visiting Santa's grotto. And, above all, Valerie had by no means got the measure of the Relate counsellor.

Diana, as she was called, had rejected Valerie's offer to play the tape that she had specially compiled as a

brief introduction to her situation. She persistently interrupted Valerie with the phrase, 'It's how we feel, not
what we think' – whatever that was supposed to mean.
And when Valerie pointed out that, since Archie was the
one who was so keen to come to the sessions, he should
perhaps be doing more of the talking, Diana had
suggested she was resisting – not missing but *resisting* –
the point of their meetings.

'I think, on reflection, that we may have moved on
too quickly,' Diana had said at the end of their last
session. 'What we need to do is take a big step back,
right back to your childhoods, when you were living
at home with your parents. Next week I'd like us to
look at how each of you perceived your parents' relationship. How loving was it? How affectionate were
they towards each other? That sort of thing. All right?
So there's a bit of homework for you to be thinking
about.'

'Actually it's a bloody awful nightmare, Jean,' Valerie
said. 'I can't tell you what it's like.'

'Poor you,' murmured Jean. 'They're not making
you fiddle around with those latex models, are they?'

'Oh God, Jean, don't, please.'

'Sorry, darling. It was only a stab in the dark. I've no
idea what it involves.'

'Nothing like that, at the moment. It's all analysis
and family history and how we feel about . . .' Valerie
suddenly felt desperately lonely. 'Did you ever not want
to, Jean? With Tony?'

'All the time, darling.' Jean gave one of her husky

laughs. 'I mean often one simply couldn't be bothered, frankly. But . . . it was always perfectly nice.'

'I just sort of clamp up,' Valerie said. 'I just feel my whole body is shouting "Don't come near me. Don't even touch me." And I feel, why should I? Why should I do it just for him, when . . .' her voice tailed off. She felt the silence on the end of the line, the absence of a reassuring chuckle, and her words hanging there in the air for both of them to pick over at leisure.

'Sweetheart,' Jean's voice was soothing. 'You just tell the woman everything. The chances are something terribly trivial's at the root of all this, something that you wouldn't even have dreamt of . . . Archie forgetting to put out the bins, or missing your anniversary. That's how it works, isn't it?'

Valerie nodded at herself in the mirror. She pressed a finger to her eyebrow and pushed upwards to see how her eyes would look relieved of the weight of crumpled eyelid. 'The thing is, Jean, as far as I'm concerned, it's only a recent idea that we should all be having these terrifically *active* sex lives.' Valerie placed the finger in the shadowy line that ran down from the corner of her mouth to her jaw. 'That's what I resent so much. The idea that you have to be doing it all the time in order to qualify as normal.'

'Val, darling,' Jean said, in a tone that made Valerie cease tracing her lines and turn away from the mirror. 'Two years with not so much as a squeeze is the other extreme, don't you think? Trust me, darling. You're on the right track.'

*

When Archie got home that night he knew, as he walked through the front door, that something was amiss. It was after eight, but there were no lights on in the hall, no lamps lit in the drawing room, and there was no sign of his wife who would normally, at this hour, have been clipping between the rooms, tidying and tucking, smoothing and plumping. By eight she was always bathed and dressed, trailing the aroma of Jo Malone bath oil through the house, transformed, as she liked to put it, from busy mother into wife and hostess.

Archie flicked on the hall lights and looked around him for clues. Valerie's handbag lay at the foot of the stairs, gaping open and spilling its contents, a sight so incongruous that his heartbeat automatically accelerated. To the right of the stairs was a clutch of abandoned grocery bags, and beyond them the shoes she had been wearing for their session with Diana, that afternoon. Archie called out his wife's name, keeping very still, and, in the frozen seconds that followed, heard the muffled clunk of an upstairs door. Without removing his coat he made straight for the stairs, craning his neck to peer up the stairwell into the gloom. Tentatively he called Valerie's name again, mounting the stairs two at a time, until he reached the point where he could see their bedroom across the landing. The door was ajar and inside the room was dark, except for a thin vapour of light leaking under the bathroom door. Archie kept moving, up the stairs, across the landing and into the bedroom, straining his eyes, check-listing the familiar shapes in the shadows, searching for irregularities. And then he was up against the bathroom door and turning the smooth glass handle.

Valerie was standing directly in front of him, wearing just a shirt and tights and clutching her tape recorder to her stomach. She looked dishevelled, dazed, but somehow triumphant.

'I've done it,' she said in a tired voice. 'I didn't think I could. But I have.'

'What have you done, my sweet?' Archie asked, scouring the bathroom like a cop at a crime scene; not yet in possession of enough information to call off the back-up and reposition the safety catch. Everything was in its place, so far as he could see, there were no spewing pill bottles, no blood-stained razor blades. He stepped slowly towards Valerie, his hands raised to either side of his chest, as if the tape recorder were a gun, and, any minute now, he might be forced to lunge for it.

'It's all right,' she said, holding the tape recorder out to him. 'It just came to me in a rush, that's all. Here, take it.'

Archie did as she said. He looked at his wife and then at the tape recorder in his hand. 'What do you want me to do?'

'Listen to it,' she said. She smiled and nodded gently. 'I did it for you.'

Tony was already sitting in their regular booth when Dave pushed through the doors of the Shuttleworth at 9.00 that Friday night.

'Sorry it's a bit last minute,' Dave said, reaching for the pint waiting for him on the table. 'I just needed a bit of a pep talk . . . I don't think the plan's working.'

Tony pushed up the sleeves of his lemon-yellow jumper and settled back on the banquette, assuming his usual position, arms spread out along the top of the seat back. Dave noticed that the buckle of the belt securing his white moleskin trousers was in the form of a gleaming gold H and, in addition to the Rolex, there was now a bracelet made of plaited thread draped round his tawny wrist.

'OK, let's have it then,' Tony said, lowering his chin and fixing Dave with his best wise but firm look.

'Should we wait for Archie?' Dave asked, glancing over his shoulder in the direction of the door.

Tony widened his eyes noncommittally. 'Could do, but then I'm the one with the relevant experience. Come on –' he made a tickling gesture with his fingers '– what's the latest?'

Dave felt suddenly weary, and strangely lonely: in a blind test, with no clues as to the specific circumstances, he might have identified the feeling as homesickness. 'Well, it's happening, just like you predicted,' he said, sagging forward onto his elbows. 'She's gone all private in the bathroom. And she's started wearing her good stuff for every day. The other day she actually wore that red dress into work – you know the red one?'

Dave made a hurried scooping motion on his chest and Tony winced obligingly.

'So. I tried the treats thing you talked about . . . I got her a coffee machine.' Dave paused to give Tony a chance to express his approval, but Tony just stared back, unmoved. 'It was a Gaggia Lever Professional. You know, they're the ones all the pros use . . . anyway, it doesn't matter because none of it's worked. And now something feels different. Before she was behaving weirdly, but she was still there, you know? It still felt like me and Billy were the centre of her world. But now it's like . . . she's gone off somewhere, on her own.'

Dave rubbed his hands up and down his face, leaving his fingers wedged up to the knuckles in his hairline.

'D'you think she is already, Tony?' he mumbled, staring down at the table. 'I mean, how long does it take? If you're a married woman and you're thinking about it, how long would you generally wait?'

Tony pursed his lips and swivelled his eyes towards the ceiling. 'I think that depends,' he said.

'How long did it take Jean?'

'Ten days.'

'Jesus.' Dave clamped his hands over his ears. 'Oh God. And I'm scared she's already come to some sort of big decision . . . what with the book and everything. Like when people have been in therapy and they suddenly realize they need to change their lives, and get bi-curious, and leave their kids and—'

Tony raised a finger, forcing Dave to pause mid sentence.

'You've given me an idea, chum,' he said. 'Chuck us your mobile. We're going to ring Anna, the one person who has the inside track on what Ruth is thinking.'

Dave grimaced. 'What are you going to say?'

'If there's a problem, Anna will obviously be aware of it. I'm going to appeal to her sense of fair play and ask her to share whatever she thinks is appropriate. Come on, hand it over.'

Dave did as he was asked and watched as Tony

punched in Anna's number and then held the phone up to his ear with a wink.

'Anna!' Tony roared, giving Dave another reassuring wink. 'Darling. Where are you? Aaah. Good. Oh, doesn't it? Well then, we were lucky to get you, weren't we? Hmm? Well, not exactly. David was just hoping to pick your brains on a slightly personal matter. Yes . . . you could put it like that. Of course. Of course we understand that, Anna. But then he wouldn't be asking if it wasn't absolutely necessary and in everyone's interest.'

Tony flashed his eyes at Dave and then there was a long, long pause during which he assumed an expression of beatific patience.

'All right,' Tony said eventually. 'But isn't there a certain obligation in extremis? Sorry? Well, I'm sure she wouldn't mind a bit . . . Jean and I have no secrets.' He extended the phone to arm's length, glared at it, and then replaced it to his ear. 'Fair enough. No, no, professional confidentiality and all that. Understood . . . Absolutely . . . Bye for now then.'

'So, that went well.' Dave grinned into his beer.

'What d'you think she meant?' Tony had the expression of someone straining to hear the first bars of a favourite song. 'What did she mean by: "I'm absolutely sure Jean wouldn't want me repeating our private conversations"?'

Dave pressed his thumbs against his temples. 'Er . . . what d'you think she meant, Tony? She meant, it's none of your business. What did you expect her to say? "Come on over and I'll give you the transcripts. Can't believe I didn't think of it before.'" He looked up and Tony was staring at him with a peculiar, almost devious smile.

'Imagine though, David . . . imagine if she had said exactly that. Look –' Tony leant forward eagerly, brushing his glass to one side. 'You need to find out what's going on inside Ruth's head, I wouldn't mind finding out what's going on in Jean's life, and I'm quite sure Archie could do with a little bit of insight as to what floats Valerie's boat.' Tony tapped the edge of the table decisively. 'Ergo – we need to get our hands on Anna's data.'

'Her *what*?'

'*Other People's Marriages*, the unabridged version, aka 'Our Private Lives Laid Bare'. Tony rubbed his hands together gleefully. 'Everything you ever wanted to know about your own relationship but were afraid to ask! It's the obvious answer, chum. Right under our noses.' Tony settled back against the banquette and smiled the long slow smile that generally preceded an admission of glamorous guilt. 'It's sitting there right now in that beige Notting Hill office. All we have to do is access it.'

Dave had a sudden vision of the three of them dressed in balaclavas and black neoprene, rifling through filing cabinets. 'Tony –' he raised his hands to indicate that this was as far as he was prepared to indulge this particular fantasy '– *forget it*, Tony. For a start, I don't need Anna's book to tell me what the problem is. I know what the problem is.'

Tony studied him patiently. 'You don't know the half of it, chum . . . you need insights. You need her innermost thoughts.' Tony dipped his chin and went for the wise but firm look again. 'You need what's on those tapes.'

'How much have you had to drink?' asked Dave. 'This is literally the worst idea I have ever heard. I'm not even going to discuss it.'

They sat there in silence for a minute, Tony adjusting his wrist decorations, Dave sloshing the remaining inch of beer around the bottom of his glass.

'How about if we go back to the mews,' Tony said, 'get Archie to meet us there and just . . . give it an airing. There's no harm in talking it through, is there?'

'OK,' said Dave, 'but you're driving.'

'Hello,' her voice on the tape said. 'It's me, Valerie.'

There was a long pause, during which the tape spooled silently. Archie lowered himself onto the edge of the bath and balanced the machine on his knee, watching it warily. Valerie stayed standing, in the middle of the bathroom, her stocking feet planted hip-width apart, her eyes fixed intently on the source of her other, echoey voice.

'I've wanted to say this out loud since I was fifteen years old,' said the voice. 'That's when I first found out. When mother told me. I've never spoken about it before, because of the promise I made to her, back then.'

Another pause. Archie glanced up at his wife who was nodding slightly, her lips twitching as if gently encouraging a shy child making a long-rehearsed speech.

'I didn't think it had affected me,' the voice on the tape continued. 'Not really. Not any more than any divorce would have done. Now I realize that isn't true. I realize what I've done is shut it all away in a place where I didn't have to think about it, but where it's been doing all kinds of harm . . . to me, and to the people close to me. Diana . . . you are always talking about the "missing pieces of our jigsaw" and having the courage to search for them and find them. Well, this is my missing piece. My father . . . my father left my mother when I was fourteen.'

There was a long pause. Archie stared at Valerie.

'He left us . . . he left my mother, for a man called Sidney Young.' There was another pause. Valerie could be heard breathing out in jerky stages. When she spoke again her voice was barely audible. 'Sidney seemed just like all our father's friends . . . charming and well-dressed and cultured. They played golf together most weekends. Sometimes Sidney took us for a ride in his car. We liked him, as I remember. Mother said that was why it had been so easy for them . . .

'We were never allowed to see my father again, of course, and we never spoke of him at home. But mother made sure we had learned the lesson – "The most important lesson you will ever learn," she said – that men were not what they seemed. That no matter how safe and loved you felt, you could never really know them. She used to say, "Don't ever forget how we all suffered because of a man," and she got her way. We didn't forget.'

The tape moaned as the Dictaphone was shifted in mid-recording, and in the background there was a clunk, like the sound of the lavatory seat being closed.

'When I fell in love with Archie,' Valerie continued,

her voice clearer and closer now, 'Mother said that I was going for the same type as father. She said that history was repeating itself before her eyes and that I was going to be used, just the way she had been. I desperately wanted her to be wrong. I told myself that it would be all right, that Archie was different, and Mother was just bitter and twisted. But a part of me . . . a part of me I couldn't control, must have believed her.'

There was silence again, only the creak and squeak of the spooling tape.

'At first I managed to push all the fears aside. But the part that believed was always there in the background, waiting and watching, and gradually . . . the thing is . . . It wasn't just the feeling that Archie might be . . . I was afraid, too, that there was something odd about me that had made him single me out . . .' Valerie's voice quivered on the tape. There was a chink of glass against porcelain and the sound of running water as she poured herself a drink from the basin. 'Now . . . now I think that what happened with my father, might have something to do with . . . almost certainly has something to do with the problems we've been having. I don't know what I can do about it. I don't see how I can make myself feel any differently when I've already tried so hard and failed. But I do know that I can't go on like this any more.'

There was a clunk and the tape stopped dead under the clear plastic window of the tape recorder. Archie stared down at the skinny width of brown ribbon that had yielded so much information in such a short space of time and then he looked up at his wife.

She was still standing, motionless, on the carpet in front of him, but now her face was wet and blotchy, her eyes muzzy and fat with tears. Archie felt a spasm of guilt that the sight of her in such distress seemed so lovely to him. He reached out and took her in his arms and, as if choreographed, they slid together down the side of the bath and onto the floor, her head resting on his shoulder, his legs arched protectively over hers.

'You're my brave girl,' he murmured, and saying the words brought tears to his own eyes. 'I wish I'd known, my love. I wish you'd told me. It would have made sense of so many things . . . your allergy to golf . . . your loathing for polo necks. Did he paint, too, your father?'

She nodded and her hair brushed against his chin, a feeling so strange and missed it felt like a memory from the womb.

'I'm not going to leave you, Val,' Archie said quietly. 'I may not be the most masculine of men, but I know what I am, and I love you in all the right ways.' He rubbed his chin from side to side against the top of her head. 'I'd prove it to you now, if it weren't for the fact that it would interfere with Diana's programme.'

He felt her stiffen in his arms. She lifted her head cautiously to look at him, and then, seeing the grin spreading across his face, she started to laugh, shaking against him, tightening her grip across his chest.

'I don't know if I can change, Archie,' she said, after a while. 'It's a part of who I am, this feeling. I may never be able to get rid of it. But I want to try.'

'That's good enough, my love,' he said. And sitting there with the rim of the bath digging into his neck, carrying the weight of his wife, feeling the damp trickle of her tears through the open neck of his shirt, Archie felt the purest sense of happiness. They stayed like that, perfectly still, for the best part of half an hour until the bleating of the mobile phone in his trouser pocket forced Archie to move.

'Is it Tony?' Valerie asked.

'Probably. Ignore it.'

'Were you meeting them?'

'Yes, but I'm not going now.'

'You go, darling. It'll give me a chance to get myself sorted out.'

'I don't want to.' Archie kissed the top of his wife's head and breathed in the powdery scent of her hair. 'I want to sit here all night. I never want to get up again.'

'Really, Archie.' Valerie pushed herself upright. 'I might be better on my own for a bit.' She leant forward and kissed him slowly and gently on the cheek. 'Besides,' she said, 'I'm not the only one who needs you.'

Fourteen

Ruth's desk was in the open-plan part of the offices, which meant that if Tim did ever want to talk to her without being overheard by half the staff, he would have to wait until they'd all gone home. The problem was she wasn't the only PJK employee who nurtured the hope that Tim might single them out one evening; perhaps offer them a lift home; possibly via one of those restaurants whose names now tripped off Denise's tongue. Every night you could feel the tension building as six o'clock came and went; see the heads turning ever more frequently in the direction of his glass-sided office. Before Tim you would rarely find a PJK employee at their desk after six thirty. After Tim the average going home time was 7 p.m., though so far no one had experienced the passenger seat of the new model BMW, apart from Denise. And that was during the tube strike.

For some reason it hadn't occurred to Ruth that the alternative to waiting until the department was empty was making contact on the internal phone. So, when her extension rang at 6.30 on Friday evening, she was expecting it to be anyone but Tim.

'Ruth?' he said, as if he wasn't quite sure it would be her. She loved the way he pronounced her name, with

a lot of emphasis on the 'oo', as if he were really savouring it, as if it were an old Russian word that had been
vulgarized over time but he knew meant 'rare blossom'
or 'spring breeze from the East'. She glanced in the
direction of his office and saw that Tim was leaning
back in his swivel chair, looking straight at her.

'Ruth, I was wondering if you were free to have a
drink with me?'

'Yes,' she said, yanking open a drawer and rifling
through it blindly. 'That'd be fine.'

'Quarterofanar?'

'Wherever you like.'

'Is a quarter of an hour long enough . . . for you to
finish up?'

'Oh, yes. Plenty.'

'I'll get the car then, and meet you in front of the
building.'

'OK. Thanks. See you.' Ruth waited until his back
was turned and then yanked her bag off the back of her
chair and raced down the corridor to the ladies' lavatories. Once inside she locked herself in a cubicle and
plonked herself down on the seat.

'That'd be fine,' she said, softly, breathing in the
Glade-scented air as if through a narrow straw. 'I can't
stay for more than half an hour, though,' she added.
'I've got other commitments. At home.'

Ruth fished clumsily in her bag for her make-up,
unscrolling the eyeliner with one hand and balancing the
powder compact with the mirror on the palm of the
other. She paused to stare at her reflection. The face
looking back at her was unfamiliar, hostile almost.

'Don't ask me,' it seemed to be saying. 'You're in

charge. Isn't this what you wanted? Isn't this why you've stayed late every night for the past week?'

A cleft appeared between her eyebrows and she prodded it with the end of the eyeliner tube. She practised smiling in the mirror, her sunny friendly smile, and then a deluxe version, chin tipped down, head at an angle, teeth concealed behind half pouting lips. The sight of it made her slam shut the compact and lean back against the cistern with her hands pressed over her eyes.

'Fuck,' she muttered. 'What am I doing?'

He'd be down in the car park now, turning the key in the driver's door – thwunk – tugging up the collar of his navy coat, closing the neck against his throat with a creamy-brown finger and thumb.

'It's just a drink,' she said to herself. 'I'll have one drink and then I'll get a taxi home. Thank you. That was very nice, Tim. Must be getting back now.'

The inside of the BMW smelt of eucalyptus and leather, with just a faint undertone of citrus. There was something jazzy playing on the CD. Ruth stared straight ahead of her, knees clamped together, handbag clasped in her lap, and prayed for inspiration.

'So, how are you settling in?' she said. Dear God.

Tim shifted his head slightly towards her, keeping his eyes on the road. 'I'm enjoying it,' he said. 'I wasn't looking forward to coming back to the UK, but I'm pleased I did.' His eyes drifted to her face and rested there for several seconds. Ruth wondered if she was sitting properly. She drew her feet in and pressed down on her heels so that her thighs lifted off the seat and looked a little more contained.

'You seem to be . . .' What was she saying? What did he seem to be? Tim was jutting an ear in her direction, waiting patiently for her verdict. 'Doing very well,' Ruth said, and pretended to be distracted by something outside the window.

He glanced swiftly at her, checking to see if that was really going to be the sum total of her observation, before replying. 'Thank you,' he said. 'And you've all made me feel very welcome. It's been a great couple of months.'

Ruth tried again. 'Your car smells nice . . . or is that you?'

'Excuse me?'

'Your aftershave I mean. Your, what do you call it? . . . I've never noticed it before.'

'Oh right. Thanks.'

She couldn't look at him, she had to keep going. 'I used to hate all that sort of thing. You know, "Men's Grooming Products". It's the way we were brought up, I suppose, to distrust those sort of men. That was all for hairdressers and Italian waiters, wasn't it? When we were, when I was . . .'

The ear was straining in her direction again.

'Anyway . . . now I think it's lovely if men make a bit of an effort with their physical . . . with their appearance.'

Tim was nodding, glancing at her surreptitiously every now and then. For a minute Ruth thought of opening the door and rolling out into the road. She'd seen it done in films and they were approaching the traffic lights, so the chances were she'd escape with only minor bruising.

'I'm sorry, Tim,' she said. 'On reflection, I think I should probably just go home.'

'Look, Ruth.' Tim's voice was low and soothing now. 'You don't have to be nervous you know. I'm not going to try anything.'

Ruth turned her head to look at him and he smiled reassuringly.

'You've been working late a lot recently.' Tim paused, widening his eyes, encouraging her to fill in the blank. 'I thought you deserved a drink, that's all.'

'That's it?' Ruth said.

'That's what?'

'That's it? You thought I deserved a drink after all my hard work?'

For a moment Tim looked confused. He turned down the jazz and flicked on the indicator. Ruth didn't say anything. She was surprised to find that in a fraction of a second she'd gone from feeling acutely anxious to really quite angry. Tim brought the car to a stop down a side street. They both sat in silence for a moment staring out through the windscreen.

'Look,' Ruth said, 'I've got myself all geared up for this. I've been waiting for this for weeks. And I'm bloody nervous. And I don't think I can sit through a drink pretending I know what I'm doing because I don't—'

Apparently there was some facility in the new BMW that made the seats recline instantly and in 0.5 of a second Tim's mouth was pressing down on hers, his hands deftly releasing her seatbelt and feeling for the buttons on the bodice of her dress.

'My flat's off Ladbroke Grove. It's five minutes from here,' he murmured. 'Why don't we make a dash for it?'

'No, thanks. Let's stay here,' Ruth said.

There was a part of her that thought staying in the car would make it less of an actual betrayal. If you were in the car it was just a fumble, surely? Also the sheer strangeness of feeling another man's body pressing against her, the unfamiliar weight and density, the unexpectedly different mouth – Tim's was sort of mushy, his lips blending into the surrounding face with no apparent definition – was taking a bit of getting used to. His hands were coming at her from the wrong places, aiming too high for her breasts, pressing and kneading where she hadn't had to endure interference for years. He was doing something with his teeth – sort of plucking at her lower lip – that reminded her of a puppy chewing its mother's ear; something to be indulged despite the discomfort and indignity.

'Um, sorry,' Ruth mumbled. Tim let go of her lip and straightened up.

'Perhaps I do need a drink,' Ruth said. 'Just a small one.'

'There's plenty back at my flat.' He gave her a wink.

'You know I'm married?' she said. Tim was tucking in his shirt, thrusting handfuls of blue cotton down the front of his starched chinos, adjusting the canvas belt with practised fingers.

'So am I. Separated, but still legal.' He grinned, and Ruth realized that this information was intended to make her feel better. As far as Tim was concerned she was looking for a bit of easy, commitment-free fun and so was he. They were both the same sort of people, confident thirty-somethings who'd got to the point where they could afford to have it all: the partner, the kids, sex with someone else, maybe more than one person. They understood each other.

'But I'm really married,' Ruth said, as Tim slid back into the driving seat and slipped the car into gear. 'I mean . . . I haven't ever. I'm actually happily married.'

Tim smiled and gave her another wink. He had a look of arrival about him; the relaxed, slightly smug expression of someone about to enjoy a richly deserved escape. Ruth suddenly had the uncomfortable feeling of having entered into a contract, the details of which were familiar to everyone at their stage of life, but not to her.

The truth was that she hadn't thought much beyond the first guilty kiss. This she had usually imagined happening at work, in the gloaming of the lift, or in the tight, corridor-shaped kitchen, where two people of the opposite sex couldn't pass without having to make some joke about getting to know each other better. Sometimes she'd pictured them on the terrace of his flat, necking like film stars against an illuminated skyline. A few times she'd imagined herself on the smoky stage of a club, with Tim sitting at a front-row table, his face pinched with desire. But the sex – beyond fleeting images of him raised up over her on toned brown arms, in the manner of a Calvin Klein ad – the reality of the sex they might have, Ruth hadn't really considered.

There would be parties, before it came to that; wonderful strangers' parties at which they'd meet on the stairs, pressing themselves into the shadows. There would be letters; hands clutched under restaurant tables and in the half dark of cinemas; long walks on deserted beaches. It had never once dawned on Ruth that the reality might be the edited, mini-break version of her fantasy – with an interval of forty-five minutes between first kiss and consummation. The only obstacle to the modern affair was, she realized with a lurching stomach, your own conscience.

'What did you expect?' snarled the voice in her head. 'You're both adults. I can't believe you really confused all that stuff, cobbled together from films and ads, with what was actually going to happen? You knew what you were up to. Don't pretend you didn't.'

'What's that?' Tim asked, reaching for her thigh, now officially permitted to roam his hands over her body at will. 'You were saying something?'

'Was I?' Ruth said. 'I think I'm just feeling a bit uncertain.'

Tim looked mildly concerned. He withdrew his hand and glowered at himself in the rear-view mirror. 'I wouldn't want you to do anything you don't want to, Ruth,' he said. 'I can take you home right now if that's what you want.'

'No, I'll be fine.'

'Ooooh. See. Don't like that, do we?' squeaked the voice. 'You want to prove you can get him now, don't you? You want to prove to yourself that a man like Tim – £150,000-plus-bonus-and-a-car Tim – would rather have you than the twenty-six-year-old from accounts?' Ruth started to hum.

'Nearly there,' said Tim, and for a split second she was transported to the front of the VW: Billy was in the back whingeing, Dave was in the driving seat, reaching his left arm behind him and feeling clumsily for Billy's beaker of juice.

'What are you thinking?' Ruth asked quickly.

'I'm thinking how lucky I am to be two minutes away from getting to know this beautiful woman a lot better.' Tim felt on the dashboard for his house keys, tapped his jacket to locate his mobile and then shot her a look that could have been described as 'intense and ready'. It was quite effective, but not as an afterthought tagged on to his standard leaving-the-car procedure. There was something about the look that reminded Ruth of an actor practising in the mirror.

'What are you really thinking?' she said. She meant it as a second chance. She wanted reassurance that after all these years of monogamy she had picked the right man, one sign to drown out the clamouring in her head. They were drawing up to the pavement. Tim pulled on the handbrake, reached for the ignition and plucked out the key, swinging it from his athlete's fingers.

'I'm really thinking I want this and you want this, so what are we doing sitting here,' he murmured, his smile set in such a way that when he undid his seatbelt and opened his door it didn't move even a fraction.

It wasn't what she'd had in mind, but it would have to do.

Back at Tony's place, the break-in plan still seemed to Dave like a risky idea, but one that, nonetheless, had potential. Archie, however, was proving considerably less open to persuasion.

'The point is,' Dave could hear Archie saying from

his reclining position on the carpet to the left of the sofa, 'I am a *solicitor*. I am not about to break into someone's flat in the dead of night and burgle—'

'Not burgle, look,' interrupted Tony. 'Research.'

Archie snorted dismissively. 'You don't even know what you're *looking* for. What exactly are you planning to do? Scroll through the whole book searching for references to us?'

'Absolutely not . . . We only need to copy the disc thingy. Dave does it all the time. You take a copy and that's that!' There was a loud clapping sound as Tony brought his hands smartly together.

'You're both half-cut,' said Archie. 'I suppose you thought I was going to drive?'

'No,' said Tony. 'We're *relying* on you to drive. We want you to be the driver because that way you can steer clear of the actual break-in, and have a stake in the information.'

'I don't *want* a stake in the information. I am perfectly happy to get my information directly from the person it concerns. As a matter of fact, I left Valerie, to come here – because you two insisted it was an emergency – in the middle of one of the most rewarding and revealing conversations of our entire married life.'

Dave raised his head from the rug and saw Tony loop an arm loosely around Archie's shoulders. 'Some of us aren't as fortunate as you, Arch,' Tony said quietly, forcing a tight, brave smile. 'Some of us are either barely speaking to, or no longer living with, our wives. Do it for us, old man. We can't pull it off without you . . . all for one, one for all.'

'This is utter madness,' Archie muttered, taking an

extra long slug of his vodka and tonic. 'How would we get in, for heaven's sake?'

'Ah.' Tony raised a finger in the air. 'You have a key.'

'What?' roared Dave. 'A key?'

'Of course. Val's on plant-watering duty while Anna's away and Richard's . . . wherever he is, so all we've got to do is pick the key up from Archie's place, en route.'

Archie's mouth gaped open.

'Well, I wasn't suggesting we broke the door down,' said Tony huffily. 'I'm not an idiot.'

It seemed to Dave that this really did change the whole complexion of things. This way it wasn't breaking in, it was more like being nosey. 'That totally changes things,' he said, spreading his hands wide as if, at long last, he'd been given the information he was waiting for.

'Even so,' sighed Archie, 'I can't see what you hope to achieve. I mean, I can just about understand Dave's motivation. But as for you, Tony . . .'

Tony closed his eyes and nodded patiently. 'I take your point, Arch. But the fact remains, and we've all said it at one time or another, we're not talking the same language as them. In general. And while it is terrific news that you are getting your sex life sorted out –' he flapped a dismissive hand in Archie's direction '– no offence, chum, but that is very, very small potatoes in the broad scheme of things. We're talking about accessing the code breaker here. Really getting to the bottom of what makes them tick.'

'Exactly,' Dave said. 'This is bigger than nosiness.'

'We *are* this book,' Tony continued. 'We are contributors. And I, for one, don't like the thought of making do with edited *highlights*.'

Archie was looking baffled now and a little flushed. He finished his drink and Dave, prompted by a look from Tony, struggled up from the rug to pour him another.

'But why does it have to be tonight?' muttered Archie. 'You can't do something like this without a plan. It would be suicide.'

Tony collapsed into an armchair and shook his head like a dog trying to get dry. 'Listen carefully. We get in the car. Drive to your house. Get the key. Drive to Ladbroke Grove. Enter Anna's flat through the front door. No one there. Go into office. Get disc. Do the . . . Dave thing. Leave. It's not the sodding Great Train Robbery.'

Archie sniffed.

'Plus, we are just drunk enough,' Dave added. 'And if we weren't just drunk enough, we wouldn't do it. We are perfectly drunk for this sort of plan.'

'That's right,' echoed Tony banging his hand on the armrest. 'The timing is PERfect.'

'What if Valerie asks what we're doing . . . when I go for the keys?'

Dave and Tony looked at each other, triumphant.

'Tell her,' said Dave, resting his chin on his chest to steady his focus, 'tell her you're dropping in on a relationship expert. Tell her you're picking up some relationship info, peculiar to you, and you fully expect it to be the making of your marriage.'

Ruth lay gripping the duvet to her chest, staring at the empty pillow beside her where, a minute previously, Tim had lain, hands behind his head, neat tan armpits exposed to the ceiling.

'Can I get you anything?' he called, the sound of an ice-maker chuntering in the background. 'How about another glass of champagne? May as well finish off the bottle.' He meant the second bottle, the one she had suggested they opened after the vodka shots, and the melon martini things.

'No thanks,' Ruth croaked, lifting the duvet a few inches and peering down the length of her naked body. 'I ought to go really.'

'Hey, what's the hurry?' Ruth jumped and yanked the duvet up under her chin. Tim was standing in the doorway of the bedroom, stark naked and honey brown to the bottom of his hip bones. 'The night is young,' he said, moving towards the emperor-size bed, 'and we're only just warming up.'

This was exactly what Ruth had feared. Whatever was considered normal sexual practice these days, Ruth was fairly sure that Tim was advanced level. As he'd swooped and reared, balancing on one knee here, adjusting his position with finger tips pressed to the wall there, angling her limbs with the concentration of a climber adjusting his rope tension, she had felt incidental to the act – a prop against which he could test his skill and versatility. It wasn't just the feeling of being involved in a choreographed routine designed for maximum physical challenge that Ruth found bewildering, it was Tim's detachment; the sense that he was on a journey all his own where no one could reach him. On the other hand, she reflected – as she jiggled silently underneath him, marvelling at his expression of controlled determination – it was probably better that it had turned out like this. Had Tim been the nuzzling, needy sort, she might not have been able to go through with it. And at least this way, she felt as if she'd been given a taster of the very latest options on the market.

'I really must go,' Ruth said, groping for her underwear beside the bed, praying Tim would let her leave gracefully. It had occurred to her that now might be the time when Tim usually liked to indulge in some shiny, ad-world-style, horse play. She could picture him kneeling up on the bed, tugging playfully at the duvet with his teeth; or rolling her up in the Egyptian cotton bedclothes and strolling around the flat with her flung over his shoulder like a carpet.

'You couldn't pass me my dress?' Ruth asked, avoiding his gaze.

Tim handed her the dress as requested and then stood, legs apart, arms folded, as Ruth manoeuvred it over each arm and rapidly secured the buttons. 'You're gorgeous, you know that?' he said. 'I don't think I can let you keep that on.'

'God, look at the time!' Ruth jumped out of the bed, cramming on her shoes as she stumbled across them en route to the bedroom door. To her relief she could see her coat draped over a chair in the hall ahead of her. She swept it up in one arm, pulled open the front door and lurched out into the corridor.

'Well, goodbye and thanks,' she called over her shoulder, as if she'd been at some late-running cocktail party. 'Got to run. See you.' Behind her she could hear Tim protesting, pleading for her to hold on a minute, but the prospect of enduring one of his puppy-sucking kisses spurred her on across the hall, down the stairs, and out onto the front steps.

Only when the door had clunked closed behind her did Ruth allow herself to stop and get her bearings. She was still drunk, of course, in that slow, dreamy way that made the commonplace seem extraordinary, and the drinker feel hyper-perceptive, like a visionary traveller on a strange planet. She noticed that Tim's car, parked next to the kerb, was a silvery blue and not the standard grey she had originally thought. She marvelled at a bus driving past on the other side of the street, skimming the branches of the fluffy lime trees overhead before coming to a throbbing standstill. All was well, she thought. She had done it, and it was over. Ruth walked down the front steps of the building and made her way cautiously across the paving that substituted for a front garden, pausing in the gateway to check which direction she should turn in. It was then that she saw Tony.

He was standing on the pavement, about ten yards down the street on the right, bent over a car. A very familiar-looking car. And there was Archie, on the opposite side, unlocking the driver's door – of course, it was Archie's car. A part of Ruth knew what was coming next, but not a part that was working fast enough to do anything about it. She watched, mesmerized, as Tony stepped away from the car and there, on his far side, leaning up against the rear door and looking straight at her, was Dave.

Ruth's first thought was that if she didn't move he might not see her, or at least not recognize her in the dim lamplight. But Dave was already pushing himself off the car with his elbows, jutting his neck enquiringly, straining his eyes in case they were playing tricks on him.

'Roo?' he called, walking towards her. 'Is that you?'

They were all looking in her direction now, Archie angling his glasses to counter the glare from the street-light overhead; Tony scrunching up one eye, a hand clamped to his brow. There was no escape.

'Oh, hi!' Ruth said. 'Fancy seeing you lot!'

Dave was standing in front of her now. He was look-ing at her strangely, warily, as if he suspected she might be booby-trapped.

'What's happened to you?' he said, running his eyes over her, causing her to glance furtively down at her chest and check her buttons. 'Where have you been?'

'Out!' Ruth said, flourishing an arm in what she thought was an appropriately carefree, fun-loving ges-ture. 'Just out with the girls. Few drinks . . . What are you staring at?'

'You haven't got your bag,' Dave said.

Ruth focused on the space next to her thigh where her handbag should have been and sighed deeply. 'Nope,' she said, forcing a smile. 'Didn't bring it. The girls paid for everything. It was their turn.'

There was a long silence then, during which Ruth began to persuade herself that it was all going to be all right. OK, her story was a bit strange, but Dave would want to believe it, almost as much as she wanted him to. And when he did – when his eyebrows gave that all clear hop, and his smile crept up the side of his face, and he said, 'Come on, Roo, let's get you home' – then she would lean against him, loop her arms around his waist, and tell him how much she loved him. Ruth looked up into Dave's face and his mouth was just beginning its slow, swing-boat arc when they both heard the click of a Chub lock as the door swung open behind her. She saw Dave's head turn slowly in the direction of the light, saw him register the figure in the doorway, the smile stuck halfway through its trajectory, and then she heard Tim's voice, crisp and confident in the night air.

'Ruth? Didn't you hear me calling? You left your handbag, you crazy girl.'

Ruth couldn't look. She kept her eyes fixed on Dave's face as Tim slopped down the steps in his Adidas slides and sauntered towards them, one tanned thigh thrusting through the gap in the hand towel wrapped around his waist.

'Ruth? Everything all right?' Tim was standing maybe two feet away now, naked but for the towel, which seemed to have the effect of exaggerating what it was meant to conceal.

Ruth nodded and stuck out her hand for the bag, keeping her eyes lowered to the pavement. But Tim was looking for a little more conviction before he was willing to hand over the goods.

'Ruth?' he repeated. 'Who is this man? Is he bothering you?'

The next thing Ruth registered was the sight of Dave and Tim embedded in the hedge outside Tim's building. Dave was on top, his elbow working like a piston, while Tim scrabbled to get a grip on the tail of Dave's shirt, occasionally delivering an awkward, flapping blow to his kidneys. During the initial seconds of the struggle Dave had established that he was 'the fucking husband' and after that there was no communication between the two men, beyond grunts and the odd sound like extreme exasperation. Once Dave lost his footing and came crashing down onto his knees, at which point Tim took the opportunity to kick him in the ribs with the toe of his rubber slide. Otherwise, they were mostly locked together, the way boxers are when resting between bouts of sparring, rocking and stumbling against each other. What struck Ruth was how ineffectual they both were, and at the same time how naturally prepared. It was like watching a couple of performers who knew the right moves but were too exhausted to pull them all together. And yet, despite the clumsiness and ineptitude, and the fact that Tim had lost his towel within the first few seconds, the spectacle was somehow profoundly upsetting. When Tony, who had been circling, saw his moment and dived in, yanking Dave backwards by his belt hooks, Ruth sank her face into her hands with relief, and discovered that her cheeks were wet with tears.

'Come on, Dave chum,' Tony said. 'That's enough now. This isn't going to solve anything.'

Out of the corner of her eye Ruth saw Tim grab his towel, wipe his arm over his mouth and, with a sidelong glance in her direction, limp towards his front door.

'Good lad,' whispered Tony, gripping Dave by the shoulders, keeping him facing down the street. Gently he persuaded Dave to lean back against the wall, and then took his head in both hands.

'Now don't you do anything hasty, chum,' Tony said, forcing Dave to meet his eyes. 'Remember what you were saying back there. Remember what you were telling me.'

Ruth could see that Dave's left cheekbone was already swollen and there was a cut just below his ear. He was breathing heavily, but otherwise there was a stillness about him she didn't recognize or like. She took a few steps towards them and Tony, seeing her approaching, let go of Dave and backed away. As he did, he gave Ruth a faltering smile that made her instantly think of the sixth-form teacher who had been delegated the job of telling her she hadn't got into drama school.

'Dave,' Ruth said, her voice barely carrying beyond her lips. 'It wasn't what you think. It was a mistake, Dave. I'm so sorry.' She stopped. He wasn't looking at her but the way his mouth was digging in at the corners made her catch her breath.

'Dave?' she whispered. 'Can we go home, please? I just want to go home. I love you, Dave.'

Ruth was crying again. She looked at her husband, staring blank-eyed down at the pavement, and remembered, for an instant, the way he had looked at her the night they met – with the sparkly-eyed, open-mouthed delight of a kid presented with a treat beyond his wildest imaginings.

'Look at me, Dave,' Ruth pleaded. 'Just look at me, please.'

He didn't move a muscle. She waited. She could feel her legs quivering against the skirt of her dress, she wanted to reach out and touch him, but was afraid to.

'We're not going home,' Dave said suddenly. Ruth nodded, relieved that he was speaking to her, anxious to be accommodating and do what was best. 'You go with the others,' he said, and she nodded again, ready to do whatever it took to make him forgive her. He still wouldn't look at her, but that was all right, that was to be expected. He was dealing with it, they were dealing with it, and it would take time but she would do anything. Anything.

'I'll get a bed at Tony's,' Dave said, 'and pick up some stuff tomorrow.'

Ruth heard the words and then, several seconds later, felt their impact. It was as if her senses were shutting down one by one: Dave seemed far away and indistinct, the other side of something invisible but as dense as stone, and everything inside her was heavy and dragging downwards, sucking out of her with a force stronger than gravity.

'Dave?' she said, and her voice sounded hoarse and drugged. 'I'm coming home with you. It didn't mean anything, Dave. It was horrible. Please, Dave.'

Dave didn't say a word. He pushed himself up off the wall, turned and walked away down the street, his ripped shirt tail flapping behind him, the hem of one trouser leg wedged at calf height, revealing the novelty socks with the cartoon reindeers that Ruth had given him for Christmas.

Fifteen

Anna woke to the sound of light tapping on her bedroom door, and by the time she had swept the hair out of her eyes Lily was standing at the foot of the bed, running a finger coyly along the pink damask cover.

'What time is it?' Anna asked, squinting at the light burning through the curtain join. 'Have I slept in?'

'Nodadall,' Lily said, smiling. 'It's early.' There was a contentment about her, a sweetness in her voice that reminded Anna of the still hopeful young woman she had met what now seemed like a lifetime ago. She was wearing a soft, coral-coloured sundress, under a boxy white jacket, and her hair was caught back above the temples with forget-me-not blue clips.

'How do I look?' Lily asked, spreading her arms wide and examining herself. 'I think it's sort of perfect . . .' she paused and raised her blue eyes to meet Anna's, 'for a visit to the lawyers in London.' Lily's face shivered with emotion. 'I've been thinking about it all night,' she said, 'and now I know that I have to do it. Even if it's just to find out where I stand. Tell me, Anna, that it's the right thing. Tell me I don't have any choice.'

With one kick Anna scrambled out from under the bedclothes and crawled down the bed towards her friend. 'Of *course* you're doing the right thing,' she said, reaching out and clasping Lily's hand. 'I've never been so sure of anything.'

Lily nodded, her roller-curled hair suspended from the clips bobbing like catkins on a branch. 'That's what I thought,' she murmured. 'Sometimes knowing when you're beat is the strong thing. You've got to be able to say you gave it your best shot and it just wasn't . . .'

'And it just wasn't possible to change another human being,' Anna said. 'I'm proud of you, Lily,' she added softly. 'I know what you've been through to get to this point.'

'Best foot forward, huh?' Lily brightened for a moment. She straightened up, tugged the shoulders of her jacket into line and then her face suddenly sagged as she contemplated some further obstacle.

'I'll stay if you want,' Anna said.

'You would?' Lily beamed with gratitude. 'You know I wouldn't get back until tomorrow.'

'I know. And I want to be here when you do. Besides, I'm getting the hang of the routine.'

Lily nodded watching her from under lightly powdered eyelids, her lips twitching involuntarily as she felt for the right words. 'I could never have done this without you, Anna,' she said. 'You know that, don't you?'

Anna did know. If she and Lily hadn't met it might have been years before Lily had plucked up the courage to confront her mistake. Maybe she never would have dared to admit it, and simply struggled on, trying to please a man who despised her for not being someone else. A whole life sacrificed.

'Perhaps,' Anna said, 'but don't forget I owe you too.'

Lily looked blank for a moment. She rumpled her pretty forehead and tipped her head to one side enquiringly.

'I mean Daniel,' Anna explained.

'Oh, gosh!' Lily shook her head dismissively. 'Thanks to me and my problems you've barely even got to see the guy. Why, I can't imagine you've had more than a few chaste kisses, let alone a chance to really get to know each other again.'

Lily raised her eyes from the bedcover and gazed searchingly into Anna's. One simple question, after all the secrets that Lily had shared with her, was surely not too much to ask? Yet Anna felt acutely uncomfortable. There was a cool, matter of factness about Lily's enquiry that she found unnerving.

'Well, I haven't been to the cottage yet, it's true,' Anna said, hugging her legs up under her chin. 'We've managed though. You didn't think we were actually walking around the lake, did you?' She laughed, but Lily's face had stiffened as if she'd been hit by a blast of icy wind. Anna saw, too late, that the prospect of her happiness had brought crashing home the desperate loneliness of Lily's own situation.

'No kidding?' Lily snapped. 'I thought you guys were going to wait. I thought that was the deal?'

'Did I tell you that?' Anna felt her cheeks smarting from the unfamiliar edge in her friend's voice.

'Sure you did.' Lily slid her a sullen look. 'So I guess he changed his mind. Or maybe you changed it for him?'

'Well, I suppose it was me. There just didn't seem

any point in waiting when . . . Look, I'm so sorry, Lily. I didn't mean to talk about me and Daniel. Especially now, when you're about to do this brave, difficult thing. Please don't feel you're alone in this. We're both here for you, you know that.'

Anna stopped. Lily had turned her back to the bed but Anna could see her face reflected in the wing of the dressing-table mirror. Her expression was blank and distant, the look of someone fathoming the depths of their misfortune and still waiting to touch the bottom.

Lily closed her eyes and let her head hang back. 'Gaaad, Anna, would you listen to me? I'm so bitter, another day of this and I'd probably turn to lemons.' She swung around and smiled, a sweet, forgive-me smile. 'I think I'd better get going and have this thing sorted out, before I become someone I really don't want to be.' Lily turned and plucked her handbag off the dressing-table stool. 'You know, Anna, even if I can't have my fairytale, the next best thing will be if you can have yours. Really. You are now my dearest and most loyal friend. I thank you.'

Half an hour or so later, as Anna made her way along the landing towards the stairs, she heard Lily in the hall below, making her peace with Mrs Gordon.

'Now, Mrs Gordon, anyone would think it was you who wanted this picnic so badly,' Lily was saying in her most upbeat, sing-song tone. 'The girls don't mind one bit if it's postponed for another day, do you, girls?'

Anna leant over the banister and saw Emily and

Maisie standing on one side of the fireplace, alongside Mrs Gordon, while Lily stood on the other.

'Nooo,' said Emily emphatically. 'It wasn't our idea anyway.'

'As you wish,' Mrs Gordon said. 'It isn't for me to bully anyone.'

Lily gave a high, dizzy laugh and, looking up to see Anna descending the stairs, called out to her.

'You hear that, Anna? You are my witness. No more bullying!'

'*She* could take us.' Emily pointed with both arms at Anna. 'We could show her where to go and everything.' And then, perhaps interpreting Mrs Gordon's silence, Emily added, 'She is a grown-up.'

Lily looked from the children to Anna and shrugged. 'Whatever. If Anna has the time and the energy and doesn't mind being stuck out on a hill in this heat. Anyway, I have to be going. You be good kids and stay out of your father's way, he's having one of his bad days.'

This observation prompted Mrs Gordon to raise her chin, as if rising above this display of disloyalty, and Maisie, seeing her reaction, lowered her face to the floor in solidarity.

'Ask her how old we are, Anna.' Emily stood on her toes as she addressed this question to Anna, who was now crossing the hall towards them. 'Ask our step-mother how old Maisie is. Or Oscar.'

'Mind your manners, Emily,' said Mrs Gordon, roughly unsnagging the collar of Emily's cardigan.

'What's so rude about that? It's only questions.' Emily wriggled free of Mrs Gordon's grasp. 'Ask her anything you like,' she continued. 'Ask her what Maisie's pony's name is. Or what our dog is called.'

Lily's eyes were lightly closed, her expression one of enforced relaxation. 'I know what your dog is called,' she murmured, through a serene half smile. 'Rufus.'

'No!' Emily raised two hands in the air triumphantly, while Maisie swished backwards and forwards in her blue pinafore dress, like a bell ringing in a tower.

'It's Ringo!' shouted Emily. 'Ringo from the Beatles. He's Daddy's friend. Don't you even know that?'

'Oh dear.' Lily raised a slender wrist to her forehead. 'Maybe I'll get something right one of these days.'

'Guess my birfday then.' Maisie beamed at her stepmother as if this were the opportunity Lily had been praying for.

'Or' – Emily flexed her brown legs in their shorts, pulling a foot up behind her and attempting to balance on one chewed flip-flop – 'tell us one thing our father has got a silver cup for. Or one thing he really likes apart from shooting and fishing and riding.'

'I told you, Emily, sweetie, I haven't got time for these games. I have to go to London on important business.' Lily sidestepped her stepdaughter and clacked smartly towards the front door, a hurt glance in Anna's direction encouraging her to follow behind.

'Do you see?' Lily hissed, as she clipped down the front steps, Anna hanging on her shoulder. 'He puts them up to it. He tells them to taunt me.' She turned sharply and gripped Anna by the arm. 'God knows what he's put into their heads. And Mrs Gordon. What if they all . . . what if they all make me look like a liar?

A bad stepmother and a bad wife and a terrible house-keeper . . .' her mouth crumpled.

'Lily,' Anna tried to sound soothing, 'that's just paranoia, surely?'

'If only!' Lily snatched her arm away and clattered on down the steps. 'I know these people, Anna. They'll turn on me when they find out. All of them: his sister, the staff, all of his friends. They'd do anything to save his reputation. Anything to keep the show on the road. I'm expendable, don't you understand? All that matters is *this*.'

Lily flung her arm wildly in the direction of the house behind them and then pressed her fist tightly to her chest.

'I'm all right, I'm OK,' she said, under her breath. 'I can do this. I'll just get in the car and go. I can do this.'

She looked frightened, Anna thought, frightened and intensely determined at the same time.

'Don't forget the tapes,' Anna said, loud enough to make Lily turn and look back at her. 'They're evidence . . . of a sort. Particularly since I'm a witness.'

'Oh, Anna, do you think so?' Lily's eyes watered. 'You'll leave them then, will you? I'll need all the help I can get.'

Anna watched as Lily picked her way cautiously down the last remaining steps and slipped into the sports car waiting on the gravel. She settled herself in the seat, turned the key in the ignition and took a long, shaky breath.

'Wish me luck,' she called, her diamond-ring hand fluttering above her head, and with that she was off, turning in a smooth arc and picking up speed as she headed down the front drive towards London.

'Do you believe us now?' cried Emily, unable to contain her excitement. 'You see, she doesn't *knooow*. She couldn't answer any of it.' She skipped across the hall towards Anna and clasped her wrist with two sticky brown hands. 'I'm glad she's gone.' Emily peered defiantly up through blonde eyelashes as she hung from Anna's arm. 'Now we can have the picnic, just us and Daddy.'

'I think we'd better leave your father to his work,' Anna said. 'He's very busy,' she added hastily, noticing how Emily was scrutinizing her.

'You know, whenever you say his name,' Emily said, 'your nostrils go all white, and you look really kind of haughty. Is that because you disapprove of Daddy?'

Anna gave a dismissive laugh which Emily appeared not to register.

'He says you disapprove of him,' she continued, her tongue pushing against the gap between her front teeth. 'He calls you Miss London.'

'Does he really?' said Anna

'Yep. He says "If Miss London drank any more bottled water we'd have to start getting it piped direct from the glacier."' Emily hesitated, her eyes darting in the direction of the library door. 'Do you want to see his study?' she whispered.

'Why should I want to do that?' Anna replied, lowering her voice nonetheless.

'Because then you might not disapprove so much.

And it's really good! Come on.' Emily slipped her hand into Anna's and before she could protest she was being dragged across the hall and into a small, dark-panelled room that smelt strongly of leather and cigar smoke.

'Look at this.' Emily skipped over to the fireplace and, standing on tiptoe, grasped hold of an engraved box on the mantlepiece. 'Daddy got this for catching the biggest salmon ever in history. It was so big that Aunt Margot fell over at the sight of it.' Emily swivelled round to check Anna's response. Anna smiled, easing the door of the study closed behind her.

'And this –' Emily flung herself across the room, landing knees first on a sofa beneath a wall smothered in framed photographs '– this is Daddy when he was young and he climbed up the Matterhorn.' She reached up a finger and planted it on the frame in question. 'And this one is when he was in the papers . . . for lying down in front of the government and not letting them dig up Penzelly Ford. And that's the salmon. Look. That's Aunt Margot having smelling salts. Only she's not really, it's just a joke. And this is Daddy out hunting on Gymcrack. He's dead now . . . you're not even looking!'

Anna glanced up from the book she had found propped open on the arm of a chair.

'Yes, I am,' she said, turning the book face down again where she had found it.

'Oh! Have you seen the wedding pictures?'

The photographs on the wall instantly forgotten, Emily made a dash for the round table in the middle of the room, and wrestled a leather-covered album from a stack at its centre. Shaking her hands briskly, like a dowager at a washbasin, she waited for Anna to take up her position next to her, and then hauled back the cover before lapsing into stillness.

There, on the opening page, was a formal black and white wedding portrait of Tyntallin and Henrietta, standing arm in arm in the archway of a medieval church. Both were smiling, mouths tight shut. Tyntallin was looking straight ahead, Henrietta's face was half-turned to gaze up at her new husband.

'I've got these,' said Emily, tracing a finger tenderly over the toe of one of Henrietta's shoes. 'The dress got cut up for curtains.' The finger hovered for a moment and then hooked the corner of the page, turning over several at a time.

'D'you want to see the other wedding?' Emily looked up at Anna, her blue eyes suddenly challenging.

She turned over another page and there, in sun-drenched colour, were Lily and Tyntallin posing against a background of azaleas. Lily's eyes lingered flirtatiously on the camera, her left hand, displaying the ring, resting above a bare knee twisted inwards, show-girl style. Tyntallin, his arm hooked tight around her waist, leant towards his new bride, his mouth stretched wide in a grin whose creases rippled out to the edges of his eyes.

Emily leant against the table, her flip-flop slapping rhythmically against the sole of her foot.

'She looks weird, don't you think?' she asked, her fingers plucking at the edge of the picture. 'No one gets married in a short dress, and it's not even white.'

The flip-flop gathered momentum as they both silently contemplated the image, and then Emily turned the page again to reveal a series of snapshots of the newly-weds. In some of them they stood, hands intertwined, on the steps of Tyntallin; in others they were lying out on the terrace, a champagne bucket placed between them. The caption read 'Honeymooning at home, hottest summer since 1956!' Emily hunched forward on her elbows and dug her ribs into the edge of the table.

'Daddy hates sunbathing,' she declared. 'And those bed things are so suburban.'

'Let me guess,' said Anna. 'Margot this time?'

Emily's chin puckered, as if she were trying to suck something off the roof of her mouth. 'It's not what people expect,' she said. 'It's just one more step towards medo . . . mediocracy.'

'Don't you think they look happy, though?'

Anna leant over a picture of them lying on their sun loungers. Tyntallin's arm reached out across the champagne bucket, the hand open, inviting Lily to take it, but her hand was already occupied, clasping a thin-stemmed glass. Her pink painted lips were slightly pursed, on the brink of taking the first sip of champagne.

'You have to be happy on your honeymoon,' Emily said, closing the album abruptly. 'Anyway, Daddy was only happy for six weeks. You can check in my diary if you don't believe me.'

She swivelled round, her head tipped to one side as it tended to be, Anna noted, before she posed one of her riskier propositions.

'That's when I heard Daddy on the phone. That's when he rang the man.' Emily's voice dropped to a whisper. 'He sounded really strict and desperate. He said, "Whatever it takes. If it means a trip to America." And then at the end he said, "Do what you have to, and keep me posted.'" Emily appeared to find this last phrase peculiarly riveting. Her front teeth hooked over her lower lip and raked rapidly up and down. 'I knew it was about her, because Daddy had to spell the name she had before she got married . . . Zelly something . . .'

Anna laughed. 'So? It sounds like he was sorting out her passport or something to do with her residency.'

'Or . . . he was hiring someone to spy on her.'

'Oh,' said Anna, trying not to smile. 'You mean like a private detective?'

Emily nodded. 'Eggsackly.' She rose up on her toes and pitched forward, gripping the table behind with her fingertips. 'What if he'd discovered something about her? Something hideous. What if he'd got in her room and looked in that box at the end of her bed and found . . .' Emily balanced, bug-eyed, her fingers barely clinging to the polished table, temporarily unable to come up with a sufficiently ghastly secret.

'You want to know what's in that chest?' asked Anna. 'Old records, things that remind Lily of where she's come from.'

'So why did she scream at us and slap Maisie really hard when we tried to have a look?'

Anna hesitated. 'Well, there's no excuse for that, of course.' She pictured Lily overwrought, opening the door of the bedroom she so badly needed to believe was still a sanctuary, to find three small figures clustered around the open box, heads bobbing as they dived for treasure. 'But you know those are Lily's private things, Emily. People can get very protective . . . of things they care for. They'd do almost anything to keep them safe.'

'Exactly so.' Tyntallin stood in the doorway of the study, his face half in shadow, a lick of smoke drifting from his lips. Anna froze. She opened her mouth to explain, but nothing came out.

'I brought Anna in here, Daddy,' Emily said, running to his side, offering him the full force of her gap-toothed grin. 'She'd never seen your pictures. She didn't know any of your achievements.'

'None of them?' Tyntallin raised an eyebrow.

'She wasn't interested, I had to make her. But then she was, a bit . . .'

'I do apologize,' Anna mumbled. 'We shouldn't be in here at all . . .'

'No harm done.' Tyntallin's tone was as brusque as ever. 'We're none of us immune to curiosity. Now. I understand you're all going on a picnic?'

Anna looked pleadingly at Emily but too late. 'Daddy, please, please come,' she chanted, hauling on his arm. 'Please, Daddy, you're the picnic king!'

Tyntallin raised an eyebrow in Anna's direction. He seemed to be amused, whether by Emily's antics or by her own obvious discomfort, she wasn't sure.

'I wouldn't dream of interfering. I'm going to take a look at the farm. Perhaps we'll come across each other during the course of the afternoon.' Tyntallin bent to look Emily in the eye before adding, 'Just you children now, you know the rules.' And then, with a quick squeeze of her shoulder, he disappeared back through the door.

Emily's eyes bulged. She scrunched up her face and put a hand to her forehead. 'Phew! Imagine if he'd heard about the private detective? Imagine if he knew we knew? Anyway, now you've seen everything, do you still disapprove?'

'It's not a question of approval or—'

'Do you' – Emily enunciated the words stretching every muscle of her face – 'or don't you? Yes or no?'

'Yes, I do,' Anna said. 'I'm sorry, Emily, but nothing you can do is going to change that.'

Sixteen

'What do you mean, "Dave is staying with you"?' Jean's tone was unusually terse, partly, Tony guessed, because of the trouble they'd had parking near the hospital, and then finding Elsie's floor. But mostly because she was going to have to do without a cigarette for the next few hours, and the last time that had happened was probably on their wedding day.

'I mean, Dave has moved out,' he said, pausing to smile at an old lady being wheeled past by a man in a green overall. 'Moved out as in considering his future.' Tony paused and lowered his voice. 'He caught Ruth coming out of some chap's flat, last night.'

'No!' Jean's reaction was somehow gratifying. Tony was pleased to have been the one to make her eyelashes flutter and her hand clutch at her polo neck. He tightened his grip on her arm as they walked with squeaking steps along the linoleum covered corridor.

'Who was it?' Jean whispered.

'Haven't a clue. Someone from her office, I'd have thought. Management obviously – Rolex, all-over tan, new model BMW—'

Jean glanced sharply at him. 'You seem to know an awful lot.'

'Well, I sort of got a look at him, in the street.' Tony pressed a handkerchief to his throbbing temple.

'You sort of got a look at him?' Jean repeated. 'You were there?'

'Yes. We were out, having a drink, and then there was Ruth and . . . whoever it was.'

'Where?'

'Not exactly sure, some new place Archie wanted to try out. Um, might have been somewhere round Ladbroke Grove.'

That really didn't have the ring of truth about it, did it? They never tried anywhere new, on principle, let alone on Archie's recommendation. And there it was, right on cue: the arched eyebrow, the dip of the chin. They were extraordinary creatures, Jean's eyebrows, so long and tapered that, were you to stretch them out, end to end, they'd probably reach all the way around her head.

'Do I detect, Tony,' Jean said, 'that you are not giving me the whole story?'

Oh, for pity's sake, he wanted to say. All right. If you really want to know, we got roaring drunk, went to Anna's house, let ourselves in and found her book on disc. And it was all going according to plan until Dave had a sudden crisis of conscience and wouldn't . . . offload it, or whatever it is you do. He started going on about how if we didn't have trust, we didn't have anything; and if we cared enough to be rooting around for clues, in the middle of the night, in a flat which we had entered illegally, then surely we could get it together to talk to our wives/ex-wives, face to face. ('You are missing the point,' Tony had yelled. 'Some of us can't. I

355

thought we'd been over this anyway? OK. Forget Ruth and Val, just offload the Jean stuff, will you?') But Dave had refused. He said that we weren't 'just-drunk-enough', we were howling, and about to make a correspondingly howling mistake. So we left Anna's flat, and went back to where we'd parked the car. And that was when we saw Ruth, followed by the bloke she had just been having sex with.

Jean was still watching him in that lazy, half-curious way that, in some indefinable sense, felt like coming home after a long, hard day. Tony knew she could tell he had the mother of all hangovers (even he wouldn't normally have worn sunglasses inside a hospital). He knew Jean would realize he had chosen this particular camel coat, both because it chimed with his image of the successful gentleman actor, and because it would tickle his mother, who thought light-coloured overcoats were recklessly impractical. He knew she'd understand that the beads of sweat collecting around his hairline were partly hangover related, and partly the result of nerves. But what Jean didn't know, and what she mustn't know, was that he had resorted to burglary in an attempt to find out more about her, his ex-wife.

The oddness of this had been brought home to Tony, by Dave, as they fumbled in the dark of Anna's office, attempting to exit the premises without the aid of Archie's mini-Maglite. Dave had cleared his throat – the way he always did on those rare occasions when he was about to say something sincere – and groped for Tony's arm.

'This isn't a criticism, mate. But have you ever thought that your interest in Jean might not be entirely normal, for an ex-husband?'

Tony had been taken aback, but naturally he wasn't about to show it. 'Certainly not,' he said. 'Every decision in her life affects me, and vice versa. Why shouldn't I be *interested*?'

At this point Dave had paused, feeling for the step up from the main room, and Tony found himself wishing that he could see his friend's expression.

'I'm not having a go, mate,' Dave continued. 'I just wondered, you know, if you should do something about it.'

For some reason Tony had a vision of a chemist sluicing blue pills into a plastic container and himself, tucked up tightly in a metal-frame bed. He decided this was his cue to get angry with Dave.

'Mind your own bloody business, David. Anyway, since when has it been a crime to have an amicable divorce, Mr . . . Divorce Police?' Tony flicked a V sign in the direction he imagined Dave to be standing, just as the door of the flat swung open, letting light from the corridor flood in.

'Bollocks,' Dave said cheerily, leaning against the door frame. 'You're not an amicably divorced bloke, you're a still in love bloke. You're in love with Jean.'

Tony shielded his eyes, pretending to avoid the glare of the light. 'That is a very serious accusation,' he said solemnly. And then, several seconds later, when he felt honour had been satisfied, 'Why do you say that?'

This made Dave snigger uncontrollably. He beckoned

Tony out through the door, locked it behind them and grabbed his friend around the neck in a pincer-like grip.

'Because, you've just broken into someone's flat, simply to find out who Jean is seeing. Because you would rather spend the night finding out who she's seeing, and what she's thinking, than give your girlfriend a seeing to. Because –' Dave gave one of his infamous eight-pint belches, forcing Tony to whip his head away like an offended lover '– because you never stop going on about how great it is to be young, free and single and then who do you call on in a crisis? Hmm?'

Dave nuzzled his friend's cheek squashing his nose flat against Tony's impressive plateau of cheekbone. 'Look . . . Maybe what you had was more important than what Jean did . . . or what anyone did. Maybe, in the heat of the moment, splitting up seems like the only thing to do. But then you come to realize all that matters is that you're with the right person when you grow old. Because, it's not like you get any Brownie points for punishing each other. It's not like it makes you *happy*. You know what?' Dave grabbed Tony round the shoulders. 'I'm glad we did this, Tone.'

'We didn't *do* anything,' Tony snapped, still straining to avoid the trajectory of his breath.

'Ahhhh, but we've achieved what we set out to achieve, haven't we? It's made us realize what's important. We've discovered that we don't need to know what they think. It's all about what *we* think . . . how much *we* care. If we can't set aside our pride and work it out . . . then what kind of men are we?'

In retrospect, the irony of these valiant words was not lost on Tony.

Jean gave a tug on Tony's arm, bringing him back to the windowless hospital corridor with an unpleasant jolt. Somehow they had made it all the way along the sixth floor to section B, crossed over the bridge to unit 3, and now they were standing outside the swing doors that marked the entrance to Lady Margaret Ward.

'Better get organized,' said Jean, rifling in the side pocket of her handbag, while Tony fished about in his wallet. She retrieved her wedding ring from the pocket, gave it a quick polish on the sleeve of her coat, and slipped it onto her finger.

'Christ!' Tony puffed, both hands embedded in his midriff. 'D'you think I've put on weight? I must have put on weight. Can't get the bloody thing over the knuckle.' He gave a low growl and lurched forward suddenly, hands braced on his thighs, his ring finger pulsing purple under the gold band.

Jean stifled a yawn. 'It's hot, that's all,' she said, holding up her own hand and fanning it backwards and forwards in the fluorescent light. 'It was always a bit tight anyway. Like your morning suit. So. D'you want to go over the highlights of our recent married life?'

'No, no. Let's stick to the basics. Boiler trouble. Takings at the shop.'

'Perhaps,' said Jean, 'we should be doing something for our sixteenth anniversary?'

'Yes, good idea.' Tony looked suddenly animated. 'What should it be then? Party at the shop? Dinner for the gang at number twenty-five? I favour something a bit bigger myself. Bit more of a statement.'

A vibration in Tony's pocket alerted him to the ringing of his phone. He took out the mobile, checked the screen, and seeing Belinda's name, switched it off.

'Bloody thing, didn't know it was on,' he said, offering Jean his arm. 'Right. Ready when you are, Mrs Alcroft.'

'You still haven't told me,' whispered Jean, as the doors of Lady Margaret Ward swung closed behind them.

'What?'

'What Dave's going to do.'

They walked slowly, scanning the cubicles on either side for a glimpse of Elsie, at the same time trying to respect the privacy of all the other Elsies and their visitors – grey-faced relatives sitting stiffly in plastic bucket chairs, or fussing over bedside lockers.

'Dave? I don't know.' Tony shrugged. 'He's not at all happy.'

'No. But then she wasn't happy either. Obviously.'

Tony surreptitiously checked his ex-wife's expression but, as ever, there wasn't one to speak of; just that very slight puckering of the upper lip which indicated she was not quite at ease.

'I told him to pay her more attention,' Tony said. 'There wasn't much more the chap could do, frankly. She'd just made up her mind to risk it all.' He paused to make way for a doctor moving at speed, a stethoscope flapping at his neck. 'If only she'd told him she was on the brink of doing something that foolish,' he hissed.

Jean lifted her chin to look at him. 'I expect she tried.'

'Well, maybe. That's possible. But why, all of a sudden, this terrific urgency to—'

'To what?'

'To change. For him to change . . . to stop being the way he'd always been. He thought she was happy. Basically.'

Jean lowered her eyes and Tony remembered, with a pang, the time she'd found the powder compact on the floor of the Porsche. How she'd turned it over in her hand, flicked it open and stared imperiously at the terracotta contents before turning her gaze on him.

'The point is,' Tony said, drawing his elbow tighter to his side, forcing Jean to tuck in closer, 'he was madly in love with her. Whatever stupid, thoughtless things he might have done. And he thought she knew that. She must have known that.'

'Maybe it felt like he didn't respect her.'

'He *did* respect her.' Tony's raised voice caused a woman sitting at a nearby bed to glare and point at a sign requesting quiet.

'All he wanted was her,' Tony whispered urgently, lowering his head towards Jean's. 'And he knew that she needed him a lot less than he needed her. That was the whole point. That was . . .' Tony racked his brains for the words the shrink had used, to no avail. 'That was the whole reason he behaved the way he did.'

'It isn't true.' Jean's voice was very quiet, so quiet Tony had to dip his ear towards her mouth. He was stooping over her now, his hand resting on the arm looped through his; to a casual observer, they would have looked like two mourners huddled in grief.

'She needed him just as much,' Jean said. 'She always did.'

'Then why? Why?'

'To make him think? To remind him he loved her?'

Tony turned his head to look at her.

'Well,' she said, 'it might have worked.'

A sudden, loud clattering from one of the cubicles caused them both to swivel in the direction of the noise. And as he did, Tony glimpsed the fuzzy halo of his mother's head, peeking above a bedside locker on the far side of the room. Just that inch or two of dandelion fluffy hair – quivering and bobbing as she busied herself with some small, invisible task – made him turn sharply away again, kneading at the tightness in his throat. Jean waited quietly beside him as he gathered himself. Then, when he was ready, she linked her arm through his and led him over towards Elsie's bed.

'Ah, look at the two of you,' Elsie said, pushing herself up in the bed. Tony tried not to look at the plastic tag encircling her tiny white wrist.

'Hello, Mummy.' Tony kissed her on the cheek. 'Here's Jean.' He beamed. 'As usual.'

Jean leaned over the bed to embrace her mother-in-law, resisting Tony's attempts to link hands.

'We've been quite busy the two of us,' Tony continued. 'Haven't we, darling?'

Elsie smiled up at her son, her Tiggy Winkle eyes sparkling with affection.

'The dogs send their love. They had a lovely weekend at . . . um. Well, they're just on particularly good form. Really . . . Fit.'

Elsie nodded enthusiastically. 'I can see you've been out walking them, love. Look at the tan you've got.'

'Oh that.' Tony looked pleadingly at Jean.

'You've discovered his little secret, Elsie,' Jean said. 'Tanning booths.'

This prompted Elsie to haul her shoulders up around her ears, and make a long astonished O with her mouth.

'Anyway, we want to know how you're doing, Elsie,' Jean said. 'Are you all set? Got everything you need?'

'Oh yes, dear. Everything I could want for. Tony sent a very nice man in a car to pick me up this morning. And he brought me a lovely fruit selection, and a whole stack of ladies' magazines and periodicals.'

Elsie nodded to herself, blinking rapidly as she tried to remember the names of some of the magazines so that she might seem more grateful. One frail cupped hand stroked the blanket, as if to reassure it.

Tony thought he was going to burst. He wanted to throw himself onto the bed and beg to have his time as her son all over again. He wanted to howl for all the wasted days; all the presents he'd given her that meant nothing to him, and little to her; all the occasions he'd thought it was more important to impress his friends and colleagues than to spend time with this woman who asked him for nothing and delighted in his smallest happiness. He wanted that dear hand to rest on his head, as it had done when he was a boy – on the threshold of a crowded room, or when a boisterous adult singled him out for scrutiny. He could still feel it, locked around his, as they crossed roads, and clipped down the corridors of public libraries – his mother a step or two ahead, always sure of where they were going. She was smaller than all the other mothers, more frightened, he knew, than all the other mothers, but more full of pride and more determined to overcome her weaknesses than any of them. When had she become a scheduling hiccup: a parcel to be dealt with by a stranger so that he could keep his squash appointment with the producer, who might introduce him to the director, who might give him a job, one day? When did he forget that there would come a time when his mother wouldn't be there?

The tightness in Tony's throat had moved downwards, and the combination of his hangover and the effort of containing the ache in his chest was making his temples throb. He wanted to sit down, badly. He needed to speak. He needed to release the pressure somehow.

'Mum,' Tony said, and no sooner had the word left his lips than his mouth cracked open like a raw welt across his face. 'Mum,' he sobbed, from the aching place in his chest, trying to muffle the strange, jagging noises with his hand.

'Oh, dear, dear,' he heard his mother say. 'Now, you shouldn't even be here when you're so busy. I'll be perfectly fine. There's lots of very nice people to talk to . . .'

Tony was shaking his head violently. He realized that it might look excessive, even disturbing, but he was unable to stop himself.

'My mum,' he sobbed. 'My mum.'

'That's right,' said Elsie softly. 'I'm not going anywhere, son.'

And that was when Jean handed him a Valium.

Seventeen

Apparently every picnic at Tyntallin was preceded by a visit to the kitchen garden, a job Emily had delegated to Anna, while she appointed herself and Maisie, rug finder and cushion collector respectively. Anna simply had to take the trug she had been given and get picking. Or was it digging?

'Some carrots would be very welcome,' Mrs Gordon said, wiping her hands on her apron. 'And a nice big lettuce, of course.' She handed Anna a small kitchen knife, her smile tightening an extra notch.

'Anything else?' asked Anna, staring at the knife.

'Maybe a radish or two.' Mrs Gordon glanced wistfully out through the glass panels of the back door and then, with a smart nod, turned and disappeared down the corridor towards the kitchen.

Anna found the kitchen garden easily enough, but that had never been her worry. What she was unsure of was how she was going to identify the vegetables, in the ground, with the exception of the lettuce. Closing the green wooden door carefully behind her, she paused to take stock. In front of her was a large walled garden with fig trees trained along three of its sides and rows of flourishing plants as far as the eye could see. Some were woven between upright canes; others grew like flames up wigwam stands of hazel, or lay couched under green netting. To her right was a covered cage containing raspberries and redcurrants, and here and there, scattered along the rows, were clouds of sweet peas the colour of violet creams.

'Right,' Anna said, tightening her grip on the trug, gazing out over the acres of unidentifiable greenness. 'Carrots first, I think.'

As it happened, the lettuce was her first successful haul. She yanked it out of the earth, pared off the roots with the knife, and laid it carefully in the trug alongside spring onions and the beetroot. The lettuce beds were in the farthest corner of the garden. In getting to them Anna had travelled up and down two thirds of the paths searching for carrot tops, diving in occasionally to pull on a promising looking handful of greenery, only to discover something quite different growing on the other end. She had suspected that this mission might prove challenging, and now she felt like a pilot who had baled out into a hostile wilderness. Anna took a deep breath, stepped clear of the lettuce bed, crouched down on the path and reached out to grasp another leafy plume. This time she pulled with her eyes shut, muttering a plea, and when she opened them she was staring at the creamy bulb of a small turnip.

'Oh, no!' she groaned. 'They've got to be somewhere round here . . .' Anna lifted her head from her hands, and as she did her eyes lit on some familiar-looking foliage.

'Ah ha!' she said, shuffling forward on her heels. 'Now, you're more like it. Might you be a . . . ?'

'I'm a potato.'

Anna swivelled round to see Tyntallin standing a few feet behind her, arms folded, face dipping towards the ground.

'If I remember correctly, I'm a Pink Fir Apple,' he continued, looking down at his boots, scuffing the path with his toe. 'Though I could be a King Edward.'

Anna froze. Her first thought was how long had he been standing there? Her second was whether or not the back of her knickers had been visible above the waist-band of her skirt. Tyntallin slowly raised his eyes to meet hers: he betrayed no sign of amusement, merely lifted his brows as if to ask if he could be of any further assistance.

'Well, I'm looking for carrots,' Anna said, discreetly dropping the turnip onto the path behind her. Tyntallin nodded, his eyes travelling slowly and deliberately to the bed directly to Anna's left. She waited, so as not to appear to need his assistance, and then followed the line of his gaze.

'Ah, yes. I see them,' she said, and without hesitating reached out to claim her prize.

'Allow me.'

Before Anna could protest Tyntallin was hunkered down beside her leaning his weight against her as he stretched across to the row beyond and gripped the feathery green tops in his hand. She could feel his hair grazing her cheek, the muscle of his thigh pressing against hers as he pulled, again and again in quick succession, until he had a bunch of carrots in his fist. Then he leant back and plucked a plant from the near row, the one she had been aiming for.

'Another King Edward,' Tyntallin said, hoisting the potato in the air and tossing it unceremoniously behind him.

He bent back over the trug, silently dusting down the carrots, snapping off their foliage and arranging them together in a tightly packed row. Anna watched, mesmerized by the brisk efficiency with which he worked. He seemed completely absorbed in his task, oblivious to her presence, and then, without warning, his grey eyes turned on her and she felt disorientated, uneasy.

'Thank you,' she said, hastily pushing herself to her feet.

Tyntallin reached up an arm to steady her, clamping his hand around her wrist, but she pulled away, gripping the trug in front of her.

'I'm going back,' she said. 'I've got everything I need.'

'If you say so.' Tyntallin lowered his eyes to the ground and wiped his face on the back of his shirt sleeve. 'Do me a favour. Tell Mrs Gordon that I picked that lettuce. She'll have your guts otherwise for taking it at the roots.'

Margot turned up in her usual fashion, unannounced and lightly perspiring, just as they were getting ready to set off on the picnic.

'Oh heavens, I'll drive you!' she said, when Emily breathlessly informed her of their plans. 'You'll need another pair of hands to help carry, if it's one of Mrs Gordon's usual efforts.'

Margot was flushed under her battered straw hat, and her chest above the neckline of her cotton dress was a rich raspberry colour, made more vivid by the thick diamond necklace nestling at the base of her throat.

'Builders,' she barked, noticing Anna's curiosity. 'Always better to wear one's jewellery when you're having work done, don't you think? Never put temptation in the way and you'll never be disappointed. So, what have we got to load up?'

In the event, Anna was relieved to have Margot in charge. A picnic, Tyntallin style, involved two baskets – one square, with sections for bottles and cups, the other deep and round – two Thermos flasks, several rugs and cushions, and a golf umbrella. Mrs Gordon loaded it all into the back of Margot's Land Rover, taking care to position the baskets so that they were wedged tight against each other. Then she stepped back and let the children scramble up onto the side benches – Oscar clasping his backpack, Maisie creating imaginary boundaries between the seats and explaining the system loudly to her brother and sister.

'Righty ho!' Margot swivelled round in the driving seat, eyes bulging in a request for clearance to take off. 'All set?' she asked, baring her square teeth, waggling her windburnt hand on the gear stick.

'No, Wait . . .' Emily was up and wrestling with the lever of the back door. 'We forgot Ringo,' she shouted, jumping out onto the gravel before anyone had a chance to protest. Two pairs of owl eyes gazed out of the shadows towards the front seats.

Margot looked perplexed. 'Is she talking about the dog?' she asked, searching for an explanation in the rear-view mirror. Oscar nodded silently. Maisie started humming. 'Oh dear.' Margot heaved a sigh. 'One's reluctant to sanction anything Mrs Gordon hasn't personally approved. You don't happen to know the form about the dog, by any chance?'

Anna hesitated. 'Well, I know he's kept in a kennel outside. In all weathers,' she added, pointedly. 'You can hear him whining sometimes, from the upstairs corridor.'

Margot was nodding appreciatively. 'That's right. He's a working dog, or Tarka hopes he will be, at any rate. You ruin them if you keep them in the house – absolute disaster.' She eyed Anna quizzically. 'Do you have animals? Much better not. They are such a bind. Unless one's looking for something to worry about, of course. Jonty and I couldn't have children, so naturally we've got hundreds of the things. Ah, here she comes.'

Emily was clambering into the back of the Land Rover dragging a sprawling, panting black mongrel by a rope lead.

'OK, ready,' she yelled, as she assumed her place on the bench, gripping the dog between her bony knees while Oscar pressed firmly down on its haunches.

'Mrs Gordon knows, does she?' Margot enquired and then, seeing the children were absorbed in a fight about whose turn it was to hold the dog's lead, started up the engine.

The appointed picnic spot was at the top of a slope overlooking a wooded valley, milky blue in the midday haze.

It was a special place, Emily informed Anna, partly because of the view ('That's the back drive down there,' she added, mischievously. 'I bet you didn't know that, I bet you couldn't have found your way home') and partly because of the bank behind them, which gave protection from the wind and made building fires 'as easy as anything'.

'Oh, the very mention of fires in this heat!' Margot said, hauling her cotton dress up to her ruddy knees and reaching for the wine. She grabbed the corkscrew, which was attached by a string to the handle of the basket, and proceeded to stab it smartly into the top of the bottle. 'Frankly, I can take it or leave it,' she puffed. 'I mean when one's abroad by a pool it's one thing, but it's rather different when one's got so much on.' She pushed the straw hat back on her head, revealing a sticky, freckled forehead, and nodded in the direction of the children. 'Glorious for them, of course. Nothing they love more than a blistering hot day.'

Anna turned her head to look down the hill. For a moment she watched the comic spectacle of Emily and Oscar hauling on the dog's lead – their bodies almost flat against the slope as they struggled to contain him – and then her eyes were drawn to the valley floor beyond, and a thin trail of white smoke rising above the trees. Behind her, Margot poured the wine and thrust a dripping glass in Anna's direction, giving her a brisk jab with the tumbler when she saw her hesitate.

'How long have you known her?' Margot asked, as Anna took the glass. 'Lily? You knew her before, I take it, in America?' Her pronunciation made the United

States sound like a rare plant species, hallowed among horticultural experts.

'No. Actually we met a few months ago,' Anna said.

'Good heavens. I just assumed you were bosom chums. Well I never . . .' Margot nodded vigorously, her eyes bunched up and twitching as she searched for inspiration in the wine swilling round her glass. 'We find her rather a mystery, you see. She was so charming and willing to start with. We really thought it was going to be a huge success, a wonderful thing all round. Still . . . it turns out that Lily is a rather more complicated girl than one assumed.' Margot shifted on the rug, bundling the hem of her dress clumsily into the space between her knees. 'Tarka would never breathe a word, of course. Never complains. But one hears the rumours. One can't avoid them. And one can see how unhappy he is . . .' She paused, her ruddy face seemed to darken a shade. 'You couldn't have a word with her, I suppose? Persuade her to knuckle down and give it a chance. I wouldn't ask, but one's at such a loss as to what to do.'

Anna hesitated. 'I'm sorry, Margot,' she said. 'But I think Lily has given it every chance.'

Margot's eyes shifted abruptly from the horizon to Anna's face. She peered at her, incredulous. 'But my dear, she's having an affair. Surely you knew? It started almost at once; within weeks of the marriage, they say. It's the reason she's never at home. It's almost certainly where she is at this very moment.'

Anna felt a sudden powerful thudding in her chest, all pity for poor, blind Margot instantly forgotten. 'Actually, Margot, Lily is in London, seeing a lawyer,' she announced, at once savouring the power of this information and regretting her recklessness in betraying it. 'Lily has been a more loyal wife to your brother than you could ever imagine, but she's not prepared to take any more. She wants a divorce.'

Anna's heart picked up pace as she prepared for the inevitable reaction to this revelation. Margot would be speechless at first, then angry; she would try to press Anna for details of Lily's plans, and doubtless insist that they return at once to the house to inform Tyntallin of her treachery. But Margot was silent and perfectly still, her eyes narrowed on the horizon.

'And I think you'll find,' continued Anna, shifting her weight in an attempt to impose herself on Margot's eyeline, 'that the divorce will be granted on the grounds of your brother's cruelty and neglect. And if you insist on supporting him, you should know that I am a witness to it, and I know everything.'

Margot continued to stare rigidly ahead. She was pushing herself up off the rug now, balancing on one quivering hand, like a nervous sprinter. 'Something's happened,' she whispered, stumbling to her feet, a warning hand drifting out in Anna's direction.

And then suddenly she was running, careering down the hill, arms pumping, her straw hat flying out behind her. For a split second Anna stared after her, too astonished to react, and then she too was up on her feet, gathering her long skirt in one hand, following as fast as her sling-backs would allow.

At first, all Anna was aware of was Margot's rolling form up ahead, her body straining like a boat in a high wind, the dull squeak and thud of her trainers. Then she caught sight of Emily, some twenty yards down the hill, and felt the first sick pulse of fear. The child stood limp and lifeless, her head lolling forward, as if she'd been hung by her shoulders on an invisible hook. Margot called out to her, the panic in her voice swinging back like an iron fist to catch Anna in the stomach. She kept calling out to her, begging for answers as she ran, and then at last she had reached Emily and was crouching down, grasping her by the shoulders.

'Oscar and Maisie? All right?' Margot gasped.

Emily nodded, then opened her mouth and wailed.

'What is it? The dog?' Margot squeezed the child tighter, gathering her up to a point like a piece of unruly clay.

Emily gagged and nodded again, pointing down the hill with a leaden-heavy arm. 'He . . .' She gulped air, struggling to catch her breath. 'He got the sheep. He . . . I couldn't stop him.'

Margot shot upright. She snatched Emily's hand and started to run again, glancing back for navigation clues from the limp figure flailing in her wake like a broken rudder. Anna ran too, trying to keep close, trying not to stumble in her heels, not knowing where they were heading or what, exactly, they were looking for. She saw Margot stoop down as she ran and snatch something from the ground – a piece of wood, or maybe a rock. And then suddenly they were standing on the lip of a hollow bowl, and below them, scattered all around on the grass, were the ragged, bloodied bodies of sheep.

None were quite dead, Anna saw. Some stumbled forward, dragging their paralysed back legs behind them, their heads swivelling in pain and fear. One lay on its side, its matted, blood-soaked coat rising and falling with the force of industrial bellows; another, propped against a rock, struggled to right itself increasingly frantically. The air was filled with a desperate, raw bleating. And right, in the midst of this awful scene, was the silent, panting presence of the dog, weaving swiftly among his prey, tongue lolling over his teeth, head sunk low between his shoulders. He paused for a moment in his circuit, darted forward, sinking his teeth into the nearest pair of hind legs, and retreated a few yards. Then, as his victim paddled unsteadily to its feet, eyes rolling back in its head, he pounced again.

Margot was already halfway down the side of the bowl, roaring commands at Ringo, pounding towards the place where he now crouched, pinning his prey by the back of the neck. Her advance, awesome from where Anna stood, appeared barely to affect the dog. He chomped down harder on the sheep's neck, in the process twisting the animal's head so that it was facing its would-be saviour, though the eyes were now closed. Beyond the dog, high up towards the lip of the crater, Anna suddenly saw Oscar and Maisie. They were standing, hand in hand, their absolute stillness somehow more chilling than anything taking place in the amphitheatre below.

Down in the bowl Margot had reached level ground and was closing on Ringo at full charge. Without breaking her stride she drew back her arm and hurled the stone she had collected earlier, cursing loudly when it hit the belly of the sheep, merely causing Ringo to adjust his grip. But now something else had distracted the dog. Something unseen. He pricked up his ears, lifted his head, and turned his gaze up towards the ridge on the right. For a split second the animal's attention was totally focused on the horizon, his nose lifted to the wind, his tongue lying still in his mouth. Then there was a sharp resounding crack, and the dog slumped, soundlessly, over the body of his prey. Instantly, Margot braked, rolling forward, hands on hips, trying to catch her breath. And at Anna's side, Emily started to scream and kept on screaming: 'Daddy, no! Daddy, no!'

On the opposite side of the crater the figure of a man carrying a gun broken over his arm stepped up to the lip and slowly, stiffly, started to make his descent into the bowl. Tyntallin exchanged no words with Margot as he passed her. He walked straight on, crouching as he came to each of the sheep in turn, sometimes combing a hand roughly through their wool coats to assess the extent of the damage. Twice he took a step back, snapped his gun closed, levelled it at the head of a sheep and fired. When he came to the dog he bent over, hooked his hand through its collar and dragged the lifeless body onto a space of clear grass, depositing it like a sack without a backward glance. Margot hovered behind him as he worked, shifting uneasily from one foot to the other. When Tyntallin finally acknowledged his sister, Anna could see, from the way she dragged her hands repeatedly through her hair, that their exchange was less than comfortable. He stood sideways-on to her, turning his head once or twice to meet her eyes, and then something she said prompted him to glance up to where they were standing. Anna held her breath. Tyntallin paused, staring up at them, then thrust the gun into Margot's hands and, to Anna's horror, started heading up the slope in their direction. Beside her, she felt Emily clasp her hand tightly, the sobbing, which had temporarily subsided, returning louder than before.

Anna prepared herself as best she could in the few seconds available, planting her feet and sucking in a deep lungful of air. This was her responsibility, at least partially, she would have to deal with it, though she didn't yet know how. She pulled Emily in closer, drew back her shoulders and tried to hold her head up. Tyntallin was already almost at the top of the bowl, and as he stepped up onto level ground and came towards them she could see the tension in his jaw, how his nostrils flared as he struggled to control his breathing, as if releasing the grip on his mouth was a risk he could not afford to take. Anna began to speak, but as she did she felt Emily pushing herself forward, still clinging tightly to her fingers.

'You didn't have to kill Ringo, Daddy.' Emily sobbed, wiping her hair out of her eyes with a snot-smeared hand. 'You needn't have shot him, Daddy. You needn't have.'

Tyntallin said nothing.

'Did he kill them all?' Emily twisted Anna's fingers in hers. 'I didn't know he would, Daddy. I didn't think he would.'

Tyntallin watched as his daughter floundered, clawing at the neck of her T-shirt, rubbing the back of her hand forwards and backwards across her wet face.

'Can we go to the vet, Daddy?' she pleaded. 'Please. Can we take the sheep to the vet now?'

'Can't you see she's beside herself?' Anna hissed, conscious that her own lip was trembling. 'Was it really necessary to do that in front of them? Did you have to be so cruel?'

He stared at her, his eyes travelling over her face with a kind of dispassionate curiosity before he answered. 'Emily and I will load up the dead animals and take them over to the shepherd to explain what has happened here. I suggest that you find your way home with my sister and take the other children with you.'

'For heaven's sake, it was an accident.' Anna took a step towards him. 'If it was anyone's fault it was mine.'

'My daughter knows the rules and she understands the consequences of her actions. I had no reason to expect the same of you.'

Anna felt the salty burn of tears. 'You're nothing but a bully,' she said. 'A cold-hearted bully.'

'No!' Emily yanked her hand from Anna's grasp, recoiling in horror. 'No. You don't understand anything. He *had* to. He has to look after the farm and us and everything. He *knows*. You don't know *anything*.' She slid across to where Tyntallin stood and, head bowed, reached up to grasp the hem of his tweed jacket.

'The dog was a killer,' Tyntallin said, placing a hand on Emily's shoulder. 'I suspected as much. And there are some things, fortunately, that one doesn't have to tolerate.'

Below them Anna saw Margot dragging an outlying sheep back towards its dead neighbours. With one last tug she hauled the carcass into position, then wiped her hands absent-mindedly on the skirt of her dress before striding off to gather up another. Anna knew she couldn't stay here, knew she couldn't sit in the Land Rover listening to Margot blustering matter-of-factly about the day's events. 'It will have taught those children a lesson they won't forget, mind you,' Anna could hear her saying. 'Never take an untrained animal on the farm. If it had been our father he'd have taken the belt to both of us.' Anna had never seen a dying creature, never witnessed a man shoot an animal, never heard a child in such distress. She knew she had to walk, alone, and then she knew where she had to go.

Though she ran most of the way, it took Anna almost ten minutes to make it to the bottom of the hill, and then she had a fence to climb, and a steep bank to slither down, before she finally set foot on the back drive. Daniel had said his cottage was on the very edge of the estate so, when Anna glimpsed a pair of high iron gates off to the right, she knew she must be close. Although it was only mid-afternoon the canopy of oak trees made the light dusky, and the atmosphere was cool and fresh after the humid air on the hill. In this cocooned, softly lit world, birds were singing, convinced that it was sundown, and, for the first time in hours, Anna felt she could breathe easily.

She started to walk back along the drive, noticing for the first time the mud-stained hem of her skirt, and the mark on her sleeve where she had wiped her streaming eyes as she ran, the angry rumble of his voice pursuing her. 'Don't go down there!' he had shouted. 'You don't know what you're doing. You will get hurt, do you hear me?' But Anna had only run faster, humming to herself to block out the sound. All she could think of was finding a way into the cottage and spending the night there, sleeping in Danny's sheets, surrounded by his belongings. In her mind, she pictured a heavy oak bed and a round wooden table in front of a mullioned window. She could see the whole scene quite clearly: the low-beamed ceiling, the silvery underwater light pushing through the leaded panes, the white roses drooping in clusters over the stone window frame. Danny's guitar would be propped up against the leg of the table; notebooks and music magazines would be strewn across its surface, the pages held open with coffee mugs. There would be a tangy smell of damp earth, roses and . . . burning wood. Anna stopped in her tracks. She lifted her eyes from the road and saw, through the trees, the tip of a thatched roof and a white trail of smoke rising from the chimney. The fire in the cottage was lit. He was there. He was waiting for her after all.

Anna darted off the drive and down the overgrown path, twisting and ducking to avoid the branches of trees, snatching her skirt as it snagged on hidden thorns. When at last she could see the cottage a few yards up ahead she stopped, breathless with excitement, and hastily shook out her hair, raking her fingers up from the nape of her neck. She would walk the last part slowly, savouring the experience she had so often imagined. Anna lifted her skirt at the knees and tiptoed forward across the grass.

The cottage was different, of course, to how she had pictured it – cruder and more run down, with a rickety wooden porch over the front door and swags of wisteria where she had seen clots of roses. Danny's motorbike was propped against a moss-coated rain barrel, and round the side of the cottage she could just see the bumper of a low-slung car. Anna drew closer, stepping across what had once been flower beds but were now a tangle of anything with the will to grow and, bending low to keep out of sight of the windows, made a crouching dash for the cover of the porch.

The door was shut tight. She stood, one hand pressed flat against her smiling mouth, the other resting on the latch, breathing in the smell of moss and damp wood. The anticipation was exquisite. A feeling deep in her stomach connected her like the current in a string of fairy lights to bright images from her past: running up the twisting wooden stairs of a Parisian hotel, hand in hand with a fiery-eyed boy; swimming outside in an inky dark pool, alone except for one silent admirer watching in the shallows. Anna breathed deeply, closing her eyes as she paused to dwell on the next picture: she and Daniel squeezed hip to hip against the bar of a pub one New Year's Eve, strangers waiting interminably to be served, chatting briefly. And then, his hand seeking hers under the rim of the counter, weaving his fingers through hers one by one.

Beyond the door Anna could just hear the murmur of a radio or a television, enough noise to cover the click of the latch and the low moan of the hinge as she slipped, unnoticed, into the cottage. Inside, the stone-floored hall was dark and cool even on this hot day. To her left was a log basket and a collection of walking sticks. On the wall opposite was a shelf cluttered with jam jars and flower pots. And to her right a deep wooden step led up into the main room of the cottage, from where the sound of the radio trickled intermittently. Anna tiptoed across the hall and paused on the threshold of the room. A soft light, stripped of the green freshness of outside, sneaked like a fog through the leaded panes illuminating a fine mist of dust. In front of the window, where she had pictured the round table, was a large, black lacquer chest, and on top of it a needle-thin white vase containing a single, crescent-shaped orchid. Beneath the chest a black sheepskin rug crept out across the floor like an ink stain, and in the middle of it something white lay abandoned: a crisp, angular shape, like a discarded waiter's jacket.

Anna shrank back. This place felt so unfamiliar, it couldn't be Daniel's. Was she in someone else's cottage? Could she somehow have made a mistake? Tentatively she craned her neck, hoping to catch sight of some object that would confirm his presence, telling herself that if she didn't within the next few seconds she would retrace her steps, or call out to the owner – the elegant, fashion-conscious, slightly intimidating female owner who must have rented this place for the summer. And then Anna heard his voice. The relief hit her instantaneously, relaxing her limbs like a drug, and was followed, in less than a heartbeat, by another sensation: a sickening, stomach clawing horror.

Danny was speaking, but the words were clenched tight in his chest, as if he were trying to talk and manoeuvre some heavy object at the same time. They came in forced, tense bursts, and then were reined in abruptly with a low moan or a sharp intake of breath. Anna didn't need to make them out to understand their meaning, and at the same time she recognized, with every nerve ending in her body, that these sounds were not familiar to her. She froze by the doorway, her ears straining over the see-sawing of the bed head. And then Danny, sucking in air like a drowning man, called out something that at first Anna could not comprehend. She heard the name he used clearly enough, but some natural morphine flooded the part of her brain responsible for making sense of words and slowed the process to a virtual standstill. Looking back, Anna often thought that, were it not for this chemical reaction, she would have turned and fled at that moment. But, as it was, she needed to see the proof in order to be able to understand.

And so, as if in a dream, Anna stepped up into the room, turned, and saw Daniel kneeling upright on the bed with his back towards her. As she watched, a hand reached up to cup him round the neck, and he flopped forward onto his elbows and then rolled over, revealing the body of the woman lying underneath him: a slim, tanned woman, naked but for the forget-me-not coloured clips in her Carmen-rollered hair. Neither of them saw Anna at first. Lily stretched out a languid hand for the cigarettes on the bedside table; Daniel let his arm flop lightly across her belly and nuzzled her shoulder with his cheek. It was only when Lily raised the lighter and lit the flame that her eyes finally met Anna's.

In all the sleepless nights that followed, Anna never quite settled on the perfect response to this moment. She knew of all the literary and film precedents, or quite a few of them. She'd imagined the screaming match, and the catfight – her dragging Lily by her hair across the floor of the cottage, while in the background Daniel begged for mercy. There were so many options, it was hard to choose. But, at the time, Anna could neither speak nor move. Like a child mesmerized by a circus trick she simply watched, transfixed, as Lily turned her head, unruffled, to gauge Daniel's response. Then he, reaching slowly for a towel, had lifted himself off the bed with the resignation of a father forced to get up in the night to attend to a restless child. Anna noticed the firm set of his mouth, the way he folded over the top of the towel and ran his fingers casually through his hair – the reasonable man living up to his responsibilities. Looking back, she could think of many things she would have liked to call him, but at the time she could only gape as he padded across the floor towards her, his eyes straying like a bored teenager's, while, in the background, Lily raised the lighter once more and calmly lit her cigarette.

Later on, Anna would tell herself that, had she found the voice to speak, she would only have come out with one of those clichéd responses: something woefully inadequate like, 'How could you?' or 'I thought you loved me?' She suspected that, in real life, when a woman finds her lover in bed with her friend, she rarely has a pithy one-liner to hand, or even a four-letter word. More likely, she finds herself in a vibrating parallel world, where her hands look too large, and voices seem echoey, and somehow she is no longer there, in the moment, but lagging way behind it, floundering like a fully clothed swimmer in high seas. And it's at this point her instinct tells her that she will only survive this pain if she runs for her life.

Daniel didn't really try to stop her. Anna saw him raise his hand, glance heavily over his shoulder, looking for guidance, and by then she was gone. Without knowing how, unaware of having opened the front door or crossed the garden, she found herself back on the path, feet flashing beneath her at a pace she would never have imagined possible, and for several minutes she was carried back along the drive at this frantic speed. Then, just as unexpectedly, her legs stopped dead underneath her, like a horse refusing a fence. Instinctively she tried to take over the forward motion, but found herself falling to her knees on the grassy verge, from where she dropped like a stone onto her side. The noise emanating from her mouth alarmed Anna at first. But gradually she gave in to it, and lay there, resigned, as her jaw strained so wide that it ached and mucus gathered in a slug trail down her cheek. Sometime later, when the wailing had subsided and become a lurching sob, she wondered if she should lift herself off the ground, but there was no energy left to summon up, and so she stayed there, with her cheek pressed to the grass and her eyes screwed shut.

Thoughts came to her like flashbulbs popping at a crime scene: the bumper of the sports car tucked around the side of the cottage; the chimney smoke she'd so often seen rising above the trees; Tyntallin's curt response to her enquiry, 'I'm sorry to disappoint you. There is no one waiting for you at the cottage.' She saw the turquoise clips in Lily's hair as she had stood at the end of Anna's bed that morning; the crisp white box jacket 'perfect for a visit to the lawyers' lying discarded on the floor of the cottage. And then she was stretched out by the lake in Daniel's arms, stroking his bare chest as she pleaded with him to keep an eye on Lily while she was away in London. 'I know you have so much to think about already,' she'd said, deliberately cautious, anxious not to make him feel nagged or put upon. And he'd folded his arms behind his head, gazed up at the

cloudless sky, and answered in a voice tight with reluc-
tance, 'Of course, if that's what you want. I'll be her
friend.'

As Anna lay there on the grass, she was dimly aware
of a vehicle approaching and pulling up on the drive
beside her. She heard the low clunk as the diesel engine
stalled, the sound of a door opening and the crunch of
heavy boots on tarmac. In the silence that followed she
waited, eyes tight closed, oblivious to her fate, and then
she felt the grating of rough tweed across her back and
behind her knees as Tyntallin scooped her up in his arms
and carried her back to the Land Rover. She had no
choice but to rest her head against his shoulder. It smelt
metallic and sweet and the jacket was warm against her
cheek. When she opened her eyes a fraction she could
see the jutting shape of his Adam's apple straining
against the collar of his shirt.

'Leave me alone,' she managed to whisper as the soft
bench seat slid underneath her shoulder and a blanket
was loosely tucked around her. She felt his fingers pushing the tear-soaked hair off her face, and then resting on
her forehead as he paused to examine her swollen features.

'I'm sorry,' Tyntallin said, as he fired up the engine,
the rattling vibrations almost drowning his next words.
'I tried to warn you.'

Eighteen

Anna learnt about the divorce from an unexpected source. She was standing in the china department of John Lewis on a Saturday afternoon in November when she overheard a conversation between two grey-haired, distinguished-looking ladies.

'It's been very tough on Margot, of course,' said the wirier of the two, gripping the strap of her shoulder bag as she bent forward to check the price of a serving plate.

'Oh, ghastly,' her friend agreed, the knot of her silk headscarf wobbling on the tip of her chin. 'All that mud-slinging. Tarka's lost a stone apparently.'

The one with the shoulder bag shook her head despairingly. 'Still, I hear she didn't get anything like what she was after.'

'Well . . . she made the mistake of thinking this was America. Of course, over there the moment you mention the word "cruelty", you can sue them for every penny. Take the lot.'

The wiry one looked at her aghast.

'Oh yes.' Her friend pursed her lips and pushed her glasses down her nose, the better to examine the underside of a reduced-price milk jug. 'Not that there were all that many pennies to be had, of course. That was her first mistake.'

'Still, I suppose he might have been forced to sell some of the contents of the house . . . that marvellous enamel collection.'

'Oh, I daresay. Luckily Tarka had his wits about him and hired . . . you know . . . the one who did Princess Diana's divorce. He wasn't standing for any nonsense, I can tell you. She took fright, of course, disappeared before any really serious damage had been done.' The headscarf lady wrinkled her nose and, after one last arm's length deliberation, swapped the jug for its larger version. 'The point is,' she continued, lowering her voice so that Anna was forced to edge closer, 'Tarka shouldn't have married her in the first place. No one knew a thing about her. It was all –' she mouthed a short word accompanied by a sharp raise of the eyebrows. 'But why he had to *marry* her I simply do not know.'

'And what's happened to her now? The American . . .'

'Well, I'm not a hundred per cent sure.' The head-scarf lady paused briefly before succumbing to the irresistible temptation of conjecture. 'I think she's gone back to where she came from, probably. She was a professional masseuse, you know,' she added, reaching across to forage in the factory reject basket.

'I'm only glad Henrietta wasn't here to see it,' whispered the wiry one. 'Thank goodness she was spared that,' and the two of them lifted their heads in unison and drifted off towards the glass section.

*

When Anna relayed the essence of this conversation to Ruth, later that evening, she was conscious that it was not being received with quite the incredulity that she had anticipated.

'I only bothered to tell you because I thought it was such a perfect insight into that narrow little world,' Anna said. 'Not because I thought there was any truth in what they were saying. Professional *masseuse*. I think we know whose side they were on.'

Ruth nodded non-committally. They were sitting in what had been Richard and Anna's flat, on the white sofa that had once been the focal point of their living area and was now the only piece of furniture left in the apartment – apart from the double bed. Now, when you talked, your voices echoed weirdly and there were shadows on the floor and on the walls where their possessions – which turned out to be, strictly speaking, Richard's possessions – had once been.

'What Lily did to me,' Anna continued, leaning forward over her crossed legs so that Ruth was obliged to look up from her glass, 'doesn't make what *Tyntallin* did any less of an abomination. Does it? It doesn't mean he should get away with it.'

Ruth was conscious that while this might have started out dressed up as a funny-thing-happened-to-me-today conversation, it was already looking very much like the me and Daniel conversation. But then all their conversations ended up being either directly or indirectly about the events that had led to them both being here, in this empty flat, more or less living together (even if Ruth was still officially at her place, she and Billy camped with Anna most nights). Lately, the unspoken rule was that you had to get to the inevitable topic by a circuitous route, so it at least felt as though they were talking about something else. But there was no fooling either of them. A careless remark about the quality of supermarket lettuce would lead, inexorably, to an angry monologue from Ruth about all the times Dave had promised her they would move to the country. A casual enquiry about how the plans for Anna's book promotion were going would – after a suitable interval – descend into fretting about whether her work was what had really sabotaged her relationship with Daniel. Last night, they had even managed to turn a chance glimpse of Belinda on the television into a debate about whether Daniel would have fancied her, as Dave had; or would he, in fact, have had better taste.

'Who cares?' Ruth had found herself shouting. 'He's a total arsehole whatever way you look at it. Stop trying to make out he's still *special*.'

The hardest part now was listening. They never tired of their own sad story – there was always more to wring out of one particular aspect of the tragedy, always the new unexplored detail – but each of them was bored with the other's self-pity and inability to see the truth. Ruth resented Anna's refusal to loathe Daniel violently, and Anna couldn't disguise the fact that she felt Ruth's misery – being self-inflicted – was less worthy of their attention. These days, when one of them was talking, you could tell that the other one was somewhere else, mentally rearranging the exhibits and testimonies in their Case for the Worst Possible Heartbreak.

'I mean,' Anna was saying, 'it's only because of the way Lily was treated that she did what she did. None of it would have happened if it hadn't been for Tyntallin. You have got to admit that,' she added, when Ruth failed to respond.

Ruth eyed the almost empty bottle of wine on the floor and wondered, as she had on so many occasions like this, if now was the time to challenge her friend's version of the events of the past summer. Anna's way of coping with what had happened had been to blame the threat that Lily was living under. In her mind, Lily was a desperate woman in need of comfort, and Daniel was a sympathetic figure who found himself caught up in a painful situation. There was no question of a reconciliation – Daniel hadn't been seen or heard of since that day – but, nonetheless, Anna seemed determined to believe that he and Lily were simply two people thrown together by circumstance, and that circumstance was the unreasonable behaviour of Tarka Tyntallin. Her strange, forced smile when she relayed this version of events to Ruth, Jean and Valerie was sufficient, at the time, to keep them from suggesting any alternative explanation.

'Oh, let her believe it, poor darling,' Jean had said as they huddled on the pavement outside Anna's flat that evening. 'What's the harm, if it helps her to forget.'

'She hasn't forgotten,' Valerie had whispered, 'she's in *denial*. Don't any of you know anything about human psychology?'

'Well, thank God, is all I can say,' Jean had continued. 'When she's strong enough to face it she will. Why rub it in now?'

'I'll tell you why,' Valerie had hissed. 'It's called closure, and closure is the necessary precursor of change. Closure is what she didn't have after Daniel disappeared, which is why she got herself tied up with him all over again. It could be Daniel, Daniel, Daniel for all eternity unless she deals with it now.'

'Did you worry about me like this?' Ruth had asked, when they finally kissed goodnight on the doorstep. 'When Dave and I separated?'

There was an uncomfortable pause and then Valerie, rummaging in her handbag, had said, 'Well your situation was more straightforward, wasn't it? You slept with someone at work and you got caught.'

Ruth examined the woman opposite her on the sofa. Anna's hair, which she had worn loose and unbrushed throughout the summer, was pulled back in a severe ponytail. She was thinner than she had been for some time but not, for once, in a way that made Ruth envious, and there was an air about her as though she were afraid of being touched, a wariness to her movements. Lately, she had taken to wearing baggy trousers and several thin layers of tops – continually plucking at the neck and wrists, adjusting them a millimetre here and there – and the glasses, which she'd only ever worn as an emergency measure, were now a regular feature. Black, with heavy rectangular frames, they made her pretty oval face look armed, secured from the threat of intruders.

'I know what you're thinking,' Anna said, scrutinizing Ruth's expression. 'You're thinking let's not get into another how-did-we-get-here conversation.'

'Actually, I was thinking just the opposite.' Ruth rubbed at the lipstick smear on the rim of her glass. 'I was thinking it might help you to go back. Find out exactly what happened after you left. You could talk to the sister maybe?'

'I know what happened,' Anna said, that same forced smile sliding into position.

'No you don't.' Ruth held Anna's eye. 'You haven't any idea. Not really. Aren't you at all interested in what happened to him?'

Anna gave a sharp disparaging laugh, turning her head away, as if to distance herself from this clumsy performance.

'Well, I'm curious. It's like a lost chapter in the story. If I were you I couldn't just leave it at that . . .' The sound of Billy grumbling from the bedroom prompted Ruth to take the bull by the horns. She took a deep breath. Anna was still turned away, her fingers tugging at the wrist of her sweater. 'Look, Anna, this horrible thing happened to you, and you haven't actually dealt with it. You've got all of us running around examining our lives from every angle but you're not . . . you haven't followed your own example.'

Anna's head swivelled slowly back to face her. For a second it reminded Ruth of a precious mask in a display cabinet, cooled by thermostatically controlled air, lit by filtered light, dusted every so often by experts with white rubber gloves and tiny sable brushes.

'You're going to have to face it sooner or later,' Ruth said quickly. 'You're going to have to admit that you got it wrong. You got it really badly wrong and you need to deal with the consequences. For your own sake.'

In the bedroom Billy's crying had built from a flat, low moan to a high-pitched consistent wail, like the sound of an air-raid siren. Ruth got up off the sofa and yanked her cardigan closed. 'Think about it, Anna,' she said, padding across the floor, 'at least there's somewhere for you to go. Some of us have reached a dead end.'

Some time later, Billy now settled, Ruth slipped back out of the bedroom like a cat burglar, closing the door behind her as if the handle were an unblown dandelion head and the frame made of wafer-thin glass.

'Sorry,' she whispered, tiptoeing back to the sofa where Anna was still sitting, still extending the boundaries of her sweater, 'I didn't mean to sound quite so . . .'

'No. You're probably right,' Anna said, the smile now gone.

'I gave in my notice today.' Ruth lowered herself cautiously onto the seat beside Anna. 'Dave said it wouldn't make any difference to him, but I thought it might. So, anyway, I rang Dave to tell him.'

Anna nodded. At least she was trying to look interested. And, to be fair, the news wasn't extraordinary. Ruth did ring Dave most days, although they had agreed that she wouldn't. 'And what did he say?'

'He said . . .' Ruth hesitated as she attempted to make something out of not much at all. 'He said "Oh." But I think he sounded pleased. He said, "Thanks for letting me know." And then he said, "How's Billy?"' Ruth smiled expectantly at Anna and Anna smiled back. There was a set pattern now, even to their gestures: Ruth would look up and Anna would be waiting with the positive expression; Anna would ask for reassurance and Ruth would be ready with a firm, 'It wasn't your fault. How could you possibly have known?'

'My mum was on the phone, earlier,' Ruth said. 'Same old thing. She said anyone else in my position would be begging him to have them back. "I don't know what you think there is to talk about," she said. "You should be down on your knees, asking that boy to forgive you."'

They smiled at each other, Ruth searching her friend's eyes for any sign of hesitation.

'I told her you've got a whole chapter on establishing what you need from a relationship, rather than rushing back in, and getting it wrong . . . And that's the point, isn't it?'

'And what did she say?'

'Oh, you know.' Ruth lowered her eyes. 'Roughly translated . . . she thinks we both need our heads examined.'

Nineteen

When Tony opened his eyes he found himself lying on his side gazing at a stainless-steel sink and next to it a steel trolley, on which there was an electric kettle, a drum of Nescafé and a long stack of styrofoam cups. It was a few seconds before he remembered that he was in a hospital, and a few more before he noticed his shoes and coat had been removed and a flesh-coloured, loose-stitched blanket draped over his reclining body. He checked that his watch was still on his wrist, for which he instantly felt guilty, and simultaneously wondered how his mother was and where Jean had got to. According to his watch it was just after five, six hours since they had first arrived at the hospital, and more or less when Elsie was due to come out of surgery. Had he been asleep then all this time? Who had put him here? Jean? Jean with the help of a troupe of male nurses?

Tony rolled over on his back and noticed for the first time the heavy, wet-sand feeling in his head. He was familiar with a Valium hangover from the early days of his marriage, when he and Jean would be dosed up, as a matter of course, for long-haul flights or high-pressure events. Lucky for him she still liked to travel prepared. He remembered now the coolness of her hand pressed against the back of his neck as she coaxed him to swallow the pill; the sound of her voice promising that everything would be all right if he would only just relax and close his eyes. A porthole window in the door beyond the foot of his bed afforded a glimpse of heads and shoulders bobbing along the brightly lit corridor outside. Lying there, watching the human traffic chuntering by, Tony found himself drifting off again, slipping back to the time when he had visited Jean in hospital, a few months into their courtship. She had broken her wrist, coming off the back of a motorcycle en route to a modelling job, though Tony hadn't given a thought to her pain at the time. All he was interested in was the fact that she had been riding pillion with a young photographer, who probably earned three times as much as he did, and who he knew to be a member of Turks Club. Tony could see Jean now, sitting pertly on the bed in the A & E unit, gazing at him from under those heavy black eyelashes while he paced up and down, railing at her for her thoughtless behaviour.

'It was only a job, Tony,' she had said, her voice back then even more velvety and patrician, or perhaps he just hadn't been used to it. 'You're being silly, Tony. You don't have anything to worry about.'

'All right,' Tony had said, dumping the photographer's lilies in the wastepaper bin beside the bed. 'Prove it then. Marry me.'

Looking back, if he were forced to analyse his feelings about becoming engaged to Jean, Tony had to admit that, as well as being excited, and proud, he was also extremely anxious. Even as she leant forward to kiss him, and he smelt the scent he knew she had

specially sent over from Paris, even as he heard her
murmur, 'You are sweet, of course I will', Tony couldn't
help feeling he was punching above his weight. Jean's
dad was a brigadier and her mother's parents lived in a
place which was open to the public at weekends. On the
one occasion they had been introduced, Tony had been
offered champagne, although it was only eleven o'clock
in the morning, and the brigadier had attempted to
engage him in a conversation about the problems of
maintaining a grass tennis court. Tony knew he could
walk the walk and talk the talk – after all that's what he
did for a living. He knew he was good-looking, and
amusing, and he knew Jean liked him enough to have
discarded several suitors, including a well-known racing
driver. But, at the same time, he wasn't completely
confident that he was a match for a woman of her cali-
bre. Jean could speak three languages, whereas he could
speak none. She'd lived in India and America and he'd
only ever been to Spain, once, on an overnight modelling job. She knew lines from poems and arias from
operas and the Latin names of flowers and how to date
an antique to the nearest ten years, and when they went
out to a club or a restaurant, or flicked through the
society pages of magazines, Jean knew people.

'Where I come from, the men have the answers and
the women ask the questions,' was how Tony had
explained it to the analyst he saw for a year or so after
the divorce. 'I wore the trousers in the marriage, don't
get me wrong. But she knew her own mind, and she had
the money, of course.'

'Why do you think your wife married you?' the
analyst had asked.

'She always said it was because I made her laugh,' was Tony's reply. 'But that doesn't mean anything, does it? I did make her laugh, but that's not the be all and end all, is it? That's not the solution to everything.'

According to his analyst, this nagging suspicion that he wasn't quite up to the job was precisely what had driven Tony to have the affairs in the first place. If he pushed Jean then she would eventually leave, so the analyst's theory went. And if she left him because he'd been unfaithful, that meant he had controlled the reason for her leaving, thereby avoiding rejection. It sounded insane to Tony at the time. He told the analyst he was just a typical man who succumbed to his natural urges; it was as simple and as shameful as that. And, in his case, there was another mitigating factor: he was second to none, so they said, at pleasing the ladies, and that particular gift was a hard one to let slip.

The analyst had looked up from his notes at about this point and said: 'Often it's easier to think of ourselves as irresponsible, than to admit we're vulnerable.'

'Whatever the hell that means,' said Tony.

'Perhaps we should talk about children,' said the analyst.

'How do you mean?'

'The fact of your not having had any. Was that a problem?'

'Worse things happen, don't they?'

'Not to some couples,' the analyst said, examining Tony over his spectacles.

'Well. Jean minded, of course.'

'You talked about it?'

I found her crying once. In the bathroom. She had a little cardigan thing in her hands.'

'And what did you say when you found her crying?'

'I said I was sorry. There wasn't much more I could say.'

'Was there any blame involved, would you say?'

'If you mean whose fault was it . . . they never got to the bottom of it,' Tony said. 'But I always knew it was mine. I knew because Jean had everything, but the one thing she couldn't do on her own . . . didn't work out. She looked like someone who was just ready to have children. Do you know what I mean?'

Later on in their sessions they had got around to the actual crisis that precipitated the break-up of the marriage. The analyst wanted to know exactly how the whole scene had unfolded. So Tony told him how he had seen Jean and the tennis coach sitting together on a bench by the courts in the nearby square. Jean, he had noticed, was smiling that particular secretive smile, and twiddling her hair the way she always did when she was interested in someone. On the basis of this evidence, that evening he had skulked in the gloaming at number 25, waiting to confront her. It had been dark for half an hour when she'd finally swung through the door like some teenager back from school, with her aertex shirt half undone and her knickers on show for all to see, and Tony had let her have it, then and there. The conversation didn't really warrant repeating, but the analyst seemed intrigued by the details nonetheless.

So she admitted it?' the analyst asked. 'I just want to be clear.'

'"Would you honestly blame me if I'd fooled around?" were her exact words,' Tony corrected him.

'And what did you say to that?'

'I said, "Yes, I bloody well would!"'

'And you made no attempt to salvage the situation?'

'Salvage?' Tony repeated, incredulous. 'Jean knew that with me there were no second chances. The point is that the moment she looked elsewhere the spell was broken.'

'Whereas when you were unfaithful . . . ?' At this point the analyst had removed his spectacles, fixing Tony with his fleshy eyes, and Tony had temporarily lost his patience.

'Doc, with respect,' he'd said, 'we're talking about two very different concepts here. You really can't compare them.'

'Do you think you're wife understood that what you did and what she did were . . . incomparable?'

'Yes,' Tony had said. 'I explained it to her.'

'And what did she say?'

'She said . . . I think she said, "I give in, Tony. You win."'

Tony opened his eyes again. Some noise had disturbed his dozing, and as he raised his head he saw that the door with the porthole window was ajar and Jean's head, and one slim leg in tapered black trousers, were poking through the gap.

'Hello,' she said softly, gripping the rubber frame of the door with white-tipped fingers. Then she turned to look over her shoulder and whispered: 'I'll deal with this. Keep us posted, would you?'

Out in the corridor Tony saw a man in a white coat

stretch his neck to peer over her head into the room. Jean pressed the door closed behind her, one hand hovering at her mouth as if she had a toothache.

'I'm feeling a lot better,' Tony said, pushing himself up on his elbows and smoothing his hair back into place. 'Sorry about the fuss. I won't let it happen again.'

Jean nodded, her eyes were lowered to the floor. 'Bunny,' she said, and that was when he knew, 'Elsie's not very well.'

'No,' he said.

'She's not well at all.' Jean discarded the hand shielding the lower part of her face and he saw that her lips were shaking. 'They say, there's nothing they can do, Bunny. They say it's gone too far. I'm so sorry.'

Tony reached out a hand to her and they clutched at each other as if the ground were shifting beneath them. He was surprised at how fragile she felt. Her ribs pressing against his reminded him of the Cunningham children, when they used to clamber up on his knee, plug a thumb into their mouths and collapse against his chest, their hearts thundering inside their soft little bodies. He remembered when he had been about the same age, how Elsie would, on the command, 'Uppy, uppy', tug his shirt up over his poker-straight arms. How he'd stand there, eyes blinking against the thick cotton, while she eased it up over his ears, and then the feel of her warm, dry hands under his armpits, the soothing chatter as she lifted him up and over the side of the bath, into the steamy water.

'Jeanie,' he said, and the sound of his voice made her pull away from him and focus earnestly on his face. 'Would you do something for me?'

'Of course, Bunny,' she said, 'anything.' Her violet eyes were foggy with tears, her long cool fingers cradled his face.

'Would you marry me, Jeanie?'

Twenty

On the phone, Margot had suggested that Anna aimed to arrive with them in time for tea.

'I'll have Jonty out of the way by then, he's off to visit the cousins,' she explained, her voice straining to be heard above a chorus of barking in the background. 'Now, you know where we are? Take a right before the Tyntallin turnoff, and if you reach the bridge you've gone too far . . .'

Whether it was because the countryside looked so unfamiliar stripped of its green cladding, or because Anna's mind was elsewhere as she drove, it was well after six, and dark, by the time she eventually turned into Margot's drive.

The house was Georgian in style and pretty as a doll's house, and as Anna stepped out onto the gravel she could see, through the ground-floor windows, an elegant drawing room, furnished with large oil paintings and sofas crowded with embroidered cushions. She hesitated, waiting for signs of life, then mounted the few steps to the front door and rang the bell, instantly triggering the cacophony of a kennel at feeding time. Beyond the door, the noise of dogs grew steadily louder and more frenzied until they were jammed up against it, jostling and yelping. Anna waited. Nothing at all happened for several minutes, then there was a sound of bolts being drawn, the door lurched open, and there stood Margot – red-faced and beaming in the midst of a swirling river of canine bodies.

'Well done for finding us!' she shouted, one arm beckoning Anna forward like a distracted traffic policeman. 'So sorry, my dear, normally we use the back door, which is why it took . . . WILL YOU GO TO YOUR BASKETS. GOTYRBASKET . . . GOO ON.' A large leg encased in tie-dye leggings lashed out, sending a couple of the smaller dogs skeetering across the floor and crashing into a plant stand. 'Come in. Come in, Anna! What did I tell you? It is a zoo here. Absolute madness. GEDOWN WILL YOU . . . GET DOWN!'

Still beckoning, Margot led the way across the hall into a large, stone-floored kitchen with wooden clothes' driers hanging from the ceiling, a cream-coloured Aga at one end and, gathered around it, three broken-down armchairs.

'Here we are!' she said, forcing the door closed behind them, to the accompaniment of hysterical yelping. 'This is where we live all winter, I'm afraid. Never go near the rest of the house between October and June. Only put the lights on so you could see what you were doing. Now, what'll you have?' Margot grabbed Anna's arm and looked her fiercely in the eye. 'I'm in the mood for a g and t. Will you join me? I think I'm rather past the tea stage.'

Anna requested a spritzer and settled herself, as instructed, in the least destroyed of the armchairs while Margot foraged in the fridge for a bottle of fizzy water

– finally opting for the one that made a slight futting noise when she twisted the lid, and pouring it from a great height.

'Now,' Margot said, slumping into the opposite chair, g and t in hand. 'It must be three months since you were last down here? Finally finished that book of yours?' Anna confirmed that she had and Margot clapped her thigh appreciatively. 'So, I suppose you must have seen the sale advertised in the newspapers?'

'What sale is that?' Anna asked.

'You haven't heard? I assumed that was why you'd got in touch after all this time. Oh, well . . .' Margot paused, gazing glumly at the floor between her slippered feet. 'My brother made the decision a month or so ago. They're starting with the contents of the house in a few weeks' time, and then . . . Of course, nothing's going to happen overnight. It's quite something to take on a house like Tyntallin, and I understand it's rather isolated for modern tastes . . .' Margot looked up suddenly and there was a dazed vulnerability about her features, like the face of a child woken from a deep sleep in strange surroundings. 'One can't blame him for wanting to make a fresh start, of course,' she added, covering the last traces of her bewilderment with a brave, gummy smile.

'I didn't know about the sale,' Anna said. 'I wanted to get in touch because it's been a while and I wasn't sure what had happened . . . to all of you.'

Margot nodded, uncertainty flickering at the corners of her smile. She looked suddenly overburdened, as if it might take her an entire lifetime to trawl through the events of the past few months, and she was ill-prepared to begin the process now.

'I know they separated,' Anna continued. 'I know that Lily went back to America. I just wondered what had gone on in between? After I left?'

'Well, let me see.' Margot turned her face to the ceiling, looking for inspiration among the rows of striped boxer shorts. 'I suppose it would have been around that time . . . Yes. I'm sure it was. She . . . Lily, presented Tarka with an ultimatum. She said she wanted a divorce, and that she was going to sue him for various alleged acts of cruelty unless he agreed to a very generous settlement.' Margot paused, her lips tightening as the focus of her memory sharpened. 'Of course, one had been prepared, in a way. But when it happened, it was so much worse than one had ever imagined. There were terrible accusations flying around . . . to do with Tarka's character and so forth.' She circled the base of the glass tumbler on her thigh. Her face twitched as she discarded some piece of information either too painful, or too distasteful, to repeat. 'Fortunately, my brother had smelt a rat, quite early on, and had the good sense to hire a man to check up on her. At first he didn't have much luck and then, just as Lily was naming her price, he started to turn up some quite astonishing stuff.'

Margot paused, settling back in her chair, dusting absent-mindedly at some old stain on her bosom.

'What sort of stuff?'

'Oh, she'd done it all before. The very same thing, apparently – married a wealthy man and taken him to the cleaners after a matter of months. It was all meticulously planned from start to finish, right from their meeting in New York. The bereavement counselling was just a cover, as it turns out, a ruse for snaring eligible widowers.' Margot glanced at Anna and shrugged. 'It is unbelievable, but rather ingenious in a way. She'd scour the obituary pages, target the most suitable candidates, set up the introduction. And then there was the man on the ground, of course, checking out the assets, deciding which of them was most worth pursuing.'

Anna shook her head. 'What? You're saying . . . ?'

'Yes!' Margot interrupted. 'Confidence tricksters! Plain and simple. After the marriage, the idea was to make it look like there had been some ghastly business going on behind closed doors, so she could get out quickly, and take a good chunk of money with her. And that's where the accomplice came in again. He was there in the background to help things along. Provide a witness to all the supposed . . . horrors.'

'Accomplice? What accomplice?'

'The fellow in the cottage, of course. Your musician friend. Oh my dear . . .' Margot gaped and put a hand to her chest. 'Good heavens, I was sure you must have known. Yes, I'm afraid so,' she continued, addressing her lap. 'It appears they'd been in league for a few years. Both of them did a moonlit flit as soon as it was clear they weren't going to get away with it. But naturally, not before they'd sold a number of valuable pieces – all carefully chosen, all of them untraceable. She was not quite the philistine she pretended to be.'

Anna shook her head vehemently. 'But this can't be right. You see, I introduced them. I bumped into Danny out of the blue. It was a complete coincidence. And then Lily happened to be having a dinner party and suggested that –' she froze. Margot held her gaze. 'But he was making an album. He couldn't have been doing that and . . . he was working on an album in a studio, just outside the village. He was there day and night, for months.'

'I don't think so, dear,' Margot said softly. 'There is no studio.'

Anna stared blinking at the glass in Margot's hands. 'I met her at a stranger's wedding,' she whispered. 'There isn't any way she could have known I'd be there, let alone that I knew Daniel. It isn't possible.'

Margot smiled at her pityingly. 'She was on the look-out for allies, my dear,' she said gently. 'I suppose Lily must have mentioned having met you, perhaps she observed that you were a sympathetic sort, and then your friend would only have had to fill in the blanks.' She shuffled forward in her chair, reaching out a hand to pat Anna's knee. 'Your coming into the picture was certainly a bonus for them, my dear. But if it hadn't been you, rest assured it would have been someone else.'

'No,' Anna said, still shaking her head. 'Why? Why choose me?'

'They wanted someone who could be set up, so to speak.' Margot smiled hard to demonstrate that there were no hard feelings, despite what she was about to say. 'Someone who would be prepared to testify on their behalf, if need be.'

Anna stared at the clock on the wall above Margot's head as she remembered the atmosphere up at the house: the tension and the raised voices; the violent out-bursts.

'But what I saw was real,' she said. 'After the dinner party. I saw him . . .'

Anna paused as she pictured that night in the drawing room, the moment when Tyntallin had lurched suddenly across the floor to where Lily cowered, terrified, on the sofa. What had he said? She retraced the scene. He was standing by the fireplace, cigarette in hand. She could see his narrowed eyes fixed on Lily, his fist clenched tightly at his side. 'Leave her out of this,' he'd said. 'Leave her out of this.' Anna closed her eyes, breathed deeply and tried again. There were the arguments in the night, the footsteps running past her bedroom door; Lily's eyes swollen from crying; all the things she had told her, the terrible things he had said and done, when no one was there to see.

'I saw it,' Anna whispered. 'She told me.'

From the chair opposite Margot watched as, one by one, Anna revisited each episode of Tyntallin's violence, reached out to touch it, and then saw it evaporate in front of her. She sat patiently, circling the gin and tonic on her knee, and it wasn't until Anna doubled over cradling her face in her hands that she spoke again.

'We're all guilty of seeing what we want to see, my dear,' she said, getting up to close the curtains over the sink. 'Don't be too hard on yourself. Really the only fool in this is my brother, trusting to the love of a stranger at his age. It's something we were taught from a very early age . . . stick with your own kind, and you won't be disappointed.'

Anna nodded weakly. She felt as if she had gone to sleep for a moment and woken up in an unreliable version of her life: a world where she needed to question all the certainties and re-evaluate all the people. Above all, she was ashamed. Margot was generous, but then Margot hadn't been there. She hadn't seen how enthusiastically Anna had embraced the role of Lily's champion; how eagerly she had condemned Tyntallin without a shred of evidence. She didn't know that Anna had nominated herself judge, jury and confessor and hungrily executed the roles, as if she, personally, had suffered at his hands. Margot hadn't been at the dining table when Anna accused her host of hypocrisy; hadn't listened to her lecture him on the importance of trust and loyalty, while all the time he had known of his wife's plans and Anna's part in them. Nor could she have suspected that her brother had chosen to protect the hostile stranger living in his midst, simply to save her from getting hurt.

'Anna, my dear.' Margot was leaning over her, peering into her face. 'My goodness, you were somewhere else altogether. I'm not the most tactful of people, but I do realize your loss in all of this. I hope I haven't upset—'

'No, Margot,' Anna said. 'I needed to know. I wish I'd known a long time ago.'

'That's the spirit.' Margot straightened up and smiled her gummy smile. 'Now, you can't come all this way without visiting the house. They've offered to feed me later, since Jonty's away, and it would be no trouble at all to add one to the party.'

'Oh I couldn't. It doesn't seem . . .'

Margot waved a hand dismissively. 'If there's one thing we've all learnt from this episode, it's that what seems and what doesn't seem is neither here nor there.

Now, don't be awkward. You're staying the night.' She walked stiffly over to the telephone, squinted hard at the display with the wary expression of someone not yet quite accustomed to cordless technology, struck a button and braced herself against the worktop. 'Even if Tarka isn't over the moon,' she said, staring blank-eyed into the middle distance, 'I can tell you, the children will be delighted to see you.'

Twenty-one

The house looked different against the chill black backdrop of a November night, more austere than Anna remembered it, and barely inhabited. The only windows lit up were on the ground floor, to the west of the entrance, so that the building seemed lopsided; a half-felled dinosaur preserving its last reservoirs of energy. The facade, that had always been illuminated on summer nights, was now shrouded in shadow, and the place had an air of shame about it – as if it accepted that advertising the grandeur of its proportions had provoked avarice in others, and that mistake was never to be repeated. Yet even so, as Margot's car swept onto the gravel and the building rose up in the headlights like a frozen wave, it still took Anna's breath away. Even now, to her profound surprise, it made her heart beat faster.

Anna stepped out of the car and, for an instant, felt her knees give way beneath her, while Margot, oblivious, chattered on about the forthcoming sale and her brother's worryingly detached attitude to the whole business.

'It's not as if he doesn't know all there is to know about every single piece that's of any value,' Margot

said, in a voice raised to compensate for the gusting
wind. 'But he seems to have lost all interest. Really, it is
frustrating. My hope,' she leant towards Anna as they
mounted the front steps, gripping her elbow confiden-
tially, 'is that they do well on the first few days and then
call the whole thing off. It's a heck of an endeavour,
mind you, as it is. If only he would ask for help. There
are plenty of local divorcees who'd be only too
delighted to lend a hand. Too *proud* you see.'

'Where will they go, if they sell the house?' Anna
asked, but Margot was already through the door, dragging off her coat as she bellowed the news of their
arrival. By the time the coat was removed and deposited
on a chair, all three children were standing in front of
her in the library doorway, each bound up like parcels
in their flannel dressing gowns, wary smiles hovering on
their faces.

'Ah ha! I thought you might be allowed to stay up
to see our visitor.' Margot tweaked Maisie's cheek as
she edged sideways past the children and into the
library. 'Now mind you don't keep Anna long. Cocktails
await.'

For a second Maisie and Oscar scanned each other's
faces, gauging the right level of reception, and then
rushed Anna at full tilt, clasping her around the knees,
giggling wildly. After a suitable interval of shouting
'Hello' in various different tones of voice, they spun
off again towards the library, and disappeared. Emily
seemed undecided as to the appropriate greeting. She
hovered shyly in the doorway, finally slinking forward
and offering Anna a polite, glancing kiss on the cheek.

'You didn't say goodbye,' she said, taking a step

back and nailing Anna with a look that she had clearly been working on.

'I didn't think you'd notice,' Anna said and then, seeing Emily's drooping lower lip, added, 'I didn't mean that. There was a lot going on. I wasn't myself.'

Emily appeared to accept this explanation. She dropped the blonde ponytail that she'd been stroking against her cheek and flipped it over her shoulder in a gesture which reminded Anna that three months are a long time in the life of a little girl.

'How have things been?' Anna asked.

'Weird,' Emily said, widening her eyes dramatically, all pretence of coolness instantly forgotten. 'Daddy wants to move, so we have to sell everything, and the stuff we aren't going to sell has to have labels on it.' The word labels was delivered with an expression of absolute incredulity, as if this were the most incomprehensible adult decision Emily had yet witnessed. In the distance, Margot's voice urged them not to dally too long in the cold.

'You're missing the white ladies!' she called. 'I'm practically onto my second!'

Emily took Anna's hand as they obediently crossed the hall towards the library. 'How long are you staying?' she asked, eyes straining for Anna's response.

'Oh, just for the night. I wasn't expecting to come here at all.'

'Why not?'

'Well,' Anna hesitated, 'I didn't want to intrude. I know your father has a lot on his mind at the moment.'

Emily was chewing on the thumb of her free hand and looking sideways up at Anna, the way a dog looks when it's protecting a bone. 'Don't you care that Daddy's selling the house?' she asked.

'Very much,' Anna said. 'I'm surprised at how much,' she added, conscious from Emily's searching expression that some more detailed analysis was required. 'It's very . . .'

'Don't say sad,' Emily interrupted. 'Everyone says sad. It's very stupid, more like.'

They paused just inside the library doors. At the far end of the room, faces warmed by the fire and the cocktails turned dreamily in their direction and Margot raised her arm in the air, jiggling a glass enticingly.

'What do you think will happen to us?' Emily asked quietly.

'Oh, you'll be fine. Your father would only ever do what's best for you.'

'That's what he said before,' Emily whispered, removing her hand from Anna's. 'That's what he said when he married Lily.'

'Anna, my dear.' Margot's raised arm waggled violently. 'Do come and get warm by the fire.'

Anna smiled in acknowledgement and, still smiling, started to walk towards the far end of the room, Emily lagging a few steps behind. Feelings jostled in her stomach, some of which she could easily label – anxiety, guilt, a faint social awkwardness – and others that slid around like black eels, refusing to yield their identity. She was acutely conscious that Tyntallin, having registered her entrance, had turned his back to the fire and was now staring stiffly ahead of him, one hand resting in the pocket of his smoking jacket, the other fingering the ever-present cigarette. Margot, chattering away, swooped towards him once or twice, batting his arm to emphasize a point, but he never moved, other than to put the cigarette to his lips and draw on it with hollowed cheeks. They were just seconds away from the inevitable reintroduction, Anna's stomach tightening that final notch, when Oscar rushed up and barred her way with an energetic star jump.

'There was meant to be other people coming, with children,' he informed her breathlessly, the cord of his dressing gown unravelling to reveal a pair of Superman pyjamas. 'But they never came in the end.'

'Family just moved down from London,' Margot explained. 'They were fussing that it might be too cold for their little darlings. Don't seem to have quite adjusted to life in the country.' Her gaze strayed for a moment to Anna's pale shearling jerkin and cream suede trousers. 'Anyway, Tarka, I'm surprised not to find at least *one* divorcee here for dinner.' Margot winked at Anna. 'A few of them have been extremely helpful, haven't they, Tarka? I think the least they could expect is a bit of Tyntallin hospitality.'

Margot cast her eyes appreciatively around the room and Anna's gaze followed, skimming the arrangements of amaryllis, the newly restored chairs upholstered in eau de nil corduroy, and the long table by the windows, once a dumping ground for newspapers, now given over to every respected country magazine title.

'Tarka?' Margot snapped her fingers. 'Wakey wakey! Good grief. You're getting as bad as Jonty. Never on the same planet as the rest of us.'

'I apologize,' mumbled Tyntallin, reaching behind him for his glass.

'I was telling Anna that there've been a few changes since she was last here. I didn't realize myself quite how much had happened, it rather brought it all home . . .' Margot looked suddenly bemused, the corners of her mouth crumpling as she contemplated the indignities of their recent history. 'He's lost over a stone, you know,' she continued, tut tutting to herself. 'Kept himself locked up in his study, wouldn't see a soul for the best part of two months. Really, there was a time when I feared he'd make himself ill. Anyway, here's to happier days.' Margot paused as Emily padded across the carpet and planted herself squarely in front of her aunt. 'And what can I do for you, young lady?'

'Could you put us to bed, please?' asked Emily sweetly, her head listing to one side.

'Bed? I thought you wanted to see Anna? Well, you don't need to go up right this minute, surely?'

'It's better we go now, Aunt Margot.' Emily pointed ominously at Maisie who stared back, wide eyes unblinking. 'Or else,' she mouthed, 'she'll have a tired tantrum.'

All eyes turned simultaneously to look at Maisie who returned their gaze with the bright-eyed confidence of someone who had never had any reason to suspect foul play. Oscar yanked up the leg of his pyjama bottom and started to scratch his knee violently.

'Oh, very well.' Margot placed her glass on the nearest table, and stretched out a practised hand in Maisie's direction. 'Looks like I'm on duty for the night. Come along then. Up we go.'

Maisie looked startled and then livid. She glared fiercely up at her aunt, her complexion transformed from milky white to thunderous red, and bolted in the opposite direction.

'Won't be long,' Margot shouted over the ensuing screams. 'Tarka, you can fill in the details for Anna while I'm sorting this lot out.'

Anna watched, helplessly, as they all disappeared down the library – Maisie wriggling in Margot's arms, Emily trailing behind and pausing in the doorway just long enough to cast a meaningful look at Anna; a look that said, 'It could have been you.'

Then they were alone together.

She assumed that Tyntallin would be obliged to say something, but he continued to stare into the middle distance, his chin slightly raised as if his collar was restricting. He seemed taller than she remembered, certainly thinner. The outer edge of his cheekbones looked sharp enough to break the skin, and his strong nose had risen up out of his face, every ridge and bump now visibly jutting below the surface. In three months, the thatch of grey hair had grown, unchecked, so that now it hung down into his bruised-looking eyes, giving him a faintly louche appearance. As Anna watched, he reached for his cigarette case, placed a cigarette in the corner of his mouth and lit it, hands cupped over the tip. She held her breath. 'Now it's coming,' she said to herself, as he slid one hand into his trouser pocket and leant back against the mantelpiece. But still he said nothing.

'I'm afraid I shouldn't be here,' Anna heard herself say. 'I'm obviously not welcome. Not that I'm surprised in the least. I should have known better than to come.'

His head turned towards her. The cigarette rested

lightly on his lower lip, two lazy, nicotine-stained fingers hovering in attendance.

'I suppose I thought . . .' she continued. 'I suppose I hoped that if we met again we might achieve some kind of closure. Or I could, at least. I'm sorry –' Anna closed her eyes and shook her head '– that's really what I want to say. Forget about the closure. I'm just very, very sorry about what happened. I was wrong. I was wrong about everything.'

Her face felt hot, her mouth parched. He was staring at her, focusing intensely on her face, the way a painter regards his subject – critically, dispassionately and yet seeing every emotion, every secret thought and feeling. 'He's appalled by me', she thought, 'mesmerized by my selfishness. He's thinking, "This woman lectured me in my own home, conspired with my ex-wife, and now she expects me to help her salve her conscience."'

'I don't expect to be forgiven,' Anna said, abruptly. 'I only wanted to apologize for having misjudged you. Even before I realized how you'd tried to protect me, I'd been thinking about what happened here . . . About you.'

The grey eyes flinched. He plucked the cigarette from his lips and took a step towards her. Anna steeled herself for the inevitable rebuke. But instead of his low, angry voice the room was suddenly filled with the sound of Margot's protests.

'Only Anna can read their bedtime story, apparently,' she bellowed as she barrelled down the library towards them. 'Would you mind awfully, Anna? I've been sent down to get you –' Margot stopped suddenly and stood, hands on hips, breathing heavily.

'Not at all,' Anna said. 'I'd be happy to.'

'Good girl . . . you know where to go then. I'll just get their hotties.'

Anna turned back to Tyntallin, but the interruption had given him a chance to gather himself and now he was facing the fire, one elbow on the mantlepiece, his head sunk low between his shoulders. His body language said everything he wasn't prepared to: he had had the courtesy to hear her out, and now, as far as he was concerned, the matter was closed. He was not angry, so much as at the limit of his patience, weary and more, Anna realized with a twinge of hurt pride, thoroughly, profoundly bored. Tyntallin reached out a hand for his glass, and for a brief second Anna thought he might turn around and say what he had been on the verge of saying before Margot reappeared. But, of course, he didn't. He simply didn't care enough to bother with the crushing put-down or the curt dismissal. The feelings she was struggling with were of not the slightest concern to him and it was only good manners that prevented him from telling her so. Anna gazed at the broad back, turned squarely to face her, and suddenly understood that, ideally, Tyntallin would rather not have to look at her.

'Anna?' It was Margot, beckoning from the doorway. 'Chop chop dear, we'll never get them settled before dinner at this rate.'

Anna was halfway along the main landing when she began to notice the drop in temperature compared with the fire-stoked warmth of the library. She had never been in the house when the weather was cold, but she knew that radiators grew progressively scarcer as you moved up towards the children's floor, and even in August their bedrooms had sometimes been chilly. From where she was standing she could see, in the hall below, her cashmere wrap draped on the chair where she had left it, just outside the library. Anna hesitated, then turned and quickly retraced her steps, down the stairs and across the hall, and was just bending to retrieve the wrap when she heard the sound of Emily's voice coming from the library. She must have dodged Margot and sneaked down the back stairs, looking for Anna to hurry her up.

Anna slung the wrap around her shoulders, walked through the library doors, and was filling her lungs to call out to Emily when something made her pause and step sideways into the shadows. Emily had said her name, but the tone in which it was spoken, the urgency in the child's voice, made her instinctively shrink back out of sight. Anna pressed herself flat against the wall of the library, her ears straining to hear the conversation taking place at the far end of the room.

'Daddeeeeee,' Emily wailed. 'Why do you think I wanted to go to bed all of a sudden? Why do you think I wanted Margot to put us to bed?' There was silence. Emily groaned with exasperation. 'So that you could have a chance to be *alone* with Anna. Obviously.'

Using the cover of a tallboy, Anna slid further down the length of the library. When her shoulder was flat up against the piece of furniture she inched her head forward and saw Emily, still in her dressing gown, standing toe to toe with her father in front of the fireplace. From this angle Anna couldn't see Tyntallin's face but Emily's was upturned, puckered with frustration, and she was tugging sharply with both hands at the hem of his smoking jacket.

'Daddy. Didn't you say *anything* to her?'

'My darling, Emily, I'm not sure quite what it is you wanted me to say.'

'Just anything! I don't know, I'm not a grown-up! You could say . . . please will you go out with me?' Emily paused for breath. 'Daddy, if there's a choice, we'd rather have Anna, even though she doesn't know anything about children, or the country, or family life.'

Tyntallin received this information with a sharp backwards jerk of his head.

'All the divorcees. They are all very well qualified, and local and everything. But the only person who likes them is Aunt Margot.'

'Is that so?' Tyntallin said.

'Yes, it is.' Emily jiggled impatiently. 'So when will you tell her, Daddy? Because she's only here for one single night.'

Tyntallin put a hand up to his face, he appeared to be pinching the bridge of his nose. Emily watched him with an expression of curiosity mingled with concern, and when she spoke again her tone was wheedling.

'We could teach her, Daddy. Maybe she could go to one of those schools like the ones they have for cooking? She could do a course on how to look after us . . . and any other things she needs to know. We could take her shopping for clothes in Exeter.' This last suggestion was delivered with the gasp appropriate to an inspired argument clincher.

Tyntallin bowed his head to meet his daughter's eyes. 'And what makes you think Anna would want to do all that for us?' he asked, without a hint of mockery.

Emily looked taken aback for a moment and then rose up on her tiptoes and thrust her face towards his. 'Because she needs a husband,' she almost shouted. 'And because she goes all snooty whenever you're around. Which means she likes you. And because you are the most legible . . . el-lergible husband, everyone says.'

Emily slouched against Tyntallin's leg and fidgeted with the button of his jacket. She slotted her thumb into her mouth, gulping rapidly as she contemplated how best to move the situation on, her gaze flitting from the jacket to his face and back again.

'Come on. It's time for bed,' Tyntallin announced suddenly. 'Don't you worry . . . everything will be fine. I promise you.' He reached out to place a hand on top of his daughter's head but she dodged it impatiently.

'Don't say that, Daddy! It won't be fine. Not if you pretend you don't even care. Why are you pretending?'

Tyntallin put a finger to his lips and then, guiding Emily by the shoulders, turned and started walking back down the library. Anna had to move quickly. She ducked behind the tallboy and, hugging the wall, swiftly sidestepped her way towards the door, the sound of Emily's high-pitched protests drawing nearer by the second.

'Why are grown-ups so difficult to make happy? It's so obvious what to do. It's *so obvious*.' Another long pause. 'Daddy?' Emily's tone had shifted again; this time it was compromising, practical. 'If you have to marry one of the divorcees, can it not be Ellen Milne? She's got

BO . . . and Felicity Milne is going round telling every-one she's going to get one of our ponies.'

Safely out in the hall Anna bolted up the stairs, so that when Tyntallin and Emily emerged from the library, moments later, she was able to call down from the land-ing, 'Emily? There you are! I've been looking for you everywhere.'

Twenty-two

On the morning of Tony and Jean's second wedding the bridal party were ensconced at number 25 Eldred Mews, while across the street at number 14, Tony was getting ready with the assistance of Archie and Dave, his two best men. The wedding was scheduled for midday at Chelsea Register Office, followed by drinks back at number 14, and then lunch over at number 25. A catering team were arriving in the next half hour, the cake was being delivered at eleven and Charlie Cunningham was rumoured to have hired some decks and put himself in charge of 'atmospheric music'. It was, Tony reflected as he loomed towards the bathroom mirror checking for nostril hair, a precision-planned event – one so carefully choreographed as to make their first wedding look like something they'd cobbled together on a whim. And that was before you'd even touched on the intricate manoeuvring that was going on in the background. That was something else altogether.

The nostrils having got the all clear, Tony shifted his attention to his chest hair, and then to the condition of his stomach. This he clenched and unclenched vigorously three or four times, and then relaxed completely, prodding and tugging the doughy overhang as if his torso were a jumper that had stretched in the wash. When he'd tired of that, he swivelled slightly to the right, eased the waistband of his boxer shorts lower down his hips and met his eyes in the mirror. The question was, had there been any significant deterioration in the past few years? Was this the body Jean remembered, or would she find him altered? Aged? Tony checked the state of his bottom – still gratifyingly flat despite the slight spreading around the waist – clenched his biceps and then bounced up and down on the balls of his feet to gauge the amount of chest wobble. Jean, of course, would be utterly unchanged: same long, blue-white legs; same jockey-narrow hips and classy, self-supporting bosoms. He pulled the waistband of his boxer shorts away from his hips and peered down into the burgundy-tinted gloom.

'Oi!' Dave's voice coming from the next-door room made Tony jump and whip his boxers up around his waist. 'What's going on in there, Tone? When are we going to have a drink? It's half past ten already.'

Tony rolled his eyes at himself in the mirror and yanked open the bathroom door. Dave was lying stretched out on the sofa that had doubled as his bed for the past few months, his bare feet dangling precariously close to a chair on which hung Tony's freshly laundered shirt.

'Feet!' Tony launched himself across the carpet and lunged for the shirt as if it were a child in the path of a juggernaut. 'David? Do you mind? This is my wedding shirt.' He hooked the hanger safely out of harm's way on the back of the door, and then retreated a few inches to check the effect. 'Where's Archie, anyway? He's meant to be here, helping me.'

'Picking up Charlotte from the dressmaker.' Dave yawned and kicked his sleeping bag onto the floor. 'Anything I can do?'

Out of the corner of his eye Tony took a brief inventory of his friend's current state. Dave was wearing his Sex Pistols T-shirt, which, it now occurred to Tony, had been his bed wear of choice since the day he moved in. His hair, woolly at the best of times, appeared to have fused into one solid fez-like lump on the top of his head, and he clearly hadn't shaved for days. If you had to sum up the overall effect, David looked like someone who had been held hostage in the jungle for several months, only with plenty to eat.

'Come on,' Dave said. 'Ask me whatever it is. I am the *co*-best man.'

Tony smiled enigmatically. He could not ask Dave, because Dave was the reason he needed Archie here. On this, Tony's wedding day, the number-one priority was to get Dave in a condition which would encourage Ruth to look on him favourably, and Archie was in charge of the grooming side. According to the plan, the very carefully orchestrated plan, by this stage Dave should have been blow-drying his hair, ideally using the products specially purchased for the occasion.

'Thanks, I think everything's under control,' Tony said. 'I tell you what would be good though.' He raised a finger in the air as if struck by sudden inspiration. 'Why don't you have a bath and a shave, then at least one of us will be ready.'

Tony glanced at his newly buffed nails and, in the most casual tone he could summon, added, 'You can borrow one of my shirts if you like.'

Apparently Tony was a bit rusty at the old nonchalance. Dave lifted his head from the arm of the sofa,
screwed up one eye and fixed Tony with the other.

'I know what you're up to, mate . . . don't even think
about it.'

'I'm not UP TO anything,' yelled Tony, over-reacting
somewhat, he realized, but he did have some ground to
recover. 'I just want my best man to look his best, if that
isn't too much to ask? If that isn't too much of an imposition?'

'Right. So you wouldn't be trying to get me all
preened and primped for the big set-up? The me and
Ruth unable to resist the love is in the air vibe, set-up?'

Tony closed his eyes and exhaled heavily. This was
going to be harder than he'd thought. Typical Dave, he
couldn't just be gracious and let them get on with sorting out his miserable life. 'In case you'd forgotten,
David, today is the day when we focus on Jean and
myself. It's just one of those boring conventions.'

'OK, fine.' Dave raised a hand in surrender.
'Seriously, though. I know you all mean well. But life is
not that simple. I can't just fall into line so that your
happy ending is perfect.'

'Oh, shut up and get in the bath, will you.'

Tony plucked his ringing mobile phone from the
table and sauntered over to the window.

'Jeanie, darling.'

'Bunny.'

'You look beautiful.' Tony pressed his palm against
the windowpane and Jean, standing at the bedroom
window of number 25, tapped her fingers on the glass in
reply.

'How's he doing, Bunny?'

'Average.'

'Nervous?'

'Yup. Ten on the scale. Eleven.'

'Have you got him all scrubbed up?'

'Er . . .' Tony leant back into the room and hearing the sound of running bathwater gave her the thumbs-up.

'Well done, darling.' Jean lowered her voice. 'Now, we need to get them both in the first car on the way back from the register office. I've told the driver to get lost for half an hour. I think that should do it.'

'Got it. Dave and Ruth, first car.'

'And Archie knows what he's got to do with Tyntallin?'

Tony nodded.

'Good. Only Anna –' Jean glanced over her shoulder before continuing '– she's been behaving very oddly ever since I told her he was coming. She seems to be memorizing a speech or something.'

'Why do you say that?'

'I keep finding her in corners, with her head buried in a sheaf of papers. Oh, I do hope there isn't going to be a scene. It never occurred to me she'd react like this.'

Tony waited as Jean gripped the phone between her ear and shoulder while she fished in her dressing-gown pocket for a cigarette. His gaze drifted for a moment towards the end of the mews, and there was Archie walking around the bonnet of his car and Charlotte stepping cautiously out of the passenger side, a long dress-bag looped over one arm and a hat box cradled in the other. She was wearing a duffel coat and a pink corduroy skirt and Tony was struck by the unfamiliar sight of her long legs in their patterned tights.

'Well I never.'

'You never what?'

'Look at little Charlotte.' Tony pointed down into the mews, and as he did Charlotte caught sight of him and grinned, half raising her overburdened arm in an attempt at a wave. 'Utter transformation,' Tony murmured, waving back. 'Look at the colour in those cheeks. I had no idea she was such a pretty girl.'

'Well, she's eating,' said Jean and then paused as, in the background, Valerie provided the full update. 'Apparently she's put on more than a stone already . . .' Jean repeated. 'And she's got a boyfriend . . . well . . . not one boy in particular. But she's going to all the parties. And having a wonderful time.'

'Good for her,' said Tony. 'How's Ruth getting on, by the way? Have you girls got her under control?'

Jean swivelled her head as if to check for Ruth's presence. 'I think she's in the bathroom with Anna,' she said, her shoulders drifting up towards her ears. 'We're working on it, as they say.'

'Jeanie, darling?'

'Bunny?'

'You didn't say you'd marry me again just to provide our friends with a matchmaking opportunity, did you?'

'No, darling. I said I'd marry you because I'm tired of looking at you through two sets of double glazing. Now, must get on, my hairdresser's just arrived. Oh, and Tony, send Archie back over for Tinks and Hopper's corsages . . . they're in the fridge.'

Tony folded the mobile shut and placed it on the windowsill. 'Right,' he said out loud, 'there is work to be done. There certainly bloody well is. DAVID?' Tony paused and when there was no answer tried again. 'DAVID? I hope you're making some progress in there. I'm timing you now. And, by the way, what's your SHOE SIZE?'

Over in the bedroom of number 25 Jean was having her hair put up the way Tony liked it, with a lifted crown and a high, almost beehive arrangement at the back. Her fringe had been straightened and trimmed, so that it fell just above her mascaraed eyelashes, and Carmen, the hairdresser, had woven a diamond T and J right at the base of the bun. Sitting slender and upright at her dressing table, blinking at herself through inky eyes, she looked like a queen insect, imperious and at the same time fragile.

'You always were lovely,' Elsie had said, reaching for her hand, her face grey against the white of the hospital pillow. 'You're everything he could have wished for, Jean. You still are, you know that, don't you?'

Tony had just been taken to the side room where he was sleeping off the effect of the pills, so the two of them were alone, probably, Jean realized, for the first time since the day they met.

'You don't have to pretend for my sake, love.' Elsie curled her papery fingers around Jean's wrist. 'It was very nice of you both to try and spare my feelings, but

I've known all along. I could see it straight away in his face.'

Jean started to speak but Elsie scrunched up her eyes and waggled a shaky finger.

'Oh, I know you've done your best. And he's put on a brave face all right. But it doesn't fool me, Jean. I can see he's lost without you. Just lost.' Elsie paused, her head bobbing gently. 'I've no right to ask. But do you think you might forgive him? Only, when I've gone, you're all he's got, you see.'

Jean had squeezed the papery hand as tight as she dared. 'I'll talk to him, Elsie, I promise. You don't need to worry.'

'You'll not let on that I knew though? It would hurt him so much.'

'I won't say a thing.'

They were silent then, for a moment, Elsie's rhythmic nods substituting for words.

'It was never anything serious,' Jean said, after a while. 'There was no one else, you know.'

'Oh, I know that,' said Elsie. 'I never saw two people so in love, even when you were divorced.'

Jean blinked hard. She yanked a tissue from the box on the dressing table and pressed it underneath her lower lashes breathing deeply through her nose. Then she swivelled her head from right to left, for Carmen's benefit, dipping her chin once or twice to accommodate the mirror being manoeuvred behind her. When the effect was pronounced perfect, the hairdresser took her leave and Jean was left alone, staring into the mirror.

Tucked into the corner of the frame was a photograph taken in her modelling days – an out-take from one of the editorial shoots she had done the year she met Tony. She was wearing a waistcoat, velvet shorts, boots, and the hairstyle that Carmen had almost faithfully recreated. Jean smiled at herself, at the glittering, hope-filled eyes, at the sober, self-conscious pout, at the giddy skinny legs which had been high kicking minutes before the camera shutter closed.

'Got a boyfriend?' the photographer had asked.

'Maybe,' she'd said.

'Well, don't let him make you give this up. A girl like you owes her services to the nation.'

And she'd laughed and planted a hand on her hip, tucked her chin over her shoulder and given him her best forbidding glare.

'Jean . . . can we come in?' The bedroom door opened a crack and before Jean had time to answer she was surrounded, the object of open-mouthed, gasp-inducing awe.

'Oh, wow,' cooed Charlotte.

'It's lovely,' said Anna. 'You look beautiful, Jean.'

Valerie blew loudly into her already soggy handkerchief and batted her free hand to indicate that she was temporarily indisposed.

'How's my bridesmaid?' Jean tilted her head and caught Charlotte's eye in the mirror. 'Not too cold in that skimpy chiffon thing?'

'No. I like it.' Charlotte smiled shyly. 'You look really lovely,' she added softly, unsure how to pitch a compliment, and Valerie's handkerchief was once again yanked from the wrist of her pink tweed jacket.

'Oh, Jean, do you remember last time?' Valerie hoisted up the skirt of her suit and half crouched beside Jean so that they were cheek to cheek in the mirror. 'Do you remember we decided Charlotte was just too little, so on the day you went down the aisle with Charlie, all on his own, in that adorable little smock. Oh, and wait till you see him in his suit today. Lottie, darling? Isn't it divine, the suit?'

'Yeah,' Charlotte nodded obligingly, 'it's really cool.'

Jean looked past Charlotte to where Anna was standing, propped against the bed. She was wearing a dark crêpe trouser suit which appeared to be slightly too big in the shoulders and made her look droopy and washed out. The front section of her hair was pulled back in a tortoiseshell clip while the rest hung lank around her shoulders. It was as if all Charlotte's vitality and weight gain had been borrowed from Anna, and in return Anna had got the angst and the parchment-white complexion.

'I'm fine,' said Anna, when finally she noticed she was being watched. 'Honestly.'

'Good.' Jean gave her hair arrangement one last pat, tugged the neck of her dressing gown closed, and swivelled round on the stool to face them. 'And how are we doing with Ruth?'

'Well,' Anna said, 'she's almost ready. And she's gone for the green dress.'

This information was met with an excited nod from Valerie and a chin dip of approval from Jean.

'But. Um. I think she might have taken a couple of Jean's pills. I'm not too sure,' Anna added, trying to sound upbeat, not wanting to alarm them unnecessarily.

Valerie's mouth gaped.

'Oh, Lord,' Jean growled, reaching for her cigarette packet, 'that's torn it.'

'What's torn what?'

Ruth was standing in the bedroom doorway wearing the green satin dress with the three-quarter sleeves, plum-coloured stockings and green suede Mary Janes – the committee's preferred outfit. She too had put her hair up for the occasion and finished it off with a plum-coloured rose. Something wasn't quite right, though.

'Ruth,' Valerie said, her voice faltering. 'It's back to front.'

Ruth peered down at herself. 'Yup, so it is,' she agreed, swinging her head upright again with some effort. 'I'll fix it. Won't take a second. I'll just –' she made a rotating movement with her hands which caused Valerie to grip her pearl choker and close her eyes. 'Look, relax, OK? I was nervous, so I did something about it, that's all.' Ruth looked at each of them in turn, her blank eyes following a split second after her head. 'Well, I was officially incontinent. I didn't actually have a *choice*.'

'Fine.' Valerie pressed her hands together in front of her mouth, fingertips fluttering. 'Don't worry about the dress for the time being, Ruth. Perhaps we should just very quickly go over what you're going to say to Dave, when you're in the car. Meanwhile, Anna,' Valerie smiled hard at Anna, as if she had made a resolution to pay her much more attention, despite all the demands on her time, 'why don't you go downstairs and make us all a lovely pot of coffee?' She gave Anna an encourag-

ing pat on the arm before adding, 'And perhaps a tiny
bit more make-up?'

Anna was relieved to be discharged, and especially to
another part of the house where she could look over the
letter, at leisure, one more time. It had arrived in the
post yesterday morning addressed simply to 'Anna', in
loopy, childish handwriting crowded together in the
centre of a rainbow-striped envelope. At first she had
assumed it was from a god-daughter, but as soon as she
opened it she saw, framed in the V of the envelope, the
words Tyntallin, Tyntallin, Cornwall, stacked one on
top of the other in neat green biro capitals. Removing
the letter from the envelope, she'd vaguely registered
that it was written on two kinds of paper: the top sheet
rainbow-hued and flimsy, while the one underneath felt
like cardboard by comparison. Then she had read from
the first sheet.

Dear Anna
    Sorry I have not got your surname. I hope
you are well. The next page is a letter that Daddy
threw in the bin in the summer, and I found and
kept. You will see that it is extremely interesting
reading! I know he will be furios that I sent it to
you, but I think you will agree it is a good idea,
when you have read it! When you came for
dinner here I thought Daddy would tell you about
the letter. But he didn't so finaly I realized I must
take the law into my own hands! It has taken
ages to find out your address so I hope you have

not got a boyfriend (I don't think so). I hope you
will like Daddy's letter and think that he is sad
and lonely but also romantic and a good catch.
Love from Emily. PS Aunt Margot broke her
ankle triping on the dogs. PPS. Mrs Gordon has
been depresed and had to go on holiday to the
Isle of White.

Anna settled herself at the kitchen table and put the
rainbow notepaper to one side. Since the first reading
she always went straight to his letter, always reading
right from the top of the page, resisting the temptation
to bolt to the end. The stiff cartridge paper was bumpy
in texture and scarred with lines, like the veins in marble, where it had been crumpled into a ball. Her eyes
skimmed rapidly over the griffin crest and the embossed
address and raced hungrily to the body of the letter. He
wrote:

August 30
Dear Anna,
    I am sure you're aware of the events that have
taken place here over the past few weeks. As you
can imagine it's been a trying time for all of us,
especially Margot and poor Mrs Gordon. Luckily
the children were so relieved to see the back of
their stepmother that they have pretty much taken
it in their stride. They now refer to her as Leevil –
which appears to cheer them up no end. I have
another name for her, and it's taking rather longer
for me to see the funny side of what has
happened. I wonder how you are faring. Now

that it's over, I find myself wishing I could talk to
you and fill in the missing pieces. Actually, I
would like to see you under any circumstances,
and I couldn't give a damn what we find to talk
about. People assume that I am bereft because of
her, but most of the time – almost all of the time
– I am thinking of you. Oh, for Christ's sake.
How can I say this?

Here some words were scored out, then the letter
continued in a looser hand.

What the hell. You probably won't have read
this far anyway. You loathed me from the
moment you set eyes on me – only a fool would
imagine that could have changed overnight. But
then I am a fool. That much has been established.
And I am, despite your appalling behaviour
towards me, foolishly, overwhelmingly taken with
you. Dear Anna. Dear, sweet, angry Anna. How I
miss your disapproval, the sight of you in your
funny little coat clipping down the drive, so full
of certainty and plans.

Although we never exchanged a civil word the
entire time you were here, somehow you gave me
hope. I even resorted to reading your early
published work, and if that isn't an indication of
my desperate state of mind, I don't know what is.

None of this makes a great deal of sense. All I
know is that it distressed me to see you throwing
yourself away on that so-called musician, and
before long I realized it wasn't only because of his

lousy character. You see, I wanted to be the one you turned to. I wanted to be the focus of your world. I wanted to make you

And there the letter stopped abruptly. A heavy line was scored through a few indistinguishable words, and then more heavy scoring trailed into an angry lightning jag covering the rest of the page.

'Anna . . . ?' Charlotte was standing at the bottom of the stairs, her head dipped shyly. 'Mum sent me down to help you . . . with the coffee.'

'Yes! Coffee.' Anna stuffed the letter into her jacket pocket and smiled weakly. She hadn't even got as far as boiling the kettle. Ever since the letter arrived she'd found the smallest task a struggle. It was impossible to switch off the noisy debate in her head, so every action, every communication had become a challenge – like making a phone call from a party in full swing or trying to talk while eavesdropping on another conversation.

'How is everything upstairs?' Anna said.

'OK. I think.'

'And what about generally?'

'Fine . . .' Charlotte looked down at her feet. 'Do you mean . . . ?'

'I mean at home.'

'Oh, it's really different.' Charlotte's blue eyes bulged as if she were about to describe a coveted pair of shoes. 'Mum and Dad do everything together now. Dad says they're on a journey, and they don't know if they'll get exactly where they're aiming for, but they're "cautiously optimistic".'

Charlotte smiled sheepishly and made her way over

to where the kettle was plugged in, lifting it with one still scrawny arm to check the weight of water, before flicking the switch to on. 'I never thought Mum and Dad were really suited,' she said dreamily. 'But now I reckon they must be . . . to have got this far. You probably always knew, though, because that's your job, isn't it?' Charlotte paused as she reached up to the shelf above and closed her hand around the base of a cafetière. 'Anna, you know your book? Does it actually tell you who you should fall for?'

Anna knew what was coming. 'In a way it does. Why?'

'Well, there's this boy called Justin, who I really like. And he's really cool, and everyone really likes him.' Anna nodded. 'And then there's this other boy called Gordon.' Charlotte's eyebrows reached for her centre parting. 'And he's OK, but he's a bit weird, and like he doesn't listen to the same music, and whatever, as every-one else. And then my friend Lucy told me that when I was ill,' her eyes flashed to Anna's face for an instant, 'Gordon would always stick up for me, and like have arguments about me. And Justin called me "stick".'

'Do you like Gordon?'

'He's OK, yeah. But he's not like a boyfriend kind of boy. He's not even like anyone I know. He's just not the kind of person you'd ever imagine . . . even being friends with.' Charlotte shrugged. 'I told Mum. She said every-one grows out of believing boyfriends come in this ideal package. She said, "Ask Anna."'

Anna watched silently as Charlotte carefully poured the boiling water from the kettle into the cafetière and then positioned the silver dome lid over the top.

'But I really like Justin,' Charlotte added with a sigh. 'Gordon's so not me, you know?'

'Look, forget Justin,' Anna said. 'Gordon is *so* you, because he sees the girl beneath the . . . "stick". In spite of the way you've treated him. In spite of everything. Who needs the boy who just sees the stick!'

'OK.' Charlotte blinked. 'I think the coffee's ready.'

Dave slipped further down into the soapy hot water and thought how much he was going to miss Tony's bathroom. It was one of those macho bathrooms, with lots of black and chrome and mirror and tobacco-coloured soap and chunky glass bottles containing stuff for slapping on your face. The bathroom in the flat he'd rented, as of next week, was a poxy internal job, with a roaring extractor fan and a peppermint-coloured bidet. He wasn't looking forward to moving and not just because of the bathroom. Even if Tony hadn't been there that much, what with getting back with Jean, it had still felt like they were somehow in this together.

Dave pushed himself up, creating a sloshing wave which splashed over the back of the bath and onto the black tiled floor. He had to get a grip of himself. He had to think of this phase as a gentle introduction to the single life, and count himself lucky that he'd had these past months to begin to make the adjustment. Besides, it hadn't been ideal living here: the sofa bed was a couple of inches too short, and the penalty for staying with Tony was having to endure the 'Don't make the same mistake I did, David' speech, at least once a week.

'Don't make the same mistake I did, David,' Dave

mouthed at himself in the mirrored wall at the end of the bath, his hand next to his mouth snapping open and closed like a duck's bill. 'Look. I've wasted three years of my life, chum . . .' was how the speech generally continued. 'It's not worth it, old boy, I'm telling you. Forgive and forget. There is no other way.'

'Maybe three years is how long it takes to get over something like this. Have you thought about that?' was Dave's response to this line of argument, at least the first couple of times. 'Anyway, what about all the perks of life as a "born-again bachelor", eh? What about throwing off the marital yoke and "accentuating the masculine"? Or, did I just dream all that?'

'Look,' Tony would then say, 'don't be a tosser, David, all right? The Belindas, and so on, were a distraction, yes. But I wasn't really happy, was I?' Then he'd put his hands on his hips and close his eyes, apparently drawing on all his inner reserves in order not to lose his patience. 'David, do you know what it's like to spend an entire weekend trying to schmooze some girl when all you really want to do is watch the telly? Do you know what it's like to discover you cannot automatically put on Frank Sinatra, or reach for a book when you get into bed, or mock the fat *Pop Idol* contestant?' And, since this was a rhetorical series of questions, Tony would barely pause before continuing. 'Listen, you're hurt, and that's inevitable. But don't be a total arse. Remember what you said to me the night of the break-in? All that stuff about not getting any Brownie points for punishing each other? Well . . . too bloody right.'

Jean was the good cop in this ongoing attempt to get

Dave to see the light. Every now and then she would sidle over from number 25, pretending to be looking for a bit of kitchen equipment that Tony had supposedly borrowed and forgotten to return. Then, after a suitable interval, she'd settle down on the sofa and, ever so casually, ask how it was all going. Not surprisingly, she was useless at the job.

'Oh, darling, couldn't you just try?' she'd beg, minutes into the decoy conversation. 'I wasn't meant to come right out with it, but really, David, can't you both put it behind you? I mean, if it were anything but sex; if she'd gambled your savings, or got into trouble with the law . . .'

'Yes, but it *was* sex,' was the obvious response. And there was no answer to that.

Lately it had all gone quiet on the pep-talk front, which led Dave to conclude that they were keeping their powder dry for the wedding day – the day on which he and Ruth would be in closer proximity than they had been at any time since that night. Of course, they'd met often enough, dropping off or picking up Billy. But, at Dave's insistence, they had never been alone together in the same room for more than a few, awkward minutes. The others all assumed he'd made the rule deliberately to punish Ruth, and that's what he'd thought himself. That is until the first time he arrived to collect Billy for the weekend, and realized he actually couldn't handle being near her: smelling the fig scent she wore; watching her tugging Billy's coat tight around him, smoothing down the little collar, trying to pack a whole day's loving into this one gesture. When they'd got out into the street Dave had had to send Billy into the sweet shop so he could cry his guts out over the steering wheel of the hire car. Dave felt sick now thinking about it. He felt sick and hollow most of the time.

'There you go!' Archie had said when he'd told him about the sweet-shop incident. 'All the feelings are still there. You just relax, let the healing process take its course.'

'Not everything mends, Arch,' Dave had said. 'This can never be fixed.'

'Well, it might not be exactly the same as it was before,' Archie had said, beaming. 'But then it doesn't have to be! You see . . . I know you don't want to hear any more Diana-isms, but probably the most important thing she has taught us is that change is not something to be frightened of. Get your head around that, and you're away!'

That was the thing with your mates. They just wouldn't listen if they thought they had the answer to your problem. And of course, it was a pain in the arse for them, having to divide their time between two separate friends instead of one convenient couple. Dave remembered only too well how cheated he had felt when Tony and Jean split up, how personally inconvenienced. It was like separating the bar of your favourite pub from the pool table and putting them at opposite ends of town.

'David.' Tony was rapping at the door of the bathroom. 'You are having a shave in there, I hope?'

Dave grimaced at himself in the mirror. 'Yes, Daddy. And what are you two up to?'

'Archie's rearranging the buttonholes.' Tony said 'rearranging' the way he might have said, 'Adding a dab of Anthrax'. There was a pause. 'What are you thinking about in there?'

'Not that.'

'Wouldn't be any harm if you were.'

'Well, I'm not.'

'Can I come in?'

'Depends. Not if you're gonna start.'

Dave eyeballed the door and, sure enough, in Tony sauntered, still wearing his boxer shorts, now supplemented with a light blue cashmere cardigan. His face was smothered in what looked like a paste form of muesli, apart from his eyes which were outlined in thick white cream.

'Jesus,' said Dave.

'Just trying to set an example.' Tony propped himself up against the basin and folded his arms. 'Want to talk about it? We've got time.'

'*No.*'

'Come oooon. We won't be flatmates after today.' Tony tapped the muesli mask tentatively. 'Just tell me what you're feeling.'

'Tony . . .'

'It can't do any harm.'

'Leave it.'

'I think you should. It might help to clarify things.'

'OK then.' Dave shot upright in the bath, sloshing another wave of water on to the floor. 'All right. If you really want to know, I feel sorry for myself. I feel angry and bitter and fucked off and sad. I miss my kid. I miss my life. I can't remember who I am without them. Sometimes it feels like a dream – a lot of the time. Today it feels very, very real, and I don't think I've ever felt so lonely. Will that do?'

Dave's mouth quivered. He gripped his lips between his teeth as hard as he could but his eyes were flooding with tears and already Tony was a blur, a moving, expanding blur.

'I'm sorry, chum,' Tony said, 'I'm so sorry.' And for the first time in his life Dave experienced the feel of pure cashmere against his bare skin as Tony knelt down beside the bath and gripped his friend in both arms.

Jean adjusted her necklace in the mirror of the bedroom closet and stood back, spreading her arms wide for their approval. She was wearing her going-away dress from wedding number one – a grey satin sleeveless sheath, fitted tight to her still slender figure – and the diamonds that Tony had provided on their fifth wedding anniversary.

'Oh, Jean!' Valerie sobbed, fanning the tears back from her eyes.

'Thank you, Val.' Jean raised a cautionary finger to remind her that they weren't in the clear just yet, that there was still work to be done. 'Now, Ruth darling, why not have another sip of coffee and we'll try again?'

Ruth, who was lying star-shaped on Jean's bed, raised her head an inch off the pillow and Anna obliged, pressing the coffee mug to her lips and tipping when she gave the signal. Then she sank back on the quilt and stared up at the ceiling, breathing deeply in preparation for delivering, one more time, the speech they had been fine-tuning for weeks.

'Dave,' she began.

'No need to pause,' interrupted Valerie.

'I'm not pausing,' said Ruth. Her voice was a flat, dull monotone, like the voice of a zombie or, as Valerie had suggested, a person with a broken jaw. 'All right, that was a pause. You put me off.'

'Start again,' said Jean patiently, glancing at her watch.

'Right. Dave . . . These last few months have been really, really, really—'

'That's far too many reallys,' said Valerie, 'two is plenty.'

'OK . . . really, really hard. I can't remember a time when we weren't together, and now I know why. Because we belong together. Because we fit, and we always have done and we shouldn't be apart. I wish I could turn back the clock.' Ruth's head flopped sideways on the pillow. 'I hate that bit,' she moaned, thrusting out her bottom lip. 'Turn back the clock. It reminds me of Sherlock Holmes. Who ever says turn back the clock?'

'Too late to change.' Valerie flapped a hand impatiently. 'If you change it now you'll lose your thread.'

Ruth closed her eyes and continued. 'Er. I wish I could turn back the clock . . .'

'But I know I can't,' prompted Anna.

'But I know I can't. All I'm asking is that you give me another chance. For Billy's sake. I never stopped loving you, Dave . . . I just forgot, for a while, what we had . . .'

Valerie gave a loud sniff and gestured to Anna to pass the Kleenex.

'And I want that back . . .' Ruth hesitated, 'not every single part of it, mind you, and definitely not the coffee machine.' She gave a low, wheezy, drunken-sounding giggle.

'No ad-libbing,' Jean said sternly, 'especially not jokes.'

'Pffffff . . . it's a bit boring though, isn't it?'

'It's not meant to be original,' Anna said. 'You can't reinvent the wheel. A take me back speech is pretty much the same from here to Bogota.'

'I still think I should *mention* some conditions.'

'No.' Valerie shook her head vigorously. 'Ruth. Please. One step at a time. As we agreed. First the reconciliation, then the new ground rules.'

'How are you feeling, that's the main thing?' asked Jean.

'Fine,' said Ruth. 'Bit sick. I just need to get going really.' She raised her arm and then let it flop with a thud back onto the bed.

'All right then.' Jean glanced warily around the room. 'If we think we're pretty much ready . . . Anna? Then I'll give the boys the signal.'

The signal was a white handkerchief waved out of the bedroom window which was reciprocated by a grinning Charlie Cunningham. After that, the bridal party and the groom's party made their way out into the mews, where they stood stamping their feet on the cobbles, bracing themselves against the chilly December morning. Waiting for them as arranged, crouched behind his tripod, was the photographer. And it was only when Jean and Tony stepped forward, arms linked, that everyone realized he had already used up a reel photographing Valerie and Archie, in what could only be described as a lovers' clinch.

Twenty-three

By 1.30 p.m. everyone was assembled in the sitting room of number 14, toasting the newly-weds with champagne cocktails. Everyone, that is, apart from Ruth and Dave – who had last been seen leaving the register office over an hour ago – and Tyntallin.

'Do you know,' Jean had said, when it became clear that he wasn't going to make the ceremony, 'I think Tarka hinted he might be running late,' but the slight rumpling of her pale, high forehead told a different story. Still, Anna didn't give up. When the vows had been said, and the time came to rush out ahead of the newly-weds, clutching her bag of rose petals, she kept glancing over her shoulder, convinced that he would come bounding up the steps dragging on his morning coat, just as they emerged in a flurry of confetti. And afterwards, as they drove in convoy back to the mews, she continued to hold out hope, telling herself that he was bound to be waiting for them on the doorstep, growling his apologies, checking his watch as if to blame its time-keeping. But Tyntallin wasn't there. He didn't appear then, or later. And now Anna was standing outside the house in the clammy cold, supposedly keeping a look out for Dave and Ruth, but actually adjusting to the realization that he had decided not to come. That he was never coming.

'What about the letter?' the last gasp of hope in her said.

'The letter? It's months old, anything could have happened since then,' answered the voice of reason.

'But if he meant it? Wouldn't he still mean it?'

'Of course not. He was in the midst of a major emotional crisis. Now that's all behind him and you've become an embarrassing reminder of a temporary lapse in judgement, like a drunken fumble at an office party.'

'Darling, you'll catch your death.' Jean was standing next to her on the doorstep. She draped an old fur coat around Anna's shoulders and then, reaching back through the front door, produced a glass of champagne. 'There,' she said, placing it between Anna's limp fingers and squeezing them tight, in that bracing way a mother touches her child when she knows she cannot make it better. And Anna, unaware that the cold had turned her lips a waxy shade of lilac, murmured that she was fine, and that Jean should go back into the warm. Behind her, in the rosiness of the house, she could hear Tony calling out for his bride and, moments later, Jean answered him amidst a surge of cheers and music.

'Don't you dare feel sorry for yourself,' said the voice of reason. 'What exactly did you think was going to happen?'

'I don't know,' whispered the dying hope. 'I suppose . . .'

'Right. So, after everything you've written, and everything that's happened, he was meant to turn up at the eleventh hour and save you from your uncertain future?'

'No. I don't know . . . Maybe I could have saved him.'

'You? That really makes sense.'

The conversation in Anna's head stopped as a car turned under the archway that formed the entrance to the mews – the same sleek, black model that had carried them all to and from the register office, with one passenger sitting stiff and upright in the back seat. As the vehicle rolled towards her, she saw that the lone passenger was Dave, and moments later, when it drew up alongside her, the reason for his rigid posture was revealed: lying across Dave's lap – mouth open, dress hitched up to her knickers – was a sleeping, or possibly unconscious, Ruth.

At an instruction from Dave the driver lowered the rear window nearest to Anna and Dave tilted towards it, eyebrows grazing his hairline. 'Hello there,' he said cheerily. 'I imagine you want to know whether we've got back together?'

Anna shrugged. She didn't, at this moment, remotely care.

'We've been in the ladies' bogs at Harrods actually,' Dave said. 'That's after we stopped off at a garage, so that Reg and I could clear the vomit off the back seat.' At the mention of his name the driver eased his neck in his collar. 'But before the throwing up really got underway,' Dave continued, 'Ruth did manage to say "They'll kill me. I'd got this whole speech prepared, about how great you are . . . which Anna made up."' Dave paused, lips pursed. 'So, cheers, Anna. Maybe you could run me

through it some time?' He ducked his head to get a
clearer look at her face. 'What's up with you, anyway?
Cooome on. So it didn't go exactly according to plan.
You did what you could. Don't beat yourself up about
it.'

'This was my last chance,' Anna said.

'Hey. Don't be like that.' Ruth made a sudden sound
like a pig at a trough and Dave stroked her hair absent-
mindedly. 'It could have been worse. After all, we've got
to . . . what would you call this? Second base? Somewhere between second and third? We've had the dress
off—'

'No,' Anna snapped, 'I mean, he hasn't turned up.'

'Who?'

'Tyntallin.'

Dave cocked an ear in her direction and shook his
head.

'The one with the house. The one with the American
wife.'

'What, the Evil Lord? Is he a friend of Jean's?'

'*Yes.* And he was supposed to be coming.' Anna's
chin sank onto her chest. 'And now he's not.'

'You mean . . . Hang on. You wanted to see him
on . . . personal business?'

Anna confirmed this with a fraction of a nod. 'I got
it all wrong,' she mumbled. 'He's not what you think.
He's nothing like what you think.'

'What *I* think?'

'He's not what I said he was. He's . . .' she closed her
eyes, she could feel a lump in her throat the size of a fist.

'Would you mind if we didn't get into this right
now?' Dave said. 'Not when I'm sitting at a very awk-

453

ward angle, with my wife unconscious in my lap. What does he look like, this bloke?'

'What does that matter?' wailed Anna.

'Well . . . has he got shaggy grey hair and smokes a fag like it was his last on this earth?' Anna caught her breath. 'Because someone answering that description is hanging around just outside the end of the mews.' Dave jerked his head back towards the archway. 'Maybe you'd better go and get him.'

Anna did not need to be told. She bolted, clutching at the fur coat as it slid off her shoulders, abandoning her champagne flute in the first flower tub she passed. The heels of her shoes jarred against the cobbles underfoot, so she reached down, still stumbling forward, and yanked them off, tossing them one after the other onto the nearest doorstep. 'Wait, please wait,' she whispered as she ran at full tilt, the fur coat bunched under one arm, a thin, spattering rain beginning to make itself felt on the stocking soles of her feet. The archway was just a few yards up ahead now. Anna ran towards it and on through it, and then she stopped dead.

Tyntallin was standing straight in front of her, propped against a tree, hands sunk deep in his trouser pockets. When he saw her, his eyes flickered, straying to her shoeless feet for an instant and then back to her face.

'I had to take Oscar to ballet,' he said. 'Then there was this . . . display. He wanted me to stay and watch.'

Anna nodded. She took a few steps towards him.

'And then I wondered if I wasn't too late.' Tyntallin was scrutinizing her face, his expression wary and hopeful at the same time. 'If it was a mistake, to turn up . . . at this stage.'

'No,' Anna said, 'it isn't too late.' She smiled, conscious that this was the first time she had ever smiled at him. Tyntallin stared back fiercely, as if he suspected her of trying to distract him. 'We were waiting for you,' she added. 'We hoped you'd make it . . .' Oh God, she thought. Say what you mean. Tell him you were beside yourself. Tell him you were counting on him coming. Tell him . . .

'I wrote you a letter,' he said abruptly.

Anna affected a look of surprise. 'Oh?'

'It wasn't much of a letter,' he paused and stared down at his feet. 'I think it said that we hoped you'd come and visit us. We've got more room now, of course. And you were always such a help . . . in the vegetable garden.' Tyntallin glanced up at her. His grey eyes were narrowed against the rain dripping off the end of his fringe. 'We . . .' he hesitated. 'The children seem to miss you.'

'I missed you,' she said, taking another step towards him. She leaned forward and took hold of the lapels of his morning coat with both hands.

'I missed *you*,' she said again.

Tyntallin closed his eyes and tilted his face up towards the sky. She saw his mouth twitch, on the brink of forming the words, and then they seemed to lodge deep in his throat, forcing him to swallow hard. He stayed like that, with his face offered up to the driving rain, for several seconds.

'It doesn't matter if you can't say it,' Anna said.

Tyntallin did not answer. He slid a hand under her hair and cradled the back of her head in his palm.

'I don't mind if you can't,' she continued, as his

other arm reached around her waist, drawing her towards him. 'But it's not as if we've got anything to be scared of. After all, there's nothing more life could throw at us,' she added as he lowered his face towards hers and she closed her eyes.

'All right, I'll say it if you insist,' he whispered. 'Marry me.'